# A Knight's Reward

## CATHERINE KEAN

"Kean's story is richly atmospheric and compelling.
You'll want to stay with these wonderful characters
long after the book ends!"

—*New York Times* best-selling author
Betina Krahn on *A Knight's Reward*

**PRESS®**

Jewel Imprint: Sapphire
Medallion Press, Inc.
Printed in USA

Previous accolades for Catherine Kean's
<u>A KNIGHT'S VENGEANCE</u>

"Medieval tales are among my favorite reads, and I am pleased to recommend A KNIGHT'S VENGEANCE to others who favor this genre as well. You will not be disappointed."

—*Romance Reviews Today*

★★★★★ <u>**FIVE STARS**</u>
Fabulous! Author Catherine Kean gives readers everything they could possibly want in this tale of heroism and betrayal. This will be one of the best historical romances of the year!
—*Detra Fitch, HUNTRESS REVIEWS*

"A KNIGHT'S VENGEANCE is a wonderful fast paced historical romance novel . . . leaves you on the edge of your seat until the very end. This is a must read for any romance reader."

—*The Romance Readers Connection*

<u>**4-1/2 blue ribbons!**</u>
"Catherine Kean will have readers riveted to the pages of her newest novel."

—*Christine Dionne, Romance Junkies*

<u>**4 plugs — "Excellent"**</u>
"A KNIGHT'S VENGEANCE is a wonderful fast paced historical romance novel. Catherine Kean brings the characters to life with details, vengeance, and honor. A Knight's Vengeance leaves you on the edge of your seat until

the very end, trying to figure out who is the villain and who is innocent. This is a must read for any romance reader."

—*Gloria Gehres, The Romance Readers' Connection*

"A KNIGHT'S VENGEANCE is a wonderfully told story about a tender love born from the hate of revenge. Elizabeth and Geoffrey's transition from enemies to lovers is entertaining and passionate. The end has a thrilling battle and heart-warming closure. A KNIGHT'S VENGEANCE captivated me with a beautiful and strong heroine, a brave and fearless hero and an exciting, romantic tale!"

—*Nannette, Joyfully Reviewed*

"Another superbly written novel by an author who's quickly become a favorite . . . a must-read. Another book for the keeper shelf and I'm eagerly awaiting this author's next novel."

—*Margaret Ohmes of Fresh Fiction*

"A KNIGHT'S VENGEANCE caught my attention from the first chapter . . . Catherine Kean has a marvelous way of grabbing one's heart and interest and keeping you in the game until the very end."

—*Lori Graham, Once Upon a Romance*

"Beautiful. Ms. Kean leads you into a fantasy world where you are taken back to the medieval century of handsome knights, daring swordfights, and steamy romance. Back to a time where honor means everything and vengeance is hard won. Vividly described, you can almost see a crumbling castle and the knights in armor. Fast paced action and intriguing dialogue keeps you on the edge of your seat, while the sensual love scenes make you swoon.

This is my first book by Ms. Kean, but certainly will not be the last."

—*Wateena, Reviewer for Coffee Time Romance*

"Fraught with friction and an extravagant degree of lusty, combative tension, A KNIGHT'S VENGEANCE is a passionate medieval romance from emerging new talent, Catherine Kean, that will evoke fond memories of the genre's golden era: . . . Kean's novel is a joyous celebration of what a medieval romance should ideally contain: passion, peril, and evocative wisps of slightly feverish conflict . . . Indeed, when all is said and done, I do believe that fans of the genre will be quite keen to read more of this up and coming author."

—*Cheryl Jeffries, Heartstrings Reviews*

"Ms. Kean delivers a medieval romance fraught with passion, treachery, and a love that cannot be denied. The characters leap off the pages into your heart. Superbly written, this is one book you won't be able to put down from page one until the end. A page-turner at its best, Ms. Kean delivers a "keeper" that you will want to read more than once."

—*Cia Leah, Romance Divas*

"This is the first book by Catherine Kean that I've read and if it is an indication of her writing style, I'm definitely putting her on my list of authors whose books I simply must read. I thoroughly enjoyed the way this whole story played out. I was breathless with anticipation with each chapter read. I highly recommend this one!"

—*Kathy Boswell, The Best Reviews*

## DEDICATION:

For my mother, Shirley Lord.
Your love is always with me.

Published 2008 by Medallion Press, Inc.

The MEDALLION PRESS LOGO
is a registered tradmark of Medallion Press, Inc.

Printed in the United States of America
Typeset in Adobe Garamond Pro

ISBN# 978-193281599-3

10 9 8 7 6 5 4 3 2 1
First Edition

## ACKNOWLEDGEMENTS:

Every day, I consider myself lucky to have such a fantastic critique group. Nancy Robards Thompson, Elizabeth Grainger, and Teresa Elliott Brown, I owe you a tremendous "thank you"—and lots of chocolate!

Mike and Megan, thank you for always cheering me on. Each book is an adventure, but you never stop me from journeying into the creative mist and wrestling my stories onto the printed page. I love you both, so very much!

# CHAPTER ONE

*Moydenshire, England*
*Summer 1194*

Someone was watching her.

Someone close by in the market crowd.

The smells of freshly baked bread, smoke from the blacksmith's fire, and dried lavender from the herbalist's stall suddenly became cloying, like a hand closing around Gisela Anne Balewyne's throat. Fear sluiced through her as she dug in her coin purse for a bit of silver to pay the baker for the loaf of coarse bread.

In her brief wander through the market, she'd almost resisted the inner cry for caution—the voice that had been her companion every day and night for the past four months. She'd nearly pushed back the hood of her drab woolen cloak, freed her hair from its leather thong, and raised her face to the warm sunshine. How she'd yearned to savor the sunlight. To pretend, for a moment, she was free to do so. That she didn't have to stay hidden within the confines of her cloak, and it did not matter who saw her face.

*It has been four months*, a traitorous little whisper had coaxed. *Ryle has not found you. He likely never will.*

Yet, despite all her careful precautions, mayhap he had.

Cold, sickly perspiration dampened her palms. Her heart lurched into a rhythm sharpened by months of simmering anxiety. She must pay for the bread, then leave the market as quickly as possible. If she were lucky, she could lose whoever watched her when she passed the throng gathered around the trainer with the two dancing bears.

"Ye all right, love?" asked the baker, a tall, broadly built man whose wife had died last year. He bent to squint at her. Gisela jerked her face away, pretending to be looking into her coin purse.

"I . . . am fine. I do have the money," she said with a shaky laugh. As her slick fingers closed on a coin, a sigh broke from her.

With a musical *clink*, the silver slipped back down into the bag.

"Mercy!" She fought the urge to toss the bread she'd tucked under her arm back onto the table, then bolt. The same voice that had lived with her for so long warned that to flee in such a way would be foolish. Whoever watched her would realize she knew she'd been found.

They might try to capture her here in the market.

They'd take her back to her husband, to answer for slipping away with little Ewan in the dark, silent hours of the night.

To pay for what she had done.

"Try to run away, and I will find you," Ryle had sneered that horrible eve months ago as blood, seeping through the slash above her right breast, stained her silk gown. Her blood glistened on his knife. "Go to your family, and I will cut them, too. You can trust no one, Gisela. This I promise you."

A brutal shudder wrenched through her. *Oh, God. Oh, God.*

*This time, he would not let her escape him.*

*This time, he would kill her.*

She forced herself to swallow the fear threatening to suffocate her. Here, now, she had no choice. She must preserve the illusion of oblivion, so in a few moments, she could elude her watcher.

Her hand shook when she dug in her purse again. She willed herself to calm, even as she rationalized how much she needed the bread. The meager portion of vegetable pottage would not be enough to feed her and Ewan that day, without the dense bread to mop up the broth.

Gisela's jaw tightened as her hand closed on the coin. Whatever had happened between her and her husband, her young son didn't deserve to go hungry.

"Here," she said, dropping the silver into the baker's hand.

"I thank ye." His voice held a kind note.

The wounded, shielded part of her heart constricted, and she blinked hard. She nodded and turned away.

His hand caught her sleeve. She jumped, even as she heard the baker say, "Take this for yer boy, Anne." He handed her a small, round currant cake.

Her gaze flew up to meet his. Of course, the baker knew her name—at least, her middle name, which she used to identify herself here in this village. Not surprising, either, that he remembered Ewan. Sometimes her rambunctious three-and-a-half-year-old son accompanied her to the market. On the good weeks, when Gisela had managed to put away the set amount of silver she was saving, she bought Ewan a sweet cake.

Not very often, lately.

The baker smiled, revealing two missing top teeth. An affectionate smile, nonetheless.

Rowdy laughter erupted behind her. Men jesting. The familiar fear roused inside her, a reminder of her watcher. She must be on her way.

Waving a gracious hand, she said, "Thank you, but I could not—"

"Go on." He pushed the cake into her palm, then patted her fingers closed around it. "Think naught of it. 'Tis my treat."

"Th-thank you."

His shoulders raised in a shrug before he addressed the farmer's wife who had elbowed in next to Gisela and asked about the rye loaves.

The currant cake cradled in her hand, Gisela walked away. Chickens clucked in crates at the stall farther on. Copper pans gleamed in the sunlight. Skirting a group of men haggling over a cow, she strode on, forcing herself to take lazy strides. Even though inside, panic welled.

A dog hurtled past her, a joint of meat in its jaws, two men in hot pursuit. She stepped aside, out of the way. Curiosity nagged at her. How dangerous to sneak a look at her watcher. Part of her didn't want to accept that her safe haven here in Clovebury, this town on the edge of Moydenshire, land of Lord Geoffrey de Lanceau, had been broached.

Yet, part of her—the angry, protective part—demanded to know who followed her.

Lingering a moment, she looked over the leather goods set out at the tanner's stall. Keeping her head down, she dared a sidelong glance down the row of stalls, skimming each of the people standing nearby to see if she recognized anyone.

A peddler in a long, tattered mantle, taking each of his steps with a wooden stick, hobbled his way through the throng.

The same hunched old man—aye, she was sure of it—had followed her to the baker's stall.

She rubbed her lips together, her mouth suddenly dry. Market day attracted all kinds of travelers, especially thieves and peddlers. If Ryle wanted to find her, he would not have sent a thug disguised as a peddler.

Would he?

The dog with the meat joint spun and hurtled back the way it had come, the men still in pursuit. As the mongrel darted past the peddler, it brushed the hem of his long garment.

He wore leather boots.

With spurs.

The mark of knighthood.

Most peddlers were lucky to be able to afford shoes.

A panicked cry flared in Gisela's throat. She turned on her heel, painfully aware of the peddler's stick rapping on the dirt.

*Thud, thud, thud* sounded behind her.

*Run, run, run!* her mind shrilled.

Squaring her shoulders, she strolled toward the trainer and his dancing bears.

Dominic de Terre cursed as he shuffled through the crowd, close behind the slender woman who, he sensed, had realized he was following her. Moving along with a steady *plod, plod*, he rued the itchy, woolen mantle that disguised him and hampered his movements. God's blood, but a man could roast like a suckling pig in such a garment.

A necessary disguise, though. One he and Geoffrey

de Lanceau, his closest friend and lord, had agreed upon, as a means to infiltrate Clovebury's market.

Someone had stolen Geoffrey's last shipment of costly silks as they were shipped down the river to his castle, Branton Keep. A king's ransom in cloth, missing.

Dominic had vowed to find the thieves—a quest that had brought him to this sleepy little town on the verge of nowhere.

The woman ahead moved with a languid grace. Despite the well-worn cloak covering her from head to toe, a peasant's garb, she moved in a most enticing way.

Like a woman he'd known years ago.

A woman he'd loved with a passion close to madness.

And left behind when he rode away to join King Richard's crusade.

Regret pierced him. He shoved aside the inconvenient remorse, for years ago, he had no choice but to leave her. Moreover, the woman he followed could not be his beloved Gisela. The village where he'd met her was leagues from here. By now, she'd be married to a good husband, with four or five children crowding around her skirts.

She trailed her hand along a row of linen gowns drifting in the breeze, then turned left, heading toward the open space where the entertainers gathered. Dominic shuffled on, keeping his gaze upon her. Idiot that he was, he should simply give up pursuit and return to the market, to see what he might overhear. His duty to

Geoffrey was far more important than chasing a wench with a sultry sway.

Yet, he couldn't turn away.

Something about this woman drew him to her.

Curiosity, mayhap.

Desire.

A grin ticked up the corner of his mouth. What man would not be enticed by a woman who swayed like a young sapling? She, however, would hardly be enticed by a scruffy peddler.

Still—

She paused a moment to watch the bear trainer. Waving a stick, the man coaxed one of the large animals to rise up on its hind legs. The crowd roared.

Switching the stick to his other hand, Dominic wiped perspiration from his brow, then flexed his stiff fingers unaccustomed to curling around the wood.

He looked back at the crowd.

The woman wasn't there.

Disquiet flickered through him. Walking forward, he scanned the rest of the throng.

*Gone.*

An apt ending, mayhap, to a senseless quest.

Just as he was about to admit defeat, he spied her, darting into a side alley. As she ran, the hood of her cloak slipped off her head, revealing a mass of blond hair.

*Gisela!*

The walking stick slid from his hand and clattered

on the ground. Before he could caution himself, Dominic broke into a run. The heavy mantle dragged against his legs, and he stumbled twice before regaining his balance. Clenching his fist into the coarse fabric, he yanked up one corner of his garment's hem.

Several men gathered around the dancing bears turned to glance at him in surprise. With a pinch of dismay, he recognized them from earlier in the morning, when he'd convinced them he was a crippled old vagrant.

He reached the entrance to the alleyway where Gisela had gone. Yards down the narrow, rubbish-strewn alley, he caught sight of a figure in brown. Her hair was again concealed by the hood, which she held in place with one hand while she ran.

"Gisela!" he called. She didn't stop, glance over her shoulder, or give any indication she'd heard him.

He sprinted into the alley. Rotting cabbages and onions littered the ground. Flies buzzed in a black, swirling cloud. Muttering an oath and batting away flies, he skidded through a slick mass of vegetables. The stench flooded his nostrils. Coughing, he covered his face with his grubby sleeve.

Halfway down the alley, he paused. The cacophony of market day carried from the other street, while in contrast, the alley seemed intensely silent. Glancing to and fro, he searched for Gisela. A sense of urgency burned in his gut. He *had* to find her. After all this time—

A scrawny gray cat scampered over a nearby pile of

broken wooden crates. One of the wooden slats shifted, then fell to the dirt. With a yowl, the feline bounded away. It disappeared down another alleyway, farther ahead.

Holding up his mantle again, he followed.

The side street led into the backyard of The Stubborn Mule Tavern. A wide dirt space—enough to turn a horse-drawn wagon—fronted the two-story, wattle and daub building with a sagging thatch roof. Glancing to his left, Dominic noted the stable's low roof also bowed in the middle, damage likely caused by heavy spring rains.

He pushed aside the mantle's hood, gasping for cool air. Wiping his brow, he scrutinized the tavern yard. His sense of urgency deepened. Could she have fled into the tavern? Not a safe place for a young woman alone, but most of the townsfolk seemed to be at the market—meaning there would be fewer drunkards inside to harass her. From her brisk run, she'd seemed desperate at all costs to elude him.

Odd, her desperation. Why did she try so hard to evade him?

Had she stolen something from one of the stalls? Surely not. The Gisela he knew had a soul as pure as unblemished snow, but then again, he'd not seen her for years.

Did she recognize his voice, but not want to speak with him ever again? Aye, that could be the crux of it. As he dried his dirty palms on his mantle, regret burrowed deeper, for their parting had been very painful. At that difficult point in his life, he had no choice but to leave

England and join King Richard's crusade. As much as he loved her, he couldn't marry her. As she well knew.

Shrugging aside his misgivings, Dominic started toward the tavern. A small, round object lying on the ground a few yards from the stable caught his gaze. He crossed to it before dropping to one knee in the dirt. With careful fingers, he picked up the object.

A broken currant cake.

The baker had handed Gisela one of the sweets.

Pushing to his feet, Dominic looked toward the stable doorway. Grayed shadows marked the entrance, concealing the interior. She could be hiding inside.

As he shifted the remains of the little cake in his palm, it disintegrated. Crumbs slipped between his fingers, like rough-grained sand. Like the years that had passed and changed them both.

He tossed the crumbs in the direction of a starling, watching bright-eyed from the tavern roof. The inevitable choice loomed before him—to step into the stable and face Gisela, or turn around and stride away, leaving the past behind him.

Years ago, he'd walked away. Every night since then, Gisela had been with him, smiling up at him while she lay in the lush meadow grass, her hair spread around her like golden fire. A bracelet of daisies dangled from her wrist as she trailed slender fingers down his cheek, over his lips, down to the front of his tunic.

God's blood, he could not walk away now.

Dragging a hand over his jaw, he exhaled a ragged breath, and then strode toward the stable.

Gisela flattened against the stable's far wall. Sunlight poked through cracks in the worn wood, slashing lines across the mounded hay in the center of the room, the implements hung on the opposite wall, the empty water trough nearby. Farther in the stable, a horse snorted, then pawed its stall.

Faint, gritty boot falls reached her, the sound of her pursuer running into the tavern yard, then coming to a halt. Hardly daring to breathe, she imagined him studying the quiet, empty yard, his face crumpled with defeat. She prayed he wouldn't think to check the stable. That any moment, she'd hear him curse, spin on his heel, and stride away.

More crunched footfalls. Coming closer, not receding.

A pause.

*Oh, God.*

The moment of silence stretched, poignant and insidious. Her pulse thundered, as loud as a musician hammering on a tabor. She bit down on her bottom lip, even as a violent shiver tore through her. The sticky residue from the currant cake burned her palm like a brand, for in her frantic dash to the stable, she'd dropped Ewan's treat. Where, she could not remember.

Mayhap her pursuer would not find it, she quickly reassured herself. By now, a hungry mongrel had probably eaten it.

Her watcher might not even have seen the baker hand it to her, and therefore, even if he did find it, the cake would have no significance.

None.

Yet, the doubt settled deeper. Like months of dust, stirred up by a cloud of ill wind, floating down to collect again in a stifling blanket.

The memory of Ryle's reddened face, twisted into that terrible sneer, again wrestled its way into her thoughts. That eve, he'd been angrier—and more drunk—than she'd ever seen him. Thank the saints, sleeping Ewan, tucked away in his chamber at the other end of the manor house, hadn't witnessed the violence.

She could only imagine Ryle's wrath when she was returned to him.

*Oh, God. Oh, God!*

Her legs shook. She pressed her back against the rough wall, into the darkest shadows. With only one route in or out of the stable, she must force herself to be patient, to be as still and silent as a tomb sculpture. Despite the smell of hay tickling her nostrils.

Despite the splinter biting into her right palm.

Despite—

Just as she covered her nose to stop a sneeze, the light in the stable's doorway dimmed. The muted thud of footfalls reached her.

Her pursuer had stepped inside.

Tension hummed inside her with the resonance of a single, plucked harp string. The air inside the stable changed. Shifted.

She sensed his presence. Determined. Inquisitive.

Familiar, somehow.

Confusion flared, even as she fought the terrified moan rising up inside her. She squeezed farther against the wall. Her hand moved sideways a fraction and bumped against a wooden-handled spade. With a loud rasp, the implement keeled sideways, then clanged onto the floor.

*Oh, God!*

"Gisela?"

The man's rich, warm voice reached out to her, without a hint of menace. Disbelief shot through her. Fie! He sounded just like Dominic.

Memories of her beloved softened the edges of her fear, reviving moments of sunshine, laughter, and love so strong and true. She had known, when she kissed him full on the lips for the last time, that she'd never love another man as she had treasured him.

She blinked, fighting tears. Of all wondrous miracles, could it be him?

Cruel reality smashed her elation like a beetle beneath a stone. How foolish, to imagine the man was Dominic. He'd gone away on crusade. He'd likely perished on the bloody eastern sands, run through by a Saracen sword. Even if he survived the battles, the journey back to England on a filthy, rat-infested boat surely would have killed him.

Nay, the man could not be Dominic.

Fear was corrupting her mind.

Yet, how did he know her given name? Not the name she used here in Clovebury, but her *real* name?

"Gisela, are you in here?" The man spoke again. His tone held an edge of frustration.

Oh, heavenly Mother of God. If she heard only his voice, she'd believe him to be Dominic.

Loneliness coaxed her to stumble out of the shadows and look upon him. *Oh, my love. Is it you?* Biting down on her tongue, she fought the urge to call out. Curling her hands against the rough wall, she struggled not to rush forward.

'Twas not Dominic, she reminded herself. 'Twas a stranger, who might well be working for her husband.

Straw rustled. The shadows shifted as the man walked farther into the stable.

"Why do you not answer me, Gisela? Are you hurt?"

Any moment, he'd round the bales of hay. He would see her. Expectation warred with a rising sense of panic. Caution had protected her and Ewan over the past four months; to foolishly risk them both now was unforgivable.

Her gaze darted to the opposite wall, searching for a hiding place.

Nowhere to conceal herself.

Yanking the bread loaf from under her arm, she tossed it onto a wooden grain barrel. Lunging forward, she picked up the spade.

A man stepped into view. The loose, ragged garments of the peddler hung from his broad frame. With only a few paces between them, standing upright rather than hunched over a stick, he looked far taller than she expected.

A warrior in a peddler's garb.

Facing him, she half-crouched, holding the spade like a pike between them.

He abruptly halted, respecting the barrier she enforced between them. He raised his hands in a gesture of surrender, even as a wry laugh broke from him. "'Tis not the greeting I expected. At least you were kind enough not to crack me over the head."

Her gaze sharpened on his face. Brown hair tangled about his shoulders, framing a handsome visage. In the shadows, she couldn't make out the color of his eyes, but they danced with undisguised mirth.

His face looked tanned, more angular, but his eyes were the same.

*Oh, God!*

*Dominic!*

Her arms trembled with the weight of the spade. It wavered, sending the metal end listing down toward the straw-littered floor. As though sensing her astonishment, he said, "Gisela, I have not come to harm you.

'Tis me, Dominic."

Stinging tears flooded her eyes. Her throat ached, as though she had swallowed a mouthful of dry straw. How she longed to drop the spade and throw herself into his arms. The compulsion to go to him burned with such force, it robbed her of breath.

However, she could never forget her husband's merciless vow. *You can trust no one, Gisela. Do you hear me? No one! This I promise you.*

Ryle knew how much she'd loved Dominic; drunk and furious, he'd cursed that love time and again. Circumstances had left her no choice but to tell him of Dominic, a wealthy lord's youngest son, whom she'd cherished and lost. If, after his return to England, he had located her husband and asked to see her, Ryle had the gift of manipulation to convince any man to do his bidding. A treachery she added to all the others for which she despised him.

Knowing Ryle, he'd fabricated a clever lie to explain why she left. He'd stitched enough concern for her into his tale to convince Dominic he must find her—and bring her back.

The anguish of her thoughts struck her like a fist. *Oh, Dominic, how desperately I have missed you. Every day, since you left me, I have wept inside. To see you here is my most cherished dream come true.*

Yet, the cautious little voice inside her repeated Ryle's threat. *You can trust no one, Gisela. No one!*

Dominic's smile had faded. Now, his expression held a tormented blend of surprise and regret.

Misery weighed upon Gisela like a sack full of rocks. How she loathed what she must do. But, she had no choice. Protecting herself, and especially Ewan, was more important than her fondest wishes.

Forcing the lie through her stiff lips, she said, "You have mistaken me for someone else."

He frowned. "Nay."

The falsehoods snarled together in her mouth like tangled thread. Still, she managed to say, "My name is not Gisela. 'Tis Anne."

Shock widened his eyes.. He shook his head, clearly grappling with her words. "'Tis Gisela. I make no mistake." The barest smile touched his lips. "I would never forget you."

A treacherous, pleasured warmth bloomed inside her. Oh, what wondrous words.

How very clever of him, if he aimed to undermine her wariness.

"My name is Anne."

"Anne is your middle name. 'Tis also your mother's name." He crossed his arms, then leaned one broad shoulder against the stable wall, a posture that implied a lazy ease, though she well knew she couldn't run past him to the door. "I remember the day you told me," he murmured. "We lay in the meadow, with the buttercups and daisies. You made me say it over and over—*Gisela Anne,*

*Gisela Anne*—so I would not forget. Do you remember?"

*Aye, I remember.* A sob rose in her throat.

From somewhere outside came men's voices. They drew near. As though hearing them, too, Dominic's head tilted. His jaw hardened before he pushed away from the wall.

Fear jolted through her. The men approaching might be his cohorts who had followed his pursuit. Reinforcements, to help take her away, if she put up a fight.

Her shaking arms failed her. The metal spade hit the floor with a loud *clunk*.

"Gisela." Dominic moved a measured step closer. "I do not understand. I thought you would be glad to see me. Why are you so afraid?"

She stumbled back. Her foot knocked the fallen implement, and she winced. "Oh, Dominic," she whispered, all of her anguish bleeding into her voice. "Please. Turn around and leave. Pretend you never saw me."

"Why?"

Shaking her head, she fought not to weep. "Please."

His searching gaze traveled over her. "Do you fear someone will find us here together?" He paused, before adding, "Mayhap your husband?"

A horrified gasp broke from Gisela. When Dominic took another step toward her, desperation spurred her into motion. She bolted for the space between him and the hay bales. The musty crunch of straw, as loud as her own breathing, filled her ears.

If she were quick enough, if she surprised him before he realized her intentions—

Just as she brushed past Dominic, his arm slid around her waist. She shrieked, struggled against his hold, but before she could draw another breath, she found herself spun around.

Kicking his shins, pounding her fists against his chest, she tried to wrench free.

Dominic grunted. "Gisela!"

With a sharp oath, he wobbled, then keeled sideways. Before she could pull free from his hold, the stable blurred around her. She was falling!

Gisela landed on her back in the mound of straw.

With a loud "oof," Dominic landed beside her. He'd shielded her fall so she did not hit the hard-packed dirt, she realized with a twinge of gratitude.

Flicking bits of straw from her face, she struggled to rise.

Leaning on one arm beside her, his face a hand's span above hers, Dominic shook his head. His broad, tanned palm splayed on her belly. "I will not let you run away, Gisela. I will have an explanation."

# CHAPTER TWO

Dominic stared down into Gisela's ashen, frightened face, barely resisting the urge to shake her. Concern and frustration twisted up inside him with punishing intensity. Why did she look upon him as though he were a fire-breathing, maiden-devouring dragon, rather than a past lover?

How different she seemed from the self-confident, sensual woman he remembered.

In the stable's dim light, he studied her. Her long, golden hair, loosened from its confining leather thong, tangled about her in the straw. Her thickly lashed, blue eyes looked huge against her pale skin. More prominent than he remembered, strong cheekbones defined her oval-shaped face, coaxing his gaze to slip down to her wide, generous lips, which parted as she sucked in an anxious breath.

He swallowed the bitter aftertaste of regret, for he remembered every luscious nuance of her mouth. How he'd lost himself in the eager brush of her lips.

That seemed an eternity ago.

Clearing an uncomfortable tightness from his throat, he dragged his gaze from her mouth. Meeting her watery gaze, he coaxed, "Tell me why you are so afeared."

Beneath his splayed hand, her belly rose and fell on a ragged sigh. Layers of woolen cloak, as well as her garments, separated them. Yet, as though 'twere yesterday, his palm remembered the softness of her skin, deliciously pliant beneath his caress and warmed by the meadow sun.

A shudder raked through him.

She must have felt it, too, for her eyes flared even more. With a gasp, she twisted sideways, clearly about to scramble across the straw. Catching her arm, he hauled her back. Meeting her furious glare, he said, "You are not making this easy for me, now, are you?"

"Please, Dominic." She trembled in his grasp, while her tone became urgent. "I beg you. Do not take me from here."

Frowning, he reached out to pull away straw dangling from her tresses. "Why do you fear I would?"

She shrank from his touch. Never before had she recoiled from him, a reaction that implied he epitomized danger, not reassurance. Anguish fueled his impatience.

When he caught the wayward straw and flicked it aside, voices again carried from the tavern yard. Two men, he discerned, from their brisk conversation.

Gisela shivered.

He gently squeezed her arm. "Are you in some kind of trouble?"

Staring up at him, she rubbed her lips together. For a moment, in her eyes, he caught a glimmer of trust. He sensed she yearned to confide in him. Then, as though catching herself, her gaze again darkened with suspicion.

Resisting the urge to curse like a drunken fishmonger, he let go of her arm. The roughness of her sleeve still prickled his palm. "I cannot help you, Gisela, if you will not trust me."

Her chin rose to a wary tilt. "How can I be certain you wish to help me? Many years have passed since I last saw you."

"True, but—"

"Nay, Dominic," she cut in, pushing up one arm, her eyes blazing with blue fire. "For all I know, you might—"

"—have been captivated by you in the market, so much so that I had to follow you, and then discovered you were my long-lost love? Aye. 'Tis the truth of it."

"If I may finish," she said softly, "you might—"

"—still, after all the years we have been apart, crave your kiss." Refusing to break her stunned gaze, he trailed his fingers down her cheek.

A gruff shout came from just outside the stable.

"Nay!" she croaked, twisting away so his hand dropped to her shoulder. She scrambled to her feet.

Dominic pushed up from the straw. When he moved, he felt the leather-sheathed knife, concealed in his boot, pressing against his calf. At least, if the situation turned threatening, he had a way to protect himself. And her.

Her spine rigid, hands curled into fists, Gisela hesitated several paces away. Ah, God. How he wanted her trust. To prove that, despite what she imagined, he was still very much the man she knew long ago.

Mayhap there was a way . . .

Reaching to his nape, he swept aside his hair, then untied the thin strip of leather he'd worn around his neck every day since they parted. With careful fingers, he drew the necklace from beneath his garments.

"Here." He offered it to her, the tattered white object at the end luminous in a slant of sunlight.

She took his necklace, just as footfalls crunched on the straw. Two men rounded the mounded hay bales— the baker accompanied by the blacksmith's assistant, whose broad shoulders and stout arms proved him a man of formidable strength. Clenched in the baker's right hand was Dominic's cane.

Unease rippled through Dominic. Upon seeing him, the baker's weathered face twisted into a scowl. The blacksmith's assistant smirked.

Dominic brushed straw from his peddler's mantle.

He did not like the looks upon the men's faces.

The baker glanced at Gisela, who had concealed the necklace in her fist. His scowl softened, betraying his genuine affection for her. 'Twas a look a widowed man would bestow upon a comely woman he hoped to woo.

Dominic's gut clenched.

"Are ye hale, Anne?" the baker asked her.

Tucking a strand of hair behind her ear, Gisela nodded. "I am fine. Thank you."

"Ye do not look fine." Thrusting an insolent hand toward Dominic, the baker said, "I saw 'im run after ye. Quite a sight, that was, seein' 'im 'obblin' along one moment, then droppin' 'is stick and breakin' into a run."

Dominic forced a good-natured chuckle. He would be wise to offer some kind of explanation, before the situation escalated into a brawl. "My good man—"

Lip curling, the baker said, "If I had known ye were a trickster, not a crippled peddler, ye would not 'ave got even one crumb from me."

A guilty flush warmed Dominic's face. "'Twas most kind of you to give me the bread to break my fast. Very generous, indeed. I will be sure to pay you for it."

The baker snorted. "Sure ye will." His gaze narrowed. "Ye may not be aware, fool, but 'is lordship, Geoffrey de Lanceau, does not take kindly ta thieves in 'is lands."

A smile tugged at Dominic's mouth. Being Geoffrey's closest friend, he knew his lord's opinions extremely well.

Having fought beside Geoffrey on crusade, helped him recover from mortal wounds cleaved by Saracen steel, and supported his recent quest to avenge his father's murder, Dominic vowed he knew Geoffrey better than anyone—apart from Geoffrey's lady wife, Elizabeth.

Pride threatened to undermine Dominic's determination not to grin. Geoffrey had many knights and men-at-arms at his command whom he might have sent on the crucial mission to find out who'd stolen his cloth shipment. But he'd chosen Dominic. The decision signified tremendous faith in Dominic's abilities—and he would not fail his friend.

Raising his hands in a gesture intended to diffuse the tension, Dominic looked at the baker, then the assistant. "Look, I meant no insult to you or your lord. My disguise was necessary, you see, to avoid knaves who tried to rob me earlier. If I may explain—"

Spitting a coarse oath, the baker threw the cane onto the straw. It landed with a *thump* by Dominic's feet.

"I had hoped to resolve this without a fight," Dominic muttered, sensing, even as he spoke, that the situation had gone beyond a peaceful resolution.

"Please." Gisela touched the baker's arm. "There was no harm done. I do not wish anyone hurt."

The baker tipped his head toward the stable doorway. "Go on, now, Anne."

She shook her head. "Not 'til I know the disagreement is over."

Lines of strain marked the corners of her mouth. Dominic suppressed an inner groan, for he'd never intended to cause her worry. "'Tis all right," he said gently.

She glanced at him. A ribbon of sunlight, streaming in through a botched repair in the wall, flowed over her, wrapping her in shimmering gold. "Mayhap if you explained that you are an old . . . friend of mine—"

Dominic doubted that would resolve the situation. Still, he gave her a reassuring smile. "I shall." He passed her the bread she'd left atop the grain barrel. "Go, now, like the good baker said."

Gisela sucked her bottom lip between her teeth, a gesture of reluctance he had adored long ago.

"Go," he said gruffly.

"I . . . Good-bye."

"Good-bye, *Anne.*"

Spinning on her heel, her hair tangling about her shoulders, she hurried away.

Her footsteps faded to silence. Flexing their hands, the baker and his assistant grinned. The stable's shadows seemed to darken with menace as the men stepped toward Dominic.

Anticipation of battle, as familiar to him as his own name, surged to life in his blood. In the east, he had fought and killed more men than he could remember. 'Twould be a shame to harm these two villagers who were riled over a misunderstanding—one, regrettably, he couldn't clarify due to his mission for Geoffrey.

With a lopsided grin, he made one last attempt to reach them. "Come now. Surely we can settle our disagreement like grown men. Shall we head to the tavern for a few pints of ale?"

The baker spat in the straw. He drew back his arm, then launched his fist toward Dominic's face.

Gisela unlocked the door of her tailor's shop, located on the ground floor of a two-story townhouse. When she stepped inside, the scent of cooking pottage greeted her. Her belly rumbled. With a sigh, she felt some of the tension slide from her shoulders.

Some, but not all.

Muffled voices reached her through the stout wall separating her shop and one-room home. She recognized the brusque but affectionate inflections of the middle-aged widow—the town midwife—who'd become a close friend and often watched over Ewan. Gisela also heard her little boy's excited ramblings. After locking and bolting the entrance door behind her, the bread loaf under her arm, Gisela stood for a moment in the shop's shadowed silence, simply listening to the swell and lull of sound.

Hanging on a wooden peg on the opposite wall, she discerned the form of a woolen gown she'd pinned together yester eve, a commission for the blacksmith's wife. On the long table underneath glinted the earthen-ware bowl in which she kept spare pins. Although she couldn't make them out in the darkness, she knew her cutting shears were there, too, along with bolts of cloth, spools of thread, and a wooden rule.

Like the sounds of conversation inside her home, the tailoring tools were familiar, an integral part of her daily routine. They should have brought her a measure of comfort. Yet, the disquiet growing inside her didn't abate.

Images of Dominic—the bold, controlled warrior cloaked in shadows—crowded into her mind to blend with her memories of him as a younger, tormented man. On her journey home, she pondered whether she'd made the right decision to leave the stable, for her shattered soul yearned to trust him, as he asked.

After the hellish past four months, would it be so wrong to trust at least him?

Running away was the safest choice. It allowed her to take refuge behind the emotional tower she'd raised around her heart in order to survive. It meant she never had to see Dominic again, if she didn't wish to.

But she did.

How desperately she missed him, craved the sound of his voice, yearned to be in his arms and know all that had happened to him since they parted.

That same, lonely part of her insisted she was a fool not to trust him. After the powerful love they forged together—proof of which was with her every day—he was the least likely person to betray her to Ryle.

Her mind spun with the weight of her thoughts. Worry plagued her, too, tightening her stomach into a painful knot, for she could not help but wonder what was happening to Dominic.

*'Tis all right*, he had assured her, before she fled. Was he truly all right?

The baker and blacksmith's assistant were furious with his deceptions, no doubt due to the recent thefts in Clovebury, committed, some claimed, by vagrants. Others blamed the rich merchants, such as Frenchman Varden Crenardieu, who wanted his own share of England; by encouraging his thugs to undermine the local traders, he took more and more control of the town.

A few sennights ago, the potter's shop was broken into, his clays ruined and his crockery smashed. The potter, a good friend of the baker's, raged 'twould cost him a month's wages for the repairs. A good reason, mayhap, for the baker to be suspicious of a peddler who was more than he initially seemed.

However, the men's manner had been extremely threatening.

A shrill cry, followed by laughter, echoed from inside Gisela's house—a reminder Ewan awaited, and of the bread she'd bought for his dinner. Struggling to harness her unsettling thoughts, she crossed to the sewing table and set down the loaf. Keeping her hand closed so she didn't drop the necklace Dominic had given her—which she'd not yet had a moment to look at—she shrugged out of her cloak. She hung it on the peg outside the door that opened into her house.

Her hand lingered on the doorknob. What if the men had harmed Dominic?

What if he lay unconscious on the stable floor, bruised and bleeding?

Gisela forced herself to exhale a calming breath as she retrieved the loaf. Angry as he might be, the baker, in all her dealings with him, seemed a fair man. Moreover, Dominic was a battle-hardened fighter. A warrior who had survived crusade and achieved knighthood was more than capable of defending himself.

She depressed the door handle. The panel swung inward, and she stepped into her home lit by candlelight and a fire in the opposite wall's stone hearth. The stone hearth, with its chimney disappearing into the unused floor above, was a rare feature for a commoner's home, which usually had a stone-ringed fire pit; it had convinced her to pay the extra rent, for with the fire venting outside, her fabrics would not smell of smoke.

Moreover, the entry to the upper story had been sealed off and the stairs removed by a previous owner, so she didn't have to worry about Ewan running up or falling down the steps.

Laughter soared in the room like bright birdsong. "Ha!" Ewan cried. "Ha!"

*Crack!* At the sound of wood smacking against

wood, Gisela jumped.

"Blocked ye again, ye red-cheeked weakling!" Ada roared. While Gisela pressed the door closed with her palm, Ewan darted into view, his gaze fixed on his opponent and his cheeks flushed with excitement. His dark blond hair, unruly at the best of times, looked completely wild.

In his right hand, he held a small wooden sword. Cornflower blue cloth wrapped around the weapon's grip—the scrap of silk Gisela saved after cutting out some commissioned garments. She'd tied on the silk with great ceremony the other day—when she played the worried lady giving a good-luck token to Sir Ewan the Bold, moments before he marched off to defeat the kitchen chair in battle.

Still unnoticed, she leaned back against the door, the bread secured under her arm. A wistful smile tugged at her mouth. A poignant ache coursed through her, for in that moment, she realized his father's hair was likely that same hue when he was a child. He'd probably dueled with toy swords, too, with equal fervor.

Ewan growled like a grumpy cat and lashed out with his sword.

"Missed!" Ada stomped into view, her plump hand dwarfing the grip of another wooden sword. Her long black braid, streaked with gray, swished from side to side, while her broad face glistened with perspiration. "'Tis thrice ye have missed me, little knight. How will ye save damsels and slay dragons?"

On the last triumphant word, Ewan jumped forward and poked her apron-covered belly.

"Oof!" Frowning, she said, "I shall get ye for that. I shall make ye quake in your boots, ye naughty little—" As though suddenly becoming aware of Gisela's presence, the woman straightened. Sweeping a hand over her girth, she blushed. "Um . . . 'allo."

Ewan's head swiveled. "Mama!" His face broke into a grin and he ran to her.

She knelt on the dirt floor, catching him in a one-armed hug. Closing her eyes, she savored his snug, return embrace. "My, what a fierce fighter you are," she said.

He drew back, his eyes sparkling. "Truly, Mama?"

She winked. "Indeed."

Raising his eyebrows, he looked over at Ada. "Can we fight again? Please?"

Wiping her forehead with the corner of the apron, Ada chuckled. "'Tis time for ye ta sup, young knight."

"Aw! But—"

"Ada is right. If you eat now, you will be refreshed for more battles."

Ewan pouted. He swung his sword from side to side. "I am not tired. Or hungry."

Gisela smiled over at Ada. "You must not miss this special feast, given to honor the young knights. That would be a shame."

Looking up at her, Ewan said, "What is served at

this special feast?"

Gisela placed a gentle hand upon his shoulder and steered him toward the battered kitchen table. "The finest cabbage pottage in the land."

Ewan grimaced. "Ugh. Pottage is—"

"—excellent for building a knight's strength," Ada said, bending over the iron pot steaming over the fire.

"Especially when served with bread." Gisela set the loaf on the table, then tore off a chunk with her fingers. She offered it to Ewan.

He shook his head. Grumbling under his breath, he slumped down on the bench drawn up to the table. His sword landed on the wood with a *thud*.

"Now, now, Button." Gisela patted his arm.

Bracing his elbows on the table, he scowled. "But, Mama—"

"'Tis better than going hungry." She handed him the bread again. "There are children in this village who go to bed at night with naught in their bellies."

Ignoring her outstretched hand, his thoughtful brown eyes gazed up at her. "Have you ever gone hungry?"

Anguish shivered through Gisela. "I have."

"When?"

Memories too painful to draw out into the here and now—or to explain to a young child who could not possibly understand—threatened to break through the mental barricades she'd managed to build day by day, month by month. The *clang* of the ladle hitting the pot's side, followed by Ada's footfalls, provided a welcome distraction. "I will tell you another time," Gisela said. "Now, you must eat."

Ewan sighed and snatched the bread from her fingers. He bit into it, just as Ada set an earthenware bowl filled with steaming pottage in front of him. Wrinkling his nose, he chewed his mouthful, while pulling at a fraying bit of the silk tied around his sword.

With a grateful smile, Gisela looked at Ada. "Thank you for looking after Ewan today."

Ada grinned back, revealing a slash of crooked teeth. "Me pleasure." Her smile wavered a little. "'E got a bit of a scrape on 'is arm, I fear, but 'tis not too bad."

Ewan nodded as he tore off more bread with his teeth. "I cried."

"Poor Button," Gisela murmured. "How did you get hurt?"

A blush stained his cheekbones. Around a mouthful of chewed bread, he said, "I fell."

"Tsk-tsk," Ada said.

Ewan's flush deepened.

"Fell from what?" Gisela resisted the motherly urge to panic. He hadn't looked hurt when she stepped into the home, so his injuries could not be too grave.

"Go on. Tell yer mama." Warmth threaded through Ada's words. She obviously tried very hard not to laugh.

Gisela quirked an eyebrow. "Tell me what happened."

Ewan shrugged, then tugged up his right tunic sleeve. A purplish bruise, along with a small, scabbed cut, marked his arm above the elbow. "Ada pretended to be a mountain ogre. I was the knight sent by the king to climb the mountain and fight her."

Covering her mouth to hide a smile, Gisela said, "Hmm?"

Dropping his tunic sleeve, Ewan flicked his hand at the table. "I jumped up here and lunged with my sword . . ." He squirmed on the bench. "My foot slipped. I hit my arm on the corner of the bench when I fell."

"We stopped playing mountain ogre after that," Ada added with a sheepish grin.

Gisela smiled before sitting beside Ewan on the bench. "I am sorry you were wounded," she said, giving him a hug. "Yet, I have told you before not to stand on the table."

His mouth tightened.

"The fault is mine," Ada cut in. "I should have—"

"Nay, Ada. Ewan knows what he is allowed to do, and what is forbidden."

The little boy looked down at the table. He swallowed.

"Please do not play on the table again, all right?"

He continued to stare down at his pottage. He bit off another chunk of bread. As he chewed, rebellion tightened his shoulders.

"Ewan." She pressed her hand over his small, white-knuckled hand, clenched on the tabletop. "What if you hit your head on the bench instead of your arm? I could not bear to see you injured."

He blew out a long sigh, heavy with resentment. "All right, Mama."

Gisela blinked moisture from her eyes. She well understood his frustrations, the sense of being constrained. How did she teach him that some risks were foolish and should be avoided, while others—like buying bread from the market—were necessary?

Her son had such spirit. If only she could let him scamper outside with other children. However, unlike Ryle's sprawling manor house where Ewan was born, which was surrounded by a lush garden, the townhouse was situated in a poorer area of the town. It overlooked a street well-traveled by farmers with horse-drawn wagons, vagrants, and customers who visited her premises as well as the other nearby shops. 'Twas not safe for Ewan to play in the busy street.

Moreover, the danger ran deeper. If Ryle or his cohorts saw him, they might snatch him. Or Ewan might inadvertently lead Ryle to this home. Then he would see them both dead.

Resisting her ever-present fear, Gisela rose from the bench to fetch a pot of salve from the table beside the two narrow pallets that were her and Ewan's beds. As she reached for the pot, she realized she still held Dominic's necklace. Now was not a good moment to inspect his gift.

Tucking the necklace into a rip in her sleeve's hem, she fetched the salve and returned to Ewan's side. She gently pushed back his tunic sleeve. The scents of lavender and comfrey rose from her fingers as she applied the salve. "There," she soothed. "A special ointment made from pickled dragon brains. 'Twill help heal your wound, Sir Knight."

A grudging grin touched his mouth. "Mama."

When Gisela rose from the bench, Ada motioned her to one side. Her hushed voice taut with concern, she said, "'Tis all right with ye, Anne, that we pretend 'e's a noble knight? 'E loves it so. 'Tis but a game, like what 'e plays with the toy knight ye made 'im. I mean no insult. I know we are all common folk."

"I do not mind," Gisela said. Glancing back at Ewan, she saw him dipping his bread into the pottage. In profile, with the light sweeping over his face, her thoughts again returned to Dominic in the stable, his visage limned by shadowed light.

What if he lay gravely wounded in the stable? Would the tavern owner help him? Or would Dominic be cast into the street, alone and suffering?

The earthenware pot shifted in her slick fingers. Being careful not to drop it, she crossed to the bedside table and set the salve down. Ada was encouraging Ewan to take another bite of pottage. Taking advantage of the quiet moment, Gisela withdrew Dominic's necklace from her sleeve.

The thin, softened leather swept like silk against her fingers, as though used to being worn against skin. Tied to the leather was a grubby bit of linen, part of an embroidered pattern of daisies.

Her hand shook. She recognized the scrap she'd torn from the hem of her shift the day they said goodbye. With tears running down her face, she'd pressed the linen into his hand as a token of her love, and to protect him on crusade.

"Oh, Dominic," she whispered. Fresh tears stung her eyes. He'd kept the little scrap all this time. Next to his skin.

Close to his heart.

With gut-wrenching poignancy, she knew he'd never have parted with the necklace unless he needed to show his loyalty to her. To prove she could trust him.

Gisela again snatched up the salve. Her whole body quivered with a tingling excitement, as though the sun had burned free of smothering clouds to illuminate a ravaged land, and she stood in its rejuvenating warmth.

She turned to face the table. "Ada, would you mind staying with Ewan a little while longer? There is something I must do."

# ChapteR ThRee

Slumped back against the stable wall, one arm cradling his aching ribs, Dominic opened his eyes. Tilting his head a fraction, he strained to hear over the restless stirring of the horse in the nearby stall.

*Footfalls.*

The light steps outside the stable indicated whoever approached was either hesitant, or knew he hadn't left and intended to entrap him. Mayhap the person meant to fulfill the baker and the assistant's parting promise: "If ye do not leave Clovebury right away, as fast as yer legs can take ye, we will come back and make certain ye leave. We want none of yer thievin' kind in our village." After delivering his threat, the baker had winced as he touched his blackening eye, a stunning punch from Dominic in retaliation for the blow to his jaw. Then, the baker turned and stalked out, the blacksmith's assistant at his heels.

For the briefest moment, Dominic hoped the footsteps were Gisela's. He wondered what she thought of his treasure and whether it meant to her what it did to him. He missed the necklace's brush against his skin, but he had no other means to prove himself worthy of her trust.

Yet, his gesture could well have been for naught. Earlier, Gisela had not welcomed him with knee-weakening kisses sweetened by the joy of a happy reunion. Instead, she reacted as though she never wanted to see him again—which meant 'twas unlikely she returned now.

A pebble rattled outside the stable's doorway. Dominic's hand dropped from his rib cage. In one soundless, careful moment, he pushed away from the wall into a crouch. Pain stabbed through his right side. He gritted his teeth, agony radiating along his bruised jaw. A groan scalded the back of his mouth, but he swallowed hard, subduing the sound. Now was not the time to dwell on his physical discomfort.

A shadow blocked the light coming in from the doorway.

His vision blurred. His pain became an eerie ringing in his ears. Shaking his head to clear his gaze, forcing himself to focus on whoever approached, he slid his hand into his boot and found the leather-sheathed knife. His fingers closed around the cool handle. As he drew it out, the thin, sharp blade glinted.

He pressed his lips together, then rose to his full height.

If he had to, he could attack with lethal efficiency. He had learned from necessity, when, his body soaked with sweat and his hauberk stained crimson with blood, he stared into the dark eyes of the enemy and knew he had but one choice: to survive.

The thought of taking another life twisted his innards. However, if whoever approached intended to kill him, survival was the one and only choice—as 'twas on crusade.

Straw rustled.

Any moment now, his assailant would round the steep mound of hay.

Edging forward, Dominic tightened his hold on the dagger. His body tensed. Pain throbbed along with the acute tension, but he paid it no heed.

He listened.

Waited.

A cloaked figure walked into his line of vision. The intruder held an object in his right hand. A weapon? "D—?"

Before his mind acknowledged the voice, he lunged. Catapulting forward, he collided with the intruder. His breath exhaled in a roar as, with his body weight, he slammed the cloaked figure against the stable wall. His left arm pinned the intruder's neck. He raised his knife, just as he realized how slight the person was, compared to the burly men he'd fought earlier.

A hard object thumped on the toe of his boot, then fell into the straw.

"Dominic!" Gisela gasped. Framed by the cloak's hood, her face looked as white as death. With the haze of attack fleeing from his mind, he recognized the rounded softness of her breasts beneath the woolen cloak, the flaxen shimmer of her hair peeking out from the hood, and her sweet scent.

"God's blood!" Lowering the dagger, he stepped back. "I am sorry."

Her mouth parted, but no sound emerged.

His exertions caught up to him. He sucked in a shaky breath, then grimaced. He forced a wry laugh. "We must stop meeting in such dire ways, Gisela, or I shall become as witless as a block of cheese."

Her trembling hand rose to her lips. She stared at the dagger. Revulsion clouded her eyes, while her fingers slid down her cloak to rest above her right breast.

"Gisela," he murmured.

She didn't seem to hear him. She continued to stare at the knife, which clearly held a terrible fascination. The horror on her face . . . It threatened to shatter him.

"Gisela!"

Her expression did not change. Her fingers pressed to her cloak, as though to stop blood gushing from a wound.

An icy chill skittered down his spine. She seemed in some kind of grisly trance. He'd witnessed men in such a state after battle, the gruesomeness of what they had encountered so overwhelming, they retreated into their own minds. Some never made the mental journey back.

Why would she react so? Surely she had not experienced battle.

Ignoring his nagging worry, he bent and pushed the knife back into its sheath. After straightening with a pained grunt, he stepped past her to retrieve the object lying in the straw a few yards away. An earthenware pot.

Dominic removed the lid and caught the pungent, herbal scent of salve. Astonishment lanced through him. She had come to tend his wounds.

She *did* care what happened to him, then.

He replaced the lid. Cradling the pot in his palm, he turned to face her. Her slender fingers still touched above her breast, but a hint of color had returned to her cheeks. Cognizance glimmered again in her eyes.

He tried not to stare, but he couldn't keep his gaze from dropping to her hand at her bosom. With wicked intensity, he remembered her breasts framed by her partly removed bodice. How smooth her breasts were, so exquisitely perfect, when he cupped them with his hands.

Had he injured her, when he threw her against the wall? Mayhap he'd bruised her lovely flesh, or accidentally cut her. "Did I hurt you?"

She made a nervous little sound before shaking her head. She snatched her fingers away. A rosy stain darkened her cheekbones.

Dominic dragged a hand over his mouth. He had to do *something* with his traitorous palm that wanted to cover the place she'd just abandoned.

Searching for words to ease the awkward silence, he said, "I did not mean to frighten you."

"W-why did you threaten me with your knife?" She shivered as she spoke and hugged her arms across her chest.

"I thought you were the baker and his friend, returning to ensure I left Clovebury."

Her gaze fixed on his bruised jaw. Compassion shadowed her gaze. "Did the baker hit you?"

"As often as I pummeled him. He got me well in the ribs, though." Dominic chuckled, but grimaced as discomfort shot through his face and rib cage. "Believe me, Gisela, if I had known 'twas you, I would never have drawn my dagger."

A tentative smile curved her mouth. "You do not intend to take me from here?"

He frowned. "What do you mean?"

She tightened her arms across her bosom. "I must know, Dominic. To be absolutely certain. You have not come . . . been sent by . . .?" Her breath shuddered between her lips. "You were not—"

"No one sent me to find you, or take you from here by force, if that is what you ask."

The faintest gleam of hope lit her eyes. "That is . . . the truth?"

Annoyance pricked him like a rose's thorns. Her distrust hurt him more deeply than he'd ever anticipated, especially after relinquishing his necklace. However, it seemed she had reason to be afraid, to doubt even him, when long ago, she'd trusted him, as no other man before, with the reward of her body's sweetness.

What had happened to her? What—or *who*—had changed his laughing, vibrant Gisela into a frightened, suspicious woman who preferred shadow to sunlight?

He would find out.

Forcing his lips into a smile, he said, "Of course, 'tis the truth. What reason would I have to speak falsely to you?"

Hope shone more brightly now in her gaze. "Promise me, Dominic."

The words reverberated in his thoughts. A memory revived, of her sitting surrounded by meadow flowers, her fetching smile tinged with sadness. *Promise me, Dominic*, she said. *Promise you will keep my memory in your soul, no matter what befalls you. I shall do the same, my love, for I shall never forget you.*

His eyes burned. 'Twas tougher this time to smile. His hand closed tighter around the salve pot, warmed by his palm. He managed to say, "I promise. I am no fire-breathing dragon, Gisela, come to destroy you. I am but a flesh-and-blood man." *And one who has missed you very, very much.*

Her gaze softened. A puff of breath escaped her, before she blinked hard. Moisture glistened along her bottom lashes. "Thank God."

"Gisela—"

A sob broke from her. She closed the space between

them, her hands fisting and uncurling as she walked. He ached to reach out and take her in his arms. To kiss her hair's silken softness. To hold her close and whisper that she never had to fear dragons ever again, for he would slay them with pebbles and straw if need be.

Would she let him embrace her? Mayhap she would think him too bold.

She probably belonged to another man, now.

Ah, what a painful thought!

Gisela hesitated before him. Her scent, perfumed with ambrosial memories of that summer meadow, teased him. Part of him begged to step away, to put distance between them and remove the temptation to touch her.

He could not. Like long ago, he was . . .

Captivated.

She tipped up her chin. Her hair slipped down off her shoulders in a golden ripple. Her moist gaze, haunted with a maelstrom of emotions, skimmed his face. Slowly. Carefully. As though comparing the man she remembered to the one who stood before her now.

Her breath rasped between her lips. Not quite a sob, but not a controlled exhalation, either. Anticipation hovered in each shuddered breath.

He was so entranced by the scent and sound of her, he didn't expect her touch. Light as a daisy petal, her fingers brushed his jaw. A tentative, almost disbelieving exploration.

"Oh, Dominic," she whispered, tears streaming

down her face. "I still cannot believe you are here."

"But I am." Ignoring the pain when he moved, he caught her hand. He pressed her palm to his skin, trapping his bruise beneath their joined hands.

She sniffled. "How—"

"I will tell you all," he promised. "Whatever you wish to know." Lifting her fingers away from his cheek, cradling them in his own, he kissed her palm. "'Tis good to see you, Gisela."

"And you," she said softly, her gaze fixed to her palm, as though she saw his kiss there, shimmering like a precious jewel.

Without looking away, he dropped the salve pot into the straw by his boots. Reaching up, he caught a stray lock of her hair, wondrously silken, as he remembered. A groan rumbled in his throat. She quivered, but didn't pull away.

*Touch her*, his mind whispered. *Kiss her, like before*.

Just when he thought to slide his arm around her waist to draw her close, he heard men talking in the tavern yard. Gisela started. Whirling away, she yanked her hood back over her head and faced the stable doorway, tense as a cornered doe.

A bitter taste flooded his tongue. How he hated to see her so changed.

"Do not fear," Dominic said. "'Tis probably farmers headed to The Stubborn Mule for a drink."

"Or the two men returning for you."

A grudging grin tilted his mouth. "If so, and there is another confrontation, I will protect you."

She glanced at him. "You are injured."

"A nuisance, aye, but I can still fight."

God's teeth, she looked about to scold him. As though he were a dull-witted child who could not even put on his own undergarments without help.

He scowled.

Throwing out her hands, she said in a tight voice, "Your wounds need to be tended. You cannot fight when you are wounded."

Nay? Ha!

"There is no other choice, Dominic. You cannot stay here. You must come home with me."

*You must come home with me.*

Even as she spoke the words, uncertainty gnawed at Gisela's frustration. Taking Dominic to her home cut a whole new facet to wove a whole new knot, one she had no idea how to face. Just the thought of him and Ewan in the same room made her stomach twist in a most unsettling fashion. However, there was no other option at this moment, apart from leaving Dominic in the stable, and she simply couldn't abandon him.

Dominic was staring at her with the most curious expression—a mixture of disbelief and pleasure. Almost as if she'd told him they must both strip off their garments and dangle upside down from the rafters.

Trust him to think such.

He cleared his throat. Keeping his voice down, to keep their conversation from whomever stood outside in the yard, he said, "Are you certain 'tis a good idea?"

Nay. 'Twas probably the most foolish idea she'd ever conceived. Somehow, she managed a confident smile. "Of course."

He pulled his fingers through his hair, wincing at the effort. The men's voices came from outside again. Her gaze flew to the doorway, tension buzzing so sharply in her veins, she wanted to scream. Reaching down, she snatched up the pot of salve—better to take it than to have to buy more—and then gestured for him to follow. She started toward the stable doorway with light, quick steps.

He muttered under his breath.

Stiffness gathered between her shoulder blades. If he made one more idiotic protest—

Straw rustled beside her, and then his strong, firm hand caught her elbow. Memories of Ryle's commanding grip lanced through her, and she instinctively recoiled, lurching, almost falling in her panic.

Dominic cursed. He instantly released her. His hand fell to his side, while his eyes narrowed, as if to shutter his concern. But it still shimmered in his gaze. "God's bloody knees, Gisela. When we are somewhere we can talk, you will tell me why you are so afeared."

Her mouth tightened at his authoritative tone. So very different from long ago, yet his boldness had likely kept him alive when others perished on crusade. Even as she recognized the toughened warrior he'd become, the maternal part of her surged to the fore.

"When we are somewhere we can talk," she said quietly, "you will not curse like a foul-mouthed sot. Agreed?" She did not want to spend days trying to stop Ewan from using the same words over and over.

Dominic's brows raised.

Fie! He had the audacity to look . . . affronted?

"Also," she said, keeping her voice low, "when others are about, you will call me Anne."

"As the baker did earlier," Dominic murmured. "Why?"

"Because in this town, that is my name."

"Ah." With a curious smile, he said, "Are you, also, disguised as someone else?"

Dread snaked through her. Shaking her head, she said, "Dominic, do not change the subject. Do you agree?"

"I do." He grinned. "I will be a very well-behaved knight."

He sounded just like Ewan—and his gaze held the same mischievous sparkle. Oh, God, was she wise to take Dominic to her home? What other choice did she have? None. "Let us be on our w—"

Laughter erupted outside.

The mirth vanished from Dominic's eyes. "Help me get out of this," he whispered, motioning to his long, filthy mantle.

"What? Why—"

"The baker and his assistant—and any of their friends—know me as a peddler. I will leave the disguise here." He handed her the knife, then unfastened the mantle and began to shrug out of it. Pain darkened his eyes.

"Let me." With a shaking hand, she helped him remove the tattered garment, aware of his breath warming the wool of her hood, and the heat of his body underneath the bulky garment. The mantle dropped to the straw. Underneath he wore a simple brown tunic, hose, and boots. Well-fitting garments that defined his broad, muscular form.

Their gazes met for a moment before he reclaimed the knife. He stepped ahead of her, shielding her body with his own. The dagger glinted.

With his free hand, he cautioned her to remain still. He edged forward to peer toward the doorway. She heard his indrawn breath when he moved in a way that strained his injuries.

A moment later, he gestured for her to join him.

"The men are heading to the tavern," he said in hushed tones. "Take my hand, and we will head for the alley." As he spoke, he turned the dagger so the flat of the blade pressed against his wrist and forearm, hidden by his tunic's cuff.

She nodded and slid her fingers into his.

Sensation glimmered where their palms touched. It

spread through her, a delicious warmth akin to the sun slipping free of a storm cloud. A sigh shivered from her lips. The brush of his calloused skin against hers, his snug but gentle grip, the memory of his touch long ago, sent awareness flooding through her. And an undeniable sense of . . . belonging.

Biting down on her lip, she looked up at Dominic, leading her toward the stable's doorway. If he'd noticed her reaction to his touch, he didn't acknowledge it, not even by the slightest glance back. Drawing her close behind him, he stepped out of the stable's shadows into the sunlight.

Dirt crunched under his strong strides—markedly different from the clumsy, shuffled gait of the peddler he had pretended to be. At a swift pace, he led her toward the narrow alley. Rowdy laughter came from the tavern. She dared a sidelong glance and saw two men stepping through the open doorway.

The weather-beaten panel swung shut.

She blew out a relieved breath.

With a wry chuckle, Dominic drew her into the alley. Glancing over his shoulder, he said, "'Twas a heavy sigh, Gisela."

"We do not appear to have been followed."

"That we know of."

She swallowed. "You mean—"

"We will not dally." While he spoke, he urged her to a quicker pace. "There may be thugs waiting for us at the street ahead."

"Waiting for you, you mean," she said. "You must be a dangerous man, Dominic."

His shoulders stiffened. Tension, now, defined his strides. As they hurried on, the smoky tang of the blacksmith's market fire carrying on the breeze, Dominic muttered, "I had not thought so."

"You had reason, though, to be disguised as a peddler. Do you have enemies in Clovebury?"

He suddenly froze, as though hearing a suspicious noise, and pressed her back against the stone wall of a nearby building. Flattened beside her, he said quietly, "We will discuss the matter later." After freeing his hand from hers, he slid the knife from his sleeve. He glanced at the entry to the alley. Tense. Alert.

A guarded secretiveness shadowed his handsome face. Resolve defined the set of his mouth. As she looked up at him, a wilder, tougher version of the man she loved, she wondered how much she really knew him. And whether he would answer her question.

Years ago, even though he was the son of a rich lord and she but a common merchant's daughter, they would have told each other anything. Promised each other anything.

Now . . .

Pressing her fingers to the building's rough stone, she tried to ignore the anguish of lost dreams. Both of their lives had changed, too much for her to hope he'd be in her life again with any more permanence than a shifting sunbeam.

Despite what they shared.

Dominic no doubt had hundreds of beautiful, wealthy noblewomen vying for his attentions. Years ago, after the arranged marriage his father and stepmother tried to force upon him, he vowed he would never wed. How he had railed in the meadow, stomping through the grass and cursing his entrapment that had naught to do with love, only his father's ambitions. To escape his betrothal to the highborn lady barely thirteen years old, he joined the king's crusade and left England.

Now that he'd returned, an older and more worldly wise man, he likely viewed marriage differently. He was probably wed to a lady worthy of his noble status, with children of his own.

Swallowing down the distressing thought, Gisela watched him peer into the alley. He grimaced, revealing the motion hurt. Then he laughed and shook his head. A mangy cat bounded past, a mouse in its jaws.

"Come on." Clasping her hand again, Dominic led her into the alley and toward the noisy market square. Musicians had started up a lively tune for an audience who clapped in time to the melody.

"Dominic, we are going the wrong way."

"Trust me," he said. "'Tis safest for us right now to be in a crowd. 'Twill be easier to lose anyone who might be following. Then, you may show me where to go."

Resentment—an emotional habit worn like a rut into her soul—welled up inside her at his commanding tone. Ryle had often spoken to her as though she had the intelligence of an iron trivet. Simply by being her husband, he believed he had the right to control even the tiniest facets of her existence.

A shudder jarred through her, leaving in its wake a painful emptiness. She shoved aside thoughts of Ryle. Dominic was not Ryle. Could never be Ryle.

Dominic glanced back at her, his brow creased with a frown. "What is wrong? Did you see someone following?"

"I am just . . . uneasy."

Compassion softened his gaze before he looked away. "'Tis not a bad thing," he said, so softly she almost didn't hear. "'Twill keep you safe."

*Safe.* She'd forgotten what 'twas like to be safe. No matter how reassured she might feel with Dominic leading the way, danger still lurked. Ahead of her. Behind her. In the market that drew townspeople from this county and beyond, some of whom likely knew Ryle. Never must she let down her caution.

They approached the market's outskirts. The bear trainer stood chatting with a group of men. Children scrambled in the dirt, chasing one another, while vendors, shouting encouragement to buy their wares, loaded more items onto their stall tables.

Dominic skirted the bear trainer and led her into the crowd between the rows of merchant tables.

With a sharp stab of fear, she saw they neared the baker's table. Had he returned to his stall? Would he recognize her? She squeezed Dominic's hand in silent warning. When he looked at her, she tipped her head, indicating the space between two nearby vendors; she and Dominic could slip through into the other section of the market.

Before she started in that direction, Dominic tugged her forward, forcing her to walk at his side, his body between her and the row of stalls, including the baker's. Dominic's arm settled around her waist. Drawing her near, bending his head close to hers, he propelled her onward.

To anyone watching, they'd appear to be a couple in love, the besotted man whispering endearments to his beloved while they shopped.

Confusion rushed through Gisela, even as his breath warmed her brow. The brush of his body against hers wreaked havoc with every emotional boundary she had established for herself. Desire, regret, the torment of their parting tangled up inside her. Her emotions unraveled, like a skein of thread tumbling from a table onto the floorboards to roll across the planks.

Fie! Never could she yield to fickle emotion. 'Twould make her careless. She couldn't afford one mistake when Ewan's safety—indeed, his life—depended on her.

Her spine rigid, she tried to step out of Dominic's embrace.

His arm tightened, curtailing her freedom. "Pretend you care for me, Gisela," he whispered against her ear.

Hot-cold tingles shivered down her neck. "Dominic—"

How could he ask that of her? How, when he no doubt loved another woman? A *lady*?

"Pretend as 'twas between us before," he coaxed with a hint of regret. "Believe, for this moment, that we were never apart. Please."

His regret burrowed inside her, an echo of every lonely day she'd missed him. She tried to swallow, but her mouth had become painfully dry. The dust stirred up by other market goers stung her eyes.

"'Tis difficult to pretend?" he said, his tone teasing. Yet, she discerned dismay, too.

"'Tis a game I have forgotten how to play," she answered, reaching up to sweep an escaping lock of hair back inside her hood. *A game of love I have not played since I lost you.*

"A pity, for a woman with eyes as blue as the summer sky."

A flush stole into her face. "Cease."

"—and lips as pink as the fleeting blush of sunset."

Her startled gaze flew to his. "Dominic!"

He grinned in a most gallant way before he kissed her brow. "And teeth as white as meadow daisies."

*Daisies.* Fighting a flood of anguish, she looked away, to catch the bemused smiles of the farmers standing nearby, who clearly saw them as a couple in love. An illusion she must stop right now. God help her if Ryle or one of his cohorts saw her with Dominic. Ryle's fury would be . . . murderous.

She pushed aside Dominic's arm. Still walking, she said, "You should not have said such."

"You do not like to be wooed? Or, were my compliments not fanciful enough for a woman of your extraordinary beauty?"

Bystanders chuckled. Gisela's face flamed. How mortifying for others to be listening to their conversation. She quickened her pace, almost tripping on her cloak. Exhaling an overly dramatic sigh—which elicited more laughter—Dominic followed.

Skirting three dogs scrabbling over a chunk of bread dropped by a child, she wondered if he remembered the afternoons they spent lying in the lush meadow, or the daisy chains she'd draped around his neck as though he were embraced by tiny suns.

"Chin up, Gisela," he murmured, matching her strides. "We are almost through the market."

"A good thing, too," she bit out, "before you resume your wretched flattery."

"I thought the daisy compliment was quite clever myself."

She rolled her eyes.

Dominic chuckled.

The crowd thinned, and then they reached the market's edge. She strode into the short alley that connected the market to a town street. To the right, a cart rumbled slowly past a line of dilapidated, two-story buildings with shopfronts opening onto the street. With a pinch of dismay, she realized her own tailor's premises looked equally as run-down.

"Which way?" Dominic glanced both ways down the street.

"Are we being followed?"

"Nay."

Clenching her hands, she faced him. "Are you absolutely certain?"

His gaze sharpened. "I am."

Gisela swallowed the fear threatening to snatch her voice. Meeting his gaze, she squared her shoulders. Her cloak's hood slipped farther from her head, revealing more of her face. With unsteady fingers, she yanked the cloth into place. "If there is even the slightest doubt we are being pursued—"

With a lazy swagger, he closed the distance between them. "I saw the baker loading more bread loaves onto his table while haggling with a customer. He was too busy to notice us. The blacksmith's assistant was not with him, nor did I see him during our walk through the market." He grinned. "Mayhap he needed to lie down after our tousle." Hands on his hips, Dominic stood near enough that his body warmth crept across the space between them, tempting her again with delicious memories of physical contact.

"Fine," she said. "Then—"

"Was there anyone else I should have been looking

for?"

His gaze skimmed her face. Like a bold, deliberate touch, she felt his attention slip from her eyes, down her nose, to her lips, then back up to her eyes. How keenly he studied her. He clearly tried to determine the source of her concern.

"Well?" he said quietly.

*Ryle*, her heart answered. *Always, we must watch out for him. Every moment of every day. Without fail.* However, 'twas not a wise moment to discuss her former husband. Shaking her head, she gestured down the street. "Follow me."

Gisela hurried past the row of shops, aware of Dominic's gritty footfalls behind her. Many of the businesses were open. The hinged, wooden boards were down, providing a table-like area to display wares. Inside the premises, the shopkeepers worked while they awaited customers.

At the tanner's shop, she spied a pair of brown leather shoes, about the right size for Ewan. His others were so badly worn, his toes would soon poke through. She had no extra coin this sennight, though, to splurge on new shoes.

Thinking of Ewan sent need racing through her— the urgent desire to know he was safe. Gisela walked faster, her cloak whispering with each step. She remembered her little boy as she'd last seen him, standing with Ada's pudgy hand on his shoulder. The wide-eyed, confused look he gave her before she dashed out had torn at her heart. Never had she arrived home and rushed out in such haste before. She must give him an extra hug tonight to make up for unsettling him.

What would he do when he saw Dominic? How would Ewan react to this bold warrior-knight, whom he had never met before? Misgiving rushed through her. What would Dominic think of little Ewan? Would he realize—

A gasp echoed behind her. She spun to see Dominic clutching his side. Sweat glistened on his brow. Despite his sun-bronzed skin, his face looked pale.

Fresh concern swept through her. "Are you all right?"

"My ribs dare to complain." His mouth curved in a wry grin. "You walk so fast, I vow the wind rushes beneath your feet."

Another attempt at flattery. However, his strained tone conveyed the extent of his discomfort. "I am sorry. I thought it best to hurry."

"If 'tis far, I should rest a moment." Stepping sideways, he leaned against a shop wall, one arm cradling his rib cage.

"My home is around the next corner." Worry pinched her. "What can I do to help? Would it ease your pain to lean on me?"

The lines around his lips deepened. "I will manage."

She frowned. "Are you certain?"

He drew himself up straight. His lips formed a roguish grin. "God's teeth, I do not wish to be seen leaning on you like an invalid. 'Twould completely destroy my reputation as a strong, lusty lover."

A disbelieving smile tugged at her lips. "That would be devastating."

He pressed his palm over his heart. "Exactly."

His bemused expression looked like Ewan's. Right down to the dimples. Her smile vanished on a wave of regret. "The sooner we reach my home, the sooner we can tend your injuries."

He nodded and carefully eased away from the wall.

Gisela slowed her strides to walk beside him. He didn't make any further complaints, but she sensed the effort it took him to maintain his indolent strides. Moments later, she motioned to her shop several yards ahead, distinguished by the painted sign depicting a needle and thread, hanging over the doorway. "That is it, there."

Dominic blew out a breath. His shoulders seemed to sag.

She hurried to the wooden door. Pressing one hand against the weathered panel, she dug in her cloak pocket for the key. Her fingers shook. When she pressed the wrought-iron key into the lock, a sense of inevitability weighed upon her, as though she stood poised to venture into a new, uncertain portion of her life.

Indeed, she was.

The lock clicked.

She slipped the key back into her pocket and pushed the door open. Motioning for Dominic to step ahead of her over the threshold, she said, "Come in."

# CHAPTER FOUR

A mélange of smells assailed Dominic when he stepped from the sunlit street into the darkened tailor's shop. He noted first the fading aroma of cooked fare. As he walked farther across the planked floor, he discerned the distinct smells of place, including the earthiness of wooden floors and walls. He also caught undertones of virgin cloth, ready to quiver free of confining bolts, sprawl in careless abandon across a table, and be cut and stitched into garments to delight and pleasure.

He inhaled again. The room's smell piqued memories of long ago days in the Port of Venice. He'd traveled there with Geoffrey and worked with rich merchants Marco and Pietro Vicenza while Geoffrey slowly regained his strength after surviving grave wounds from crusade.

More recently, Dominic had toiled alongside Geoffrey at Branton Keep, unloading shipments of fine silks and other fabrics Pietro sent from Venice.

When the shipments arrived, that is.

Dominic halted in the middle of the shop, aware of voices coming from a room beyond. Ignoring the ache in his side, he squinted in the shadows to take in the whitewashed walls, the table covered with tailor's implements, and the half-finished gown hung on the wall. A rolled length of brown wool rested on the table, alongside other bolts of fabric. He crossed to them and then trailed his fingers over the cloth. Far from the quality of Geoffrey's imported fabrics. None were silk.

Why, then, had he thought he caught a hint of expensive Eastern silk?

He reached up to rub his brow. Pain lanced through his rib cage, almost sending him reeling against the table. He grunted, then winced at the answering twinge in his jaw. With his senses chafed by pain, he couldn't completely trust his perceptions. He'd imagined the scent of silk, no doubt, because his thoughts had drifted.

Cold, clammy sweat collected between his shoulder blades. Under his breath, he prayed his knees wouldn't buckle. Just as he wiped perspiration from his upper lip, the door to the street closed. The room plunged into inky shadow, streaked here and there by sunshine piercing through holes in the wall.

"I will fetch some light." Gisela's voice wavered.

Was she worried about being alone with him in the dark? A mischievous voice inside him dared him to roar like a wild beast, to make her shriek, but somehow, he doubted 'twas the right moment for jest.

The chamber's air shifted as she swept past him. Her floral scent blended into the surrounding smells. He turned, following her scent. Savoring it like perfume.

Gisela did not seem to need light to guide her—she obviously knew the room's layout in minute detail—for a moment later, there came a soft *click*. Light streamed in through a doorway to an adjoining chamber. Surrounded by a bright stream of light, Gisela looked at him. "Wait here."

"Why?" he asked, before he thought to caution the question.

Looking at him, she pushed back her hood, revealing her hair's silken tangle. Resolve gleamed in her eyes, while another emotion—wariness, mayhap—hardened her expression. Without answering, she stepped into the chamber beyond and shut the door.

Dominic sighed. Why did she not invite him into the rest of the premises? Why must he wait here, in this empty room, like an unwanted pup?

He should march across the floor, yank open the door, and stride through . . . But, his wobbly legs might not carry him that far. And, if he guessed correctly, the connecting room was Gisela's home. Someone had cooked the fare he smelled earlier. Who shared her lodgings? A friend? A relative? Or even . . . a husband?

Anguish pressed upon Dominic's soul. Aye, could well be a husband. A comely young woman like Gisela wouldn't be without a companion. Far wiser, then, for him to wait for an invitation, than to barge in like an arrogant ass. He didn't need any more bruised ribs.

Hushed conversation reached him. Gingerly folding his arms across his chest, he turned to half-sit on the table. How wondrous to take weight off his unsteady legs.

He closed his eyes to the room's shadows. Let the quiet seep into him.

Listened.

The voices rose, one childlike and insistent. Three people were in the room beyond. Gisela, another woman, and . . . a young boy.

Dominic's eyes flew open. Was the child the woman's, or Gisela's?

He uncrossed his arms and pushed to standing, just as the inner door opened. Gisela stepped through, a cautious smile on her lips. She'd removed her cloak, revealing a worn, woolen gown that disguised rather than accentuated her lovely figure. Holding a tallow candle, she walked toward him. "You may come in now."

"I have triumphed in my initial test?" he quipped.

She frowned. "Test?"

"Trial by endurance," he said. "Waiting here, all alone, for you to return and fetch me." He grinned, despite the pain in his jaw. "Sheer agony, I assure you."

Her worried frown intensified. Raising the flickering candle close to his face, she peered into his eyes. How exquisite she looked, her features softened by the golden light, the dewy pout of her lips tantalizingly close—

"Dominic, did one of the men hit you about the head?"

"Mmm?" He snapped his gaze back up to hers. God's blood, but he could lose his soul in the beauty of her eyes. Thickly lashed and the color of an Eastern sea, they glimmered with the most intriguing secrets.

"Dominic."

Still holding her gaze, he winked. "Gisela, I was teasing you."

"Oh. I see." Lowering the candle, she stepped away. Even in the shadows, he saw her blush. She gestured to the doorway. "Please. This way."

He followed her to the threshold. Warmth and light enveloped him as he stepped into the small room beyond. The dirt-floored chamber was sparsely furnished, surprisingly so, considering Gisela's merchant parents were fairly well off. His gaze skimmed the rough-hewn trestle table and bench, the smaller table in the kitchen area for preparing food, a cupboard, side table, and two lumpy straw pallets pushed against the right wall. A fire crackled in the hearth.

His gaze returned to the trestle table and the black-haired woman wearing a stained apron, who eyed him with suspicion. In front of her, protected by her arm across his chest, stood a young boy of about four years old. His eyes were blue, just like his mother's. His dark blond hair, however, was inherited from his sire, whoever the man was. Wearing a brown tunic and hose that looked a bit too small, the boy carried a cloth doll under his arm—a knight, judging by the toy's garments.

The woman nudged the boy, who was peering down at Dominic's spurs. With a little jump, the lad executed a bow. The woman curtsied.

If his ribs were not aching, Dominic would have responded with a gallant bow in return. Instead, he dipped his head. "Good day."

Gisela gestured to the woman and boy. "Dominic," she said, "I would like you to meet Ada, a dear friend of mine."

The woman nodded. "'Allo."

A curious tension seemed to define Gisela's posture before she motioned to the boy. "Dominic, this is Ewan. My son."

The boy was hers. For one stunned breath, Dominic wondered if he looked upon his own child. Nay. He and Gisela had made love only twice. 'Twas unlikely she had conceived. However, from the boy's age, Dominic guessed she'd married and got with child shortly after he left England.

Her husband must not be here at the moment. He'd return, however, to slide his arm around her, kiss her, and draw his son in to join the embrace.

Fighting the unwelcome numbness flooding through

him, Dominic smiled at the boy. "Hello, Ewan."

The boy stared up at him with wide-eyed curiosity. Distrust also glinted in his gaze that shifted from Dominic to Gisela.

"Ewan," Gisela said in gentle reprimand. "Say hello to Dominic."

The boy's lips pursed. Dominic barely resisted a grin. The little lad had a stubborn streak, a trait acquired from his mother.

"Button."

The child's shoulders hunched. His eyes narrowed beneath his dark lashes, before he said, "Mama says you are her friend."

"I am."

"She says you are a knight."

"Aye."

Awe brightened the boy's gaze. *"Really?"*

Dominic nodded, then fingered perspiration-damp hair from his brow. He was sweating like a goose turning on a spit. Hardly the way to make a favorable impression.

"Mayhap you should sit down," Gisela said quickly. She gestured to the battered bench drawn up to the table. "Ada, is there any pottage left?"

"There is." The older woman turned to the fire.

With a grateful groan, Dominic sank onto the bench that squeaked at his weight. He spread his booted legs out in front of him. With slow, very careful movements, he rested his elbows back on the table. His entire body sighed with relief.

Standing by the fire, Ada cast him a disparaging glance before looking back at the steaming pot.

Closing his eyes, Dominic ran his hand over his face. He could only imagine how he looked to the older woman—like a ruffian dragged in by kindhearted Gisela. He vowed to hold true to his promise to be on his most chivalrous behavior. Above all, he must remember not to curse. That was a sensitive issue, it seemed, for Gisela.

He heard her walk across the chamber and whisper to Ada, and the *clank* of the ladle. Yet, the rasp of an indrawn breath, along with the sensation of being scrutinized from head to toe, forced Dominic to open his weary eyes. Ewan stood barely a hand's span away, his little fingers clasped together. They twitched with barely contained excitement. The toy knight, tossed aside in haste, now lay facedown on one of the pallets.

Ewan sucked in his plump bottom lip. "My knight's name is Sir Smug."

Sir *what?* "I see. How did he get such a fine name?"

"My mama made him for me. She tried to sew him a smiling mouth, but she could not get it quite right. She said he looks a bit smug."

Dominic barely smothered a laugh. "He is perfectly named, then."

After a silence, the boy blurted, "If you are a knight, where is your sword?"

Ah. An astute question. "'Tis in a safe place."

A frown clouded Ewan's face. "Does a knight not wear his sword all the time?"

"Most of the time."

"Ewan," Gisela said, casting Dominic an apologetic smile. "Dominic would like to rest quietly for a moment. He is wounded, you see."

"You were in a fight?" Ewan's eyes were enormous now.

Ridiculous pride welled inside Dominic. "Indeed, I was. I fended off my assailants with my bare hands. I learned all manner of fighting, you see, when I was on crusade."

"Crusade!" Ewan gasped. "You fought with the king?"

Dominic nodded.

The boy edged even closer. An excited flush reddened his cheeks. "When were you on crusade? Did you meet King Richard? What does he look like? When—"

"Button! What did I tell you?"

"Mama."

The little boy looked so disappointed, Dominic could not resist a chuckle. "'Tis all right. He is merely curious."

The barest smile touched Ewan's mouth. Anticipation still glimmered in his eyes while his hands twisted into the front of his worn tunic. "Did you . . ." He gnawed his bottom lip. "Did you ever—"

"Pottage, milord." With a brisk *thud*, Ada set the bowl down on the table beside Dominic, a deliberate attempt, no doubt, to cut short the conversation.

Dominic smiled at her. "I thank you, good woman."

She snorted, sounding remarkably like a rheumatic

horse, then looked at Ewan. "Why do you not come with me for a moment? Your mama is running out of flour. We will go to my home and fetch some."

Ewan shook his head. "I want to stay here."

"I might have a sugared cake for you." Ada reached for the lad's hand. "I will see what I can find in my kitchen."

Snatching his hand away, Ewan said, "I am not going. I want to show him my wooden sword."

Gisela walked over, carrying cloth bandages and the ointment pot she took to the stable. "Another time, Button. Now, you will go with Ada." Worry shadowed her gaze as she looked at Ada. "He must wear his mantle. Do not let him push down his hood. He must stay covered up."

"Of course," the older woman replied in a soothing tone that implied she'd discussed the matter several times before. "We are only going five houses away. He will be fine."

Dominic frowned. Five houses away? For such a short distance, and on such a fine summer day, the boy did not need to wear his hooded mantle. Why did Gisela insist upon it? Why did she also keep covered up when outside? He longed to ask, but 'twas not his affair.

Scowling, Ewan crossed his arms. He did not budge when Ada fetched his mantle, cut from coarse, mud-brown wool. She held it out, clucking her tongue. At last, rolling his eyes, the boy relented and shoved his arms into the garment that looked several sizes too big.

Gisela stepped forward to murmur in Ada's ear. Dominic pretended not to listen.

Drowning in his overlarge mantle, Ewan met Dominic's gaze. "I have to know," the little boy said in a whisper. "Did you ever . . ."

Dominic arched an eyebrow. He anticipated the rest of the question. Did you ever kill a man? Fight a Saracen? Dine with the king? "Aye?"

"Slay dragons?"

*Slay dragons?*

Dominic barely caught an astonished laugh. His eyes watered with the effort. Somehow, he forced a solemn expression. "Indeed," he said, "I have."

Gisela waited until the outer door closed. Then, she released a heavy, pent-up breath.

Sitting on the bench only a hand's span away, Dominic chuckled.

"Do not laugh so," she said, trying not to frown. She removed the lid from the ointment pot, releasing the strong, herbal scent.

"Ewan is a charming boy."

*Aye. He takes after his father.*

"He is," she said, lining up strips of linen bandages beside the pot on the table, "but you should not have told him you slayed dragons."

The bench creaked as Dominic stretched back farther. "Why not?"

She straightened to glare at him. "'Tis a lie."

"Is it?"

Gisela's mouth tightened. Did he take her for a fool? "I have never seen a dragon. Nor has anyone else I know. Do you mean to tell me such creatures with fangs and wings are real?"

An indulgent grin softened Dominic's mouth. "Dragons come in many shapes and sizes, Gisela. Some are loud and dangerous. Others, more insidious."

Loud, dangerous, and insidious. All of those qualities applied to Ryle.

"What I am trying to say," he went on, his tone quiet yet intense, "is that not all dragons are fire-breathing monsters with wings and fangs. Some come in the guise of fellow men and women. Some could be better described as obstacles that keep us from what we desire most. However, they are dragons just the same."

Fie! There was such truth to his words—which meant he, too, had encountered dragons who scarred him. His father and stepmother. The Saracens he faced on the eastern battlefields. All fit his description of dragons. So did the men he fought today.

"What you imply, then," she said, "is that your wounds were caused by a brush with two angry dragons."

A wry smile tilted Dominic's mouth. "Something like that."

She arched an eyebrow. "The cut on your cheek was caused by a scratch from a dragon's claw?"

"Nay, a blow from a wing, I vow," Dominic said.

"And your hurt ribs?"

"A consequence of trying to climb up the dragon's back. I planned to run up its scaly spine to its head and stab out its eyes, but it threw me off."

She smiled. "A dangerous ploy."

"I have never been afraid of a little danger."

His words ended on a velvety huskiness that reminded her of a lazy afternoon long ago, especially the breathless moment before he kissed her and eased her down in the sweet-scented grass. A tingling sensation skittered across her breasts.

Quite apart from his voice's raw sensuality, he spoke with hidden meaning. He told her, in his own way, she could confide in him. He would help her vanquish her dragons.

A silent cry welled up inside her. How she wished she could melt into his embrace, tell him all that had happened to her and why she couldn't trust anyone. He, of all people, deserved to know. However, she simply . . . could not.

Dominic's intense gaze had not left her face. A painful sense of vulnerability—of unbearable longing for him—swept through her.

Somehow, she forced a careless grin. "Well, Sir Dominic the Mighty Dragon Slayer," she said, "we had best take care of your wounds before they fester."

Remorse glimmered in his eyes for a moment before he nodded.

Gisela picked up several long, linen strips. "If you remove your tunic, I will bind your ribs."

He reached for his garment's hem. As his hands moved, she had a sudden memory of him taking off his tunic in the meadow. He'd drawn the garment over his head and then tossed it aside, revealing the sun-bronzed planes of his torso. Dark, curly hair sprinkled across his chest. For a vivid, stunning moment, she recalled the springy texture of that hair beneath her palm and the heat of his muscled body as he lay back in the long grasses, his lopsided grin encouraging her to explore his nakedness.

Drawing in a shaky breath, she blinked down at the table. She fiddled with the other bandages, barely seeing them, trying to force aside the tantalizing image in her mind.

Beside her came a whispering sound, followed by a gasp. "God's blood," Dominic groaned.

She dropped the bandages and turned to face him. His tunic bunched about his raised arms, imprisoning his movements. The lower part of his face hidden by the fabric, Dominic gazed at her with desperation.

"I am as helpless as a trussed rooster."

An astonishing thought. She laughed.

Dominic scowled and wiggled his arms, clearly trying to shift the tight fabric. He groaned again.

"Careful! Your ribs—"

He grunted like Ewan in one of his petulant moments. "You must help me."

"Of course. Hold still."

She moved closer. His thigh was no more than two fingers' width from her legs. But she stopped short of physical contact. That, she couldn't do.

From his tangle of tunic, he mumbled, "How mortifying. I cannot even undress myself."

She smiled. "I will not tell anyone."

"Especially Ewan. If he knew that I was not in truth a brave, skilled knight, but a helpless idiot—"

Gisela rolled her eyes. "Dominic." Leaning forward, she reached for his tunic's hem. Simple to catch hold of the right side, but the left . . .

Fighting the urge to blush, she reached across his splayed legs. 'Twould be much easier to stand between his parted limbs, but . . . she simply could not be so brazen. Biting down on her lip, she groped for the tunic's left edge.

"Be sure you grab the right sections of cloth, Gisela."

She huffed. "Do not be ridiculous." Her fingers were nowhere near any part of him that might be inappropriate.

Especially *that* part.

Oh, God! Why did she even *think* about *that* part of Dominic?

Her face burned. She hoped Ada and Ewan did not walk in while she helped Dominic, or she would owe them a very good explanation.

"I was only trying to be helpful," Dominic said, his voice close to her ear.

Ha! Indeed.

Her fingers slipped over his bare waist, tempting her with the feel of taut muscles and his skin's smooth warmth. Tamping down a shiver, she caught hold of the left side of his tunic. "Keep still," she said, more briskly than intended, while she began to draw up the hem.

The movement caught her off balance. Gisela felt herself pitch forward. She must *not* fall onto him!

With a startled squawk, she let go and stumbled back.

Dominic sighed. "Gisela—"

Impatience thinned his voice. The effort of holding his arms up at an awkward angle was no doubt aggravating his injuries.

Her fault, for being foolish.

Shoving aside her inhibitions, she stepped around his right leg, into the vee between his legs. The fabric of his hose brushed against her gown, a sensuous pull of cloth against cloth.

His gaze sharpened. "I did not think you would come so close."

"'Twill be easiest to remove your tunic," she said matter-of-factly, glad her tone did not betray the tiny tremors racing through her.

"Mmm."

Bending at the waist, she reached for his tunic's hem

again. At this angle, her forehead bumped against his raised arms. When her fingers skated over his bared waist again, his breath rushed out on a hiss. Ignoring a fresh wave of awareness, she slowly drew the material up. With gentle movements, she eased out one of his arms, then the other, and pulled the tunic over his head. It landed on the table with a muted *plop*.

He blew out a relieved groan. His arms lowered to his sides, drawing her gaze to his bare chest. His tanned skin flowed over honed muscles. Several pinkish scars marked his torso—healed wounds from past dragon fights. None, though, as deep as the scar on her breast.

She swallowed hard, sensing his keen gaze upon her. *Look away, Gisela. You are a commoner and 'tis not proper to stare. Dominic is no longer your lover. He belongs to a lady.*

Oh, God, but she couldn't tear her gaze away. Her fingers ached to journey over his skin in a deliberate caress, to trace each scar and rejoice he was still alive, and to discover whether the memories she cherished of him were still true. How she longed to touch him.

*Do not, Gisela. Do not!*

She started to turn away.

With faint scrapes, his booted legs shifted inward. Trapping her.

She gasped. Her gaze locked with his.

Crossing his arms over his naked chest, Dominic smiled up at her.

"Dominic—"

"My limbs felt very weak," he said with a mischievous little grin. "Thank you for helping me to regain my strength."

What cheek! "Release me."

"Aye, Sweet Daisy. When you tell me why you are so afeared."

*Sweet Daisy.* His special name for her long ago.

Rebellion and desire warred inside her. He had no right to imprison her in such a manner. However, the lovesick, lonely part of her yearned to surrender to his demand. To draw strength from his strength and risk confiding in him. To know that for one, brief moment, she didn't have to shoulder all of her burdens alone.

"Go on, Gisela," Dominic said, his voice as soft as the luxurious silk Varden Crenardieu delivered to her days ago, now hidden in the storage area under her shop's floor. "We are alone," Dominic went on. "No one else will know what you tell me."

Warmth from his legs seeped through her gown's thin wool. How easy 'twould be to lean forward, slide her arms around his neck, and melt against him.

But once she confided in him, she could not take the words back. They would flood out, as blood had gushed from her breast and stained her bodice crimson. He would know, then, how very different she was from the woman he loved years ago.

He might be driven to confront Ryle . . . and then Dominic would die.

Gisela's heart ached. She mentally stitched together her resolve and leveled him a cool look. "Your wounds are more important right now than what I would tell you."

He smiled. The sly twist of his mouth suggested she wouldn't deter him that easily. "My wounds will still be there after you have confided in me."

She almost laughed at the stubborn tilt of his jaw. Setting her hands on her hips, she frowned at him. "Why do you insist on being a difficult patient? You are in my home, Dominic. I vow you owe *me* an explanation. Most of all, why you were in disguise."

He chuckled. "What a tough little daisy you have become."

*Out of necessity*, her mind answered, *for Ewan*. She flattened her lips to smother the words and reached over to snatch up a linen bandage. Dangling it in front of him, she said, "'Twould be easiest to bind your ribs if you stand."

He squinted up at her for a long moment. "As you command, Sweet Daisy. While you tend me, I will confide my secrets to you. Then, you will share yours with me."

Dominic pushed himself up from the bench, gritting his teeth against the sensation of daggers piercing his ribs. Gisela's scent still lingered in the space she'd vacated the instant he eased his legs apart. She'd shot away like an arrow fired from a bow.

Now, she stood a short distance from him. She twisted the bandage around her slender fingers, fashioning the length of cloth to her purpose before she neared him again. Gnawing the lush curve of her bottom lip, she examined his ribs before closing her eyes on a little sigh. A sound of reluctance.

Disappointment dulled the awareness still sparking in his veins. Had she changed her mind about treating him because he'd entrapped her?

Before he could ask, she quickly stepped forward, extended her arms on either side of his torso, and stretched the bandage out behind him. For the barest moment, her breasts brushed his chest before she drew back, binding the cloth around his rib cage.

He inhaled sharply, stunned by the sensations elicited by that brief contact.

She paused. "Did I hurt you?"

*Aye, you are causing me tremendous torment.*

"Nay, Daisy. I am deciding where, exactly, I should begin my tale."

Gisela stood so close, he could dip his head and kiss the crown of her head. Her tresses shimmered like the purest gold, while her fragrance drifted to him, delicate, yet . . . captivating. Her essence, sweet as wildflower nectar, tantalized him in a way no other woman had, before or after her. "It sounds very important," she murmured, slipping more of the linen around his torso. When her warm fingertips brushed his spine, he shuddered.

"Indeed, 'tis," he said, clearing the huskiness from his voice. "I would not have been in disguise otherwise."

Her hand stilled. "Dominic, were you involved in some kind of misdeed?"

*Nay, but I may be, if you keep tormenting me with your hands.*

Mentally sweeping away his inappropriate thoughts, he smiled down at her. "I am not a hunted criminal, if that is what you ask. I came to Clovebury because I was ordered here by my good friend and lord, Geoffrey de Lanceau."

"*The* Lord de Lanceau? Who lives with his lady wife and son at Branton Keep?"

"The same." Dominic could not contain a proud grin. "As you probably know, Geoffrey is lord of most of Moydenshire."

Awe glistened in her eyes. As well as an inkling of . . . dread?

"So," she said, "you are his spy."

Dominic nodded.

She exhaled a shaky breath. Her fingers felt damp against his skin. Ah. He had startled her with his revelation. Knowing he was a man of great importance, she viewed him differently. She probably worried about botching the bandaging.

He must reassure her immediately. "I am still the same Dominic you knew long ago," he said, "despite my allegiance to de Lanceau."

She did not look at all convinced. After tying the bandage, she reached for another. "If I may ask, what brings you to Clovebury? Did you come to investigate the recent spate of robberies?"

A frown touched Dominic's brow. "I did not know of such robberies."

Shaking her head, Gisela continued her bandaging. "Many of the shop owners fear their premises will be broken into and their goods destroyed. The break-ins usually happen at night, and are committed either by local thugs or vagrants. The potter's shop is among those recently vandalized." Raising her gaze, she said, "He is a good friend of the baker's."

"A good reason, then, for him to distrust strangers," Dominic said.

Surprise widened her gaze before she again lowered her lashes, golden against her fair skin. When her fingers touched his torso, and an answering shiver broke through him, he said, "My quest for de Lanceau could well be connected to these robberies. However, I do not know yet. I have been tasked, you see, to discover who stole Geoffrey's shipment of cloth sent to him by river."

"What kind of cloth?"

"Silks. Bolts of the finest, most luxurious fabric . . ."

His voice trailed off. She gaped up at him with a most curious expression. A touching blend of suspicion and dismay.

Her mouth, parted on a silent gasp, snapped shut. Blinking hard, she again looked at his bandages. But, from her distant gaze, he guessed her thoughts were not on this moment, but elsewhere.

"Gisela?"

"Mmm?"

He caught hold of her upper arms. She stiffened. Her hands, about to sweep the linen around his back again, dropped to his torso. The warmth of her fingers pressed to his skin . . .

He must not allow himself to be distracted.

"Do you know about the stolen silks?"

A sharp little laugh broke from her. "Me? Why would I?"

"You are a tailor. You earn your living from making garments."

Her gaze fell to her hands, curled against his chest. She gnawed her lip again. "Dominic—"

"I only ask, Gisela, because a client may have asked you about sewing garments from silk." He gently squeezed her arms. "Not because I suspect you are involved with stealing Geoffrey's shipments or any other wrongdoing."

A shaky breath rushed between her lips. She slowly nodded. "If I seem . . . shocked," she said, each word spoken with care, "'tis because I hate to think there are folk in this town—a place I consider my home—who would steal from Lord de Lanceau." Her throat moved with a swallow. "I cannot believe it."

"'Tis the truth."

Her body quivered in his hold, proof of how much the thought unnerved her. "Is that why you were disguised as a peddler? To try to find the thieves?"

Dominic nodded. "Geoffrey decided 'twas the best approach for now, rather than send out a contingent of men-at-arms. The thieves might run, then, with the silks—making it more difficult to find the stolen cloth. 'Tis vital to recover all of the missing bolts." He grinned. "I hoped to linger about the market, to eavesdrop on the local gossipers. Then, I saw you."

A flush stained her face. "I thwarted your plans."

"Nay. Merely delayed them." Squeezing her arms one more time, he released her and glanced down at his bandages. "Are you almost done?"

"Aye." With gentle hands, she resumed wrapping the linen about his ribs. Not too tight. Loose enough for his chest to expand and constrict with each breath. As though, somehow, she knew the secrets of good bandaging. Of course, having a rambunctious son, she likely learned by tending his wounds.

"If you hear any word about the silks—or mayhap a customer brings some to you to be made into clothes—you will tell me, aye?"

"Few in Clovebury have the means to buy silk, Dominic," she said quietly.

"Geoffrey's shipment is in this town somewhere. It left the town farther upriver, but did not reach Branton.

Clovebury is the only riverfront town in between."

After knotting the last bandage, she tucked the ends into the rest of the wrappings. "How does that feel?"

"Much better. Thank you."

"If you sit again, I will tend your jaw."

He almost answered he could tend the injury him-self—even a simpleton could rub on some salve—but he found himself dropping back down on the bench. Hold-ing the pot, she leaned closer and dabbed ointment on his wound.

The salve's strong scent assailed him. Yet, it carried the soft undertone of her fragrance. A reminder that she, above all, was the reason he spoke of the silks in the first place.

"What I have told you about Geoffrey's stolen cloth, you must keep to yourself," he said in clear warning. "You must tell no one."

One hand on his chin, she was leaning back to in-spect his wound. Her gaze slid to his. "I will not."

"That is a solemn oath, Gisela, healer of Sir Dominic the Mighty Dragon Slayer?"

She rolled her eyes and laughed. "'Tis."

"Good." He smiled at her. "Now, Gisela, 'tis your turn to share your confidence with me. Tell me what— or *whom*—you fear."

# CHAPTER FIVE

Refusal rose in Gisela's throat, scalding like hot soup. The salve on her fingers suddenly felt cold, as if a breeze had invaded her home and chilled her skin. Breaking her gaze from Dominic's, she stepped from between his legs, pressed the stopper into the pot, and set it down on the table.

"You *must* tell me," Dominic said.

His voice, taut with emotion, forced her gaze back to him. The angles of his cheekbones looked harsher, all teasing boyishness gone from his expression. A steely tension surrounded him. He would look this way in the moments before he charged into battle.

Looking back at the table, she picked up a clean bandage and dried her fingers. She struggled to deny the command in his stare. Fie! Refusing him was akin to denying the sun's warmth. Impossible.

Their gazes locked. Such resolve gleamed in his brown eyes. His need for answers obviously consumed him.

A similar consuming heat, rooted in the love they'd once shared, bloomed within her. Gisela struggled to smother it, to quell the other emotions taking root— longing, desire, and regret. She moistened her bottom lip with her tongue and set aside the bandage, while fighting to bolster the courage that had kept her and Ewan alive. "Dominic, please, I cannot—"

"Who has wounded you so?" His tone almost a growl, he said, "Who, Gisela? Your lover?"

Tears burned her eyes. "I have no lover." *I have loved no man, Dominic, but you.*

His gaze sharpened to a piercing stare. "Your husband?"

She had anticipated the question. Still, a gasp jammed in her throat. The room blurred around her. Her fingers skidded blindly over the table, seeking hold, finally clamping to the edge of the scarred but service-able oak. A wheezing sound broke from her.

The bench creaked. Before she could wave him away, Dominic stood beside her. His hands pressed to her shoulders.

"Gisela," he whispered. Such fury crackled in his voice. It turned her innards as cold as a bleak winter night.

The heat of his palms warmed her through the gown and shift she wore underneath. His touch thawed some of the numbness inside her, threatening to melt it. Oh,

God. If only she could accept the comfort he offered.

"You fear your husband," Dominic said quietly, as if he needed her to confirm what she'd unintentionally revealed.

*Deny the truth*, part of her shrilled. *Do what you must—say what you must—to keep Dominic from knowing about Ryle.* However, Dominic's touch, offering trust and compassion, held a coaxing persuasion all its own.

"I call no man 'husband,'" she bit out. "Not anymore."

"What happened?" he whispered.

Misery, anger, and shame tangled up inside her. She fought a sob.

Dominic spat an oath. He gently massaged her shoulders; he must have felt the tension cinching her muscles into knots. "Tell me what he did to you, Sweet Daisy."

*Nay!*

Gisela twisted in his hold. His hands fell from her shoulders, and his arms dropped to his sides. He did not, however, step away.

Her bottom pressed against the table's edge, she faced him now. Her gaze met the swell of his bandaged chest. His masculine scent rose from his skin, tempting her with memories of lying naked beneath him, of the mingled fragrance of their bodies when they made love.

Fisting her trembling hands, she looked up at him.

He didn't scowl or quirk a domineering eyebrow. Nor did his gaze sharpen with command. He stood absolutely still, his silence more powerful than words, for he clearly believed he had a right to stand so close. Long ago, with the meadow grass beneath them, the wildflowers watching over them, the sun streaming down upon them, he'd become integral to her existence. As vital as rainwater to a daisy.

"Gisela," he coaxed.

His breath warmed her brow. She fought for emotional detachment. For the safety of distance. Forcing out the words, she said, "I cannot."

Dominic's gaze darkened. "Do you fear he will know what you have told me? I will never betray you."

She hated the bitter words burning her tongue. But she had to force Dominic away, to quell the dangerous emotion into submission, before it crested beyond her control. She'd rather die than give Ryle the opportunity to kill Dominic. "What is between my former husband and me is not your affair."

Instead of recoiling in anger, an indulgent smile spread across Dominic's face. "Aye, Sweet Daisy, 'tis. Ever since I laid eyes upon you in the market."

*Why? You belong to another woman. I mean naught to you.* Throwing up her hands, she cried, "You cannot help me!"

"How can you be certain? I know Geoffrey very well. Mayhap he can intervene."

"Nay! Ry—H-he . . . is a very dangerous man. His temper—"

"Is *he* the cause of your fear? How, Sweet Daisy, did

he show you this fearsome temper?"

She looked away. How her disfigured breast ached. The pain cut into her with the bite of a dagger. She longed to press her fingers over the scar, to ease the discomfort, but 'twould only rouse Dominic's suspicions further.

Her gaze fell to the side table beside her pallet. His necklace lay there, the bit of embroidered linen very white against the oak. She had no right to keep his memento. Brushing past him, she crossed to the table, collected the necklace, and handed it to him.

With a wry glance down at his bandages, he said, "Will you put it on for me?"

"Of course." Stepping behind him, she fastened the jewelry. Her fingers brushed his tangled hair spilling over his broad shoulders. Magnificent shoulders that bespoke years of physical training required of a knight. Would he notice if she lingered, just for a moment, and appreciated his beauty?

*Gisela, do not be foolish!*

He turned to face her, his fingers touching the ragged scrap that brushed the edge of his bandages. "I have missed my necklace. It seemed as though part of me were missing."

*Do not say such lovely things.* Blinking away the threat of tears, she said, "I am astonished you kept it all these years."

He smiled. "Your token brought me luck in battle." His tone softening, he added, "I am certain it brought me back to you."

*Oh, Dominic!*

Before she realized his intent, he touched her cheek, a caress so exquisitely tender, she wanted to weep. "Be honest with me, Gisela. Are you are afraid to speak to me because your former husband knows where you live? You fear if he learns you confided in me, he will be angry with you? That he will come here to confront you?"

How dangerously close Dominic came to the truth. While she could never tell him the truth, she refused to let him believe Ryle lived nearby and she was too weak to try to elude his influence. "He does not live in Clovebury. Neither does he know where I live." Her voice hardened. "He will never know."

A curious light warmed Dominic's eyes. "With every word, Gisela, I grow more and more intrigued."

Fear tingled in her veins like shards of ice. She'd said too much. He owed his allegiance to de Lanceau, who, if he knew she'd fled from Ryle, could well order her returned to her husband. 'Twas the law.

"Please. No more questions." She turned away, forcing his hand to drop from her cheek.

Before she took two steps, he said very quietly, "You ran away."

Gisela swallowed, the sound impossibly loud. Panic shrieked inside her. She froze, her mind scrambling for a reasonable explanation to undermine Dominic's words. But, when she glanced back at him, she saw acknowledgment in his gaze. He *knew* he'd guessed correctly.

*Oh, God!*

Through a haze of shock, she heard her shop door open. Footfalls pounded on the planks.

Exhaling a sharp breath, Dominic glanced toward the inner door.

Ewan rushed into the house, his hood askew. He held up an earthenware pot. "Mama! Ada gave me some honey."

"What a wonderful treat," Gisela said. She glanced at Ada, plodding through the open doorway, wiping perspiration from her brow. "I wanted to buy some this week, but after the farmer raised the price on his cabbages—"

The older woman waved a hand. "Ye do not 'ave ta explain. I like ta make this young 'un smile."

Ada's grin was so infectious, Gisela smiled back. She hoped her little boy did not sense her strain. Looking back at him, she said gently, "Did you say thank you?"

Ewan swung to face Ada. "Thank you."

"Ye are most welcome, little knight."

Gisela cast Dominic a sidelong glance. A taut smile curved his mouth before he picked up his tunic. Ada's narrowed gaze skimmed over his bare back, lingering where the muscles rippled at the edge of the linen strips. The bandages looked flimsy, somehow, compared to his strength.

Gisela forced down an offer to help him with the tunic. Dominic didn't want Ewan to perceive him as weak. Unless Dominic asked for assistance, she'd let him don the garment on his own.

Scampering over, Ewan thrust the pot at Gisela. "May I have some honey on a slice of bread? Please?"

"Aye, in the morn, to break your fast."

"Aw! Can I have some now?"

Gisela tousled his hair, much in need of a cut. Tomorrow, if she could convince him to sit still long enough, she might trim his locks. "Did you not just eat some pottage?"

"Aye, but . . ." His lower lip stuck out. "I am still hungry."

Despite the strain still humming inside her, Gisela chuckled.

"He is a growing lad," Dominic said while easing the tunic over his head. Gesturing to his untouched bowl of pottage on the table, he said, "One reason why I did not eat the portion Ada gave me. 'Twas a kind offer, but I am already a grown knight. I would rather Ewan ate it."

The little boy grimaced. "I hate pottage."

Dominic winked. "'Twill help you grow into a big, strong warrior."

Ewan's little chest puffed out. "I *am* a warrior. One day, I will be a knight."

Smoothing a hand over his tunic-clad chest, Dominic paused.

Gisela sensed his astonished glance in her direction. He no doubt wondered how Ewan aspired to be a knight when he wasn't of the privileged class.

Oh, but he *did* have noble blood.

Sadness threatened to snatch away Gisela's smile. Refusing to look at Dominic, she rubbed Ewan's shoulder. "I will fetch your bread. Why do you not remove your mantle and hang it back on the peg by the door?"

Ewan thrust the honey pot into her hands. Gisela strolled past the trestle table toward the smaller, oak table where she prepared food. Beside it stood a battered cupboard, standing on four squat legs, where she stored vegetables and salted meats. Dominic's gaze followed her—she felt his stare so intensely—but she resisted the temptation to look back at him.

When she cleared the trestle table, an object on the floor ahead caught her gaze: Ewan's toy sword. Adorning the grip was the scrap of blue silk she'd given him the other day.

Varden had given her the silk.

Quite possibly de Lanceau's stolen silk.

If Dominic came around the table and saw the sword—

Her strides slowed, while her sweaty fingers tightened around the honey pot. Would she be wisest to tell Dominic of the bolts of silk concealed beneath her shop's floor? To admit she didn't realize the cloth might be stolen when she agreed to sew the sumptuous garments Varden commissioned?

*Do not speak of it! If you tell Dominic, de Lanceau will send his men-at-arms to investigate. Whether the silk is stolen or not, you risk losing the payment Varden promised.*

*You need that coin to flee north—as you have dreamed—*
*and begin a new life, where Ryle will never find you. Surely*
*Ewan's life is more important than your qualms.*

"Ewan!" Ada's scolding voice broke into Gisela's
thoughts. "Did ye not hear yer mama? She said ta 'ang yer
mantle up on the peg, not leave it in an 'eap on the floor."

Half-listening to her son's grumbles, Gisela drew in
a steadying breath. She must do whatever was necessary
to ensure her little boy's future. As much as she once
loved—*still* loved—Dominic, Ewan was completely
dependent upon her. Not just for food, shelter, and comfort. For survival.

Picking up the sword and untying the silk would
draw attention to it. She must hide the sword.

*Where?*

As she glanced about the small kitchen area, Dominic said, "So you wish to be a knight, do you, boy?"

"Aye." Ewan sounded faintly defensive.

"You will need to learn to fight. To work very hard."

Ewan snorted. "I practice every day."

"Do you, now?"

Gisela's frantic gaze settled on the shadowed area
beneath the cupboard. She pushed the sword with her
foot. The toy rasped across the dirt floor. She prayed the
sound wouldn't be audible over the conversation.

"I have my own sword," Ewan said. "I will show you."

*Nay, Ewan! Nay!*

With a swift shove, she sent the sword skidding

under the cupboard.

Her son's footsteps sounded close by. "Mama, have you seen my sword?"

Setting the honey pot on the food table, she faced her frowning son. "Nay, Button." An unwelcome twinge in the vicinity of her heart chastised her for lying to her own child. Surely, though, ensuring his safety justified a little falsehood.

Ewan's frown deepened. "I am certain I left my sword in here." He studied the floor.

"I did not see it." Anxious to distract him before he peered under the cupboard, Gisela gestured to the bread. "We will look for it after you have eaten."

Scooting closer, his face shadowed with disappointment, Ewan muttered, "Sir Dominic does not believe I am a warrior, Mama."

She put her arm around him and tried not to smile at the insulted pride in his gaze. "I am sure he does."

Dominic cleared his throat. He sounded as though he struggled to suppress a chuckle. "Mayhap Ewan can show me his sword-fighting skills another day. I must be on my way."

Ewan twisted in Gisela's embrace so his shoulders pressed against her belly. Sliding her arm loosely around his torso, she said, "Dominic, are you well enough to leave?"

"After your excellent care, I should be."

Gisela blushed. "I did not do much." *Except stir up his suspicions and unwittingly reveal you ran away from Ryle.*

Yet, she saw no hint of their prior conversation in his expression. "I feel far better than I did when I arrived. You are an excellent bandager. Where, if you do not mind my asking, did you acquire such a skill?"

Ada. But Ada would not tell.

Gisela sensed the older woman's concerned gaze, but resisted the urge to glance at her. Forcing a careless shrug, Gisela said, "I have tended a few of Ewan's wounds."

Tipping his head back, her little boy squinted up at her. "When did I need linen bandages?"

Regret clawed up inside her. She'd told another lie, more easily than the first. But she wasn't going to admit she was forced to care for her own wound after Ryle stabbed her. If Ada hadn't come upon her and crying Ewan that rainy afternoon, after Gisela collapsed on the grassy verge on the town's outskirts . . . If Ada hadn't kindly taken them into her home, bought Gisela salve and fresh bandages, and taught her how to tend her wound . . . Gisela shuddered. She didn't want to think what might have happened.

Dragging in a shaky breath, she said, "'Twas a long time ago, Button, when you were small." Patting his shoulder, she looked at Dominic. "Before you leave, would you like some bread and honey?"

"Thank you, but nay. I have already stayed longer than I ought."

Ada made a sound of complete agreement.

"Also, I have much to do this day."

Gisela nodded, for she didn't miss the hidden meaning in his words. He intended to resume his search for de Lanceau's stolen shipment.

"If you need me, *Anne*, I plan to get a room at The Stubborn Mule Tavern." Smiling pleasantly, he bowed to Ada, his movements clearly hampered by his injuries. "Good day to you."

"Good day, milord." She dropped into a stiff curtsy. With a loud sniff, she said, "Since I am on my way home, I shall accompany you out."

Gisela expected Dominic's expression to darken with irritation. He merely grinned, clearly enjoying the woman's tart tone. "How thoughtful of you, Ada."

Surprise widened the woman's eyes. She blinked like a stunned owl.

Still grinning, Dominic faced Gisela. When his keen gaze fixed upon her, her arm instinctively tightened around Ewan. "Good day to you, young warrior," Dominic said. His gaze held hers for a long, breath-stealing moment. "Good day, Sweet Daisy."

Ada's breath whooshed out. "Sweet Daisy? Why, you are an impertinent, mischievous rogue."

Dominic chuckled. He sauntered past her, through the open doorway, and out into the darkened tailor's premises. "Are you not going to accompany me, Ada? Do not disappoint me. I shall be devastated."

Muttering under her breath, Ada stomped after him. The door slammed behind her.

Ewan tugged on Gisela's sleeve. "Mama, why did he call you 'Sweet Daisy'?"

Gisela tore her gaze from the wooden panel. Still, she half-listened for the sound of the outer shop door closing. To know at last, she and Ewan were once again alone.

"Mama?"

"Years ago, Dominic and I were very close . . . friends," she said softly, guiding Ewan into the kitchen area. "'Sweet Daisy' was his name for me."

"What does a daisy look like?"

She looked at her son, standing beside her, his expression serious. "You do not remember the daisies growing in the grass by our old home?" she asked.

Ewan shook his head.

She sensed his thoughts turning to the beautiful manor where he, she, and Ryle had struggled along as a family. Her happiest moments were when Ryle was traveling to promote his cloth business, and she and Ewan spent carefree days in the garden, playing on the swing she made for him in the cherry tree, chasing a ball around the grass, and counting the sparrows that swooped down to eat crumbs from their lunches.

Fie! She did not want to discuss their old home today.

"Mama—"

Gisela picked up the knife and bread loaf. "I will make you a daisy." She cut a slice and then opened the honey pot. Using the tip of the knife, she put a dollop of honey in the center of the bread. "The center of the daisy is bright yellow like the sun," she said. Then, with more honey, she drew rounded petals. "The rest of the flower is white."

"Like snow," Ewan said. "Remember, a few months ago, when the snow made it hard to walk to the market?"

Gisela smiled. "Aye." She pushed the bread toward him. "Daisies thrive in meadows and fields where there is lots of sunshine. They are such happy flowers."

Indeed, Dominic had commented so when he linked together daisy stems to make her a necklace. She still had that fragile, delicate daisy chain in her box of treasures.

Ewan chewed a big mouthful of bread. "I think I will like daisies." His expression turned thoughtful. "Mama, do you think dragons eat daisies?"

Sadness wove through her. "Aye, Button," she said softly. "I do."

# CHAPTER SIX

The next morning, sunshine streamed in through the open window of Gisela's shop while she sat on a wooden stool stitching the pinned sleeves of the gown for the blacksmith's wife. Earlier, Gisela had drawn her work-table away from the wall and pushed it into the space by the window, to take advantage of the natural light—and thus not waste her dwindling supply of candles.

A warm breeze swept in over the fold-down board fronting her premises, stirring the linen shifts and girls' dresses she'd hung on each side of the opening. From outside came the gritty footfalls of passersby, the squeaks and rumbles of wagons, blended with snatches of conversation. Somewhere close by, children shrieked and giggled, likely playing a game in the street.

Another yawn broke past Gisela's lips. Her penance for working so late into the night. She had not been able to continue with Varden's commission until Ewan fell asleep, Sir Smug tucked in beside him. Her little boy lay with one arm curled under his tousled head, the other resting on his wooden sword—no longer tied with blue silk—lying atop his blanket. "I am sleeping as a knight on crusade," he'd said in such a serious tone.

She'd nodded, tucked the worn blanket about him, and lain beside him until his eyelids drifted closed and his mouth drooped in sleep. Then, as quietly as possible, she retreated into her shop, raised the floorboards to reveal the concealed storage space, and carefully removed the luxurious silk. Burning far more candles than she could afford, she'd measured, cut, and stitched the shimmering blue cloth that reminded her of a summer sky.

Ewan's roar echoed inside the living area, startling Gisela from her recollections. "Ha! You will never defeat me, stupid dragon! Slink away, O beast with stinky breath, or you will feel the bite of my sword!"

Shaking her head, Gisela smiled. How he loved Sir Smug and the cloth dragon she'd made him from fabric scraps. From the sounds of things, quite a battle raged in her home.

Smoothing a wrinkle from the gown's sleeve, she blinked fatigue from her gaze. She raised the fabric closer to her eyes to catch a tricky stitch . . .

The light in her shop window vanished.

A customer? She glanced up.

Dominic stood outside, his hands braced on either side of the window frame. Standing at such an angle, his broad body blocked most of her incoming light. The majority of his face and torso looked in shadow. Leaning forward, grinning, he murmured, "Good morn."

The gown dropped from her fingers. A wave of sensation whooshed through her—surprise, delight . . . Guilt. A damning blush rushed to her cheeks. "Hello, Dominic."

His smile widened, revealing his pleasingly straight teeth. "You did not expect to see me?"

She cleared an awkward croak from her voice. "I did not know quite what to expect after yesterday. You did not say you would visit my shop this morn."

Oh, God. She hadn't meant to sound petulant—as if she'd anxiously counted every passing moment since he left and wondered when she'd see him again.

Although she had.

With such passionate intensity, she'd pricked her finger three times yester eve, and had to wait for the blood to dry before she could continue her sewing.

"Surely you did not believe I would simply vanish after finding you again?"

How softly he spoke. Yet, each word seemed to sink down inside her, like gold coins tossed into a lake.

Fie! She could not read more into his words, or hope that whatever they had shared before could ever be theirs again. "I thought mayhap your . . . affairs might keep you away."

Dominic shook his head. Drawing one hand from the window, he pushed windblown hair from his eyes. Sunlight struck him full on the face and torso.

Gisela gasped again. "Your tunic!"

Dominic laughed. "Quite fetching, is it not?"

The wooden stool scraped on the planks as she jumped to her feet. No longer did he wear simple, plain garments. Today, he wore a wool tunic the rich, dark blue of a twilight sky. Red and silver embroidery twined about the collar and sleeves. Stepping around the table's edge, she moved between it and the window for a better look.

"Where did you get such a tunic?" she whispered. "'Tis magnificent." Her fingers itched to skim over the luxurious fabric and gauge the texture and softness.

His roguish smile invited her to touch. "I packed the tunic in my saddlebag." He waggled his eyebrows. "I donned my best hose. Would you like me to pose for you?"

"Um . . . Well, I—"

Stepping away from the shop front, Dominic placed one hand on his hip. He thrust the other out with a dramatic flick of his hand. Face tipped up to the sky, he pranced in a slow circle, right there in the street.

How utterly ridiculous he looked, a muscled warrior posing like a puffed-up cockerel. She pressed her hand to her lips, but a giggle broke free on a mortifyingly loud snort, and then she laughed like a silly girl, as she had all those years ago. How natural it felt to laugh so . . . as though she were destined to enjoy Dominic's antics.

Facing her, he chuckled.

Still giggling, she wiped the corners of her eyes with her fingers. "Dominic," she murmured.

His gaze softened with tenderness. How devastating he looked in his refined garments, with the sun streaming over him. His clothes bespoke the privileged life into which he, as a lord's son, had been born.

Years ago, her parents had bought her several exquisite gowns, not to please her, but to show off her breasts and slim waist in hopes of a proposal from one of their merchant associates. Ryle had bought her sumptuous finery. Now, such garments were so far beyond her means, she didn't even dare remember the feather-light brush of silk against her bosom.

Her hand trembled. Hot, stinging tears moistened her eyes. The boundary between laughter and sadness seemed treacherously fragile, akin to the parchment-thin husk of a seedpod, dangerously close to splitting apart. Years of anguish, regret, and struggle—carefully buried in her heart—threatened to slip loose, to plant new roots in the banished reaches of her soul. To grow, once again, for the sun.

"Well? What do you think?" Dominic swept a hand to indicate his clothes.

She blinked hard, forcing the betraying tears aside, and smiled brightly at him. "Magnificent."

Looking pleased, he smoothed the front of his tunic.

"Why are you dressed so?" she asked. "Or, should I say, since you are no longer an old and crippled peddler, *who* are you today?"

He laughed before executing a careful bow. "I am Dominic de Terre, a wealthy merchant, traveling south to the Port of London," he said. "I am most eager to buy Eastern silks." He winked. "Have any you would care to sell me?"

Her pulse lurched, just as a soft scrape sounded behind her. She turned to see Ewan lingering in the doorway to her home, holding Sir Smug to his chest. The toy knight's head, covered by a gray woolen helm, stuck out above the little boy's clasped hands, while his cloth-booted legs dangled against Ewan's belly.

"Button." Tilting her head, she ordered him back inside the house.

Standing firm, he shook his head. "I heard Dominic." His gaze slid past her to the open shop window.

"He is Sir Dominic, to you," she gently corrected.

"'Tis all right. He is a fellow warrior, so he does not need to call me 'Sir,'" Dominic said with a chuckle, his voice rumbling from the window. "Good day, Ewan."

"Good day." Clutching Sir Smug tighter, the little boy stepped farther into the shop.

Gisela frowned. "Ewan, remember what I told you."

His mouth pinched with stubbornness.

"Ewan," she repeated.

"I found my sword," he said, still looking at Dominic.

His gaze slid back to Gisela. "I cannot find the bit of cloth you gave me, though. 'Tis gone."

*Aye, Button. Yesterday I burned it in the fire.*

"Do not worry. I will find you another." She gestured to the house.

Her son's gaze sparked with defiance. "That cloth was very soft. I liked the color. I want the same again, Mama. I like bl—"

"Button, go, as I asked you. If I must tell you one more time—"

While she intended to scold, her words emerged far sharper than she intended. His eyes widened. Regret dissolved her last words.

His chin quivered. Rebellion, though, still brightened his gaze. "I am tired of being indoors."

Her heart squeezed. "I know, Button, but—"

"How long must I stay inside this house, Mama? Every day 'tis the same." His voice broke on an angry sob. Squishing Sir Smug in his hands, he scowled, and then threw the toy on the floor. "I want to go home. I do not wish to see Father—he shouted too much—but I want to go back to the big house with the swing. There, I could run outside whenever I liked. There—" He stamped his foot with a frustrated cry.

How keenly she felt his frustrations. Turning from the window, Gisela went to him, crouched, and slid her arm around him.

Crossing his arms, he jerked away. He stood in

profile, staring at the wall, his face set in a mutinous
scowl. Tears glistened along his eyelashes.

*Oh, Button. You have never drawn away from me before.*

The fragile part of her wept. Her little boy was growing. Changing. Testing her, it seemed, in front of Dominic.
Pressing her lips together, she steeled her fortitude. Focused
on the courage and instinct that kept him safe.

Never could she forget those.

Aware of Dominic's gaze upon them, she rubbed
Ewan's back, a soothing habit he'd enjoyed since he was
a baby. "Right now, you must go inside our home, as I
bade. Later, we will speak of what troubles you."

"Always later," he grumbled.

She sighed. If only she could explain the dangers to
him. He could not possibly understand, for he was only
a child. Moreover, she had done all she could to protect
him from the horrors of the night Ryle cut her breast.
And, God help her, from Ryle's murderous threat.

Reaching out, she picked up Sir Smug. After
straightening the knight's helm, she rose to standing,
then handed him back to Ewan.

Her son looked at her. His intense gaze clearly revealed he understood she wanted him to go back inside.
He took Sir Smug. But he didn't budge.

A frustrated scream welled inside her. "Ewan." She
set a firm hand upon his shoulder and steered him toward the doorway.

Ewan struggled. "Nay! I will not go!"

Light in the room shifted, telling Gisela that Dominic had left the window. She sensed his entry into her shop before booted footfalls sounded on the floorboards. Step by step, he came toward them with those bold, swaggered strides.

Ewan's struggles ceased. His face lit with curiosity as he glanced at Dominic.

Gisela tensed. She braced herself for Dominic to urge her to let Ewan stay. Wasted words. She wouldn't yield, no matter how persuasive Dominic might be. If her little boy were to stay safe, he must heed her. Being solely responsible for his welfare, she must follow through with her demand that he return inside the house; if she gave in now, she showed Ewan that by disobeying, he got his way. A very dangerous precedent. One day, his disobedience might get him killed.

Ewan shrugged off her hold. "He has come to see my sword," he said, raising his chin to look up at Dominic.

An indulgent smile touched Dominic's mouth. "Nay, little warrior. I have come to tell you to heed your mother."

Astonished warmth filled Gisela's belly. *Oh, Dominic.*

Ewan balled his hands and looked about to erupt in another temper tantrum.

"Do not look so," Dominic said gently, touching the little boy's shoulder. "Your mother cares for you very much. If she wishes you to remain in the house, there is a reason for her order. You should obey."

"I do not want to."

"I know." Dominic dropped to one knee, his garments whispering with the movement. Looking at Ewan, he said, "Sometimes mothers know things they cannot tell their children."

"Why not?" Ewan asked.

"Pardon?"

"Why can they not tell their children?"

"Ah." Dominic nodded. "An excellent question. Being a mother is a very important duty. Not every woman can be a mother, you know, for there are a great many tasks she must oversee. Most of all, she must do what she feels is best for her young one. Even if, at the time, she cannot tell her son why, and her son does not understand."

Gisela pressed her shaking hand to her mouth. She couldn't have explained better herself.

Ewan frowned.

"Do you know how lucky you are to have such a caring mother?"

Looking down at Sir Smug, the boy shook his head.

"My mother died years ago. She was a very wise woman, just like your mother." Dominic's tone softened. "Every day, I miss her."

Ewan's gaze moved slowly to Gisela.

"Do as she has asked you," Dominic said quietly.

The little boy pouted. "But I have not shown you my sword."

"I will be back to see you." Dominic patted Ewan's shoulder. Holding the boy's gaze, he leaned close to his ear. "If you go now, without a fuss, I will tell you the story about the maiden and the dragon next time I visit."

His eyes bright, Ewan said, "Tell me now!"

Dominic shook his head. "Now, you will obey your mother."

Ewan looked one last time at his knight, then up at Gisela. He turned and, with obedient steps, went back into the home.

Dominic rose. His tender smile suggested he might enjoy being a father one day.

*Oh, Dominic, if only you knew . . .*

"Thank you," Gisela murmured.

He nodded, still staring at the doorway through which Ewan had disappeared. "He is a good child. He reminds me so much of myself, when I was young."

*That is because there is much of you in him,* a voice inside Gisela answered, rousing a new tangle of emotions. No matter how difficult it might be—no matter what obstacles her revelation might toss in her path toward freedom—she must tell him. He deserved to know.

The moment stretched ahead of her in the quiet room. When his attention returned to her, she clasped her unsteady hands together.

"Dominic," she began, half-aware of voices outside in the street. One sounded familiar. Brusque, as gravelly as a table dragged across dirt, it carried over the *tramp* of approaching footfalls.

*Varden Crenardieu.*

"Aye, Sweet Daisy?" Dominic said.

"—you men wait outside." The voice, heavy with a French accent, came from just outside her shop door. Still, after several meetings with the rich merchant, his voice sent misgiving pooling inside her like icy water.

Even more so, after Dominic's tale about de Lanceau's missing cloth.

Her stomach twisted. What wretchedly bad timing for the French merchant to arrive while Dominic stood in her premises—almost directly over the silk stowed under the floorboards.

Oh, God, if Crenardieu mentioned the commissioned garments . . .

Her heart thudding against her ribs, she turned to face the doorway. A broad shadow blocked the embrasure before Crenardieu stepped inside. Tall as Dominic, his imposing stature was accentuated by a forest green cloak draping in shimmering folds from his shoulders to his ankles. Trimmed with black fur, the sleeves and hem glittered with gold embroidery clearly meant to flaunt his trade and his wealth. His black leather boots creaked as he walked.

"*Bonjour*, Anne." Glancing from her to Dominic, he strode farther into the room. The rings on his fingers glittered as he fingered his straight, blond hair back over his shoulder.

"Good day," she answered.

"You are well this fine morn?"

"Aye, thank you."

"And your son?"

Every visit he asked after Ewan. How she loathed his interest in her little boy. It implied, somehow, her son was important to him. Yet, she needed Crenardieu's payment, so she must tolerate his unwelcome questions. Forcing a smile, she said, "He is well, thank you."

"*Bon.*" A curious smile touched the Frenchman's mouth before his attention again shifted to Dominic. His gaze lingered and then trailed in a slow, deliberate perusal over Dominic's body, all the way down to his boots. The scrutiny was so pointedly thorough, Gisela shuddered.

"*Bonjour* to you, monsieur." Varden's pale fingers twitched, as if the glittering gemstone rings on his fingers suddenly started to pinch. "I did not realize you were with a client, Anne. I apologize if I interrupted a negotiation."

"You did not," Dominic said, before she could utter one word.

"Ah. *Bon.*" The Frenchman's smile broadened. "I do not believe we have met, monsieur—?"

Stepping forward, smiling in return, Dominic extended his hand. "Dominic de Terre."

The Frenchman shook hands. "Varden Crenardieu." Again, his gaze skimmed over Dominic in blatant appreciation. "*C'est magnifique,* your tunic. English wool, or Flemish?"

"English." Dominic chuckled. "I see you know your cloth."

*"Oui."* Varden's chest seemed to expand. He set his bejeweled fingers upon his waist, separating the edges of his cloak to reveal his embroidered gray tunic and hose beneath. "Cloth is my trade. Here in Moydenshire, no other man can match my supply of fabrics."

"Indeed." His face alight with astonishment, Dominic raised his eyebrows. "Even Lord Geoffrey de Lanceau?"

Wariness flashed in Crenardieu's green eyes, but his smile didn't waver. "From what I have heard, Lord de Lanceau runs a fine wool trade from Branton Keep. I have also heard tales of the excellent silks he imports from the continent." He shrugged. "Since I have never met him, or seen his selection of fabrics, I cannot say whether my stock matches his. Yet, I can assure you, monsieur, my goods are the finest from the Fairs of Champagne."

"I see," Dominic murmured.

"If you need a particular fabric, in a particular color, I can find it."

Gisela clasped her trembling hands so tightly, they turned numb. Crenardieu's words were virtually an invitation for Dominic to mention his search for de Lanceau's missing shipment.

She *had* to divert the conversation. Quickly. Before one question led to another and the damning revelation of the silk in her shop.

"'Tis fortuitous that we met this day," Dominic said, "for I, too, am a merchant in need of cloth for one of my clients."

Crenardieu's gaze brightened. His fingers twitched again, indicating he anticipated an exchange of coin.

Sweat beaded between Gisela's breasts. *Now, Gisela!*

Clearing her throat, she drew Crenardieu's attention. "Milord, I do not mean to interrupt, but may I fetch you a drink? Some mead, mayhap?"

Crenardieu waved his bejeweled hand. "*Non, merci.* I intended to stop by only a moment." He gestured to her worktable. "All goes well with the garments I commissioned?"

*Oh, God!*

She nodded, fighting the anxiety lancing through her. Did her panic show in her expression? Did Dominic sense her disquiet? She hoped not.

"*Bon,*" Crenardieu said.

*Please, go, without asking any more questions. Please!*

The Frenchman glanced at Dominic before half-turning toward the open doorway. "Was there aught in particular you wished to discuss with me?"

*Naught!* Gisela's mind shrieked.

Dominic's head dipped in a determined nod. "I am looking to buy silk. Not any silk, mind, but the finest Eastern cloth. 'Tis of such wondrous quality, it feels like down against one's skin." He smiled. "Do you know where I can purchase some?"

# ChAPTER SEVEN

Dominic carefully studied the Frenchman's expression. He waited for some sign of deception, of a struggle to control a flare of surprise. The man's eyelids did not even flicker with a hint of disquiet. Nor did his oily smile waver.

Gisela, however, seemed to grow more pale. Why? Mayhap the disagreement with Ewan had upset her more than Dominic realized.

Or, there was more to her dealings with Crenardieu than a simple commission. One not evident in her shop—not hanging from a peg on the wall, or spread out on the worktable. What was she sewing for him that he didn't wish others to see? Undergarments?

Laughter tickled Dominic's throat. Rubbing his hand over his jaw, he managed to suppress the chuckle.

"What color of silk do you require?" Crenardieu asked.

"Blue. The hue of cornflowers. 'Tis the color of my client's lover's eyes." Geoffrey's lady wife's eyes, actually, but Crenardieu didn't need that tidbit of information.

The Frenchman smoothed a crease from his cloak's sleeve. "I do not have such cloth in my stock at the moment. However, I can make inquiries."

His bland tone implied he wouldn't expend much time or effort searching. Disappointment ran like cold rainwater down Dominic's spine. Still, he steeled himself against revealing his dismay to this merchant, who seemed as trustworthy as a ravenous snake. Glancing at his nails, Dominic said, "Never mind. Mayhap one of the other merchants in Clovebury will assist me."

The Frenchman's lips flattened. "Monsieur de Terre, none have the suppliers or the resources I do."

Dominic barely resisted a grin. As he suspected, the Frenchman didn't wish to lose the potential sale. He wanted to know if Dominic could pay his price.

"My client is very wealthy," Dominic said. "He is most determined to have the blue silk." With a lazy shrug, he added, "If I cannot find what I want here, I will go to London."

"As I said, I will make inquiries." Crenardieu hesitated, one hand in the air, his fingers splayed in contemplative silence. "If I do find cornflower blue silk—?"

Dominic smiled. "I will be most grateful and in your debt. You may name your price, for I will pay it."

"How shall I contact you? Are you lodging in the town?"

"Aye, at The Stubborn Mule Tavern." Even as he spoke, Dominic tamped down unease. Crenardieu might send thugs to investigate him. However, 'twas a necessary risk, for he mustn't give the Frenchman any reason to doubt he was a rich silk buyer. Crenardieu would expect a traveling merchant to lodge at the local tavern. "If I am not in my room," Dominic added, "leave a message for me on the wooden board by the bar."

"Very well." Crenardieu gave an elegant bow that indicated, in its effortlessness, the high circles the Frenchman frequented. "Good day to you both."

With a swirl of his cape, he walked out.

Silence settled inside the shop, marked by the dust motes floating in the streaming sunlight. Even Ewan, inside the house, seemed to have gone quiet.

Gisela stared at the doorway, her expression an odd blend of relief, regret, and . . . resignation.

"A charming man," Dominic said, not bothering to suppress his sarcasm.

Gisela smoothed her hands over her gown. "A rich man," she said quietly, "who has tremendous influence in Clovebury and throughout Moydenshire."

*He also has influence over you, Sweet Daisy.* The thought brought a surge of blazing jealousy—and protectiveness.

"He is a client of yours?" Dominic asked.

Her shoulders rose and fell on a sharp breath before

she nodded stiffly. "He pays well. As I am certain you have noticed, there is a great deal Ewan and I need."

"You should want for *naught*," Dominic growled, unable to keep the anger from his tone.

Gisela stood very still. He sensed her drawing herself up, hardening her will against memories she loathed to share. "At one time," she murmured, "I had all I ever wanted. I have tasted heaven, Dominic." Her mouth trembled into a smile. "If that taste, however wondrous, is all I am given, then 'tis enough."

Tears glistened in her eyes. Sunlight fingered in through the window to play over her hair and the delicate curves of her face. How lovely, yet sad, she looked.

Swallowing down an anguished groan, Dominic wondered when she had tasted such joy. With him? With the man she married but then grew to fear? Had the bastard cherished her and manipulated her into loving him, and then crushed her?

He could not abide such a thought.

Their gazes locked. Her wide-eyed gaze shimmered. How beautiful she looked, proud, alone, caressed by the sunshine.

Only a few spaces stood between them. Dominic stepped closer. He had to. He couldn't resist the desire to touch her. He yearned to hold her in his arms and soothe the torment in her eyes.

He reached for her, ignoring the twinge of his healing ribs, his hands splayed to slide around her waist.

Her head tipped back, while her body swayed slightly, as though to accept his embrace. She looked up at him, her lips slightly parted. For a kiss.

*For a kiss!*

Blood pounded at his temple. His mouth flooded with the delicious, remembered taste of her. Gisela's lips had opened like a flower bud beneath his. He had tasted her and drowned in her ambrosial perfection.

Desire sprang hot in his groin. Gisela said she had no husband. However, if she ran away, she remained bound to the man by law. She still belonged to the husband she feared.

*Step away!* his conscience shouted. *She is no longer yours to kiss. You did not marry her years ago, and now she is beyond your grasp.*

How he ached to press his lips to hers. To again taste her sweet essence. Need rushed like floodwater through his veins, so excruciatingly powerful . . .

"Sweet Daisy," he whispered.

She inhaled a shivered breath. Beneath the golden veil of her lashes, her eyes darkened with yearning. Ah, God, she wanted his kiss. Wanted it as much as he!

Dominic reached for her. Every muscle in his body anticipated her fragrant softness in his arms . . .

Her hands shot up, her fingers splayed like spent petals about to drop to the ground.

She denied him! *Denied him!*

Fighting the surging heat inside him, he lowered his

arms to his sides. "What—?"

A scuffling noise came from behind him. He hadn't noticed the sound before. Yet, she had.

Following her gaze, Dominic turned. Ewan stood in the doorway.

"Mama, is that man gone?"

Gisela's head dipped in a jerky nod. With a swipe of her fingers, she dried her eyes and smiled at Ewan. Through months of practice, it seemed, she'd learned to hide her unhappiness from her son.

"I am hungry."

*As am I,* a voice inside Dominic growled. *Starved for my Sweet Daisy's kiss.*

Gisela crossed to the little boy. "I will fetch you some bread and honey after my appointment with the blacksmith's wife."

"The blacksmith's wife?" Dominic ground out.

Gisela's eyes flared with surprise, no doubt because of his surly tone. She gestured to the garment draped over her worktable. "I promised to finish her gown this week. She is coming by for a fitting."

Footsteps crunched outside the doorway and then a woman walked in, her sturdy shoes rapping on the planks. Her face as brown and wrinkled as a dried apple, she smiled at Gisela. "'Allo."

Gisela smiled back. "Good day."

*Go away, Apple Wench. Leave us to finish what we must say to one another.*

Biting down the words, Dominic said to Gisela, "I will take my leave and return at a more convenient time. I will see you anon." He nodded to Ewan. "Little warrior."

The boy scowled at him. "You cannot go. You promised to tell me about the maiden and the dragon."

Dominic couldn't resist a grin. "I did. And I shall, when I next see you."

He strode past the woman, now chatting to Gisela, and out into the dusty street. A horse-drawn cart rumbled by, its wooden wheels grinding up a cloud of dust. Waving it out of his face, he headed down the street toward the shops Gisela had led him past the other day.

Forcing aside tantalizing thoughts of kissing Gisela, he recalled Crenardieu strolling into and out of her premises. Mentally blocking out the cacophonous street sounds around him, Dominic pictured the Frenchman's stance, gait, and mannerisms. With each stride, Dominic's posture changed. His stride lengthened to convey the arrogance of a wealthy man who used his coin to manipulate those around him.

Dominic smiled. Astonishing how coin had the power to win over a man.

Or, indeed, a woman.

"Mama, when will we see Dominic again?"

"Hmm?" Gisela murmured, a length of thread between her lips.

Perched on the wooden stool in her shop, his legs swinging to and fro, Ewan set his chin in his hand. Candlelight played over his features. "Mama, you are not listening to me."

A weary smile tugged at her mouth. Withdrawing the thread, she set it down along with her bone needle on the almost finished gown on the table. Ewan had been very good all day. She'd closed up her premises a short while ago, which meant she was due to give him some attention—and fetch him some food.

"I do not know when Dominic will visit again," she said, crossing to Ewan's side. "He is a busy man."

"Doing what?"

*Looking for thieves, a search that might lead him here to the hidden silks.* Ignoring her nagging conscience, she said, "He had tasks to attend in the town."

"What tasks?" Her son's curious gaze urged her to blurt out all she knew.

"If Dominic wishes you to know, he will tell you."

Ewan pouted. "Do you know?"

She could not resist a smile. "Aye."

The little boy slid down from the stool and set his hands on his hips. "Why did he not tell me? I am a fellow warrior. I would not tell."

"Of course, you would not." She winked at him. "You are very good at keeping secrets. I am proud that, as you promised, you have not told anyone my true name.

You are indeed a champion of keeping secrets."

Ewan squirmed. His face reddened. "Well . . ."

"Well, what?"

"*Some* secrets."

"You have not revealed to anyone where we put your special baby blanket. You remember, the one with the embroidered hen and chick on the front."

His gaze shifted to the other side of the room. "Um . . ."

"Did you?"

"I showed Ada. She said sometimes she is cold at night. I thought she might like to borrow it."

"Oh, Button. That was sweet of you."

His little shoulders thrust back. "I will be a knight one day. 'Tis my duty to be kind to maidens."

Ada, who had birthed six children and survived two husbands, was far from a "maiden." Gisela fought to suppress a giggle.

Ewan's mouth tightened. "I also showed her . . ."

"Aye?"

"Your necklace."

Gisela gasped. Shock and anger swirled inside her like a flurry of fallen petals. "Ewan!"

"I was careful, Mama."

"I asked you not to touch it, Button," she said, unable to keep the frustration from her voice. How foolish to cherish something as common as a daisy chain necklace . . . But she did.

"Mama, I am grown up now. I know how to be

careful."

"The dry petals are very fragile." Her stomach twisted at the thought of the delicate flowers ruined. "Ewan, you were wrong to disobey me."

He blinked hard. "The necklace is fine. I promise."

She must check. She had not looked at it since Dominic found her in the tavern's stable.

Catching hold of Ewan's hand, Gisela pulled him through the doorway into the house. She crossed to her pallet, raised the top edge, and withdrew a plain wooden box. Kneeling on the pallet, she raised the box lid.

Inside, atop an assortment of other mementoes, was a folded swatch of linen. She carefully opened it, revealing a dried daisy chain. Shriveled and spidery, the blooms still held a hint of their snowy white color.

Ewan knelt beside her. "See?"

"I see," she said softly, remembering how Dominic had lovingly made her the daisy chain. "Still, you are not to touch it."

"Why not? 'Tis just a silly string of flowers."

Gisela rewrapped the necklace and returned it to the box. "Nay, Button, 'tis far more. The day I . . . received this necklace is the day I conceived you."

His eyes widened. Then he frowned. "What does consee . . . cons—"

Out in her tailor's shop, a knock sounded on the door.

Gisela sighed. "Who could that be? Ada is not coming by this eve. She is helping to deliver a babe."

"Dominic?" Ewan jumped to his feet.

"I shall see. You stay here." After tucking the box back in its hiding place, she walked through to her shop, pausing to shut the door to her home behind her. She crossed her unlit premises, set a hand on the outer door's handle, and called, "Who is there?"

"A handsome messenger with a surprise."

*Dominic.*

Her pulse jolted. Joy and desire rushed through her. She shouldn't be so thrilled. He was not her lover and never would be again. Their near embrace earlier—caused by frayed emotions and revived memories of their past, lost love—were best forgotten. Still, her hand shook when she drew the bolts and unlocked the door.

The scent of food—warm bread, fresh pastries, and roasted meat—wafted inside before the door fully opened. Still clad in his fine garments, Dominic stood on the threshold. Tucked under his arm, he carried a bulging cloth sack.

"Hello again," he murmured.

"Dominic."

With a slight flinch—no doubt because his ribs still hurt—he lifted up the bag. "I hope you have not eaten. I brought enough fare to feed the king's army"—he winked—"and their hungry hounds."

Gisela bit her bottom lip. She should protest his kindness. If she accepted his generous offer, she became indebted to him, and she couldn't afford to repay him for the food.

Thrusting up a hand, Dominic shook his head. "I know what you are thinking. Please, do not refuse my gift. 'Tis freely offered, with no demands or persuasions."

How well he still knew her. She couldn't hold back a little laugh.

Oh, the fare smelled heavenly. And 'twould be so much nicer than eating the hard, day-old bread.

Gisela motioned him inside.

He brushed past her into the unlit shop, bringing with him the mouthwatering scents. She pushed the door shut, secured it, and inhaled deeply once again.

"Do not linger, Gisela," Dominic called over his shoulder while he strode toward her home. "The food will be cold afore you get to it."

She shook her head. How deftly he took control of the situation.

As he still had a hold on her heart.

Before she took two steps, the door to her home crashed open. Ewan appeared in the embrasure, his toy sword clutched in his hands. Feet planted apart, his weapon poised to attack, he yelled, "Who goes there?"

Her hand over her pounding heart, Gisela said, "Button, you know 'tis Dominic."

Dominic raised his hand, curtailing her protest. "'Tis I, Sir Dominic." Not a trace of mockery underscored his words.

"Sir Dominic who?" Ewan shouted.

"Dominic de Terre, sworn knight of King Richard."

"Hmm," the little boy said, sounding highly suspicious. Adjusting his hold on his sword, he said, "Come into the light, where I can see you better."

"As you command," Dominic replied.

Gisela rolled her eyes. "Ewan, stop being silly. You know Dominic. These dramatics are unnecessary."

"On the contrary. He is protecting his home and a lovely maiden," Dominic said, halting in the swath of light spilling into the shadowed shop. "Do you accept me, little warrior?"

Ewan squished up his nose. "We-elll—"

"Let me in, and you may have two custard tarts."

"Custard tarts?" The boy beamed. "Two?"

"Aye. As well as sausage pastries."

Ewan immediately lowered his sword. "Come in, Sir Dominic."

"Why, thank you, little warrior."

"On one condition," Ewan said, holding up a finger.

"Hmm?"

"You must tell me your story. The one—"

"About the dragon and the maiden." Dominic laughed. "Agreed."

With an earsplitting whoop, Ewan scampered away, swishing his sword to and fro.

"I hope you will keep your promise," Gisela murmured. "Otherwise, he will be a very unhappy little boy."

"I will keep my promise," Dominic said, entering her house. He headed to the table, set down the sack, and began to unload the contents—as though he belonged in her home.

Shrugging aside a peculiar tingle, Gisela closed the door and strolled to the table, her gaze upon the cloth-wrapped packages.

After tossing his sword on his pallet, Ewan hurried toward the food. "What did you bring? Where are the custard tarts?"

"Here, I believe." With a flourish, Dominic drew apart the edges of the cloth. "There you are, my sweeties." He picked up a larger package and opened it. "Chicken, freshly roasted." Another parcel emerged from the sack. "Fresh bread from the baker's oven."

Gisela's mouth watered. "How did you visit the baker's shop? He must have recognized you."

Dominic's lips curved in a smug grin. "A young woman tended the shop, likely his daughter." He winked. "I plied my charms on her. She was akin to quivering jelly afore I left."

He was teasing. Still, ridiculous jealousy bubbled inside Gisela. "I see."

Dominic winked again. "A well-deserved ploy, I vow, to get what I want."

His voice softened to the whisper of silk. A sluggish tension coursed through Gisela, tightening her belly with anticipation. She tried to resist—oh, how she tried—but she could not deny the pull of his stare. Their gazes locked. Held.

Gisela's breath caught. Her whole being felt suspended, captivated by Dominic's gaze, poised to dive into something wonderful.

Something forbidden.

A loud *thud, thud* echoed, akin to her heart falling and shattering on the floor by her feet. Again, Ewan pounded his fists on the table. "What else did you bring?"

Dominic's attention slid away, but the slow, sensual awareness still glided in Gisela's veins. Picking up a smaller, cloth-enclosed package, he said, "Cherries, dates—"

"Dates?" Gisela exclaimed. "They are very expensive."

"—and honey." Dominic withdrew a large earthenware pot.

Gisela sank onto the nearest bench. "Oh, my. What a feast."

"Fit for a lady," Dominic said, "and her knight."

Delight warred inside her with a crushing sense of dismay. What a chivalrous gesture, for Dominic to bring such a meal. Yet, she couldn't easily forget 'twas all a pantomime in which they pretended to be what they were not. She was no lady, Ewan no knight, and Dominic no rich, cloth-buying merchant.

How many nights she'd lain awake, listening to her son's steady breathing, wishing she could give him a better life. And for Dominic to be able to cover the table with treats so far beyond her means—

"Can we eat now?" Ewan asked.

Dominic chuckled. "Take what you like."

The little boy's hands plunged into the chicken. He grabbed a leg, slick with grease, and sank his teeth into the flesh. "Mmm."

"Slow down," Gisela said. With a wry laugh, she realized he probably hadn't heard her over his delighted sighs and groans.

"What tempts you?" Dominic murmured, pushing the chicken toward her.

Her mouth filled with the promise of delicious tastes. She selected a chicken leg, drew it to her lips, and inhaled the scent of succulent meat. The last time she ate chicken was at a feast held by one of Ryle's merchant friends. In January.

She bit off a morsel with her teeth and chewed. Her eyes drifted closed.

The bench creaked beside her.

"Good?" Dominic asked.

"The best fare I have tasted in months."

He smiled at her in a kind, but knowing way. She averted her gaze to look again at the moist chicken. At what she'd denied herself and her son so she could save for their move north. *For good reason,* her conscience reminded her. *All the more reason to indulge now.*

Suddenly, she could no longer hold back the urge to seize the temptations before her. She bit off more chicken, chewed, and then snatched another bite, ignoring the juice running down her chin. "Mmm. This tastes wonderful."

"Mama, taste the dates." Ewan chewed noisily.

"And the sausage pastries."

He'd taken one bite of the chicken, one from the pastries, and was reaching for another date, his mouth smeared with evidence of all he'd tasted.

Wiping her chin, Gisela laughed.

Around a mouthful of semi-chewed fruit, he said, "Dominic, tell the story."

"Button, mayhap Dominic wishes to eat first."

"'Tis all right." He tore off a chunk of bread. "'Tis a fine moment to tell my tale. Did I tell you 'twas told to me by my mother? 'Tis one of my favorites." His voice softened. "I will always be grateful she shared her stories with me. One day, I will pass them on to my children."

Gisela swallowed hard, for grief etched Dominic's features. Clearly, his mother's death still pained him. Gisela remembered him speaking fondly of his mother, of how she bravely faced the illness that sapped her strength. "I am sorry she died," Gisela whispered.

"As am I." He shrugged and the anguish in his gaze faded. "Long ago, she used to say, there lived a very beautiful woman. Tall and slender, she was the loveliest in all the land."

"Like my mama." Ewan grinned around a big mouthful of chicken.

Dominic nodded before scratching his chin. "Somehow, I cannot remember the woman's name. Let me think—"

"Gisela!" the little boy yelled.

Heat warmed her face. "Nay, I do not think—"

Dominic snapped his fingers. "Well done, Ewan. Her name *was* Gisela."

She snorted. "I suppose in your tale, roosters could lay silver coins?"

Dominic grinned and swallowed his bite of bread. "Her beauty was so extraordinary, the villagers knew she was the one—the maiden to be left as an offering for the fearsome dragon ravaging their lands."

Ewan's eyes grew enormous.

A shiver trailed down Gisela's spine, as though she felt Ryle's hands upon her. The way Dominic said "dragon" suggested his story held a hidden meaning.

"The woman refused her fate. However, the villagers feared the dragon's wrath. They believed giving her to the beast was the only way to pacify it. Before she could run away, they tied her hands, dragged her to the old oak tree near the dragon's cave, and bound her to the trunk. They ignored her pleas for mercy and left her to become the creature's slave."

Ewan grimaced. "Ugh."

"Indeed." Dominic pulled off another morsel of bread and held it between his fingers. "The beast was hideous. As big as a stable and a hundred times as smelly."

Ewan clapped a hand over his nose. "Ew!"

"The dragon had glowing yellow eyes, huge fanged teeth, and claws like sharpened daggers. When Gisela saw it lumbering toward her, she almost fainted with fright.

She tried to get free, but her bonds held fast. Breathing fire and smoke, the beast mocked her attempts to escape. It slashed her bindings with its claws, picked her up in its jaws, and carried her back to its cave. There, she became its slave. She toiled amongst the bones of its prey, always aware the dragon might gobble her up, too."

"She could run away," Ewan said. "When it slept."

*As I ran,* Gisela thought, *while Ryle dozed, slumped over in a drunken stupor, the bloody knife resting on the table beside him.*

His expression grim, Dominic shook his head. "She longed for her freedom, but the dragon kept her chained. When it no longer chained her, it kept close watch upon her. Only after many weeks did the beast cease watching her so closely. One night, she slipped away, taking a lantern to light her way."

*As I fled, Button, with you in my arms and Ryle's knife in my bag. I sold his wretched dagger to buy you food. I went hungry, but I did not care. I cared only that you were safe.*

"What happened?" Ewan asked.

"She fled far away, where she thought the dragon would never find her. She began a new life. She met a young farmer and fell in love. For the first time in months, she was happy."

Refusing to look at Dominic, Gisela discarded the leg bone and took another piece of chicken. Strange, how his tale seemed to mirror her life. A coincidence. Naught more.

Ewan groaned. "You are not going to tell about them kissing, are you? Ugh! What about the dragon?"

Dominic laughed. "The beast was furious when it realized Gisela was gone. It stormed off into the surrounding lands, looking for her, destroying all in its path. One day, it found Gisela and her beloved farmer."

"Uh-oh," Ewan said.

"Aye. The dragon demanded she come back to its lair. Gisela refused. Desperate to help her, the young farmer offered the dragon as much sheep as it wanted to eat, in exchange for her freedom. However, the selfish beast coveted her. It narrowed its eyes and roared fire."

*As Ryle will roar at me when he finds me—right before he kills me.*

Gisela sensed Dominic's gaze upon her. The chicken in her mouth seemed tasteless, its flavor obliterated by bitter fear.

"Gisela could not go back to her life of slavery," Dominic went on. "She would never leave her young farmer, and she did not want the dragon to kill him or anyone else. In secret, she took one of the farmer's knives. When the dragon tried to take her in its jaws, she pulled out the dagger and plunged it into the beast's heart. The mighty dragon bellowed and thrashed its tail, but she had delivered a mortal blow. It died. Gisela and her farmer rejoiced."

Ewan rolled his eyes. "Remember, naught about them kissing."

"All right," Dominic agreed. "However, they lived

long, happy lives together. Never again were they threatened by dragons."

"I liked that story," Ewan said. "Did you, Mama?"

Gisela set aside her chicken, unable to stop the cold tremor rippling through her. "Aye, Button. 'Twas an imaginative tale."

She doubted a woman could single-handedly slay a fire-breathing dragon. As, despite how she loathed Ryle, she doubted she had the physical strength to defeat him.

"Imaginative, true," Dominic said quietly, "but 'tis astonishing what one can accomplish, when one's desires are strong enough."

"Like me, eating two pieces of chicken!" Ewan piped up.

Gisela raised her lashes to meet Dominic's gaze. How intently he studied her. A smile touched his lips. Did he smile because he thought she resembled the Gisela in his story—because he believed he knew what she had endured? Did he want her to confront her dragon like the woman in his tale?

Fie! Dominic couldn't know what she'd suffered at Ryle's hand, and the very real danger he still posed to all of them. Not unless she told Dominic, or showed him her damaged breast.

Oh, God, she couldn't bear for him to see her scar and recoil in revulsion. Not only was she as common as a roadside daisy, but disfigured. Even less worthy of him than years ago.

A wave of anguish snatched her breath away. The

intimacy of her small, dingy home became a weight pressing down upon her. Rising from the bench, she said, "I must make certain I locked up my shop. I will be back in a moment."

"Do you have any more stories?" Ewan asked Dominic, stuffing yet another date into his mouth.

Gisela stepped into her premises, leaving the door ajar to let in light. While Dominic and Ewan's voices carried from inside her home, she drew a slow breath and crossed to her worktable. She pressed her fingers into the gown's coarse wool. With each finished project, she brought her and her son closer to their new life.

To freedom.

Her hair tumbled forward as she bowed her head and slowly rolled her shoulders to ease her tension. Once she completed Crenardieu's commission, she'd have enough money to take her little boy far away from Clovebury. The realization held much less pleasure than days ago.

The thought of leaving Dominic behind, of never seeing him again, hurt so very, very much. Worse than the memory of Ryle cutting her.

Yet, what other choice did she have?

None.

Staring down at her fingers, she swallowed, her throat painfully tight. She had to forget Dominic . . . because she'd loved him years ago.

And, God help her, because she still loved him.

*"Do not lie to me, Gisela. You still love Dominic, aye?"*

*Ryle sneered, crouched naked on their bed, his hand closed around her neck and pinning her down on the pillow. His face glistened with sweat. "You want Dominic in this bed, not me. You dream of him, not me. Your body aches for him, not me."*

*"Ryle," she gasped. "You . . . are hurting . . . me."*

*His lips curled. He snatched her fluttering hand from the bedding and shoved it between his legs. Her fingers connected with soft, flaccid flesh. So very different from Dominic's manhood.*

*Tears scalded her eyes. She writhed, desperate to break free.*

*Ryle's mouth contorted on an oath. His fingertips dug into her neck, punishing her.*

*"Please—" she croaked.*

*Again, he pushed her hand to his groin. "This is because of your treachery. Your fault. Yours! I swear to you, Gisela, if I ever see Dominic, I will kill him!"*

With a strangled cry, she broke from the horrible memory. She straightened, sucking in a ragged breath, her whole body shaking. Still, she could feel Ryle's fingers biting into her flesh.

Uncurling her hands from the gown on the table, Gisela massaged her neck, eager to erase the awful sensation. How she despised the power Ryle held over her. Would she ever be truly free of him?

Aye. She would.

Drawing in slow, even breaths to regain her calm, she snipped a stray thread from the gown and hung it on the wall peg. She smoothed the fabric's folds, her hands steadier than before, and smiled, comforted by a sense of pride. While cut from common cloth, the simple, well-made garment would last for years—unlike the frivolous fashions of the courts that changed as oft as the seasons.

Dominic's lady wife no doubt had such a wardrobe.

Anguish crested again. *Enough, Gisela. Far wiser to go back inside your home and cherish your remaining moments with Dominic, before you and Ewan travel north.*

Tidying her hair with her fingers, she steeled herself to face Dominic again—aware, suddenly, of the silence in her home.

She turned. Dominic lounged in the half-open doorway, one shoulder braced against the embrasure, his arms folded across his chest. She knew, even before their gazes met, that he'd thoughtfully studied her for a few, quiet moments. Caught up in her thoughts, she hadn't heard him approach.

How mortifying for him to have witnessed her in an unguarded moment. That she might have unwittingly revealed her dangerous secrets.

"Are you all right?" he asked.

She managed a cheery smile. "Of course."

"You are not saying that to spare my feelings, are you?" He looked faintly sheepish. "If you hated my tale—"

She shook her head.

"Ah. You ran away, then, because 'twas too close to the truth."

How softly he spoke. However, the hard undercurrent to his words revealed he struggled to control his feelings. The snarled emotions seemed to reach out to her, an echo of the torment churning inside her.

How her heart ached! "Dominic—"

"Ewan is fine. He is sitting by the fire with Sir Smug, eating a custard tart." Dominic pushed away from the doorway, his face taut. "You must know, Gisela, that you can trust me." He withdrew his necklace from beneath his tunic, holding it in one fist. "*This* must prove how much I cared for you. How I *still* care."

Helplessness coursed through her, as merciless as the pain piercing her soul.

"Tell me what happened to you. I want to help," he whispered, his voice raw. "Let me."

"Nay."

"Why not?"

She rubbed her quivering lips together. How did she tell him that to spare his life, she must keep her terrible secrets? He wouldn't understand. "I must go check on Ewan."

She tried to slip past Dominic, but his arm snaked out to slide around her waist, drawing her against him. He ensnared her not just by physical contact, but by memories of the joy, pleasure, and sheer freedom of being loved by him. The scent of him, clean and male, tugged at every thread of her restraint.

His lips brushed her hair. "Tell me," he pleaded.

Crushing agony whipped through her. Thrusting up her chin, clinging to her resolve like a broken shield, she met his impassioned gaze. "Because I still care for you," she said, her voice breaking, "I cannot."

He frowned.

Before he could say a word, she pulled from his hold and hurried into the house.

Bowing his head, Dominic muttered an oath. *Because I still care for you, I cannot.* What, exactly, did Gisela mean by that?

He plowed both of his hands into his hair, seizing fistfuls of it before tipping his head back to stare at the shadowed ceiling. His palm still burned where it had pressed against her waist, her body as vibrant as sunlight in his embrace.

A groan broke from him. Wants and needs warred with loyalties to king and lord that had defined his existence from his earliest aspirations of knighthood. With the demons of loneliness and distrust mocking him, his loyalties no longer seemed clear.

Days ago, he hadn't hesitated to accept Geoffrey's order to hunt down the thieves with ruthless perseverance. However, now, he also felt bound to pursue the fear haunting Gisela. To slay her demons.

To have her, again, for his own.

Years ago, he fervently believed knighthood, honor, and duty were a warrior's greatest rewards. How eagerly he'd accepted the challenge of leaving all he knew—and his despicable betrothal—behind to champion his king on eastern battlefields. Is that why Gisela didn't trust him enough to confide in him, because he'd abandoned her to go on crusade?

His jaw clenched. Aye, in his choice between true love and duty, he'd chosen duty. The only decision he could have made, with his father and bitch of a step-mother—barely two years older than he—coercing him into marrying a stranger.

*Speak no more of that commoner Gisela!* his sire had raged. *She is—and can be—naught to you. You will wed a noblewoman and beget heirs as I expect of my sons. The betrothal is already arranged. Your brother would not have questioned my decision. Neither should you.*

*Listen to your father,* the sharp-tongued witch had agreed. *You are a great disappointment to him, you know —unlike your brother. You never gave your mother one reason to be proud before she died. Surely you will not dis-appoint your sire, too?*

The memory brought a bitter smile to Dominic's lips, for after telling them what he thought of their manipulating his life, he revealed he *had* accepted his duty—not to them, but to his king. Like past warriors in the de Terre lineage, he would fight for the crown. Since he might die on crusade, his betrothed would be wise to find herself another husband.

His father, clearly stunned, couldn't deny the merit of such a decision. What sire did not want his son to be a battle hero?

"Eat up that last bit of tart," Gisela murmured, her voice drifting into the shop.

Ewan grumbled. "Mama, my tummy is full."

"'Tis only three small bites, Button. Do not waste such a wonderful sweet."

Dominic lowered his arms, shaking out the tension locked between his shoulder blades. Gisela's gentle tone brushed Dominic's soul like a caress, stirring a deluge of regret. While he'd eagerly anticipated the adventures of crusade and escaping his betrothal, he'd known, when it came to Gisela, his decision would wound him for the rest of his life.

As much as he'd loved her, he couldn't ask her to wait for him to return. He might not survive the Eastern battles. He might be so badly injured that even if he did return to England, she'd no longer want him.

Now they had found each other again, did she fear their love would rekindle tenfold, consuming them both in its intensity? She claimed she had no husband, but the man clearly held sway over her. Did she worry about being unfaithful—and her husband learning of her betrayal?

*Husband.* Dominic ground his teeth. What he would give for information on the man who had claimed Gisela for his own.

Mayhap he should make a few inquiries.

As he fingered his hair back into place, Ewan came through the doorway to his side. "Why do you not come back into the house?"

Dominic smiled. "I will, but only for a moment. I must be on my way."

Ewan's expression turned solemn. "Are you angry with Mama?"

"Nay." Putting his hand on the little boy's shoulder, Dominic guided him back into the home. Gisela stood by the trestle table, wrapping up the parcels of food. She didn't look up, but her tensing posture told Dominic she was aware of his approach.

Her hair tumbled forward in a shiny, golden swath as she reached for the cloth sack. "There is quite a bit of food left."

"'Tis yours," he said.

Her head jerked up. Astonishment shone in her eyes, which looked overly moist. "All of it?"

"Aye."

"Oh. I . . . We could not. I mean—"

He smiled. "You have a growing warrior to feed."

She hesitated, then murmured, "Thank you."

Dominic fought a tug at his heart. Were those tears in her eyes? Before he could ask, she spun on her heel and carried several packages to the cupboard.

Ewan pulled at Dominic's sleeve, claiming his attention. "I want another story. Do you have any more tales about dragons?"

"Another day, little warrior. I must bid you good eve."

"Aw!"

Returning to the table, Gisela said, "I will see you out."

Dominic strode through her premises. He waited by the door while she drew the bolts, unlocked the panel, and pulled it open. The evening breeze gusted in.

How foolish to have forgotten the fine mantle, which matched his tunic, in his room at the tavern. Yet, he was only half-aware of the cool summer night. Gisela stood so close. Directly behind him, one slender hand upon the door's iron handle, waiting for him to walk away so she could lock up her shop again.

Ah, God, how acutely he sensed her—her fragrance, her body warmth, and the fear she kept tightly leashed.

He fought the pressing need to face her. The hope that, before he left, she might change her mind and tell him all. If he turned now, he'd see her robed in soft light and shadow, her lovely features set with familiar, touching stubbornness.

He'd not be able to leave without kissing her.

"Good night, Gisela." Without looking back, Dominic strode into the inky street. A soft "good-bye" followed him before he heard the door shut and the bolts slide into place.

Darkness swallowed him like the mouth of an enormous beast, concealing all but the areas limned by moonlight. He trudged on through the streets, following the distant shouts, clapping, and rowdy laughter until he came to The Stubborn Mule Tavern.

He looked forward to a stiff pint of ale.

As he crossed the dirt yard by the stable, his gaze fell upon the men standing outside the tavern door. Light streamed over the exquisite green cloak of a man turned in profile, handing coins to a smiling, loose-hipped bar wench.

Crenardieu.

Dominic smiled. The Frenchman would know as much as anyone about Gisela. Or, should he say, *Anne*.

# CHAPTER EIGHT

Twirling a daisy between her fingers, Gisela strolled farther into the meadow grasses.  Butterflies danced ahead of her, lifting from the wildflowers to form a white veil, drawing her on into the meadow.  Bumblebees ambled from bloom to bloom.  How good the warm sunlight felt upon her back.

Someone was watching her.

Someone close by.

Unease shivered through her.  She turned, tensed, ready to run.  A man strode toward her, the long grasses dragging with a soft hiss against his legs.  Her pulse quickened.  At first, she couldn't make out his features, barely dared to hope . . . but as he neared, she knew her heart spoke true.

Dominic!

He grinned, so handsome in the brilliant sunshine.  She couldn't resist smiling back.  She started toward him, her *steps light, joy glowing within her. Drawing near, she threw herself into his arms. He embraced her, pulling her snug against his broad chest, spinning her around so her feet left the ground. How wondrous it felt to be in his arms.*

*"I love you," he said, kissing her cheek. "I love you, Sweet Daisy."*

*"As I love you." Tears began to stream down her face. "I have missed you."*

*Gently, he set her down. How safe she felt standing in his arms. Cherished. Complete. His gaze heavy with desire, he swept his hands into her hair, holding her head between his palms. Her breath seemed to float up like a butterfly, then suspend, waiting . . .*

*He lowered his head, and his lips brushed hers. She should not kiss him. Must not. There was danger in kissing him, no matter how much she wanted to. Her conscience cried a warning. Yet, his delicious touch stole every word of her refusal. He kissed her slowly, deeply, and she couldn't deny kissing him back. He tasted of sweet promises. Of pleasure. Of love that knew no end.*

*He exhaled a ragged breath before urging her down to the ground. Her body draped easily, like tumbled silk, onto the bed of crushed grasses. She ached for his touch, his kiss, the pleasure he'd shown her long ago. Her yearning seared like scorching sunshine. Oh, how she wanted him.*

*He plucked the daisy from her hand. Holding the bloom between his fingers, his trembling hand slid down to her bodice. "Lie with me, Gisela. Be mine. Now. Always."*

*Her skin longed for his touch. However, caution welled, intruding on her anticipation of bliss. "Dominic—"*

*"Sweet Daisy." His hand slid lower, to her cleavage. There, between her breasts, he tucked the flower. Trailing a finger over the upper swell of her bosom, he said, "Tell me what happened to you. Tell me."*

*Hopelessness crushed her rush of pleasure. "Dominic—"*

*"Tell me."*

*His hand skimmed down to her right breast. Horror bloomed inside her, insidious as a weed, choking the last of her joy. She tried to speak, to warn him, but she couldn't force air into her lungs.*

*The fabric of her gown disintegrated, as though burned away. Her scarred flesh lay bared to him.*

*Dominic's face crumpled with revulsion. He looked at her, his gaze harsh with loathing. He pushed her away.*

With a gasp, Gisela's eyes flew open. She blinked away the wetness clinging to her eyelashes while she heaved in another breath. Her body shivered through an anguished aftershock.

As her groggy mind began to clear from the dream, she realized she didn't lie on her pallet. The scent of silk rose from beneath her, accented by the acrid tang of candle smoke. Her forehead rested on her curled arm.

She'd fallen asleep at her sewing table.

Gisela shoved up to sitting, wincing at the crick in her neck. Sensation returned to her numb arm like hundreds of pins poking into her. She massaged her flesh, staring in dismay at the unfinished gown, creased by her slumber. Thank the saints she had not drooled all over it.

How *could* she have fallen asleep? She *knew* she couldn't waste one moment finishing Crenardieu's commission.

The squeaky rumble of a cart reached her from outside. The townsfolk were beginning their morning routines, which meant she had slept for quite a while.

"Stupid, stupid!" she muttered, swiping damp hair from her face. When she slid off her work stool, she caught the glisten of wax at the upper corner of her table. Overflowing from the candle holder, the wax formed a milky pool. Moments away from damaging the silk.

Lurching forward, she whipped the fabric out of harm's way. As she moved, her foot caught the stool's edge. With the *screech* of wood against wood, it tilted sideways and fell over with a *thump*.

Gisela groaned. She might have woken Ewan. She must work quickly, now, to stow the fabric before he came to investigate. So far, she had managed to keep the hiding place beneath the floor a secret from him. 'Twould be best if he never knew.

With clumsy hands, she folded the silk. If she damaged the expensive cloth, she'd owe Crenardieu most of her hard-earned savings. From this point forward, she must be more careful. She wouldn't fall asleep again.

Crouching by the opening in the floor, she tucked the gown beside the cut pieces of the flowing, ankle-length cloak and the bolt of remaining silk. Just as she reached for the planks to cover the cavity, the door to her home opened.

She set down the floorboard and hurried to the door, catching it before it opened too far.

His hair an adorable mess, Ewan blinked up at her, rubbing his eyes with his fists. "Mama, I heard a noise."

"I knocked over the wooden stool. 'Tis all. Why do you not go back to sleep?"

His sleepy gaze darkened with a frown. "When did you wake up?"

"A while ago." Not quite the truth, but not quite a lie, either.

"Can I sit with you in your shop?"

"Mayhap this afternoon." She gestured to his pallet. "Go on. I will wake you later."

He slowly pivoted on his heel, as though to obey her. Before she guessed his intent, he whirled and darted past her with a cheeky giggle.

Gisela rubbed her tired brow with her hand. "Ewan!"

She knew the exact moment he saw the hole in the floor, because his footfalls slowed. Turning, she saw him crouched at the edge, peering in. He glanced back at her, his eyes shining. "'Tis a secret hiding place."

Gisela nodded. "Now you have seen it—"

"Are there dragons down there, Mama?"

The question was so unexpected, she laughed. "Nay, Button."

His hands clenched. "Are you certain? Mayhap I should get my sword and have a look."

"Nay, you should not." The last thing she needed this morn was for him to scramble into the cavity and not want to come out. Knowing him, he'd claim it as his fortress. Walking past him, she knelt, picked up a plank, and slotted it back into place.

"Aw, Mama!"

Three more boards and the floor returned to normal. "There." She brushed off her hands. Giving him a pointed look, she said, "You must not tell anyone about this hiding place, all right? 'Tis another secret you must keep. Promise me."

Staring down at the floor, Ewan scowled. "I did not even get a good look."

"Promise, Button."

"All right! I promise."

Gisela headed to her worktable, aware of Ewan stomping along behind her. She swept a small pile of silk scraps, wax, and blue thread onto the planks before crossing the room to fetch the broom. She turned to see Ewan fingering through the pile, holding a lump of wax.

Fie! He'd be after another bit of silk to replace the one she tied to his sword days ago and then destroyed. A disaster.

"Button, please go and get dressed while I sweep up here."

His fingers curled around the wax, concealing it. "I

want to watch."

She whisked the broom over his bare toes, and he squealed in surprise. "Hey!"

"I might sweep you up by mistake if you stand there." *Whisk.* "Ha! Got you again."

Laughing, he scampered toward the doorway. "Catch me now, if you can."

Gisela pretended to pursue him, and he disappeared through the doorway. Resisting a chuckle, she swept up the discards, carried them into the house, and stoked the fire. She tossed the silk into the crackling flames. With a smoky hiss, the evidence disintegrated.

Humming under her breath, she strolled past the pallets and gave the lump under Ewan's blanket a nudge with the broom. "Got you."

His head poked out the other end. "Aw, Mama!"

After replacing the broom and blowing out the candles in her workroom, she made them both bread and honey, then helped him don his tunic and hose. Fatigue weighed down her eyelids and made her limbs ache, but she shrugged her discomfort away. She pulled Ewan's tunic down over his head and planted a noisy kiss on his cheek. "Aw, Mama!" he groaned again, but his eyes sparkled with delight.

Gisela smoothed a crease from his sleeve, unable to resist a sigh. How had she not noticed that the tunic she made him two months ago was already too short through the sleeves?

Never mind. Right now, she had other priorities. Once she'd got them both far away, she would have all the days she liked to sew him clothes.

Ewan plopped down on the bench so she could fasten his shoes. Swinging his legs, looking down at her crouched by his feet, he asked, "Where are we going?"

She caught hold of one foot and pushed on his shoe. "We have some errands to attend. Then, we will return home so I can work."

"I want to play outside. Remember that big field—"

"Not today."

He huffed. "You never let me play outside."

*And for good reason, Button. One day, you will understand and forgive me.*

After fastening both of his shoes, Gisela rose, ignoring his frustrated glare. She smoothed a hand over her weary brow and disorderly hair. Today, even if she were able to let him romp in the field, she couldn't dally. She must finish the commission for the blacksmith's wife. There were preparations to make, too, for as soon as she received payment from Crenardieu, she intended to take Ewan and flee.

Leaving Dominic behind.

The thought brought a fresh stab of torment. Struggling to ignore it, she slipped her cloak from the peg on the wall.

"Mama, can I bring Sir Smug?"

"Of course." Draping her cloak around her shoulders, she said, "Fetch your mantle, Button. I will wait for you by the outer door."

While she walked through her shop, she cast a quick glance around to be sure she hadn't missed any blue threads. A yawn tugged at her mouth, but she smothered it with the back of her hand. A moment later, Ewan trudged into her shop, the toy knight tucked under his arm. As he neared, he yanked his mantle's hood up over his head.

"I am glad Sir Smug can come, too. He is bored with being inside. He wants an adventure."

Gisela smothered a chuckle and drew up her own hood. "Come along, then, my two little warriors." She gave Ewan's hood an extra tug, to ensure his face was completely covered, then opened the door. They stepped into the street, and she locked the door behind them.

Dust and stones kicked up under her shoes while they walked. Dogs scampered into alleyways looking for scraps, while grubby children tossed rocks in a made-up game. Ewan stared longingly in their direction, almost stumbling over his own feet.

With brisk strides, Gisela headed toward the shop district. The scent of baking bread, yeasty and enticing, led her to the right street.

"Mama, you walk too fast."

She caught Ewan's hand, urging him along when he wanted to investigate a mound of sticks. A few premises away, past a crowd of early shoppers, she spied the shop run by a kindly husband and wife. She often purchased thread and cloth buttons from their well-stocked establishment. They'd even referred several customers to her.

The front window was open. Relief brought a smile to her lips.

Ewan's fingers wriggled in hers. How easily he became distracted. "Mama—"

"Not now, Ewan."

She skirted two men chatting while eating pastries likely purchased from the baker.

"Mama!"

The distress in her son's voice made her glance at him. Ewan's anxious gaze darted from her, then away. Holding Sir Smug tight to his chest, he scooted closer to her side.

A reaction she knew well.

Glancing back, she saw Crenardieu striding past the two talking men, his cloak almost skimming the ground. His bright gaze slid from her to Ewan.

Warning buzzed in her mind. The way he looked at her son seemed almost . . . possessive.

Facing the Frenchman, she drew Ewan against her. Without the slightest protest, he obeyed.

Crenardieu smiled. "*Bonjour.*"

"Good morn." She nodded politely, hoping to continue walking. Before she could step away, he moved to block her path.

Warning shrilled more sharply. Others in the street

were watching them. Most likely Crenardieu's thugs.

*Do not let him see your fear*, she told herself, forcing her chin higher. *Find out what he wants and be on your way as quickly as possible.*

Crenardieu seemed to sense her discomfort, for he smiled. "I would like to speak with you. Do you have a moment?"

*Nay*, her mind answered. But she couldn't refuse him. She needed his payment. Smiling in return, she said, "Aye."

His hand touched her elbow—a hold that sent shivers racing through her—and he guided her to the side of the street. They stopped beside an empty shop. An iron padlock secured its splintered front window. Gisela remembered the merchant who'd sold pots and pans from this premises, which was recently broken into. His wares ruined, the man had closed up his shop and left Clovebury.

The blackened space at the bottom right of the window yawned, vacant and eerie.

"Now then." The warmth of the Frenchman's smile didn't reach his eyes. "I meant to visit you later today. I did not expect to see you wandering through the town."

Again, his gaze dropped to Ewan. With her arm, she nudged him behind her, removing him from Crenardieu's view. "Ewan and I had some shopping to finish this morn," she said.

The Frenchman nodded. "How are you faring with my commission?"

"The gown is almost done. Both garments will be finished next week as you asked."

Crenardieu's lips tightened. "Ah. But, you see, I need them in two days."

Despite her best efforts, a stunned breath burst from her. "*What?*"

"I will collect the items from you before dawn, along with the remaining silk. *Oui?*"

Her stunned mind scrambled to form a reply.

"A regrettable change in plan. Yet, 'tis so."

She fought the angry panic heating her face. Forcing a civil tone, she said, "You know I cannot work on your commission during the day. You told me not to. You swore me to secrecy, although you have not explained why that must be so."

A dark flicker sharpened the Frenchman's gaze. For an instant, she regretted daring to toss out the challenge. Yet, it had slipped out before she could smother it. "'Tis not necessary for you to know. Your task is to create the gown, with the fine skill for which you are known."

His flattery only deepened her unease. How she longed to ask if the silk was stolen—to have an answer to the question gnawing at her conscience. However, to do so might jeopardize her dealings with him. If he resented her suspicion, he might take away the unfinished garments, and the money he promised would be lost.

"Tsk-tsk! Do not look at me so, Anne—as though I ask you to commit some kind of crime. 'Twould be a shame to spoil my customer's surprise for his mistress, *oui*, if word got out about the commission?"

"True," Gisela answered, even as a chill wove through her. "Did your client ask for the garments to be finished sooner?"

The Frenchman's head dipped in the barest nod.

"Mayhap if you explain to him that to do my best work, I need until next week—"

Crenardieu shrugged, his luxurious cloak whispering with the movement. "I did not foresee a problem. If you cannot complete the garments—"

*I will find someone else to do the work, and you will not receive payment,* her mind finished for her. "I will do as you ask."

"Good." His smile thinned. "I would hate for the wrong people to learn you are unreliable. Or," he said quietly, "exactly where you are."

His words pummeled her like chunks of melting ice. A tremor shook her, so powerful, she almost keeled into the wall.

Placing her palm against the stone, she used its strength to fortify her. She struggled for calm. "What do you mean?"

Another grin, deliberate and cold. "Come now, *Anne.*"

His emphasis on her false name sent fear screaming through her. Oh, God. Oh, God. Did he know her true identity?

If he knew . . . who else did?

Desperation tightened her breathing. She barely restrained the urge to whirl, grab Ewan's hand, and run. However, the willful, wounded part of her bared its teeth in defiance. She had done all this man asked of her. She didn't deserve his goading. She'd not cower to his bullying, especially in front of an audience that, she noted, was watching their exchange with expressions of both amusement and outright curiosity.

Crenardieu might have no idea who she really was. He might be testing her, to gauge her reaction, because he'd heard a rumor from one of his associates.

*Pretend you do not know what he is talking about. Bluff through it. You can do it, Gisela.*

By sheer strength of will, she managed a puzzled smile. "Your words confuse me. You know my name is Anne."

"Aye." Cruel humor glittered in his eyes. "But is it your *real* name?"

Ewan tugged at the back of her cloak. "Mama! Your name is—"

She spun. "Ewan," she snapped, so fiercely, his eyes widened with shock. She wept inside at the hurt in his eyes, as well as the crushing dread she could scarcely contain. When she turned back to face the Frenchman, she squeezed her son's hand. Later, she'd apologize for shouting at him. At this moment, she needed her verbal claws to protect them both.

Looking Crenardieu straight in the eye, she said, "Please say what it is you wish of me. Otherwise, I ask that you let me be on my way, so I can finish your commission."

Admiration lit his gaze before he glanced away. "Those of us in the cloth trade know each other well. Those connections are an important part of our business." He adjusted one of his gemstone rings. "'Tis well known Ryle Balewyne is looking for his runaway wife and son." Crenardieu's gaze locked with hers. "For you."

She tried to force a denial between her teeth. But she couldn't get a sound past the fear jamming her throat.

"Do not fail me," the Frenchman said as he turned away. "Two days, *Gisela*."

# CHAPTER NINE

The scent of dried grasses filled Dominic's nostrils. Ahh. He lay in a summer meadow, his cheek tickled by the greenery, his body cocooned in a breeze alive with the buzz of a happy insect. God's holy fingernails, but he was drunk with the pleasure of the meadow . . .

The drone intensified. Something landed on his arm. Pinched.

"Ow!" Dominic's head snapped up. The meadow swam. A merciless ache crashed against his forehead, a sensation akin to being whacked by a board. Groaning, he fell back to the ground.

Nay, 'twas not the ground.

He cracked open his bleary eyes as his befuddled senses began to sharpen. He lay in the small, dingy room in The Stubborn Mule Tavern. A fly—which disappeared through the ill-fitting shutters at the window—had just bitten his forearm. He lay flat on his belly, his fine mantle squashed into a makeshift pillow, his hands curled into the musty-smelling pallet that served as his bed. He sprawled like a drunkard who'd collapsed after a night of overindulgence.

Dominic groaned, his stomach protesting every slight movement. God's teeth, he *was* a drunkard!

Drunk as a brandy-soaked pudding.

Yet, the contents of his belly felt like curdled custard—and equally as volatile.

Unable to restrain another groan, he pressed his palms flat against the pallet. It rustled as he slowly sat up, the events of the previous night filtering into his foggy mind. How many drinks had he bought Crenardieu? Seven? Ten? The obnoxious Frenchman, who grinned at the barmaid each time she strolled by, drank like a leaky keg and never seemed to get addled. Nor had he revealed any good information. Horribly disappointing, when the whole point of imbibing in the first place was to loosen the man's tongue and wrest details from him.

Especially what Crenardieu knew about Gisela.

*Gisela.* A smile softened Dominic's frown. How he longed to see her. *Needed* to. The keen ache resonated in his soul, always more intense when he had too much to drink and his mind wandered to "what ifs" and "what might have been."

The reason he had imagined himself in a meadow,

no doubt.

Dominic swiped at straw dangling in his eyes, then brushed off his wrinkled tunic. Once he got to his feet, he'd go see Gisela. An excellent plan. The best plan he'd devised since . . . Never mind.

Rubbing his throbbing brow, he steeled himself to stand. He would walk to her home. Step by step. One boot in front of the other. Simple.

With an awkward shove, he rose, careening three steps sideways and almost tripping over his saddlebag. He barely avoided the ink pot and quill on the floor, left out from when he penned Geoffrey a quick missive. Dominic steadied his balance. A belch erupted from down in his belly. God's knees! That explosion of sound would bring the tavern's rafters crashing down on him. He might need more bandaging from Gisela.

Hmm. Not an entirely unpleasant prospect.

Just thinking of her warm, gentle hands moving over him again . . .

*Behave, Dominic.*

He sucked in a breath, shuddering when the linen bandages he still wore tickled his skin. After rubbing his hands over his face, he attempted to smooth his hair. It felt like a rat's nest. He had not been in such a state since Geoffrey and Lady Elizabeth's wedding celebrations. However long ago that was.

Squaring his shoulders, he fixed his gaze on the doorway and started toward it. *Thud, thud,* went his boots. *Gurgle, gurgle,* answered his gut. At least he was moving forward, even if not in an entirely straight line.

He stepped out into the shadowed hallway, made his way down the creaky staircase—bypassing slumbering drunkards and empty ale mugs—and walked out into the tavern yard. He squinted against the bright light. The tavern was quiet now, slumbering like a blowsy strumpet, very different from last eve when the revelry had tumbled out through the open door.

Filling his lungs with fresh air, he headed into the alley and toward Gisela's shop, stopping on the way to buy a pastry from a street vendor. He ate as he walked. A good idea, to eat. His belly felt more stable already. The fog cleared from his mind.

His steps lightened when he entered the street near Gisela's premises. Anticipation glowed inside him, for soon he'd see her lovely face tinged pink with a blush. The graceful sweep of her hair he longed to touch. The proud, yet beautiful, tilt of her chin.

Brushing stray crumbs from his tunic, he glanced toward her shop.

Closed.

He came to an abrupt halt in the middle of the street, wobbling a moment. A young boy pulling a small cartload of firewood grumbled under his breath and veered past, as did the mongrel at the lad's heels.

Misgiving lanced through Dominic, tainting his excitement with a sense of dread. He shrugged the unease away. No doubt there was a reasonable explanation for Gisela's shop being shut. Mayhap she had gone to meet with a client.

Mayhap Ewan was ill.

Mayhap Gisela was unwell. He'd sensed something amiss last eve. She might not have wanted him to know of her ailment because she realized he would insist on staying to care for her. Thus, he wouldn't be able to pursue his mission for Geoffrey.

Dominic sighed. Even after years apart, she knew him well. He would, indeed, have stayed. He'd always loved her stubborn, independent streak, but if he didn't look after her, who would?

Even before he willed his body into motion, he was striding toward the building. He fought the urge to slam his shoulder into the door and break it from his hinges. Hardly the way to impress Gisela. Not wise, either, considering his healing ribs. Moreover, the rash act would attract attention from passersby, who would view him as a dragon rather than a protector; he did not care for another round of local justice.

Curling his hand into a fist, he knocked three times.

A muffled oath came from within, followed by the scrape of furniture across the floor.

"Who is there?" Gisela called from inside.

He smiled, his anticipation burning anew. "Dominic."

Another oath. Had she really said "Oh, my *God!*" with utter horror? She'd speak that way about a poisonous, five-headed snake.

"I . . . Um . . . Just a moment" she called.

He frowned. "Are you well?"

"Aye!" she said, before he had finished speaking. Through the door, her voice sounded breathless. As though he'd caught her in a clandestine act.

His frown deepened. Curiosity nagged, turning his excitement into suspicion. He had no right to know . . . but what *was* she doing in there?

Pressing his fingers to the rough wooden panel, he tipped his head close to hear. Impossible, with the horse-drawn wagon rattling by.

He remembered the first time he visited her shop, how she'd sat at her sewing table, sunlight illuminating her face, her expression one of intense concentration while she smoothed out the gown. The image distorted. He saw her standing back against the table, hands splayed in crushed fabric while her body arched up to meet her lover's hungry kiss. As her eyes closed and her head tilted back in rapture, the man pushed down her gown to reveal her breasts' luscious swell.

Thumping noises came from inside the shop. Then, more scraping.

Dominic's fingers curled against the door. The wood, weathered to a browny-gray hue, mocked him with its solid blankness. He saw no crack, no broken knot, through which he could peer in and see what was transpiring.

The urge to break down the panel roared again.

*Nay.* She was probably with a female client who needed to try on a garment for fitting. That explained the closed shop and Gisela's delay in letting him in.

She would not be with a lover.

He willed himself to be patient.

*Forget patience!*

He pummeled the door again. "Open up, G— " *Careful, Dominic, you idiot!* "Anne."

Inside, the bolts on the door slid back. The lock clicked, and the panel creaked open. Gisela leaned into the small space between the door and the embrasure. Wispy hair poked out from her loosened braid. How he longed to tuck those strands back into place. To touch, just for a moment, the silk of her tresses and her cheek's soft curve.

A flush stained her face. "Dominic."

"Aye."

Her slender hand flitted over her bodice, a nervous gesture that encouraged his gaze to skim down to her bosom.

Relief shivered through him. Her breasts were neatly restrained within her gown. The same one, he remembered, she wore yester eve. As he became fully attuned to her presence, he noted shadows under her eyes and the weariness lining her features.

"You look tired."

She straightened, pushing her shoulders back. He tried not to notice the tempting thrust of her bosom. "I am fine." Arching an eyebrow, she said, "You look like you slept in your clothes."

He followed her gaze to his creased tunic. "Actually, I did." Bestowing upon her his most charming grin, he said, "May I come in? I will tell you of my night drinking at the tavern."

Dismay flitted over her face. She blinked and seemed to gather her composure. "I . . . I am sorry, Dominic. 'Tis not convenient. Mayhap you could come back later?"

Her apology sounded most gracious. Behind her encouraging smile, however, he sensed desperation.

She wished he would be on his way.

Why?

Pretending he had an entire day to dawdle, he shrugged. He toed a stone with his boot. "I did not realize you were with a client."

"I am not."

"Your shop is shut." He paused before adding, "I was worried. I thought you or Ewan might be ill."

Nodding, she gnawed on her bottom lip. Dominic let the moment drag. Tilting his head to one side, he looked at her, coaxing her to elaborate.

She averted her gaze. Then, after a long moment, she said, "I needed to catch up on my work today. The noises from the street are a distraction, and—"

Still talking, she removed her hand from the door to finger aside her hair.

The perfect opportunity.

He stepped forward. Shoved the panel. It swung inward, hit the wall, and bounced on its hinges.

"Dominic!"

He brushed past Gisela, his gaze scanning the room's interior. Candles flickered on the worktable. He noted sewing implements scattered on the table's surface. A half-finished chemise. The wooden stool, pushed to one side.

Scowling, he spun to glance behind the door. No one else occupied the room. Not even Ewan.

"All that scraping and thumping . . ." he said under his breath.

"Why did you barge in?" Gisela demanded behind him. "I told you 'twas not convenient."

He turned to meet her flashing blue gaze. She stood with her hands on her hips and her chin thrust forward. She looked so indignant, he almost bent at the waist in a gallant apology.

"I had to be certain you were not in danger." Thank God his drink-hazed brain didn't fail him. "For all I knew, someone stood behind you, threatening your life."

"Fie! Why would you assume that?"

Ah. A very good question. The thumping and scraping sounds were likely caused when she moved the wooden stool across the planks. What other explanation could there be for the noises?

Dominic scrambled for an explanation that didn't make him look a complete fool. "You told me yourself thugs are preying on shopkeepers in this town. They might have been robbing you of your cloth, and any other items they could sell elsewhere."

Her gaze softened. "True."

"I had to be certain, Gisela," he said more gently. "I would never forgive myself, Sweet Daisy, if aught terrible happened to you that I could have prevented."

A heart-wrenching expression shadowed her features. Misgiving? Regret? Mayhap both of these, blended with stubborn resolve. For a moment she looked desperately . . . alone.

Only once before had she looked at him so: that blue-skied summer day he'd said good-bye. He'd embraced her, kissed her with all the love in his soul, and said he'd never forget her. She stood in the daisy-strewn meadow, the breeze tangling her hair, her face wet with tears. Still, silent, she watched while he turned and strode away.

Dominic hadn't looked back—even when her sobs threatened to bring him falling to his knees. He couldn't bear for her to see him weep or sense the pain splintering his soul, For all the joy she'd given him, he must let her go, to find another man and fall in love again. He could promise her naught when leaving on crusade. She deserved a good marriage. To be happy. Treasured.

The anguish of their parting cut through him again. He longed to slide his arms around her, to draw her close, to comfort her with the warmth of their touching bodies. How alive he'd felt when they embraced.

Would she let him hold her? Just this once? "Gisela . . ."

Her name broke from him in a rough plea. She drew a shaky breath, as though the emotion in his voice grazed a wound inside her.

Shaking her head, she stepped away. Again, she wore her invisible shield, enforcing an emotional wall between them. "Please, Dominic. I did not lie when I said I had much work to do." She gestured to her worktable. "The blacksmith's wife liked her gown so much, she asked me to sew her a new chemise."

He nodded, trying hard to dismiss his disappointment. His gaze slid to the chemise, awaiting her skilled attentions. As much as he yearned to touch, taste, and feel her again, he must respect their lives were very different. Very . . . separate. They both had commitments other than the love they once shared.

"I will return later, as you suggested."

"Ewan is with Ada today. He would like to see you, as well. If you return by early eve, we can eat together."

"I would like that." He winked. "I shall have to remember more stories about dragons."

A smile touched her mouth. "Until this eve, then." While she spoke, she turned to face the open doorway, encouraging him, with her body language, to leave.

"Until this eve."

Gisela pushed the door closed, secured it, and leaned

her brow against the wood. A tremor jarred through her. How close Dominic had come to discovering her deception. She'd managed to stow the silk in the hidden cavity and replace the panels, but only just.

She stared down at her feet peeping out from her gown's hem. There, by her right shoe, lit by the sunlight fingering in through a crack in the wall, lay a strand of blue thread.

She squeezed her eyes shut. If Dominic had seen it . . .

But he hadn't. She would finish the gown and cloak as Crenardieu demanded. If—and only if—Dominic discovered her duplicity, she and Ewan would be long gone from Clovebury.

*I would never forgive myself, Sweet Daisy, if aught terrible happened to you that I could have prevented.*

Each of her steps leaden with guilt, she walked back to the worktable. Dominic had spoken with such sincerity. For one, fleeting moment, his words had melted through her fear.

How she wished she could confide in him, especially after Crenardieu's threat to betray her to Ryle. Could Dominic help her—more importantly, help Ewan—escape the danger hovering over them like a dragon poised to attack? Could she possibly barter with Dominic, exchanging what she knew about Crenardieu and the stolen cloth for her and Ewan's safe passage out of Clovebury?

Or, if she told, would the truth shatter all? Dominic's revulsion, straight from her nightmare, filled her mind. He'd despise her for not being honest when he first told her about his mission in Clovebury. Furious, he might arrest her. He would take Ewan away.

*Oh, God, she could not bear to be separated from her son!*

Fear became a brutal knot against her breastbone. Without her protecting Ewan, every moment of every day, Ryle would find a way to get to him. Her charming, clever former husband would manipulate his way into Dominic's circle of acquaintances. Ryle would murder Ewan. And then, Dominic.

She couldn't let that happen.

With stiff hands, she whisked the chemise from the table. After hanging it back on the wall peg, Gisela crouched, raised the loose planks, and withdrew the silk gown. It shimmered in her hands, taunting her with its exquisite beauty.

When she laid the gown on the table, the fabric rustled. It sounded like rain falling on a spring afternoon.

One day, soon, she'd feel rain on her uncovered hair. Wipe it from her upturned face. See it sparkle on Ewan's eyelashes.

A smile touched her lips as she shifted the gown.

*Freedom*, the sound whispered. *Freedom*.

After Gisela's shop door closed behind him, Dominic stopped in the street. A relief, that she was hale, and he had no cause to worry. He looked forward to sharing a meal with her and Ewan later.

Still, he couldn't dismiss the unease chewing at him like a mischievous hound.

Something was wrong.

He sensed it as acutely as the dust rising from the road in a hazy cloud.

Massaging his right shoulder, he tried to ease his aching, fatigued muscles. His suspicion could well be the result of being overtired from his night at the tavern. Fatigue had the power to influence one's judgment. While Gisela seemed uncomfortable at times during their meeting, he had seen naught in her shop to justify his anxiety.

Yet . . .

A peddler, leading two heavily laden horses, ambled past. Farther down the street, two women strolled along, heads bent together, caught up in their private conversation. A group of men crouched beside a cart with a broken wheel, clearly trying to decide how best to repair it.

He glanced back at the men. His gaze fixed on the dark-haired, broad-shouldered one standing behind the wagon. The lout faced the street, his face partly covered by a floppy leather hat.

A chill coursed through Dominic.

The man was one of Crenardieu's lackeys. He'd hovered close by the Frenchman at the tavern. Where he stood, the man had a clear view of Gisela's shopfront.

No one could come or go without him noticing.

Gisela was being watched.

Or, was Dominic the target of Crenardieu's spying?

The chill inside Dominic transformed to burning anger. No one had followed him that morn. Addled as he was, he was certain of it.

Why, then, would Crenardieu send a man to spy on Gisela? He'd not waste his hired thugs unless she was important to him somehow.

How? And why?

A silent growl rumbled in Dominic's chest. He would find out.

The man looked up, squinting toward Gisela's shop. Straightening his tunic, Dominic acted as if he was merely casting a casual glance down the street. He must be very careful. Whatever he did, he mustn't endanger Gisela.

Fighting the impulse to lunge at the man, Dominic sauntered past him and down the street. Balling his hands into fists, he focused on the *crunch* of dirt beneath his boots.

Mutters erupted from the direction of the group of men. Moments later, an answering *crunch* sounded behind Dominic.

As he'd hoped.

A grim smile curved his mouth. He walked on. The footfalls continued.

Ahead, an alley veered off the street. Dominic turned into it. A mound of wooden crates stood stacked against the side of a building.

*Perfect.*

Darting forward, he crouched beside the crates and pressed his back to the stone wall. The cold seeped into his clothing and bandages.

Footsteps sounded in the mouth of the alley.

"*Merde,*" the man said softly, then started in.

*Five strides,* Dominic counted. *Six. Seven . . .*

The lackey's shadow fell upon him. Dominic leapt to his feet and threw his weight against the man. The lout's hat fell off as they crashed together into the opposite wall. Dominic gritted his teeth against the pain jarring through his ribs.

"What—" the thug spluttered.

Dominic shoved his arm against the man's throat. Glaring into the lout's eyes, Dominic said, "Now, you and I will talk."

# CHAPTER TEN

Crenardieu's thug choked out a curse, spittle glistening at the corner of his mouth. He struggled in Dominic's hold while his fingers clawed into Dominic's tunic.

The oaf had the strength of a mad bull. 'Twould be difficult to keep him restrained for long.

Dominic blocked a kick. He snarled in the man's face. "Why are you following me?"

The lout's gaze narrowed. Jerking his head to one side, he wrenched sideways. Dominic knew that trick well. He'd used it himself a few times—especially in the dark streets of Venice—to escape unwelcome confrontations with thugs.

Dominic pressed his arm tighter against the man's Adam's apple. The lackey stiffened. Eyes wide, he flattened back against the rough stone. He swallowed, and his throat moved against Dominic's sleeve.

"Answer me," Dominic said between his teeth. "Why are you following me? Why are you spying on G—" —he remembered at the last moment— "Anne?"

The man's harsh breath fanned across Dominic's cheek. The barest glint of acquiescence shone in his eyes, before he pressed his lips together.

He spat in Dominic's face.

The spittle landed on Dominic's nose. "Tsk-tsk. Not very nice." Ignoring the cooling wetness on his skin, he leaned harder against the man's throat. "Now, I ask you again—"

Stones skittered to Dominic's right. The thug's gaze shifted in that direction, and Dominic risked a glance. The lout's friends might have come to his rescue.

A little peasant boy ambled into the alley after a ball. The toy bounced off the wall and rolled toward the crates. His gaze on his prize, the grubby-faced child toddled closer.

Dominic clenched his jaw.

The thug twisted. Dominic sensed the man reaching for his belt. No doubt, to draw a knife.

*God's blood.*

The boy suddenly seemed to realize he was not alone in the alley. Eyes huge, he looked up. He stumbled to a halt. His face paled.

A woman's voice carried from the street. "Pip? Where did ye go?"

Concern sharpened her words. How easily Dominic imagined Gisela in such a situation, calling for Ewan who had disappeared from view. Dominic's mouth flattened. He was not a parent, but no man could be immune to a mother's worried voice. Peasant or lady, when they feared for their children, all women were equals.

Dominic glared back at the lout. Smug triumph glinted now in the man's eyes. A warning cry seared through Dominic's anger-hazed mind. The thug intended to draw blood. Despite the child standing so near. Despite possible risk of injuring the boy.

"Run away, son!" Dominic shouted to him. "Go!"

"Mama," the child whined. His eyes welled with tears as he glanced from the men to the ball lying close to Dominic's boots. His dirty face clouded with indecision. He seemed torn between what was wise and what he wanted.

"God's teeth," Dominic muttered. He'd never forgive himself if the boy got hurt.

Geoffrey wouldn't forgive him, either.

Swallowing bitter disappointment, Dominic stepped away from the lackey, just as the blade of a knife glinted in the man's hand. Dominic darted back, his boot heel thudding against one of the broken crates.

"Pip?" A woman stepped into the alley. Her gasp echoed. "Oh!"

Spinning on his heel, the thug faced her. Then, he shoved his blade into his belt and sprinted past.

"Mama." The boy rushed toward his mother. Wailing at an earsplitting volume, he buried his face in her patched skirts.

Dominic dragged a hand over his face, wiping away the oaf's spittle. His emotions were wound so tight, he felt like yelling, too. That release of pent-up emotion would be most welcome.

However, he'd have another opportunity with that lout. He would make certain.

Dominic stooped and picked up the ball. The woman had swept her son up into her arms. Cooing to him, she hurried back to the street. Safe in the sunlight and crowds, she stopped and hugged the little boy tight.

Dominic approached her. "I believe this belongs to your son." He held out the toy.

Bewilderment registered on the woman's face, weathered from long days toiling outdoors. "Milord." She tried to drop into a curtsy, but he waved a hand. With a shy nod, she took the ball. "Thank ye."

Turning his face out of his mother's skirts, the boy beamed.

Dominic smiled back. He could not help it. The child's delighted grin was immensely . . . gratifying.

One day, his own son would look upon him so.

He shook aside the peculiar thought. Such notions held no purpose when he had a great deal to do—above all, send a missive reporting his progress to Geoffrey.

Nodding to mother and child, Dominic spun on his

heel and strode away.

Smoothing a hand over her gown, Gisela opened her shop door. A gust of late afternoon air swept in, swirling over the freshly swept planks. She inhaled a slow breath, savoring the smells of the living town. How she'd hated spending her day shut inside, cloistered to the outside world, enslaved to her commission for Crenardieu.

Soon, she would no longer be forced to any man's will.

She cast a careful glance about her premises. Twice she swept the floor to be sure no threads remained. She even moved the table and wooden stool, to be extra certain. Dominic would discover naught out of the ordinary.

*He will never know I lied to him about the silk,* she reminded herself. *However, he will know the truth about Ewan. That, I cannot keep any longer from him.*

A hot-cold shiver trailed through her. She crossed the room and, with sweaty hands, placed the broom back in its usual corner. Aye, she would tell Dominic. Today. When they had a quiet moment to talk. She'd come to the decision that afternoon when her only companions were needle and thread. No matter how difficult the truth might be, Dominic deserved to know.

Guilt gnawed, along with intense anticipation. Was it fair of her to tell him and then vanish? Nay. He would resent her. Mayhap even come to hate her. Gisela's eyes burned, for the thought of hurting him in such a way made her soul weep.

*You know there is no other choice, Gisela. Not if you want to protect Dominic from Ryle's viciousness.*

Again, the memory of Ryle's contorted face barged into her thoughts. She squeezed her eyes shut, trying to block him out, but his violent roar echoed in her mind, followed by the sharp pain of his dagger piercing her flesh. Shuddering, pressing her hand to her scarred breast, she fought to defeat the memory. Fought, with her strength of will, as she should have fought that eve, if only she hadn't been so weak.

Reaching out, she grasped the worktable. Her fingers clutched its solid strength, until the memory dissipated and her shaking subsided.

She forced up her chin, ignoring the lingering pangs of dread. With freedom so near, she would *not* be cowed by memories of Ryle. Dominic would arrive soon. She must bolster herself for what she was to tell him. Moreover, she needed to plan what she and Ewan would take when they fled.

She went through into her home, her gaze straying to the bread, cheese, and bowl of hazelnuts on the table. A simple repast, but 'twould do. With it she would serve the last of the mead she kept in the cupboard. Good to drink it up, since she wouldn't take it with her and Ewan. They must take only what was light and easy to carry.

Booted footfalls echoed in the shop. "Hello?"

*Dominic.*

Her pulse began an erratic thunder. "In here." She crossed to the doorway, drying her suddenly damp hands on her skirt.

How bold and handsome he looked, poised in the light streaming in from the doorway behind him—as though he commanded the sun. He no longer wore the embroidered tunic, but a simple, well-fitting one the gray of a winter sky. As he neared, her gaze took in his hair's unruly tousle, the graceful curve of his lips, and the stubborn purpose about him.

How much he reminded her of Ewan.

A breath shivered from her, for, as it did that morn, concern glinted in Dominic's eyes. Gesturing to the street outside, he said, "The door was open."

Surprise skittered through her. "I wanted to let in some fresh air."

His head dipped in a half nod. "Did you have visitors?"

"I only finished working a short while ago, and then I opened the door. No one came or went."

"Ah." His gaze skimmed the room, pausing to linger on the chemise hanging on the wall peg. She'd hoped to sew more on it that afternoon, but would have to return to it that eve. If she worked through the night, she could finish it along with Crenardieu's commission.

Reaching back, Dominic swung the door closed. It clicked shut, and the room plunged into shadow, lit only by the fading sunlight fingering in through cracks in the walls.

Gisela frowned. "Why did you shut the panel?"

His gaze narrowed, but he did not answer.

"Please open it."

"In a moment." His attention shifted from her to the chemise before he strode to it, his boots loud on the planks. His expression thoughtful, he caught the sleeve in his fingers and examined the unfinished cuff.

*He will notice you have not worked on it today. He will be suspicious,* her mind shrilled.

Alarm shot through Gisela like hot sparks. She must distract him. Quickly!

"Dominic, what is going on?"

He hesitated, long enough to send a shiver coursing through her, before he glanced in her direction. "I might ask you that question."

"W-what do you mean?" She tried to sound puzzled, but her words died on her tongue.

"Your shop is being watched."

"*What?* By whom?"

*Ryle. He has found you. He has come to kill you.*

She fought a blinding surge of panic. Nay. Ryle wouldn't merely watch her; he'd storm in and unleash his temper.

"Crenardieu's men," Dominic said.

She exhaled on an oath. Crenardieu didn't trust her, after all. He suspected she might bolt before she finished her commission for him. Did he think she'd steal the silk and sell it?

Or, did he expect her to betray him to Dominic?

Resentment welled inside her, so sharp, she almost choked on it.

Releasing the chemise's hem, Dominic turned to face her. "Why, I wonder, would Crenardieu guard your shop?"

"I do not know," she managed to say. *Liar!* her conscience screamed. *How can you speak falsely to the man you love? The only man you will ever love, until the day you perish?*

A sad, taut smile touched Dominic's mouth. "I vow you do know, Gisela."

A sob lodged in her throat. Aching loneliness filled her soul. She sensed the emotional distance furrowing between her and Dominic, cleaving like an axe through the loving trust that had defined their relationship before.

Fie! Circumstances were different now. How could she not speak falsely, when her lie would save Dominic from Ryle?

She crossed her arms and rubbed her sleeves with her hands. "Crenardieu has no reason to distrust me." That, at least, didn't further embroider her falsehood.

"So you say. Yet, from early morn 'til I came in just now, at least two men stood in the street and kept watch on your premises. They pretended to be repairing a broken wagon. I pursued one of them and tried to wrest an explanation from him, but he was not forthcoming. A short while later, he was back in his spot, watching."

"Oh, God," she whispered.

"Crenardieu would not order his thugs here, Gisela, unless he had reason."

She tried to speak, but desperation froze her mind. All the words that might rush to her defense evaporated like dew.

Dominic's gaze challenged hers. "From the moment we met, I sensed you withheld something from me. 'Tis more than your running from your husband."

A tremor shook her.

He stepped forward, his fierce strength of will rolling toward her out of the shadows. "Are you indebted to Crenardieu in some way? Is that why he watches you?"

Trying to swallow down a moan, she shook her head.

He raked fingers through his hair. His face contorted as though his next words were unbearably painful. "Are you and he . . ." He clenched his eyes shut before opening them again. "Are you his . . . lover?"

"Never!"

"Does he fear my relationship with you, then? That I might take what he believes is his?"

A frantic laugh bubbled inside her. If only Dominic knew how perfectly his words related to the hidden silks. "Honestly, Dominic, I would rather eat a slug than lie with Crenardieu."

A faint smile tilted Dominic's lips. "Good. Otherwise, I would be very disappointed in you."

Gisela smiled back. Warmth spread within her, akin

to a flower unfolding and reaching for the sky. How she loved Dominic's wry humor. How she loved . . . him.

*Tell him now, Gisela. Tell him what he deserves to know. Before you lose your courage. Before Ewan scampers through the doorway.*

Drawing a trembling breath, she said, "Dominic, you were right about a secret. One I have kept from you far too long. I shall deny you the truth no longer."

# CHAPTER ELEVEN

A sigh broke from Dominic, a sound expressing the relief whooshing through him. At last, Gisela confided in him. 'Twas best she reached this decision on her own, rather than him having to coerce her.

Letting his hands fall to his sides, he stepped closer. "Thank you, Gisela, for trusting me."

She gave a jerky nod, causing her hair to shift about her shoulders. He remembered the brush of her tresses against his hands. The way, years ago, she had looked up at him, her blue eyes shining with limitless love and trust.

When she looked at him now, he saw wariness in her gaze, as well as haunting shadows of anguish. Whatever she was about to tell him was difficult for her.

Silence spread through the shop like a thick blanket. "'Tis about Crenardieu," he gently pressed.

"Um . . . Nay."

He frowned. "What do you mean, nay?"

Her lashes dropped a fraction, veiling the spark of her eyes. "Crenardieu has no part in what I must . . ."—she shivered and clasped her hands—"what I will tell you."

Disbelief weighed like a stone in Dominic's gut. He'd been so sure about her revelation. His gut instincts screamed she had information about the missing silks and that Crenardieu was responsible for stealing Geoffrey's shipment.

His frown deepened, for Gisela's hands were quivering. An awkward giggle escaped her. "Now the moment is upon me, I do not know how to begin."

Her wobbly voice melted some of his irritation. Glaring at her was hardly the way to encourage her to share what she knew. He must assure her, with words and comforting gestures, that he wouldn't cast judgment upon what she told him. "Why not start with how you came to bear this knowledge?"

She blinked, tears sparkling along her lower lashes. "Bear this knowledge," she repeated softly with another laugh. "Oh, God."

Her shrill tone grated on his nerves. *Patience, Dominic.* Setting his hands on his hips, he studied her, barely resisting the urge to place his hands upon her shoulders and persuade her with a caress.

After inhaling a tremulous breath, she said, "'Tis about . . . us."

"Us," he repeated. Confusion tangled with a wild, yearning anticipation. Memories flooded into his mind, careening one over another.

"What happened between you and . . . me years ago."

He squinted at her. "'Tis not about the silk?"

"Silk!" Her face whitened. "Why would you think that I—"

"Why would I not? Every thread of information I have discovered so far leads me to Crenardieu. And, Sweet Daisy, to you."

"Me?" Her breathless whisper seemed to reverberate in the room.

"Aye. You."

Her hand fluttered to her throat. Her lips parted. She clearly intended to refute him, but no sound emerged. Not even the faintest, choked protest.

Anxiety widened her watery eyes. Then, her gaze sharpened with determination. She whirled and marched to the door, her hair swaying to and fro against her back.

He scowled at her. "Gisela!"

She flinched, but didn't halt or glance back at him.

"Do not run from me." He stormed after her.

"Run? Why should I?" she shot back. "Show me the louts who are spying on me. Ask *them* about the accursed silk. They will know far more than I."

He might have believed her, except she was now shaking from head to toe. And her voice . . . Her desperation revealed all. Her will might be strong, but her body betrayed her.

Gisela grabbed the door handle. Yanked the panel open.

Striding up behind her, he clamped his hand over hers. Shoved the door closed with a firm *click*.

She stood very still, clearly frozen by the subtle but meaningful show of force, her breathing coming in uneven gasps. Pressed lightly against her back, he felt each inhalation and shudder. She stared at his hand covering hers as though unable to tear her gaze away.

Dominic couldn't help but spread his fingers wider upon her skin, to touch more of her. To *feel* her. He wanted to groan aloud with the pleasure of touching her.

She swallowed. As he looked at her taut profile, the petal-smooth column of her neck begged for his kiss. His gaze moved down, to her tantalizing cleavage at the top of her bodice, and he fought his own shudder. Ah, God, he couldn't help but stare.

He hauled his focus back to her face—the delicate line of her jaw, her rose-pink mouth, her smooth cheek . . . perfection in each curve. No well-bred noblewoman's profile could be more exquisite.

"Crenardieu's men—" she said in a strained whisper.

"I do not wish to ask them," he said just as softly. "I wish to ask you."

*As I wish to feel you. Taste you. Kiss you.*

He inhaled, drawing in the essence of her. Warmth, sunlight . . . Completion. Closing his eyes, he let the scent of her wash through him. Like the summer sun, her being burned through the tangle of his restraint. Singed him with a need. He pressed closer. His torso brushed her back. His groin nudged her bottom.

*Ah, God! To touch you like this, after so very long!*

"Dominic," she gasped. Her spine arched, an attempt to sever the intimate contact. Yet, the movement forced her supple body to glide against his, fluid and tantalizing, like sunlight skimming over water.

Intense, consuming heat flooded through him, focusing where their bodies touched. He could hardly breathe. He stared down at the crown of her head, mesmerized by her shining gold hair that led his gaze down, again, to her bosom.

How perfect her breasts had felt in his palm. Warm. Ripe.

He dipped his head and kissed her hair.

A sigh wrenched from her. "Stop."

"Why?"

"Please." No more than a whisper, ragged with anguish and . . . desire.

Dominic clamped his jaw against the voices inside his head urging him to heed her plea. She was married. Forbidden. Yet, she herself denied any commitment to her husband, and Dominic *must* know what she kept from him. Chivalry had its place in the ways between men and women, but he'd been patient long enough.

He removed his hand covering hers. How he missed

her skin's warmth—but only for a moment. When she uncurled her fingers and they slipped from the door handle, he placed his hands upon the curve of her hips. Her gown's coarse fabric—very different from the clothes she wore in the meadow that summer—grazed his palms.

Anticipation rippled through him. *I care not that you are dressed in commoner's garb. I know the delicate silk of your naked skin. I have caressed it. Tasted it. Kissed the sun-warmed patch below your—*

"Nay!" she cried, as if attuned to his wanton cravings. She twisted in his hold, darting sideways faster than he imagined possible.

Her hands curled at her sides, she stood several steps away. Her eyes glittered, not with fury, but passion.

"Come back, Gisela," he whispered.

"Do not touch me again." A sobbed plea.

*A lie.*

"I must," he answered, closing the space between them. "No longer can I deny myself."

She stepped backward. "Nay! To touch me—"

"—'Tis all I have wanted to do since I first saw you in the stable."

"'Tis dangerous! I will not allow you."

"Aye, Gisela, you will." He closed the last paces separating them.

The backs of her thighs hit the sewing table. She flinched. "Oh, God," she said, looking frantically for a place to run.

Dominic stepped in front of her. He took her face in his hands and gently, but firmly, tipped it up.

Her eyes huge and wet, she stared up at him, tears glistening like rainwater on her face. Her hands came up to clutch his arms.

Lowering his voice to a husky rasp, he said, "Never will I regret wanting to kiss you. Or for desiring you as I did years ago."

Moisture brimmed along her lashes. "Dominic—"

"You are *mine*, Gisela. You always will be."

"Walk away," she said on a sob. "Forget me."

"Never." He pressed a tender kiss to the hair tangling over her brow.

She thrust her shoulders back, fighting him even in her desire. Misery shadowed her gaze like a black cloud obliterating the sun. "*Please!* Trust me when I say—"

"Trust me, Sweet Daisy." Coaxing her chin upward even more, he leaned his body against hers. With a gasped protest, she dropped back to sit on the table's edge. The wood squeaked at her weight.

Before she could squirm away, he nudged her legs apart with his knee. Cloth whispered, the sound akin to an impassioned sigh.

A flush stained her face. "You are a bold man."

He smiled. "Aye." What irony, that days ago, when she tended his ribs, she stood in a similar fashion between his legs. Then, she had treated his physical discomfort. Now, he must tend her. He wouldn't ease bodily pain, but assuage her emotional torment rooted in their parting long ago.

"Dominic, if you do not let me rise this instant—"

He chuckled. "You will what?" He kissed her temple. "Beat your fists upon me?"

She glared at him, but reluctance defined the set of her mouth. "I could not hurt your sore ribs."

"Scratch my eyes out, then?"

Desperation lit her gaze. "Fie! How could I wound you? How, when I still . . ." Her voice faded. She bit her lip, obviously trying to stifle her unspoken words, and looked away. "Oh, Dominic."

"Mmm?" He waited, holding her face in his hands. He kissed her eyebrow. Her eyelid. The salty path streaming down her face.

"Dominic," she moaned.

"Sweet Daisy." Dipping his head, he brushed his lips over hers. A tender memento of the love they once shared.

The instant their mouths touched, awareness catapulted through him. The stunning force of it snatched his breath, made him draw away for the barest moment. He shuddered, humbled by the sheer power of the physical connection.

The fierce passion between them remained, despite their years apart.

*Gisela is yours, as she was before*, his mind whispered. *Prove that then, now, and always, she is the purest half of your soul.*

She, too, must have felt the jolt of desire. She went very still. Blinking tears from her damp lashes, she gazed up at him with longing and reticence. Then, her gaze fell to his mouth. Yearning darkened her eyes.

An answering need coursed through him in a swift, potent surge. He kissed her again. His mouth swept over hers, urging her to kiss him back. Asking her to return the pleasure he offered her. Demanding she acknowledge the desire between them.

A ragged cry broke from her. She seemed unable to resist any longer, for her eyelids closed. Her lips parted, accepting all he offered. Taking, yet giving in return.

Their lips moved in perfect rhythm. As perfect as years ago.

Give. Take.

Nibble. Suck.

"Gisela," he groaned. His tongue slid into her mouth. With a hungry sigh, she curved her body to meet his thrusting tongue. Her fingers, clutching his arms, curled into his tunic sleeves. Her grasping fingertips dug into his skin.

"Gisela." He kissed her faster. Deeper. Never could he devour enough of her sweetness. He bent closer, his hands sliding from her face into her hair. His fingers buried into the silken strands, holding her head firm, holding her closer to his body and heart.

Their sighs and kisses echoed in her shadowed shop, the melody of their long-ago love.

She tore her mouth free, her breath coming in harsh pants. "Dominic." In her voice, he heard both delight and despair.

"Shh." His hand slid from her hair to sweep over the curve of her shoulder. "Gisela, I have missed you."

"As I have missed you." With a hesitant touch, she caressed his face. Her gentle fingertips trailed over his healing bruise.

He smiled and kissed her thumb. Then, dipping his head, he kissed her cheek, her jaw, the velvety line of her neck.

"Nay," she breathed, her head listing back. "Wait!"

He blew on her neck and was rewarded by her gasp. Her hand fluttered, a feeble attempt to stop his sensual barrage. Resisting a grin, he caught her fingers and kissed them before pressing little kisses along her bodice's edge. He savored her soft, scented skin that obliterated all but the pleasure of her.

He nibbled a path back up to her mouth. Ravenous, seeking, her lips meshed with his. He kissed her with matching fervor. When a pleasured purr rumbled in her throat, he skimmed his other hand down over her shoulder to her bodice. Sliding his finger between the fabric and her skin, he touched the upper swell of her breast with his fingertip.

She tensed. With a strangled cry, she drew back.

Panic widened her eyes. Her breaths sharpened with urgency. His heart constricted, compassion and tenderness melding with his desire. Did she hesitate because they'd been apart so long? Did she believe, somehow, she no longer measured up to the young maiden he had loved? That he wouldn't find her pleasing?

In his eagerness, he hadn't wooed her enough to vanquish her unease. To show how much she still meant to him. He lifted his fingers away, then squeezed her hand still entwined with his. "'Tis all right, Gisela."

She shook her head, her hair spilling over her shoulder. "We should not be kissing or . . . caressing." Shifting her bottom on the table, she tried to scoot sideways.

He didn't budge. Resisting a grin, he noted she could not escape him unless she slid backward on the table. In that instance, he would simply grab her skirts and yank her forward again.

Shoving her free hand to his chest, she said, "Please move aside."

"What happens here, now, is between us." He softened each word. "Only us."

"You do not understand."

How distressed she sounded. Her tone was vastly different from the dulcet coaxing with which she'd seduced him in the meadow. However, he sensed that passionate lover still lived on, in her thoughts, memories, and secret dreams.

"No matter what happened while we were apart, our feelings are still true," he murmured. "You cannot deny that."

She gnawed her lip. Her fingertips curled into his tunic. How close her hand was to catching the linen on his necklace pressed against his skin.

Anguish shivered across her face. Again, she pushed at him.

"Touching you," he said quietly, "is merely acknowledging what is true."

"Nay, touching me is *wrong*."

"Why?" How he loved her skin's luscious softness. Of their own initiative, his fingers moved in lazy circles against her flesh, as though he traced a flower petals.

She trembled. "Dominic."

"You are mine, Sweet Daisy."

"But—"

"*Mine.* Then, now, and forever."

While he spoke, he skimmed his hand down over her bodice. His mind flooded with the delicious memory of her breast molded to his palm. A groan of intense longing burned inside him.

He cupped her breast.

His thumb met a hard ridge beneath the fabric.

Shock plowed through him. At the same moment, a gasp tore from her. She recoiled, her body so rigid, she might have been stabbed in the back.

He wrenched his hand away, staring at his palm. Blood pounded hard at his temple.

What had he felt?

Merciful God, *what?*

A scar? Surely not. Yet, he well knew of such wounds. While on crusade, he'd tended injured knights, even stitched their skin closed to encourage healing. He'd helped Geoffrey survive near-mortal wounds that now were only scars.

To think of her enduring such pain . . .

"Gisela?" In the silent room, Dominic's anguished whisper sounded like a scream.

Raising his head, he looked at her. She sat with her arms folded over her bosom in a defensive posture. Her beautiful face contorted with grief.

"What happened to you?" He forced each word through his teeth.

She met his gaze with a blank stare. "Will you move away now?"

"*What?*"

"I said, will you move away now?"

His shock disintegrated, became cresting anger. Fury blazed—that she seemed so distant. That she held within her such terrible anguish. Above all, that she'd suffered through such an injury.

"I will not move." He tried to speak calmly and keep his fury tightly leashed, but he couldn't stop his tone from roughening. "Tell me what happened."

Shrugging, she looked across her shop. Her body trembled, but she held herself taut, pride in the thrust of her chin. The pride of a woman who had faced . . . unspeakable horror.

Tears scalded his eyes. What had she endured? What had happened to his Sweet Daisy?

Vile possibilities seared through his mind. Clamping his jaw, he struggled to keep a clear mind and not make false assumptions. "How were you wounded? In an accident?"

A bitter laugh broke from her. "Nay."

*Someone had intentionally cut her.*

Dominic's stomach twisted. Bile scorched the back of his mouth. He wanted to vomit. Scream. Slam his fists into the wall and smash it into splinters.

"Who hurt you?" Disbelief pounded like an anvil against his skull. "*Who?*" Shocking realization crashed through him. "Your . . . husband?"

She flinched with such force, the table jolted. "I told you before, I have no husband."

"The man you wed. He hurt you?" Dominic repeated, his voice rising. "*Did he?*"

He waited, unable to breathe. Scarcely able to see past the red haze flooding into his line of vision.

Silence strained, tight as a thread about to snap.

She nodded.

A roar tore up from Dominic's gut, ripped through him, exploded from his lips with such ferocity, he reeled. "Gisela!"

She flinched again. "Now you know, Dominic. I am flawed, for the rest of my living days."

Her flat tone cut worse than a dagger. Did she hold herself responsible for her husband's cruelty? How could she? The man was clearly a monster.

Dominic's hand itched to seize a knife, to face her former husband man to man, to gouge a wound of equal size on the bastard's body. How could he have disfigured a woman as beautiful as Gisela? Or any woman?

"Let me see your scar."

Her watery gaze snapped to his.

"Let me see. I must know what he did to you." Even as Dominic spoke, his hands reached for her crossed arms. He eased them away from her body.

He half-expected her to fight him, lash out at him, even. Yet, she sat motionless, resignation in the set of her mouth, while he eased his fingers inside her chemise, next to her skin. He gently drew aside the fabric to expose her breast.

God's. Holy. *Blood!*

A puckered scar sliced the swell of her flesh. The pinkish gouge ran in a near-diagonal line, down her breast to the center of her rib cage. Not a light grazing of the knife, but a deep cut—the twisted bastard's mark of possession.

Oaths flew from Dominic's lips.

She struggled. "Dominic—"

"Who is he? What is his name? Where will I find him?"

"Dominic!"

He clutched her shoulders. "*Where? Answer me!*"

At the same moment, over the rage thundering in his ears, he heard the shop door creak open. A woman's startled cry. A child's gasp.

"Mama?"

# CHAPTER TWELVE

At the sound of Ewan's voice, Gisela jumped. Oh, God, she could only imagine how her and Dominic's encounter appeared to her son—and what thoughts must be racing through his mind.

Stifling a dismayed cry, she wrenched out of Dominic's grasp and yanked her bodice to cover her breast. She shoved him away. This time, he didn't attempt to thwart her, but moved in a graceful back step-turn that somehow conveyed the interruption rattled him as much as she.

Dragging his hand over his mouth, Dominic faced the open doorway where Ada and Ewan stood. A flush stained his cheekbones. A muscle twitched in his jaw, and she sensed him trying to quell his frustration.

If only she could appear as controlled. Her emotions seemed as fragile as tattered parchment.

Forcing a smile, Gisela slid off the table. "Ewan."

Her little boy stood pressed against Ada's skirts, his expression a gut-wrenching blend of shock and rage. Her hand pressed to her mouth, the older woman gaped.

Gisela swallowed down bitter regret. While she was immensely glad of the interruption, she never, ever wanted Ewan to discover her and Dominic having a disagreement. Months ago, she had vowed to protect her son from strife. Today, she had failed him.

"'Tis all right, Ewan." Gisela started toward him.

Her son's gaze riveted to Dominic. "What were you doing to Mama?"

The harshness of Ewan's voice made Gisela pause. He did not sound three-and-a-half years old, but much older. She clasped her sweating hands together. "We—"

"We were . . . having a discussion," Dominic said.

The little boy's mouth flattened. "I do not believe you."

"Nor do I, milord," Ada said with an indignant sniff.

"You were shouting." Ewan's whole body quivered with pent-up emotion. "You tried to hurt Mama."

Behind Gisela, Dominic groaned, a sound of distress. "Nay, little warrior."

"I *saw*. I thought you were a knight. A man of honor."

"I am." He raised his hands, obviously trying to calm Ewan's fury. "Believe me—"

"Knights do not hurt damsels. Especially mothers."

"Ewan, I did not lie to you. I was not hurting your mother. Why would I wish to do so?"

Scowling, the little boy stepped away from Ada. Fisting his hands, he loosed a fierce yell.

His cry held such pain—the ache of betrayal along with the anguish of shattered trust—Gisela stretched her arms out to him. Instinct propelled her forward, to take her son in her embrace, kiss him, and whisper comforting words.

Before she could slip her arms around him, he bolted past her. His footfalls pounded on the planks. Blinking hard, she watched him pull open the door to the living quarters and disappear inside.

"Ewan?" Gisela whispered.

Behind her, Dominic cursed. "I will go after him."

Gisela whirled. "Do *not!*"

Dominic frowned. "I will not have him believing I was doing you harm."

"I will speak with him. I will explain." *How?* Her mind shrilled. *What will you say that shall make a difference to Ewan? He is a child. How can he possibly understand the complex relationship between you and Dominic?*

"I *want* to speak with him," Dominic said, his tone barely a civilized growl. "Are you saying I cannot?"

Frustration became a cruel fist digging into Gisela's ribs. Before she could reply, Ada touched her arm. "Are ye hale? Did he hurt ye grabbing at yer bodice?"

Waving away the woman's concern, Gisela said, "I

am not hurt."

Ada flicked her black braid over her shoulder and turned to the open doorway to the street. "Good. I will scream fer 'elp."

"Nay!" Gisela cried. 'Tis all she needed, to attract more suspicion from Crenardieu's men—or to have Dominic beaten again in misguided heroics.

Glancing back, Ada scowled. "Do not feel ye must protect 'im. Even if 'e is a lord, 'e—"

"Thank you, but I am certain we can resolve this situation on our own." Brushing past the older woman, Gisela shut the door.

Ada's lips pursed. Planting her fists on her hips, she said, "I saw 'is 'ands upon ye. 'E was yellin' in yer face." Her indignant gaze slid to Dominic. Jabbing a finger at him, she said, "Before ye say one word, milord, do *not* try ta be clever and tell me ye was shoutin' because she did not 'ear ye. Anne 'as perfectly good 'earin.'"

"I would not dare to be clever with you, Ada," Dominic muttered. "You are right. I did shout. While I should be chivalrous, drop down on one knee, and offer a gallant apology, I will not."

Ada's brows raised.

When Dominic's sharp gaze settled on her, Gisela shivered.

"Anne and I have important matters to resolve between us. I raised my voice because I lost my patience with her."

"Ooh! So ye cannot control yer temper, then?" Ada crossed her plump arms.

A tight smile curved Dominic's lips. "In this instance, nay. I am not a man who likes to be teased—"

"Ha, milord! Teased?" the older woman snapped.

"—with the barest snippets of information. She owes me the rest. I will have it."

The sheer determination in his voice sent a shudder raking through Gisela. Part of her—the idiotic, naïve part—had hoped with Ada and Ewan's arrival, Dominic would cease questioning her about her scar. However, their conversation seemed far from over.

In his opinion, mayhap. She had other pressing matters. Giving Dominic a pointed glance, she said, "I am going to check on Ewan."

"I will come with you."

"He is my son." *Not* just your son, her mind corrected. *Be fair, Gisela*—

A *thump* sounded inside her house. She hurried across the shop. Booted footsteps came after her. *Dominic*.

Spinning to face him, she snapped, "Ewan is very upset. Please. Wait here—"

A shrill cry erupted inside her home. The little boy ran out, brandishing his wooden sword. His face scarlet with fury, he lashed out at Dominic.

*Whack*. The flat of the sword hit Dominic's thigh.

"Ewan! Stop," Gisela cried, grabbing for his sword arm.

*Whack*. "Take that!" Ewan yelled.

Gisela caught her son's elbow. "Cease! Right now, or—"

A flash of blue pinned her gaze and froze the rest of her words. Tied around the sword's grip was a length of cornflower blue silk. Ewan must have picked it up off her shop floor when he discovered the lump of wax. He'd hidden the cloth so she wouldn't take it away.

"Nay," she whispered, making a frantic grab for the sword.

With a loud *smack*, Dominic's hand closed over the toy's blade, halting it in mid-thrust.

"That is enough, Ewan."

Dominic's authoritative tone sent tremors racing through her. She prayed he had not seen the silk, that she would have a chance to untie it and stuff it into her gown.

"Let go of the sword," Dominic said.

"Aye, let Mama have it, Ewan." Gisela's pulse drummed a frantic rhythm.

A sob broke from Ewan.

"I know you are unsettled, Button. I will explain all. I promise," Gisela soothed, rubbing his shoulder. "Right now, I want you to give me the sword. I will keep it safe for you."

With a reluctant nod, Ewan released the toy. Gisela grabbed for it.

Too late.

Faster than she thought possible, Dominic flipped the toy weapon toward him. Holding it by the blade, he raised the grip to eye level. The silk trailed down in a blue wisp.

He fingered the scrap. "Ewan, where did you get this?"

She begged for him not to answer, even as he sniffled out, "M-Mama."

Very slowly, very deliberately, Dominic's gaze slid from the silk to her. "Indeed, we still have much to talk about."

When Gisela's face went ashen, Dominic fought a flood of disbelief and fury. Her reaction told him a great deal. Most of all, that 'twas no coincidence Ewan had blue silk adorning his sword.

She knew of de Lanceau's stolen silks. *She knew!*

How long had she known? Was the cloth in her possession? Here in her home? When he'd taken her into his confidence days ago and told her of his mission, had she listened, even offered him encouragement, while she hoarded the prize he sought?

Whatever the truth, she had lied to him. A dagger-sharp ache gouged Dominic's soul. How could his Sweet Daisy betray his trust?

Lowering the sword, Dominic glared at her. She still stared at him, her eyes enormous in her pale face. Ewan cried against her skirts, while she rubbed her hands over his back. Her soothing, protective gesture said a great deal, also—most of all, how much she loved her son.

His own mother had comforted him in such a manner when he was a child. "There, there," she'd murmured, patting him while he bawled about a stubbed toe or losing his favorite toy horse in a bramble patch. After a moment, she pushed him back enough to turn up his face and dry his tears with her thumbs. "Save some tears for another time, now." She winked, a twinkle in her warm brown eyes. "How about a story to cheer you? I know an exciting one about a maiden and a dragon . . ."

He forced aside the cherished memory. His personal sentiments must not—indeed, *could* not—overshadow the important duty Geoffrey had bestowed upon him. Gisela had withheld information vital to his mission, while knowing she committed a crime.

With brisk tugs, he untied the clumsy knot holding the silk to the sword. He sensed Ada's stern, curious gaze upon his back. From where she stood by the door, he doubted she saw much of the interchange with the toy weapon—or the silk bound to it. Good. The fewer who knew the damning truth, the better.

After closing his fingers around the cloth, he held out the sword. "Your weapon, little warrior."

Ewan turned his splotchy face away from Gisela's skirts.

"The battle between us is over. A draw."

A puzzled frown wrinkling his face, the little boy sniffled.

"When I get back, you and I will talk. Warrior to

warrior. All right?"

Ewan stared at him a long moment, dried his eyes on his sleeve, and nodded. Reaching out, he took back the sword. "You said, 'when I get back.'"

Dominic managed a firm smile. "Aye."

"Where are you going?"

He refused to let his smile waver as his gaze slid up Gisela's arm and bodice to meet her worried gaze. "Your mother and I need to finish our discussion."

Her throat moved with a swallow. "Later, mayhap—"

"*Now.*"

His growled order clearly shocked her. Her spine stiffened. Her hand stilled on Ewan's shoulder. How Dominic hated speaking harshly to her. Yet, no longer could he hold back the bloody thorns of emotion stabbing him.

He yanked up his tunic sleeve and tied the bit of silk around his wrist, tucking the ends under so they did not dangle. Spinning on his heel, he faced Ada. "You will stay with Ewan."

Her eyebrows arched. "Will I?" Her lips pursed. "Ye may be a lord, and ye may well 'ave me 'ead for speakin' me mind, but ye are a bossy, arrogant, no-good—"

Raising the edge of his tunic, Dominic withdrew a small, leather pouch. It jingled as he drew apart the top and turned it upside down. Silver coins spilled into his palm.

Ada gaped. Her mouth worked several times without emitting a sound. Then, she scowled. "Oh, ye are devious. Ye try ta bribe me, now?"

"Nay, good woman. I pay you to look after Ewan while his mother and I go for a walk."

A soft rustle alerted him that Gisela no longer stood motionless. He sensed her scrambling to think of a way out of her predicament. One she'd brought upon herself.

Anger lanced through him. She should have told him the truth days ago.

Dominic reached out, caught one of Ada's hands, and dropped the coins into it. "Until we return."

Ada's gaze shifted from the coins to a point past his shoulder. No doubt she exchanged glances with Gisela. "But—"

"Good. 'Tis settled." Dominic turned back to face Gisela, who appeared to be edging inside the house. "Fetch your cloak."

Resistance glinted in her gaze. "Will we be long?"

He almost laughed at her challenging tone. "That depends on you." *And, God help me, what I decide to do with you, Sweet Daisy, once I know the truth. Not just what you wish to tell me, but all of it, right down to the last, sordid detail.*

Her mouth pressed into a stubborn line, but she reached out, took her cloak down from its peg, and pulled the wool about her shoulders.

"Where are you going?" Ewan looked up at him. Concern shone in the little boy's eyes.

"Not far." Dominic ruffled the boy's hair.

"Why do you look angry?" Ewan shuffled his feet. "You look like you are going to shout. Like Father."

Dominic grimaced. Never did he wish to be compared to Gisela's former husband.

"Ewan—"

"I do not like it when you look so. It makes my tummy go squishy."

*Squishy?* Dominic suppressed a groan. "Your mama and I need to clarify some issues. Then, I hope not to be so . . . annoyed."

Gisela crossed to his side, garbed in her cloak. She yanked the hood up into place.

Dominic reached out to tuck in a stray length of her hair. "Walk by my side, as though we are associates taking a casual evening stroll."

"How else would I walk?" she muttered, striding toward the door.

He matched her pace. "Not like that."

Gisela threw up her hands. "Dominic!"

"'Tis best if Crenardieu's men do not follow us," he cut in. "You will arouse suspicion if you march along as though you wish to pummel someone—namely me."

The barest smile kicked up the corner of her mouth.

Ada gave a gleeful snort.

Hands on his hips, he leaned closer to Gisela. The scent of her hair, her body, her sweetness, posed their own challenges to his determination, but he pointedly ignored them. "I am trying to be chivalrous," he said, in a voice only she could hear. "I wish to hear your explanation, understand why you deceived me, and know how you came to have the stolen silk. However, if you insist on thwarting me, I will haul you from here, tie you to my horse, and take you to Branton Keep to answer to de Lanceau himself." He paused, letting his words sink in. "Your choice."

"I have not refused to go with you," she said between her teeth, mutiny in her eyes.

"Do as I ask, then." Brushing past her, he opened the door and gestured to the shadow-robed street. "After you."

She stepped over the threshold and moved aside to let him pass. With a nod to Ada, he drew the door closed. He tipped his head in the direction of the market square and, as he had suggested, she walked at his side, her shoes rasping on the dirt.

The end-of-day breeze held a heavy note, redolent of the coming twilight. As he strode along, he cast a discreet glance up and down the street. No sign of Crenardieu's thugs. Either they had gone to report to him, or they had snuck away for their evening meal.

He quickened his strides a fraction, encouraged when Gisela did the same. While he wished to speak to her alone, without Ewan or Ada to distract or interfere, he didn't want to be out after dark. His dealings with Crenardieu last eve had shown him a glimpse of Clovebury's seedy underbelly. Once was enough.

He crossed through the market, over to the streets

on the other side, past houses and shops until the glint of
river water appeared ahead. He'd discovered this pictur-
esque spot while walking the bank, searching for clues
as to the silk theft. How apt, that his wounded heart
brought him here.

"Will you please tell me where we are going?" Gisela
said, a catch in her voice.

"Just up here." The stone wall running along the
roadside—a remnant of ancient Roman conquerors—disintegrated a few yards on. A passing cart, veering out
of control, must have careened into it, leaving behind a
gaping hole. Crumbled rocks trailed into the wildflowers
and weeds growing alongside, as if the stones tried to bury
themselves again in the earth, to return to familiar ground,
rather than risk being mortared back into the wall.

Turning his body sideways, he stepped through the
jagged opening into the meadow that led down to the
riverbank. Facing Gisela, he extended his hand to help
her. She looked at his outstretched fingers, an expression of both longing and determination tightening her
features, before she braced her slender hands upon the
crumbled stone and eased herself through.

Dominic snuffed a sting of disappointment that
she did not allow him to assist her, then turned on his
heel and started across the meadow. Shadows, lightened
here and there by patches of fading sunshine, flowed like
gray cloth across the grasses and wildflowers. Greenery crunched beneath his boots, stirring up hidden

creatures—not vibrant butterflies or giddy bumblebees, but small, buzzing insects.

Behind him, he heard the whisper of grasses brushing against her cloak, accompanied by her footsteps. Years ago, she'd followed him so, her strides lazy and coy, her smile as bright as spring sunlight. Now . . .

He glanced over his shoulder. A pensive frown on her face, she scanned the slow-moving river, the wooden bridge spanning the banks farther down, the trees and cottages on the opposite bank. She rubbed her arms, as if to warm herself.

"Head for that tree. 'Tis shielded from the road." Dominic gestured to the ancient willow gilded in the orange hues of sunset.

Gisela followed him beneath the broad, spreading branches. She stood in the shadows, looking down at the tangled tracery of roots, as though there lay the answer to her dilemma.

At last, the moment had come. The moment he got his answers. Anticipation ate at him, creating an uncomfortable ache in his gut.

He waited until she looked up at him, then raised his cuff to reveal the silk encircling his wrist like a bracelet. The edges of the fabric were not frayed; this indicated the scrap wasn't torn from a larger piece of cloth, but neatly cut. Only well-sharpened shears left such a neat edge.

"How did Ewan come by this blue silk, Gisela?"

"I guess he . . . picked it up."

"He said you gave it to him."

Gnawing her lip, she shook her head. "I did not. He must have taken it from the pile of scraps on my shop floor. I did not notice." Self-condemnation crept into her gaze. "I should have. I should have expected him to sneak some of the cloth for his sword."

"You know the whereabouts of the stolen silk."

After a long moment, she nodded. "Some of it."

"'Tis hidden close to your home?"

"Under the floor of my shop."

"God's teeth!" No wonder the planks had sounded odd in places. But, he'd assumed 'twas was due to wearing of the floorboards and the building's poor construction.

"When he first gave me the bolts, he told me to keep them hidden to protect them from thieves. He reminded me of the many break-ins over the past few months."

"He," Dominic repeated. "You mean Crenardieu."

"Aye."

*French snake!* "How did you come to know him?"

She folded her hands, her fingers moving in a restless pattern as though trying to escape confinement. "One morn, he came to my shop. He said he had heard of my fine work and asked me to make some garments for him. I agreed. I had no reason to decline." She paused. "Then, one eve, he returned with two bolts of blue silk."

"I *knew* he was involved with the stolen shipment," Dominic growled. "Something about his manner—"

"I did not know at first that the cloth was stolen,"

she said, words rushing from her lips. "I thought he had bought the fabric for a wealthy client. With his connections, he could buy any cloth he wanted."

"True," Dominic said, "yet, surely you were suspicious. Silk is rare and costly."

"Indeed, when I heard of the stolen silks, I had my suspicions, but I kept them to myself. I did not want him to know I distrusted him. I did not want to lose . . ." Her voice trailed off before she looked across the meadow. Her fingers moved with a more frantic rhythm.

"Lose what?" Dominic demanded. "His confidence? His patronage?"

"Nay." Her lovely face tautened. "His payment."

An exasperated cry tore up from Dominic's gut. "Payment!" She had betrayed him out of *greed*?

Shocked fury threatened to obliterate his rational grasp of the situation. While her admission sank into his consciousness, his heart rebelled. Avarice hadn't blemished her soul years ago. Surely her moral fortitude hadn't changed so much, especially when she was responsible for raising a child.

Moreover, the humble residence she called home and her worn garments contradicted all impressions of a greedy woman who spent every coin she earned.

"I know what you are thinking," she said, her voice cutting into his thoughts like shears. "You believe I acted upon greed."

"That is, indeed, what I thought."

Gisela's body went rigid. His words clearly hurt her. "I *needed* his money, Dominic. From the first day Ewan and I arrived in Clovebury, I hoarded my income. Coin by wretched coin. Not an easy task, when I earned so little, but I promised . . ."

Her words broke on a sob. He resisted the urge to reach out and touch her arm.

"Promised what?"

She thrust her shoulders back. He glimpsed rage in the watery gleam of her eyes. "—to keep Ewan safe. To do whatever I must to protect him."

The discomfort in Dominic's belly did an awful twist. "I . . . see."

"Do you?" Her tear-soaked gaze fixed on him. "How can you possibly understand? You, with your fine clothes, coin to splurge on your every whim, and the friendship of a powerful lord. You want for *naught*."

The desperate fury in her voice flayed so deep, he almost flinched. *Aye, Sweet Daisy, I did want. I wanted you. Always, you.*

He opened his mouth to speak, but she slashed the air with her arm, ordering him to silence. "You saw what my husband did to me," she said in a fierce whisper. "The night he cut me, I made a vow. I swore I would *die* before I let him hurt me again." She shook with the effort of her words. "Never would I let him kill Ewan."

"*What?*" Dominic choked out. "Kill . . . Ewan?" Horror made him stagger back a step. "Why—?"

Touching anguish shadowed her gaze. She looked at him as she had long ago, with a bittersweet tenderness. "Ryle wanted to hurt me. To wound me . . . in the worst possible way." She shook so fiercely, she looked about to topple over. Dominic caught her elbow and guided her back toward the tree. With a shuddered sigh, she leaned against the trunk.

When her head tilted back, her hair slipped in a golden ribbon over her bosom. Her chest lifted and fell on a tortured breath, and he fought the need to stare at her right breast, its grim scar concealed by her gown. How he longed to know every detail of the night Ryle disfigured her.

"Gisela, why would your husband wish to kill his own child?"

Her lips formed a sad smile. "He was jealous."

Dominic frowned. "Of the child?"

"Aye. Of the affection I showed Ewan. Of the wonderful, pure love . . . from which he was conceived."

Her soft voice and the shadowed atmosphere tugged him into the realm of long ago. He forced the recollections away, saying, "There were difficulties in your marriage, then, after you gave birth to Ewan."

Her expression hardened. "There were difficulties before. Ryle. He . . ." Her lips pressed together, suggesting her next words were difficult.

"'Tis all right. You can tell me," Dominic coaxed.

"He was . . ."

"A monster," Dominic said.

She nodded, strands of her hair catching in the bark and glinting in a stream of sunlight. "He also was . . . impotent."

Dominic's hand, half-raised to tug her tresses free, froze. "Impotent."

Her eyes wet with tears, she nodded again.

Dominic's frown intensified. How could her husband be impotent? He got her with child. She birthed his son. Mayhap she mistook the word "impotent" for another, such as "intolerant" or "impatient"? "Gisela," he said most gently, "impotent means he could not . . ."—he cleared the awkward catch from his throat—". . . sire a child."

"I know." She blinked, her long lashes sweeping down over her eyes before their brilliant blue held his gaze again.

How intently she stared at him—a look that implied her words had monumental significance. An odd sensation tingled through Dominic, an inkling that she kept a knowledge just beyond his comprehension.

He exhaled an unsteady breath. "Let me be certain I understand. Your former husband could not . . . You and he did not—"

"Couple," she said.

"Not once?" he blurted, before he could stop himself.

A flush stained her face. "Not once."

"Not even on your wedding night?"

"Not even then," she said quietly. "He tried." A

shudder racked her, before she stared down at the ground. "He could not manage to . . . That is, his manhood would not . . ."

"Swell?" Dominic said.

Her face turned scarlet. "Not like yours."

*Not like yours.* Heat flamed in his groin while his delighted mind registered what she revealed in those three words. She remembered his body. Recalled the pleasure between them, and the intensity of his desire for her.

He cleared his throat again. "Ah." When had his wits evaporated like a puddle on a summer's day? She seduced him with memories, but she still hadn't provided him answers. Giving himself a strong mental shake, he said, "'Tis still not clear to me, Gisela. If your husband did not couple with you, how did you get with child?"

He waited for her response, tension cresting inside him. Gisela became pregnant by having an affair. Married to a man who couldn't pleasure her, she'd deceived him, which would explain his vicious treatment of her.

A tiny smile curved her mouth. Her expression seemed to say, *Still, Dominic, you cannot guess? The answer is very simple.*

Suddenly, the answer materialized in his mind. The shock of it slammed through him, seemed to shake the roots beneath his feet.

"Ewan—" he said hoarsely.

"Aye, Dominic. He is your son."

# CHAPTER THIRTEEN

Gisela waited, hardly daring to breathe, while her revelation settled between her and Dominic like dust blown off years of secrecy. He stood frozen, a myriad of expressions playing over his angular features, among them astonishment, disbelief, and . . . wariness.

"Ewan is my son," he repeated, each word spoken with great care.

"He is."

Dominic's mouth flattened. "Are you certain?"

Part of her had expected such a question. "There is no doubt," she murmured.

"None at all?"

She shook her head, trying hard to quell the buried love threatening to spill over from her soul and run down her face in a deluge of tears. "You are the only man I lay with, Dominic. There was no other." *Because, Dominic, no matter what happens in the coming days, you are the only man I will ever love. You always will be.*

He still looked wary. Anger glinted in his eyes. "In all the days we have been together, you never once mentioned this to me?"

She'd expected this question, too, and the painful guilt that followed. "To be honest, I was unsure . . . how to tell you." *Or, truth be told, how you would react to my disclosure.*

He raised an eyebrow.

"I could not very well say at the table the other eve, 'Guess what? Ewan is your child.' Could I?"

Dominic laughed, but the sound held no mirth. "You could have found a moment to tell me."

"I wanted to." Misery tightened her voice. "I promised myself I would, but only when I could speak with you alone."

"Ewan does not know?"

"Not yet."

Dominic studied her a long moment, and she guessed he was mulling the truth of her words. "When did you realize you carried a child?" he asked.

*Our child,* her mind cried. *Our son, Dominic. The proof of our love.*

"I knew several sennights after you left." She swallowed hard. "Oh, Dominic, how desperately I wanted to share my news with you. Not because I expected compensation of any kind," she added quickly. "When I lay with you, I knew full well I might conceive. Yet, I vowed if I were gifted with your babe, I would care for it. Love it. Cherish it." She hesitated, forcing herself to continue. "To know I would bear your daughter or son . . . 'Twas both exciting and very frightening. Even though we had said good-bye, and you had no doubt left for crusade, I journeyed to your father's keep. I could not bear . . . not to."

Memories of that difficult, painful visit whispered anew in her mind.

"Go on," Dominic said.

"At first, the guards refused to heed me. They said you no longer lived there and ordered me away. When I begged them"—she bit down on her lip—"they sent a messenger into the keep. Moments later, I was escorted into the great hall, where a woman greeted me. She said she was your stepmother."

Dominic's expression darkened. "A scheming bitch."

Gisela recalled the young lady's austere beauty and smug gaze. "She asked me what I wanted. When I told her I wished to contact you, she smiled. 'You must be Gisela,' she said. I was surprised, for I did not realize she knew of me . . . and then I . . . could not help myself. I burst into tears. After I confided in her"—Gisela drew a shaky breath—"she said there was no way to send you a message. Even if there were, I should rid myself of your bastard and forget about you, because . . ."

Oh, how the remembered words hurt! Like daggers, each one.

"*What*, Gisela?"

"You never wished to see me again."

He dragged a hand through his hair. "God's blood! Never did I say—"

"If you returned from crusade, you would marry a lady of your own noble class. Not a common little whore like me." A sob tore up from her.

"Gisela!" Anguish etched Dominic's features. "I am sorry."

"I left knowing our love had truly ended," she said, trailing a hand over her belly. "That all I had left of you —of *us*—was our child. A babe I wanted very much."

A sigh broke from Dominic, a sound akin to the willow leaves stirring overhead.

"When my parents learned I was with child," she went on, "they were shocked. My family was well known in the county. They had hoped to marry me to one of their wealthy clients and thereby expand my father's influence in the cloth trade. No man would want me pregnant with another's babe."

"Your dragon of a husband married you."

"Ryle was an associate of my father's and many years older than I," Gisela bit out, unable to tamp down her loathing. "He had no children. His previous wife died. He offered to accept my babe as his own, in exchange for my help running his business. My father had taught me to manage the accounts. Ryle wished me to do the same for him."

Dominic stood silent for a long moment, a tall, brooding presence in the darkening shadows. The wind, whispering through the leaves again, sounded like the hushed gossip of finger-pointing old crones. "I had no choice, Dominic," she said, speaking the words she had silently told herself a hundred times over. "My parents wanted to avoid a scandal. To leave and try to begin a trade on my own, with no money and a babe to feed and clothe, was foolish. Ryle was a rich merchant. He promised to care for me and my child."

"I understand, Gisela." Dominic's voice sounded flat and as emotionless as a barren winter day.

"Really?" she whispered, the torment of her choices turning her voice to pure pain. "I felt naught for him. He was a stranger to me in all ways. I stood beside him during our nuptials, but felt only . . . emptiness." *Because I loved you. Every part of me longed to be with you.*

"'Twas not so unpleasant the first few months," she went on, "or those after Ewan was born. Ryle traveled a great deal, sometimes to the continent to visit the Fairs of Champagne and purchase cloth, or other parts of England to meet fellow merchants. I looked after his manor home and the accounts, while raising Ewan."

"An ideal situation, to outsiders."

*Nay, my love, for each day, I craved you. I begged that, by some divine miracle, you would survive the horrors of battle and return to England, to be with me.*

"Ideal until the profits did not match his reckless spending," Gisela said with a shiver. "When Geoffrey de Lanceau settled at Branton Keep, and his cloth industry thrived, Ryle lost clients. De Lanceau became rich, while Ryle struggled to keep customers."

"Ah," Dominic murmured.

"Ryle grew angry. He began to drink, his one goblet of wine in the evening becoming five or six. When I begged him to stop, he hit me, hard enough to send me sprawling on the floor."

She forced words through chattering teeth. "I told him I would leave. He said if I dared to run away, no matter where I went, he would find me. He would hurt my parents, until they told him where I could be found."

"Gisela!"

"Then, after raising his fist to hit me again, he wept and apologized. He said he loved me, and promised to be a better man."

Dominic shook his head.

"I tried to keep him content. I asked the servants to cook his favorite meals. I kept up with the accounts. Then, one eve, I . . . I made a mistake."

"What do you mean, 'a mistake'?"

"In the ledger, I . . . incorrectly subtracted a sum. I swear, I did not mean to. Ewan was teething and restless in the nights, and I had not slept well. I miscalculated. Ryle found the mistake. Drunk and angry, he accused me of trying to cheat him. He said I planned to steal the money to run away, to be with another man." *To be with you, Dominic. Because you gave me your son. Because you loved me in ways Ryle could not.*

"Gisela, 'twas not your fault."

She shrugged off the soothing reassurance of Dominic's words. "I am to blame. I should have checked my sums."

"He should never have taken out his anger on you."

Gisela tried very hard not to cry. How she yearned to accept the concern in Dominic's gaze, to melt against him. Yet, how could she turn to him when in all likelihood, he would destroy her dream of a new life? As de Lanceau's spy, Dominic had no choice but to tell his lord what she had done—and see her punished.

"Did Ewan see Ryle attack you?" Dominic asked softly.

"Nay. He was asleep upstairs. Oblivious. For that, I am forever grateful. For him to have witnessed Ryle's fury . . ." She rubbed her chilled arms, her breast hurting anew with the remembered pain. Again, she smelled wine on Ryle's breath as he loomed over her, his handsome, sweaty face twisted with malice.

*"Speak true, Gisela. You intended to deceive me."* His breath roared from him, hot as fire, scalding her with the force of his rage. *"Admit it!"*

*"Nay! Ryle, I am sorry,"* she cried. *"I am sorry."*

*She stepped back, anxious to stay out of range of his swinging fist. His lips curled away from his teeth, stained red from his drink. His eyes cinched into slits.*

She knew that look. She woke in a cold sweat from dark dreams because of it. Fear turned her innards to water.

"Ryle, I am sorr—"

His hand snapped out. She raised her hands to try to deflect the blow. Stumbled back.

His fist did not strike her.

Instead, his hand locked around her arm. His fingers clamped onto her sleeve, digging into her skin despite the layer of shimmering silk between their flesh.

"Please," she gasped. If only he had hit her and been done with his cruelty. The glint in his eyes promised more.

His other hand reached to his belt. His dagger hissed from its scabbard.

She froze. Surely he would not . . . "Ryle—" Her plea sounded like someone else's voice. A woman consumed by terror.

"You will be sorry," he said between his teeth. "You will never deceive me again."

The knife glinted, a silver flash of light that seemed to reflect off every surrounding surface. The light transfixed her, imprisoned her with sheer horror. What did Ryle mean to do? Was he going to kill her?

Run! her mind screamed. Get away while you still can.

Even as her mind shrieked, she remained frozen. Frantic thoughts clashed, undermining her instinct to bolt. If she fled, would he come after her? Or, would he storm up the stairs and use the knife on Ewan?

Her breath locked tight in her lungs. Several times,

Ryle had vowed to hurt anyone she loved if she ran away. He was cruel enough to wound a sleeping child. Another man's son.

Sobs welled inside her. With every ounce of willpower, she forced herself to remain motionless. Curling her hands into fists, she watched the knife plunge down in a bright arc.

With a sickening rasp, the blade whisked across her bodice, cutting silk and flesh as though they were soft cheese. Pain careened into her mind. Blood, thick and warm, spewed between her breasts, down to her belly, sticking her delicate chemise to her skin.

A crimson stain ribboned across her bodice.

She stared down at her blood-soaked gown. A strange sound echoed in the chamber. A gasping, wheezing noise.

The sound of her own breathing.

The agony of her cut flesh . . . Hideous pain! She bit her lip to keep from screaming. Never would she reveal her anguish. Ryle must not have the satisfaction of knowing how much he hurt her. Nor would she wake Ewan and have him see her injury.

The suppressed scream scorched her throat. With a trembling hand, she fingered the torn silk. A cut with neat, clean edges, she noted dully. The sign of a deadly sharp knife.

She glanced up, wavering as the room spun at a peculiar angle. Squinting down at her, Ryle met her gaze. The menacing force of his glare commanded her to cower before him, crying, bleeding and wounded.

Never again would she yield to this beast of a man.

Never!

*When she continued to stare, his squint hardened. She dropped her gaze—she did not want to—but to outright challenge him in such a rage was foolish. Better to use her remaining strength to find a way to defend herself if he attacked again.*

*There. The flower vase he had bought her as a gift. She would smash it over his head. Somehow, she must reach out and grab it.*

*Ryle exhaled a rough sigh. The knife winked again. As her arms instinctively flew up in self-defense, the dagger landed with a* thump *on the table beside them. After running a hand through his silvery hair, he reached for his wine.*

*Relief weakened her legs. They threatened to give out, to send her collapsing on the floor.*

*Drawn by grim fascination, her gaze slid to the knife. Blood glistened on the blade. Her blood, cleaved from her breast. God, oh, God, how it hurt!*

*Vomit burned her mouth. The slick, crimson liquid on the knife began to spread, growing like a murky pool across the table. Wider, wider, it grew, covering the table, consuming . . .*

"Gisela," Dominic said from nearby.

The scarlet haze in her mind slowly faded to the mottled green of tree shadows. Dominic's arms were around her, supporting her, Gisela realized dully. He stood behind her, holding her about the waist, supporting her while . . .

While she moaned like a little girl lost in a nightmare.

"Shh," he murmured against her hair.

She clamped her lips together, curtailing the last of her desolate cry. The breeze whispered through the leaves overhead, altering the shadows beneath the willow with new patterns of light and dark. Sunshine slipped over the twisted roots plunging like fingers into the soil. Those roots anchored the tree. Sustained it through drought and storms. Grew deeper over time and helped it flourish.

Dominic's arms tightened about her, reinforcing her with their muscled strength. Another moan, of unbearable longing, bubbled inside her. How wondrous to be pressed against him.

How dangerous, to defy the physical distance between them.

She released her pent-up breath. "W-what did I say?"

"Enough," he said, his breath a warm gust against her hair.

Anticipation swirled from her nape down to her toes. The breeze whispered again, bringing with it the smells of grasses, loam, and river water, mingled with Dominic's scent.

Closing her eyes, she savored the forbidden essence of him. His masculine scent personified joy, pleasure, passion . . . all she'd left behind in the meadow the day they parted.

*Step away*, her reason commanded. *You must. Your*

*emotions are too fragile. Your love for Dominic can never be as it was. Do not torment yourself.* However, before her traitorous body could obey, her head tipped back to nestle between his shoulder and neck.

He drew in a startled breath. Clearly, he hadn't expected the contact. As he inhaled, his upper chest brushed her back. A low groan burned her throat, for even that touch made her crave him. Tears stung her closed eyes.

*Step away, Gisela.*

Before she could break from his embrace, his arms shifted. Instead of easing her away, he tightened his hold. For this one moment, it seemed, he agreed to indulge her, while she gathered her tattered emotions.

A gallant gesture. One true to his noble nature.

*Oh, Dominic.* Tears slipped past her lashes.

"Gisela," he whispered.

Her eyes fluttered open. "Mmm?" How husky her voice sounded.

Turning her face, she glanced up at him . . . to find his mouth a breath away. The slightest nudge forward, and their lips would touch.

The memory of their kiss in her shop swept through her. Her skin tingled, recalling the hungry softness of his mouth, and his groans when the kiss deepened.

How would he taste in this secluded meadow?

As though attuned to her thoughts, his gaze dropped to her lips. Desire sparked beneath the dark sweep of his lashes.

His mouth tightened. Turning his face away, he looked out across the twilight field. "'Twill be dark soon. We must start back to your home."

Dominic strode ahead of Gisela toward the disintegrating Roman wall. His thoughts reeled with the impact of what she'd told him of her husband's viciousness—and what he'd deduced from her fear-induced near-collapse.

As he walked, he seized a grass head and ripped it from its stem. His warrior instincts roared for retribution. To think of Gisela disfigured, controlled, crushed by a man like Ryle . . . It explained much about the changes in her from years ago and why in desperation she might make wrong choices—among them, lying to him.

Still, he couldn't deny his anger, almost as fierce as his hunger for her. She'd deliberately withheld information about Geoffrey's stolen cloth and Ewan's paternity. What other secrets did she keep? In what other ways would she betray his trust?

*Cease, Dominic*, his heart cried. *Left with few choices, she did what she thought best to protect herself and her child.*

That much was true. What Ryle had inflicted upon her was unforgivable. Dominic scowled. To think of Ewan, his son, living in the same home as Ryle . . .

Ewan. *His son.*

Bewilderment plowed through Dominic, causing him to almost stumble over his own boots. In all his dalliances with women, he'd never imagined himself a father. Was the boy *really* his son? Had Gisela invented her story about Ryle's impotence and Dominic being Ewan's father in hopes of bettering her circumstances with him?

Nay. Ewan was his son. In his gut, Dominic knew.

Fury still simmered that she hadn't divulged the news earlier. But, weaving into his anger, was a sense of wonder and—

"Dominic?"

He half-glanced at Gisela, trying very hard not to look at her mouth. Her lips were as much temptation as if she stood before him naked.

"What are you going to do?"

She spoke bravely, but he caught the anxiety threading through and around each word.

She fell back. A few paces ahead, he turned to look at her. A sudden memory of her on the day they said good-bye superimposed itself over her standing in the shadowed meadow.

Aware their voices might carry to the road, he crossed the trampled grasses back to her. In hushed tones, he said, "We will return to your shop, where you will show me the silk."

Her stare did not waver. "What will you do then? Tell Lord de Lanceau?"

Dominic nodded. "I must."

"Will I be"—she hesitated—"arrested? Will I be imprisoned in his dungeon?"

"I do not know." An honest, if vague, answer. As much as Dominic could tell her right now.

He knew Geoffrey well enough to plead for Gisela, to insist her actions were those of a mother desperate to protect her son.

Dominic swallowed. *His* son.

Geoffrey, also, was the father of a young boy, his lady wife pregnant with their second child. Geoffrey would understand a parent's protective instincts. Apart from that, Dominic couldn't say what his lord would believe, or what might transpire.

"Will he take Ewan from me?" Gisela asked, her voice as thin and brittle as dried flowers. "I beg you, do not take him from me."

Dominic fought the need to embrace her again. How he wanted to kiss her, to yield to the volatile emotions twisting up inside him. Yet, nightfall gathered across the sky. 'Twas not safe for them to delay.

"We will discuss this later," he said. "We must get back before dark. Come."

He started for the wall again, and her reluctant footfalls sounded behind him.

As they neared her shop, and she drew her key out of her cloak pocket, Dominic glanced about. Still no sign of Crenardieu's watchers. The Frenchman must need them elsewhere this eve.

She unlocked the door, and they stepped inside. The panel to the main part of the house was closed, and light fingered through the cracked wood. Ewan and Ada's voices, raised in lively conversation, came from beyond.

"Arr!" Ada roared. "I will eat you bit by bit, Sir Smug. I will save your toes for last."

"You will not eat my toes," Ewan yelled back, "or any other part of me! Prepare to fight, dragon!"

A mighty battle cry echoed, at the same moment Gisela closed the door. She secured it before removing her cloak and crossing to her home's entrance.

"Gisela," Dominic said. She was not going to escape showing him the silk.

"I will let Ada and Ewan know we have returned," she answered, "and fetch some light."

She opened the door. For a moment, she stood surrounded by a golden aura.

"Mama!"

Ewan's delighted tone touched deep within Dominic. One day, would the little boy greet him with such joy? Or, would Ewan hate him, for revealing his mother's deceptions to de Lanceau?

"I missed you, Mama."

"I missed you, too, Button," she murmured, before the door shut, leaving Dominic in near-darkness. Voices carried, softer this time, before the panel again opened and Gisela stepped through holding a burning taper.

She nudged the door closed with her foot, headed to her worktable, and lit the candles. Dominic waited, aware of the stiffness of her movements. If she foolishly refused to show him the hiding place, he would go over the floor plank by plank, on his hands and knees, until he found it.

Wiping her hands on her gown, she walked near to where he stood. She knelt and pressed her palms to the worn boards.

He stared down at the crown of her head, shining in the candlelight. At the elegant sway of her body, outlined by her shabby gown. He remembered kissing the soft dimples and hollows of her back, as perfect as a Roman sculpture's. How he longed to kneel beside her, catch her chin, and tilt her face up for a kiss. To tell her whatever she'd done, he could forgive her—because he loved her.

But, she had lied to him. More than once.

With a grating rasp, the panel beneath her hands shifted. Blackness gaped beneath.

He dropped to a crouch, bringing his face to the same level as hers. Her lashes flicked up. Her gaze held his for an instant before she again looked at the plank, gave a slight tug, and drew it free.

He reached for the neighboring board. The edges were perfectly smooth. The planks joined without the slightest space in between. Whoever had constructed the hidden storage area—likely a smuggler and one of the shop's previous owners—was a clever craftsman who ensured the cavity remained invisible to all but those who knew its location.

A grudging smile tugged at Dominic's mouth. No wonder he had not found it. While he knew precisely how to investigate Crenardieu's deceptions, the nuances of plank floors were a complete mystery.

Gisela withdrew two more boards. Then, sitting back on her heels, she pointed into the opening.

Blue silk shimmered. A small fortune in cloth.

Shaking his head, Dominic said, "Do you have any more hidden in your shop?"

"Nay."

"Are you absolutely certain?"

Her jaw tightened. She nodded once.

"This silk is only a small part of Geoffrey's shipment. There are many more bolts, somewhere." Giving her a pointed look, he said, "Do you know where Crenardieu hid them?"

"I do not." She looked down at her hands, clasped in her lap. A shrill giggle erupted from her home—Ewan's laughter—and she exhaled a heavy sigh.

Dominic reached into the hiding place and examined the contents. Neatly folded atop two bolts of silk were a gown and a partly finished silk cloak. Exquisite garments.

"What was your agreement with Crenardieu?" he asked, inspecting the bolts.

"He will visit tomorrow morn to collect the garments

and remaining cloth."

"At that time, he will also pay you," Dominic said.

"Aye."

Dominic smiled.

Gisela's eyebrows arched. Misgiving glinted in her eyes. "I know that look."

"I vow you do."

With a little huff, she pushed up to standing. "What do you have planned? I must know."

*Must.* Ah, what a subjective term. He had made it quite clear to her, days ago, that he *must* discover the location of the stolen silks.

He stood and brushed off his hands on his tunic. "When I return later this eve, we will discuss this further. Right now, there are matters to which I must attend." Of primary importance, he must write a missive to Geoffrey detailing his findings. The more men-at-arms Geoffrey could send to Clovebury by dawn tomorrow, the better.

"Dominic, we will discuss your plans now."

A stunned laugh shot from him. She was telling *him* what to do? "Fie! You are overbold, Gisela, considering your circumstances."

She didn't avert her mutinous gaze or look the slightest bit embarrassed. Indeed, she looked even more resolute. "I respect your duty to de Lanceau, but you cannot be rash in this instance. 'Tis not only your life you jeopardize, Dominic. Think of Ewan."

Dominic's mouth tautened. Lowering his voice to a

gravelly whisper, he said, "I do, Gisela. He has been in my thoughts every moment, since you told me he is my son."

Distress flickered across her features. He'd not meant to speak so harshly, but the words had slipped out, laden with frustration and resentment.

"I know you are angry with me," she said quietly.

He raised his hands, palms up. Now was not the time for an emotionally wrenching discussion. He had a great deal to do.

"I cannot fault your rage," she went on, her gaze pleading, "but Ewan must not suffer for decisions I made. He must not come to harm. I will protect him, with my own life if need be, if you tell me what you intend to do."

Admiration softened the edge off Dominic's annoyance. Her love for Ewan shone brightly in her eyes. Whatever transpired, Dominic had no wish to endanger their son's life.

Or hers. Regardless of her crimes, he wouldn't fail to protect her, like the chivalrous knights Ewan admired.

"I am sorry, Gisela, but I cannot tell you yet."

"Why not?"

"You might betray me."

She jerked back as though he had bellowed. Her face paled. "To Crenardieu? Never!" Standing tall, she clenched her hands by her sides. She looked as determined as Ewan when he attacked with his wooden sword.

Mayhap he was a witless fool, but he believed her. She wouldn't deliberately betray him. However, betrayal occurred in the most subtle of ways. A wrong word, an unintentional glance, a gesture—

"You do not trust me," she said before Dominic could reply. "I cannot blame you. Yet, please believe me when I say Crenardieu is a very dangerous man."

"I know."

"He and his hired thugs control Clovebury. They will kill you, if they sense you are conspiring against them."

"Then they must not find out." Crouching again, Dominic reached for the boards to cover the hiding place. "I will return shortly." Raising a brow, he looked up at her. "I trust you will let me back inside?"

Gisela scowled. "If I do not, you will merely find another way in."

He chuckled at her surly tone. "Very true." The planks back in place, he rose. "Do not admit anyone while I am gone. I will return as soon as I can."

Without another word, she let him out. Twilight had turned the street into a land of shadows, on the cusp of darkness.

He began to walk away.

"Dominic," Gisela called after him. "Be careful."

"Mama, where is Dominic?"

As her hand dropped from the door handle, Gisela glanced to where Ewan sat cross-legged on the floor in front of the pallets. Ada sat opposite him. Between them they held the cloth dragon and Sir Smug, poised for more rambunctious play.

"I heard Dominic a moment ago. Is he still in the shop?"

Expectation brightened Ewan's eyes. He obviously wished to see Dominic again—to have his "warrior to warrior" talk. A bittersweet pang dimmed the unease pressing upon Gisela's soul. When they told him Dominic was his father, he would take the news well—one good element from the unraveling string of disasters.

"Dominic had to leave," she said, managing to smile. "He had some business to attend."

Ada's brows drew together. "Now? 'Tis nightfall."

Ewan rolled his eyes. "Dominic *is* a grown warrior."

"And a rogue," Ada said under her breath, while straightening the kink in the dragon's tail.

The little boy frowned at Ada. His expression turned thoughtful. "Mama, you told me 'tis not safe to be out in the town alone, especially after dark."

She had, indeed, told him such, for his own safety. She didn't want him, in a moment of rebellious curiosity, to sneak out at night to explore while she lay sleeping. "Aye, Button."

"Does that mean Dominic might be in danger?"

*Oh, my.* She bit down on her tongue to suppress a groan. "As you said, he is a grown warrior. He has the fighting skills to defend himself if he is attacked by dragons." Or two-legged thugs loyal to Crenardieu.

Ewan nodded, as though satisfied with her answer. With careful fingers, he straightened Sir Smug's cloth armor.

Ada's questioning frown remained.

Breaking the older woman's gaze, Gisela moved to the table, picked up a chunk of bread, and raised it to her lips. The yeasty scent turned her nervous stomach. With a sigh, she set the morsel down beside the bowl of hazelnuts and poured herself a mug of mead.

Gisela sipped the warm liquid, forcing it down when it threatened to choke her. Still, the sense of dread—the gut-squeezing uncertainty that rushed through her when Dominic strode away—lingered. What was he arranging that he didn't want to confide in her? Were her moments of freedom—her moments with Ewan—drawing to an end?

The coolness of the earthenware mug seeped into her fingers, matching the cold knot in the pit of her stomach. If only Dominic hadn't discovered the truth about the silk until after she completed her deal with Crenardieu. If only she had the Frenchman's coin, enabling her and Ewan to flee north tonight.

What selfish, deceitful thoughts. She would surely writhe in purgatory for such musings—after she had rotted to nothingness in de Lanceau's dungeon.

Oh, God, she couldn't stand by, counting the moments until Dominic returned, while her life became tightly bound to circumstances she couldn't control. Waiting was its own kind of hell.

"—and Sir Smug should clean his weapons after this round of fighting," Ada was saying. Clothing rustled, followed by loud grunts—the sound of the woman pushing to her feet. "Whew! Me arse is numb from sittin' on the floor."

Ewan giggled.

"We will call an 'alt to our battle for a while. Aye?"

Gislea turned in time to see her son's face crumple into a disappointed scowl. "Aw. Sir Smug wants to fight some more."

"Of course 'e does. 'E is a knight." Ada rolled her eyes at Gisela. "'E will battle e'en more fiercely, though, after a brief rest in 'is camp." She peered down at the little boy. "Ye did set up a camp for 'im, did ye not?"

Ewan glanced about. "Um—"

"Right, then. I think ye 'ad better make one. Let me know when ye 'ave finished."

The little boy twisted where he sat, clearly searching for a good location. Concentration sharpened his gaze, an expression similar to Dominic's before he left earlier.

Rubbing her bottom, Ada crossed the space between her and Gisela. "'E 'ad some bread and cheese," she said, gesturing in Ewan's direction.

"Thank you."

Ada nodded, but the worry lines didn't soften around her mouth. "If ye do not mind me askin'," she said quietly, "what is botherin' ye?"

The woman's motherly gaze urged Gisela to release her turmoil on a good, satisfying cry. 'Twould not be the first time Gisela had wept on the woman's shoulder; months ago, in Ada's home, while her slashed breast healed, she'd cried far too often. Now, tearfully confiding in Ada and possibly jeopardizing her well-being was not only unwise, but unfair.

"I am fine," Gisela said, hoping she sounded convincing. She must try to keep a focused perspective and decide what to do.

Ada clucked her tongue. Muttering under her breath, she reached into her pocket and withdrew the money Dominic had given her. Holding the silver in her creased palm, she said, "Take it."

Gisela stared at the coins, enough to feed her and Ewan for a couple of sennights. Yet, Ada earned a modest living as a midwife. "'Tis very kind," Gisela said, "but Dominic gave that coin to you."

"Ye have a young 'un ta clothe and feed. I have only meself." Ada's tone softened to a whisper. "Ye may not wish ta tell me, but I know ye are in trouble. That clever-tongued lord, 'e brought the trouble with 'im, aye?"

"Nay, he did not—"

Ada snorted a breath and set the coins down by the bowl of nuts. "I am not daft. I see the way 'e looks at ye, when 'e thinks ye do not notice."

Gisela glanced at Ewan. Chatting to Sir Smug lying

prone on the floor, her son carefully folded a linen rag into a makeshift pallet.

"If that Dominic 'ad 'is way, ye'd be off in the nearest field, havin' a good ol'—"

"Ada!" Gisela blushed.

The woman's mouth pursed. "Ye know I speak true."

Gisela looked down at the marred tabletop. After her confessions earlier today, Dominic would not look at her with desire again, only bitterness and dismay.

Ada fingered the coins. "Ye may not want ta tell me what is between ye. But, if I may speak plainly, ye deserve better 'n' what ye 'ave in Clovebury. Take the coin. Use it ta go away from 'ere . . . and 'im."

Pain, swift and sharp as an arrow, pierced Gisela. Running now would be another betrayal of Dominic and an admission of cowardice. "'Tis a bit more complicated—" she began.

"Mama," Ewan called.

*Crash.*

Gisela whirled in the direction of the noise. Ewan stood beside her pallet, his eyes huge. The lid of her special box dangled from his hand. The box's contents lay scattered across the floor.

By his feet lay the remains of her daisy-chain necklace.

Dominic walked at a brisk pace down the inky streets.

From an alley to his left came scuffling sounds, followed by the *crack* of splintering wood and raucous laughter. Another *crack*. Cheers erupted. Clovebury's thugs were already at work, like nighttime parasites feeding off the townsfolk's vulnerabilities.

His strides slowed. He listened, assessing the various sounds. The ruffians were either demolishing a wagon or breaking into one of the local businesses.

As de Lanceau's loyal knight, he should investigate. Do his best to scare the criminals off. However, he'd be one man, fighting—judging by the different voices—at least four others. Did he risk confronting the ruffians when he might be injured or killed and thus would not be able to fulfill his duty to Geoffrey—or help Gisela and Ewan?

Days ago, he would have drawn his dagger and rushed into the fray. Before he reunited with Gisela and learned Ewan was his son, choices were much clearer. Now . . . Other responsibilities spoke louder than his battle-honed instincts.

Shutting out the continuing smashes and laughter, he continued down the street. Of primary importance, right now, was writing and sending the missive to Geoffrey.

Then, he'd try to round up a few men to help him thwart the thugs.

Strains of music and the drone of lively chatter guided him to the tavern. Despite the early hour, the door stood open and light spilled onto the dirt yard. The mingled

smells of wood smoke, ale, and sweat accosted Dominic
as he stepped past the men lolling half-drunk at the closest tables and wove through the standing crowd until he
reached the rickety staircase. Snatching the tallow candle
from the nearest table, he hurried up the stairs, entered
his room, and bolted the door behind him.

The sounds of revelry from the main room crept in
under the door and through the cracked panel. Ignoring
the distraction, Dominic dropped down onto the straw
pallet and set the candle on the floor beside him. He
reached for his saddlebag and drew out his quill, ink,
and parchment. Pressing the skin to the floorboards,
he began to write. The quill scratched across the parchment, obliging him with deft black letters.

*My dearest friend and honorable*
*Lord Geoffrey de Lanceau,*

*With utmost pleasure, I write to tell you I*
*have discovered some of your stolen silks. They*
*were concealed in a most unexpected location.*
*The remainder of the stolen shipment remains*
*missing, but I am certain I have discovered the*
*ringleader of the thieves, a Frenchman by the*
*name of Crenardieu. I vow he can tell us*

*where the rest of the silks can be found.*

*With utmost urgency, I ask you dispatch*
*men-at-arms to Clovebury. Tomorrow morn he*
*will be meeting—*

A knock sounded on the door.

Dominic frowned at the wooden panel. "Who is there?"

"Who de ya think, luv?" cooed a female voice.

The barmaid.

Dominic smothered an oath. Not only had she rushed to fulfill Crenardieu's every demand last eve, she'd made her interest in Dominic blatantly clear. He'd refused. However, she must have seen him arrive and decided to pursue him again.

Nails scratched on the door. "Are ye not goin' ta open up?"

Shaking his head, he shoved to his feet. He could hardly finish his missive with her making such a cacophony. He drew open the panel, holding it firm with one hand while he leaned the other on the rough-hewn embrasure.

The woman stood in the shadowed hallway, holding a tray bearing three ale mugs. Her brown-eyed gaze glided over him with undisguised lust. "What ye doin' all alone in there?" Her gaze fixed on his right hand. Glancing over, he saw black ink stained his thumb and forefinger. Luckily the scrap of blue silk, still tied around his wrist for safekeeping, had slid down out of sight.

He winked at her. "You found me out."

Her eyes brightened with mischievous delight. "Did I?"

"I am writing my lover a bawdy letter."

She giggled. "Ooh, ye are a naughty one." Balancing the tray on her hip, she leaned closer, displaying her breasts squeezed into a grubby linen bodice. "A rich merchant like ye likely 'as lots o' lovers."

Dominic chuckled, playing along. "Well—"

"Does this 'un live far away . . . or close by?"

"Close by. If you will excuse me—"

Her foot shot into the space between the embrasure and door, preventing him from closing the panel. "Let me in, luv. I will gladly 'elp ye with yer letter."

"A gracious invitation," he said. "However, I am managing very well on my own."

She smiled, revealing all of her crooked, browned teeth, then tapped her head. "I am a clever 'un, ye know. All the men tell me so."

"Of course, you are." God's blood, but she was making a polite rejection difficult for him. "I regret, though, I cannot dally right now. Mayhap later—"

Clucking her tongue, she took one of the ale mugs from her tray. Smiling again, she offered it to him. "Some ale, then, ta 'elp ye while ye work?"

If she went away, aye. "Why not?" Remembering he

had given the silver in his coin pouch to Ada, he stepped back to grab his saddlebag. Faster than he thought possible, the bar wench slipped inside his room, her greedy gaze taking in the quill, ink, and parchment.

Warning sparked, but he shrugged it aside. He did not know any barmaid who could read. Still, after taking the ale from her, he guided her back into the hallway where he dug a silver coin out of his bag. "Thank you."

"Thank *ye*, luv." Grinning at him, making an elaborate show of her efforts, she poked the coin into her cleavage.

A bosom not half as enticing as Gisela's.

He gave the wench a last smile, turned back into his room, and locked the door. Sipping the dark ale, he finished his missive and signed it with a flourish. He rerolled the skin. Picking up the candle, he tipped it toward him, causing a fat drop of wax to fall upon the parchment's edge to form a seal.

Laughter swelled from the downstairs room, followed by the *thump* of fists upon tables. Men were placing bets. Occupied with their wagering, they wouldn't notice him making arrangements with one of the farmhands to deliver the message. He would hire the lanky, blond-haired lad who complained last eve to all who cared to listen that he never earned enough in a season to buy his betrothed a ring. A man like him would know the local roads better than anyone, especially at night—and the fastest route to Branton Keep.

Raising his ale mug, Dominic downed the rest of the brew. He stood, tucked the parchment under his tunic, and stepped out into the hall, securing the door behind him. At the top of the stairs, he paused to glance over the crowded, smoky room below. There, near the door, stood the farmhand. His handsome face pinched into a scowl, the young man shoved a hand through his hair, then swallowed a long draught of ale. Slamming his mug down on the nearest table, he stepped out into the night.

Dominic's boots pounded on the steps. He brushed past the men gathered around the bottom stairs. One he recognized. The baker.

Under his breath, Dominic prayed the man hadn't noticed him and would not cause a confrontation. Dominic headed for the open doorway.

"Oy!" called a familiar voice behind him. "Coo-eee, luv."

Glancing over his shoulder, he spied the bar wench hurrying toward him, her breasts jostling with each step. He raised his hand in a fleeting wave before heading outside.

The night air enveloped him, almost smothering in its intensity. He halted in the middle of the yard. On the soundless breeze, he caught the scent of stabled horses, along with the mustiness of earth and moldering wood.

He scanned the dirt yard for the young man. There. Walking to the back of the tavern.

"Leavin' ta visit yer lover?" The maid stood silhouetted in the doorway. Light outlined her curves, yet she was a poor imitation of how he had seen Gisela surrounded by a golden aura.

With a sultry giggle, the wench approached him. "Did ye finish yer letter?"

"I did." He smiled before starting in the direction of the young farmhand. "I am sorry, but I must—"

Close by, he heard footfalls. He swung around, reaching for his dagger. Two of Crenardieu's thugs emerged from the darkness. They grinned. Not pleasant smiles, but the teeth-baring smirks of louts who'd been waiting for him.

Warning seared through him with almost painful intensity. Where were Crenardieu's other men? Waiting for him . . . or threatening Gisela and Ewan?

He tamped down a surge of unease. "What do you want?" he said, glaring at the thugs. "'Tis dangerous to startle a man in such a manner. I might have mistaken you for thieves and accidentally stabbed you." *Play the rich fool merchant*, his instincts screamed. *Continue your persona from last eve. Keep them talking, while you decide what in hellfire to do next.*

More footfalls.

He glanced back at The Stubborn Mule's doorway. Crenardieu stepped outside. He had lurked inside, waiting also. Invisible in the crowd.

Sweat beaded on Dominic's brow. He mentally calculated the distance to the alley. If he could keep the men talking and edge backward, he could dart into the streets.

He *had* to get away. He *had* to send the missive to Geoffrey.

If these thugs found the parchment on him . . .

"Crenardieu," Dominic said with a feigned laugh. "Call off your mongrels, will you?"

The men scowled.

The Frenchman's lips formed a smug smile. Looking back at the barmaid, he said, "*Merci.*"

"Me pleasure. 'E 'as the letter on 'im," she said, toying with her bodice.

Crenardieu handed her coins. Curling her fingers around the money, she smirked at Dominic.

She had betrayed him. *God's blood!* What had she said to the Frenchman?

"What, pray tell, do you want with me, Crenardieu? Is this your way of saying you wish to continue our discussion from last eve?" Dominic flexed his fingers on his knife, preparing to bolt for the alley. "If so, I really think—"

The rasp of a boot heel, no more, behind him.

An object slammed into his skull.

Dominic staggered. The tavern spun before him, then listed at an odd angle. Lights flared behind his eyes, searing his eyelids.

"Fool," Crenardieu muttered.

All went black.

# CHAPTER FOURTEEN

Gisela dropped to her knees before Ewan, amongst the treasures strewn around her. A cry burning her throat, she picked up the fragile daisy chain. Dried petals and stems crumbled in her fingers.

*Ruined.*

"Mama," Ewan wailed. "I did not mean to break it."

She forced down the grief threatening to erupt in a scream. Blinking back tears, she closed her fingers around the mangled treasure and looked up at him. "I know, Button."

His little face crumpled on a sob. "I only wanted the wood."

Gisela sighed. He had found the delicate, twisted bit of wood on one of their jaunts to the market. After he'd played with it and lost interest, she tucked it into her box, along with a lock of hair from his very first cutting, his first shoes, and other assorted mementos.

"I wanted a log for Sir Smug's campfire," Ewan said with a sniffle.

Spying the wood beside the pallet, she picked it up. "I understand, Button, but I told you before not to go in my box without asking."

Ewan sobbed again.

With an awkward huff, Ada dropped to her knees beside Gisela. "'Tis my fault. I told him to make a camp." She started gathering the fallen items. "If I had known—"

"Do not blame yourself," Gisela said, retrieving the little shoes made of tan leather.

With a loud sniffle, her son dropped to a crouch, bringing his face to her level. He pushed the box toward her. "I am sorry, Mama," he said again and threw his arms around her. His words muffled against her neck, he said, "I will make you another daisy chain. An even better one."

The anger inside her dissolved. Tears streaming down her cheeks, she slid her arm around his waist, drew him snug against her, and buried her face in the soft tangle of his hair. "You are, indeed, a most honorable knight," she murmured.

His little body trembled on a sob. "I love you, Mama."

"I love you, too."

"Even though I opened your box?"

"Aye." She kissed him.

Another noisy sniffle drew her gaze to Ada, who dabbed her eyes with her sleeve. "Look at me! I am blubbering like a babe," she said, laughing.

"Come on," Gisela said, giving Ewan one last kiss. "Let us tidy up these things."

Together they gathered the items and returned them to the box. All but the tattered daisy-chain necklace.

"Mayhap it can be repaired," Ada said, glancing down at the shreds in Gisela's hand.

"I do not think so," Gisela said. "'Twould be easiest to make another."

"Easiest, mayhap," Ada agreed, "but 'twould never be the same."

The poignant note in the woman's voice squeezed Gisela's heart. Ada spoke true. Never could Gisela replace the love and memories woven into the necklace Dominic had made her.

After tucking her treasure box away, she went to put the daisy chain on the table, for she wasn't ready to toss the bits into the fire. As she gently set the fragments down, a loud hammering started on her shop door. She jumped and glanced over at the panel that separated her home from her premises. Dread slashed through her.

"'Tis Dominic," Ewan said, rushing to her side.

"I expect so." She dried her clammy hands on her gown. "Yet, he does not usually knock in that way."

*Before, when he visited you, he did not realize you had de Lanceau's blue silk. Now, he knows the truth. Dominic has come to tell you what to say when Crenardieu visits tomorrow—and reveal your fate.*

"I shall go with you to the door," Ewan said.

Gisela shook her head, a dull ache spreading inside her. "Button—"

"Ye should stay 'ere with me." Ada reached over to pick up the bowl of hazelnuts. She pushed the coins underneath, hiding them from view. She winked at Gisela.

Another knock sounded—more of a fist slamming on the wood.

Gisela scowled. Dominic had no right to demand her in such a way.

*Oh, but he does. You are a criminal, Gisela. Quickly! Let him in. Do not make him even more angry with you.*

She stepped into her premises, shut the panel behind her, and hurried to the outer door. Her shaking fingers touched the top bolt. But the tiniest flare of doubt made her hesitate. "Who is there?" she called.

"Open the door, Gisela."

*Crenardieu!*

Oh, God, what could he want?

Dominic would be returning at any moment. If he saw Crenardieu, and believed she meant to betray him by handing over the silks to the Frenchman—

She had to turn Crenardieu away.

"I am busy at the moment," she said. "Please return in the morn, as we arranged."

Muttered voices came from outside, followed by a

grisly *thud*—the sound of something hitting the door.

A man groaned.

The sound raised every hair on the back of her neck.

"Gisela," came a hoarse voice.

"*Dominic?*"

"Do *not* open—" he yelled, before his voice abruptly broke off.

Fear shot through her veins like hot, sharp pins. She pressed her ear to the wooden panel and strained to hear. "Dominic? Dominic! Answer me."

"He is here, Gisela," Crenardieu said. "Let us in."

"What—Is Dominic all right?"

"*Oui.*"

A muffled roar sounded beyond the door—the sound of a man trying to call out— followed by a scuffle.

Worry compelled her to snap back the bolts, unlock the door, and yank it open, despite Dominic's warning. He was in danger. The lethal tension outside oozed in through the cracks in the door, circumventing the barricade between them.

What was happening to Dominic? Had Crenardieu discovered he was working for de Lanceau? If so, Dominic was in grave peril.

She dropped her forehead to the rough wood, begging for a clear mind, trying to ignore the frantic *thump* of her pulse. If she didn't obey Crenardieu, what would he do to Dominic? She couldn't stand here in her shop, listening, while the Frenchman's thugs further wounded or killed the man she loved. The man she would *always* love, even if they could never be together.

However, if she obeyed the Frenchman and let him in, he might take the silk. He'd promised to pay her for the gown and cloak, but he could refuse to do so—and she had no way to force him to honor their agreement. His lips twisting into a disdainful smile, he would accuse her of conspiring with Dominic to entrap him.

Moreover, if she let Crenardieu inside, she had no means to barter with him for Dominic's well-being.

"Gisela," Crenardieu said, sounding impatient.

More scuffles.

"Who else is with you? What they are doing to Dominic."

A tug on her sleeve. "Mama?"

Ewan stood beside her. His wide-eyed gaze slid to the door.

"Ewan!" Ada hurried up to them. "You *must* heed me."

The little boy wrenched away from the older woman. "What is happening outside?"

Gisela seized his hands and tried very hard not to yell. "Go back in the house with Ada. Do not come out, no matter what you hear."

"But—"

"Obey me," she said fiercely. "Please."

Again, he looked at the door. "Dominic is in trouble."

"There is naught you can do," she said. "You must

be a strong warrior now, Button. Ada needs a knight's protection."

The woman nodded while turning him away from Gisela. "We will look after each other, all right?"

Harsh voices came from outside, followed by a loud *thud*. The panel jarred.

Gisela's hand flew to her mouth. Surely Crenardieu wouldn't order his men to crash down her door. He must know how much repairs would cost her.

"Crenardieu!" she shrieked.

Another *thud*. Wood cracked. The top bolt's wrought-iron fastenings pulled away from the embrasure.

"*Mama!*"

Stumbling backward, Gisela pushed Ewan and Ada toward her home.

*Thud*. A loud splintering sound. The bolt flew off and clattered on the floor.

"Crenardieu!" she yelled. "Cease!"

Another *thud*, and the main door lock broke. The lower bolt gave. The panel slammed inward, groaning on its hinges.

Crenardieu stood on the threshold. His furious gaze pinned Gisela where she stood. Behind her, the door to her house slammed.

The Frenchman stepped into her shop. With a sharp jerk of his head, two men followed, hauling Dominic along between them. Head drooping, he staggered. He looked barely able to walk.

"Oh, God," Gisela whispered, unable to suppress a sob.

Wavering from side to side, he raised his head. A nasty, purpling bruise encircled his right eye. Blood dripped from his lower lip. The two men yanked him farther forward, sneering when he grimaced.

"Gisela," he rasped, his voice eerily slurred. "Be . . . w—"

"Dominic," she sobbed, starting toward him. "What have they done to you?"

Crenardieu flicked his hand. The thugs released Dominic. Wobbling on his feet, he straightened. He attempted to push his shoulders back, but the effort seemed too great. He dropped to his knees.

Gisela gasped and rushed to his side. She knelt before him, pushing matted hair from his face. With gentle hands on either side of his jaw, she raised his chin to look into his eyes. Sticky wetness dampened her fingertips.

Blood.

Tears blurred her vision. "Dominic."

His mouth formed a weak smile.

"Why did they do this to you?" Anger gnawed the edge off her fear. "How dare you hurt him like this?" she said, glancing first at the thugs, then over her shoulder at Crenardieu.

"How dare I?" Crenardieu chuckled. "I had good reason."

"What reason?" she said, even as fear numbed her.

The Frenchman knew about Dominic's mission. He knew Dominic intended to capture him and his men.

She held Dominic's gaze, but his eyelids fluttered. She sensed him hovering on the edge of unconsciousness, and his internal battle not to surrender to the pain. His fingers curled into her sleeve, as if to stop himself from collapsing.

Under his breath, he muttered a few, urgent words. Fie! She could not understand him.

*I love you*, she told him with her gaze, sweeping her thumbs over his stubbled jaw. *Dominic, how I love you*.

A soft rustle drew her gaze back to Crenardieu, who drew an object from his clothing. He held a rolled parchment, once sealed with wax. The seal was broken.

Sneering, the Frenchman unfurled the skin. "'My dearest friend and honorable Lord Geoffrey de Lanceau,' he read in a scathing tone. "'With utmost pleasure, I write to tell you I have discovered some of your stolen silks.'" His sharpened gaze bored into her. "Imagine. He is not a fool merchant looking to buy silk for a client. He is de Lanceau's spy."

"How do you know he penned that note?" she said. "Someone could have given it to him."

"Show her."

A ruffian reached down, grabbed Dominic's hand, and held it out for her to see. Black ink stained his thumb and forefinger.

"He wrote it," Crenardieu said. "A bar wench at The

Stubborn Mule also saw him writing it."

Dominic mumbled again, louder this time. She stared down into his swollen face. "Tell me again," she pleaded. "What?"

"Be . . . ware," he wheezed. "R—"

The closest thug kicked him. Dominic groaned.

"Stop!" Gisela shrieked. "You have wounded him enough."

The two men looked at each other and chortled.

More voices drifted in from the open doorway. There were other lackeys outside. Standing guard. Or waiting for instructions.

God above, she would fight them.

Easing away from Dominic, she rose to her feet and faced Crenardieu. "Why did you injure Dominic and bring him here? Is this your idea of a cruel jest, to mistreat a man so?" Her voice shook with rage. "Whatever you want from me, I will not cooperate."

Crenardieu's face twisted into a leer. "Really?"

"Really." Despite the fear churning inside her, she glared at him. "If you want the blue silk, you will leave now. Dominic stays with me. You will not harm him again. Do you understand?"

Her body trembled with the vehemence of her words.

Crenardieu raised his eyebrows and laughed. "I do admire your spirit. Especially"—his gaze slid to her right breast—"after all you have been through."

Her breath jammed in her lungs. Foreboding rushed

from her scalp to her feet, leaving a ghastly chill in its wake. How did he know about her scar? *How?*

With a pained moan, Dominic struggled to stand. "Gisela. Rrr—"

The two men yanked him to his feet, just as rough laughter carried from outside.

*That laugh.*

It tormented her in nightmares. It woke her in the night. It wove into every glimmer of her dreams.

*Oh, God. Oh, God!*

Her breathing became a frantic wheeze. Bile flooded her mouth. An eerie whistling sound filled her ears.

"*Oui*, Gisela. I vow there is one man who will make you cooperate," Crenardieu said.

She watched, paralyzed with terror, as a tall, silver-haired man stepped into her shop.

*Ryle.*

# CHAPTER FIFTEEN

His body racked with pain, Dominic registered being bound and tossed belly-down across the back of a stationary horse. Gritting his teeth so tightly his jaw popped, the sweetish odor of horse burning his nostrils, he stared down at the ground. Or, what would be the dirt and stones of the town road if he could bloody well see like an owl in the dark.

Fighting intense dizziness, he slowly inhaled and exhaled. After dragging him out of Gisela's shop shortly after Ryle's entrance, the thugs had tied Dominic's hands behind his back. The rope bit into his wrists, mocking any intentions of escape. The bastards also tied his legs—below the knees and at his booted ankles.

Anger burned. He welcomed the rage, fed it with every ounce of his remaining strength. He would break free from his bonds. He would knock the thugs' heads together, and then pummel Crenardieu with the same enthusiasm his men had shown Dominic.

After dealing with them, he'd return to Gisela and rescue her and Ewan from Ryle. Like the knight Ewan—his *son*—envisioned him to be, he would be victorious. Never again would Gisela live in fear of her former husband.

He remembered the moment she saw Ryle. The utter horror that filled her eyes and turned her face skull white would haunt Dominic forever.

*I will fight your dragon, Gisela, despite his fangs, wings, and claws. Even if it means my death. This, I promise you.*

Regret lashed at him, more painful than the ropes binding him, for he'd not been able to spare her from facing the brutal bastard again. Ah, but he had tried. Spurred by a tremendous surge of fury, he lunged straight for Ryle. Dizziness had slowed his reactions, and Crenardieu's lackeys had quickly subdued him.

He couldn't wait to trounce them in return!

Simmering rage and excitement burgeoned inside him. His mind spun with the sensation, akin to being drunk on potent liquor. A dissonant ringing sounded in his ears and threatened to drown out the conversation of the thugs preparing to ride.

"Keep watch on him," Crenardieu muttered from nearby, followed by the creak of a leather saddle. The

Frenchman had climbed onto his horse. "Two of you ride in front of him, two in back. If he tries to escape, knock him senseless."

"Why not hit him now?" one of the thugs said. By his voice, Dominic recognized the dark-haired lout he'd confronted in the alley. The man laughed, as did his friends.

*Go on, have a good chuckle. To repay your cruelty, I shall make you eat dirt.*

"*Non*, fool. You struck him too hard last time. I want him alert enough to answer my questions."

The ringing in Dominic's ears grew louder. He sensed himself on the verge of collapse, teetering on the precipice of unconsciousness.

*Nay*. Oblivion was cowardice. He *must* stay awake. Unconscious, he was as useless as a one-legged mule.

Despite his predicament—and his injuries—he couldn't have wished for better circumstances. With luck, the men would take him to the place where they had stored the rest of the stolen cloth. Therefore, he must go along with their plans for him. Not meekly, though. That would make them suspicious. While he must offer enough resistance to prove he loathed their treatment of him, he wouldn't escape before he knew their hideout.

Close by, a horse whinnied, followed by the *clip-clop* of hooves. Dominic's horse started to walk. The sound of hooves striking dirt echoed inside his brain. He squeezed his eyes shut, trying to find equilibrium in the animal's stride, which jostled him about like a sack of beans. Had the thugs deliberately given him this ill-paced nag for additional torture, or was he only imagining its clumsiness?

God's blood, how many miles would he have to endure, his head to the ground and his arse in the air?

He might have indulged in a wry groan if the horse hadn't stumbled. Pain shot through his skull. The discomfort slowly dimmed, fusing into a memory of Gisela lifting his head and her beautiful eyes widening with shock.

*Gisela.* Sweet Daisy. Was she all right? What had happened to her and Ewan after Ryle entered her shop?

Dominic bit back an oath. He stared down into the darkness, blinking against the grime drifting up from the road. *I will come for you, Gisela. I will not abandon you, as I did years ago. This, I promise. I pledge my life upon it.*

Her fingers clenched together, Gisela stood by the table in her home. Ewan sat on the bench beside her, wrapped in Ada's comforting embrace. A few yards away, Ryle stood with his back to them, ominously silent, his gaze traveling over the interior.

Fear shrieked inside Gisela like claws scraped across slate. The shrillness superseded the chatter of the two louts Crenardieu had left behind in her shop to stand guard—even though he'd confiscated the silk.

At first, she'd refused to reveal the cloth's hiding place, but when Crenardieu's thugs started to batter down her home's door—threatening to beat whoever was inside unless she obeyed—she relented. Ryle at his side, Crenardieu watched her remove the floorboards, whereupon he ordered his men to take the silk and garments and replace the planks. Then, he forced her to let him into her home. After a smug glance at Ewan, the Frenchman strode out, ordering the two men to stay behind.

"You have what you want!" she shrieked. "Let Dominic go. Leave us be."

Crenardieu merely smiled at her. He spoke to the men who were lounging by the shop door, drinking from a shared flask, and left.

Beside Gisela, Ewan sniffled. Ada murmured, "There, there."

Gisela fought a moan. She, not the older woman, should be embracing Ewan. Yet, panic pinned Gisela's feet to the floor. Her limbs felt hewn from stone, her spirit entombed within an unresponsive body. She tried, but couldn't wrench her gaze from Ryle.

Sickly sweat trickled down between her breasts. The insides of her shoes felt as cold as snow. *Fight, Gisela!* her spirit cried. *Do not cower before Ryle. Do not let him destroy you and Ewan.*

She struggled to cast her son a reassuring glance. She couldn't. Ryle stood in almost the exact spot where Ewan had spilled the contents of her box, his fine boots planted apart, one hand on his hip. His other hand clasped a leather flask, from which he had drunk several times.

Ryle's silver-gray hair swept the shoulders of his cloak, which draped down to his ankles. Even in the murky light, she discerned the fine quality of the wool woven at the cuffs with silver thread. A costly garment. She wondered just how much coin he had spent to find her—and what he'd paid Crenardieu to reveal her whereabouts.

The cloak's inky black—the hue of the darkest, most dangerous night hours—not only enrobed Ryle, but seemed to magnify his physical presence. He looked taller than she remembered, more imposing, as if his anger and hatred made him grow into even more of a monster. She knew, while she stared in mute terror, he would not be denied whatever he desired.

And he wanted her to suffer.

His head turned. He glanced down at her and Ewan's pallets pushed against the wall, at Sir Smug lying nearly naked in the make-believe camp. Her attempt at an independent life suddenly seemed a pathetic illusion, as insubstantial as the fire made from a bit of wood, and the bed made of folded cloth. Like Sir Smug, she was vulnerable to Ryle. Her dreams of freedom were exposed, in danger of being trampled beneath his boot.

*Fight, Gisela!* her spirit screamed. *You must. Have you forgotten what he promised for Ewan and Dominic?*

Ryle closed the flask and put it inside his cloak. "So this is where you have been hiding, *wife*." He did not glance at her. Neither did he raise his voice, but the calculated quality of his words frightened her more than his screaming temper.

*Will he kill me now? Or will he kill Ewan first, to spite me, and then murder me?*

"You cast aside all I offered you—my manor, fine clothes, the prestige of a rich merchant's wife—for *this*?" Ryle waved his hand, indicating the pitiful furnishings and dirt floor. His shoulders shook in a disbelieving laugh.

*Fight, Gisela! For your son. For Dominic.*

Forcing words through her wooden lips, she said, "I did."

Ryle's chuckle faded. His shoulders stiffened. Gisela sensed anger pouring from him, but still, he didn't turn and face her.

"You should not have run away," he said.

She shuddered at the whipping lash of his words.

"I warned you," he said, too quietly. "I told you what would happen."

"Father," Ewan said, shoving off the bench beside her.

Alarm jarred her into motion. "Nay—"

Ryle whipped around, his eyes flashing. Thrusting a finger at Ewan, he roared, "Do *not* speak to me!"

Ewan recoiled. His little body lurched back into Gisela. Confusion and fear clouded his face.

Ryle's mouth twisted on a sneer. "Sit."

Ewan scrambled back onto the bench. A sob broke from him. Clucking her tongue, Ada put her arms around him again.

Warning bubbled inside Gisela, urging her to watch her words. Yet, months of worry, living in hiding, and scrounging to make ends meet converged into one, powerful spirit that refused to stay silent. "Never speak to Ewan that way again."

Ryle's head jerked. His sharp gaze fixed on her, bored into her, with enmity. "Why in hellfire not? He is my son."

*He is not. He is Dominic's son, as you well know!* However, she could not say that aloud. Ewan did not yet know.

"No child deserves to be treated in such a manner."

"A child should be taught what is right, and what is wrong," Ryle said with an ugly smile. "Just like a wife."

*Oh, God. Oh, God.*

She clenched her fists, her mind whirling for a distraction. "What do you want, Ryle? Why did you come here?" Good. Keep him talking. Keep him occupied.

His smile did not falter. "I want what is mine." His gaze traveled down over her worn gown.

"I have never been *yours*." How she meant those words, voiced from the very depths of her soul.

"You are, Gisela." Ryle leaned forward as he spoke, looming like a dragon preparing to exhale flames. His breath reeked of liquor. "You fooled the people of this town by hiding behind the name Anne, but you are the woman I married. The priest declared us man and wife.

Remember? You belong to me."

*Belong.* Like a garment, or a shoe, or some other possession.

"You will come home, Gisela." He reached for her, his broad fingers splayed to close around her arm.

She lurched backward, bumping into the end of the bench, almost keeling over. "I will never return with you. Never!"

"You will!" Ryle grabbed for her again.

"Stop!" Ewan shrieked, leaping to his feet. Tears ran down his face. "Do not shout at Mama."

Ryle shoved a dismissive hand at him, ordering him to be silent. His boots creaked as he lunged again. His fingers clamped around Gisela's wrist in a bruising grip.

She gasped. His harsh fingers felt like a manacle. Pain and panic spiraled from the place he grasped, flooding through her in a punishing wave. A vision of him raising his arm, striking her a fierce blow across the side of her face, flashed through her mind.

If he struck her unconscious—as he had before—she couldn't protect Ewan.

She struggled to free her arm, vaguely aware of her son running from the table. With an irritated grunt, Ryle tightened his hold.

"Ryle!" she gasped again. "Stop."

"Ewan," Ada said, sounding worried. "Do not—"

"Let go of Mama!" Ewan yelled.

Ryle laughed. Still holding her arm, he turned in

profile to face her little boy. Ewan stood with his sword raised, ready to attack.

Gisela drew a shaky breath. *Oh, Button.* Did he hope to save her from Ryle? She blinked away the tears stinging her eyes.

"Look at you," Ryle sneered.

The boy's fingers tightened on the sword. "Let go of her."

"Ewan!" Ada called, clearly trying to draw his attention.

The boy shook his head. "He is hurting Mama. I will not let him."

"You will stop me?" Ryle laughed. "You are not even four years old."

Scowling, Ewan said, "I am a little warrior."

"*Little warrior,*" Ryle mocked. "Did your mother call you that?"

"Leave him alone!" Gisela choked out.

"Did your mama fill your head with stupid notions of being a knight?"

"Nay, not Mama," Ewan said. "Dominic."

Ryle's face whitened. His mouth compressed into a line before his face turned scarlet. "*Dominic!*"

"He fought on crusade. He went into battle with King Richard. He knows all about being a warrior knight—"

Fear seized Gisela's heart. "Ewan—!"

Before the cry left her lips, Ryle struck out. His fist flew toward her son.

"Nay!" she screamed, struggling to get free.

A grisly *thud* echoed.

Ryle howled. "Little whoreson!" His face contorted into a pained grimace, and he shook out his arm.

Stepping back, Ewan raised his sword again. Pride glowed in his eyes.

"Ewan," Ada said, pulling at him. "Come over 'ere, now, with me—"

Ryle's hand flexed. He was going to lash out again at Ewan. Harder and faster than before.

Gisela's gaze flew to the table. *The bowl.*

Holding her breath, she waited.

The very instant he moved, she jerked back on her arm. He lost his grip, and she broke free. Snarling like a beast, Ryle glanced at her, but she threw her weight against him, shoving him off balance.

He stumbled sideways.

Gisela grabbed the earthenware bowl, scattering the coins underneath. As Ryle straightened, she smashed the bowl into his head. Chunks of pottery and hazelnuts rained onto the floor.

Ryle froze. His whole body taut, his hands splayed in surprise, he stared at her. Murderous rage glowed in his eyes.

*Oh, God. Oh, God.* She had not hit him hard enough. Now he would—

Ryle reached up to touch his head. His eyes glazed. Rolled backward. He slumped to the floor.

Ewan rushed to her and flung his arms around her

legs, his sword bumping against the back of her calf. "Mama, I was scared."

"You were *very* brave," she said, kissing the top of his tousled head.

"As were ye, Anne. Or, should I say, Gisela." Ada crossed to them and peered down at Ryle's prone body. Wrinkling her nose, she said, "If I were ye, I would 'ave run away from 'im, too. 'E well deserved that knock on the pate, and the wretched 'eadache 'e will 'ave when 'e wakes."

Aftershocks of panic rippled through Gisela. "I cannot say how long he will be unconscious."

Ada grinned. "As long as ye need. Ye have more bowls, do ye not?" Spinning on her heel, she hurried toward the kitchen area.

A knock pounded on the door. "What goes on in there?" demanded one of Crenardieu's men.

Ewan shivered. Gisela's arms tightened around him, while she scrambled for an explanation to pacify the thugs. "We—"

Ada raised her head from a cupboard. "We need 'elp!" she shouted.

Gisela stared at the older woman. "*What?*"

With a brazen wink, Ada held up several stacked bowls. She jabbed a plump finger in the direction of the door.

Gisela swallowed. Two more men to render senseless. Yet, 'twas a good plan.

"Hide under the table," she whispered to Ewan, steering him toward safety. "Aye!" she shouted to the men beyond the door. "My"—she forced out the despicable word—"husband has collapsed." With her foot, she pushed pottery shards and hazelnuts under Ryle's bent arm.

After setting one bowl on the table within Gisela's reach, Ada pressed back against the wall, her face lit with gleeful determination.

"I want to fight," Ewan grumbled.

Voices sounded outside the door. The men were clearly debating whether or not to come in.

Raising his sword, the little boy glared at the panel.

"Not this time, Button. Go under the table. Hurry!"

"I am not a coward." His gaze darkened with indignation.

*God above!* "Of course not. I"—*could not bear to see you hurt, my precious son*—"want you to conserve your strength. Your fighting skills are needed in other battles."

A delighted smile spread across Ewan's face. "Oh. You are very wise, Mama."

She smothered a wobbly grin as her son scrambled under the table. Flattening himself to the floor, his sword beside him, he peered at her.

The door slowly opened. A scowling thug—one hand clutching the flask, the other on the pommel of his sword—stepped inside.

"'E collapsed?" the man said, looking down at Ryle.

"Please," Gisela said, wringing her hands and doing her best to sound frantic. "Will you see if he is all right? I feel so . . . helpless. I do not know what to do."

The man hesitated a moment. Setting aside the flask, he dropped to one knee beside Ryle.

"What is wrong?" muttered the other guard, nudging his way in. He bent forward, his drink-reddened gaze fixed on Ryle. Stooping, he picked up a chunk of crockery. "Why, 'e looks like 'e woz—"

With a shrill whoop fit for battle, Ada shoved the door closed and dashed forward, bowl raised. Both men turned, their eyes wide with shock.

Gisela grabbed the bowl from the table. The cool, glazed earthenware felt slick against her sweaty palms.

With a grisly *clunk*, Ada's bowl connected with the bloodshot-eyed lout's head. It shattered. Bits of pottery dropped onto the floor while he howled and staggered sideways, reaching for his sword.

Spitting a curse, the kneeling man began to rise. Gisela sucked in a breath. Raising her arms high, she brought her bowl slamming down. Anticipating the blow, he twisted away at the last moment. The heavy earthenware smacked into his shoulder. Bone cracked. He roared in agony and cradled his wounded arm.

Gisela shuddered at the sound of the man's pain. Remorse poked at her conscience, but she forced it aside. Qualms had no place in this fight. She would not kill the thug, only stop him from pursuing her and Ewan. Their lives—and Dominic's—justified desperate measures.

A sharp cry drew her gaze to Ada. Before the red-eyed lout could turn his weapon on her, Ada kicked him in the groin. Shrieking, clutching his crotch, he careened into the wall and slid partway to sitting. Fisting both hands together, Ada slammed them down on his head. He crumpled to the floor, his sword landing with a *clang*.

"Ha!" She smacked her hands together. "Got ye."

Adjusting her grip on her still-intact bowl, Gisela snapped her gaze back to the man before her. Glaring at her, his shoulder positioned at an awkward angle, he struggled to draw his sword. Gisela lifted the earthenware high. The lout stepped back to avoid her strike, but his boot heel hit Ryle's arm. He stumbled, at the very moment Gisela brought the bowl arcing down. With a loud *crash*, it connected with the man's skull and shattered into pieces. He wavered, before falling across Ryle's body. He lay still.

Ada grinned. "Well done!"

Gisela wiped her palms on her skirt, relief rushing through her. "Thank goodness 'tis over."

Ewan crawled out from underneath the table, leapt up and down, and waved his sword in the air. "Mama, you are warrior, too."

*A warrior.* Aye, indeed.

"Thank you, Ewan. Now, fetch Sir Smug and your mantle. Quickly, now." Stooping, Gisela picked fallen coins off the floor and set them back on the table with the others.

"Where are we going, Mama?"

Gisela glanced back at him. He had not budged. "You and I must leave. I want to be far from here before these men awaken."

A smile brightened Ewan's face. "Are we going on a journey? Like the bold knights in the *chansons?*"

"Aye. Now, fetch your things, so we can begin." While she spoke, Gisela hurried to the pallet, lifted it up, and withdrew her box, as well as a jangling bag of silver—her entire savings, carefully hoarded. She stuffed the items into a cloth satchel, donned her cloak, and slung the satchel's strap over her shoulder. She turned to check Ewan's progress. Humming under his breath, he was shoving his arms into his outer garment. Never had he put on his mantle so fast.

As Gisela crossed to him, Ada scooped up the coins on the table. Intercepting Gisela, the older woman pushed the money into her hands. "Take this and go far from 'ere," Ada said, her gaze earnest. "'Tis enough ta pay yer way ta the next county."

Gisela looked down at the mound of coins. Ada was right. This silver, added to what she'd saved, would be enough to begin a new life. Nowhere near as much as Crenardieu had promised her, but enough.

In her hands, she held freedom.

As though attuned to her thoughts, Ada said, "If that Dominic cares for ye, 'e would not want ye ta be in danger, or yer son."

Lowering her voice to a whisper, Gisela said, "His

son, too."

"His—" The woman's eyes widened. "Oh." She glanced at Ewan, back at Gisela, and then at Ryle sprawled on the floor. "Oh!"

Gisela blinked hard, fighting to stifle her distress. "Ada, are you certain you can spare the silver?"

"Fer you and yer sweet boy, aye." Ada patted Gisela's hands. The woman's lips formed a shaky smile. "Hurry, now."

Drawing an unsteady breath, Gisela took a last glance about her shop, her home for the past months. Her gaze settled again on Ewan, standing by the door, sword in hand and Sir Smug under his arm. He stood guard over the fallen men.

"Thank you," Gisela whispered to Ada. "I will repay you."

The midwife flicked her hand. "Nay, Gisela. Now, be off with ye, afore I 'ave to wallop these louts again. And afore ye say it—or start ta think it—I will not be 'ere when that French idiot returns. 'E does not know where I live. I shall stay out of sight and all will be well."

"Mama, come *on*," Ewan called.

Gisela dropped the silver into her bag of coins, pushed the satchel's strap up on her shoulder again, and hurried to Ewan's side. With a last wave to Ada, she said, "Let us begin our journey."

# CHAPTER SIXTEEN

As though emerging from a smothering fog, Dominic gradually became conscious of noises around him: boots scraping on dirt; mutters and laughter; and the crackle of a fire.

No longer did he ride on the nag's back. He lay with his eyes closed, facedown on an earth floor that smelled of mold and rotting leaves. A draft swept over him, coming from somewhere in front of him—a doorway or an open window—chilling his brow and his hands, pressed to the . . . dirt.

He bent his fingers slightly, curling them into the soil until he felt it scrape up under his nails. Thank the holy saints he was not delirious and imagining his circumstances. He shifted his hands ever so slightly, causing his fingertips to drag on the hard-packed earth. The mild discomfort brought the faintest smile to his lips. Good. He still had sensation in his hands. His arms might feel as heavy as stone, but no bones were broken.

With discreet movements, he flexed his toes and then his leg muscles. Relieved his body seemed to be fully intact, he risked turning his head a fraction. A snarled lock of hair fell down over his face. Ignoring the brush of hair against his tender black eye, he squinted in the semidarkness. A newly stoked blaze, ringed by stones, burned several yards away. Several of the thugs sat talking.

Careless bastards. They didn't realize he was awake. They had unbound him, expecting him to be unconscious for a while. A mistake he must use to his advantage.

Wherever he was.

Self-condemnation stabbed him like a vicious knife. He'd vowed to stay awake, to glean vital information that would bring about victory for Geoffrey. He'd promised to save Gisela and Ewan. Yet, he'd succumbed to his infirmities. He had failed Geoffrey. Gisela. Ewan.

*Failed them all.*

He tried to swallow, but his parched mouth, still tasting of his bloody lip, refused to oblige. An image of his sire forced its way into the haze of Dominic's thoughts. He tried to ignore it, but the vision persisted, as ruthless as the man he called Father.

Again, as years ago, he stood on the windswept battlements of his sire's keep. Shrugging his shoulders in that familiar, terse way, his father said, "You disappoint me, Dominic. You will never be an equal to your brother." His mouth, so quick to offer praise to Dominic's older sibling, flattened with disapproval.

The anger and resentment of that day returned. "Father, he and I are very different."

"God's blood, will you *listen* to me? When will you cease living like a reckless fool and accept you have obligations? You are a lord's son. *My* son. 'Tis your duty to this family to fulfill the responsibilities of your lineage. To do otherwise is to fail us all. To fail *me*."

"With all due respect, Father, someone needs to tend to Mother. She . . . Her illness worsens each day."

"I know." Dominic's father stared across the landscape, his silver-brown hair the same color as the stone behind him. "She fills your head with stories. Tales will not win battles, Dominic, or subdue an enemy. Only a skilled warrior can be of use to his family and his king."

"I can wield a sword and shoot a bow well enough, Father."

His sire exhaled an impatient breath. "Not as well as your brother."

A *thump* sounded—a log shifting in the nearby fire. Dominic blinked, rousing from near unconsciousness. He willed his groggy mind to focus. His forehead throbbed with the effort.

He mustn't let his thoughts drift again. He must focus on escape. On fulfilling his mission for Geoffrey.

On returning to Gisela's home to take her and Ewan to safety. On triumph, not failure.

His narrowed gaze fixed upon the men by the fire, chatting with their heads close together. He silently willed them to stay that way. Once he gathered his strength, he'd leap up, rush over, and—*crack!*—slam their heads together. Two dealt with, a few more to—

Footsteps approached. The draft swirled over Dominic's body, sending a shiver dancing down his spine.

"He is awake."

*Crenardieu.*

Dominic shut his eyes, opening his uninjured one only the barest crack. The Frenchman's expensive leather boots appeared in Dominic's line of vision. Crenardieu halted less than a hand's span from Dominic's face, so close he saw the fine dust coating the Frenchman's boots.

The thugs by the fire lurched to their feet.

"Idiots," Crenardieu snapped. "I told you to inform me when he awoke."

"We did not realize."

"He made no movement," another man said. "Not a sound."

"*Non,* he is more clever than that," Crenardieu muttered. Before Dominic could recoil, the Frenchman drew back his foot and kicked Dominic's arm. He bit down on his tongue not to cry out.

"Sit up," Crenardieu commanded.

*Burn in hellfire,* Dominic silently snarled. Closing his

eye, he lay completely still, pretending to be oblivious.

An ominous *creak*, followed by the whisper of fabric, warned him Crenardieu had moved. Was he going to kick again? Dominic opened his eye again to see the Frenchman squatting before him, his cloak pooled about him on the dirt.

Their gazes locked.

Crenardieu smiled. "I give you one more chance, *oui?* Sit up."

Dominic forced his mouth into a return smile, while he coiled his aching body to spring. "Actually, I am quite comfortable here." He patted the cold floor. "Far better than that clumsy horse."

Crenardieu growled. His fist flew toward Dominic's head.

Shoving up with his hands, Dominic leapt back to a crouch; he gasped as the room spun before coming back into focus. The Frenchman's fist met only air. When his face twisted with fury, Dominic kicked out. His foot slammed into Crenardieu's knee. Astonishment registered in the Frenchman's eyes before he fell backward, his hands flailing.

Pain screamed through every muscle in Dominic's body, but he rose to standing. Squinting, he looked for a door, a window . . . any way out of the building which appeared to be a dilapidated hut.

"Stop him," Crenardieu spluttered.

Men rushed toward him.

Metal hissed—the sound of a drawn sword.

"God's teeth," Dominic muttered, darting past the fire. His body protested every movement. The annoying ringing in his ears resumed.

The thugs surrounded him.

The tip of a sword pressed against his neck.

Dominic froze. The room whirled, making his stomach pitch. He sucked in a breath, fighting the need to vomit. He would *not* retch in front of these men.

Crenardieu edged into view, his sword level at Dominic's neck. An exquisite blade, newly sharpened. One slash, and Dominic would not have to worry about his aching limbs ever again.

*Failed, again.*

"The rope," Crenardieu said, not taking his gaze from Dominic.

The dark-haired thug brought over a length of frayed cord, wrapping one end around his hand while he walked. The rope whispered, a sinister sound that raised the hairs at the back of Dominic's neck. His legs threatened to give out.

"I am of no use to you. I will not betray de Lanceau."

As the Frenchman stepped back a few paces, the thug moved forward, letting the rope's free end dangle toward the ground like a snake.

"Brave words," Crenardieu said. "But I will get the information I want from you one way"—he gestured to the rope—"or another."

Holding tight to Ewan's hand, Gisela hurried down the street. The surrounding buildings stood silvered by watery moonlight. With each step, her satchel bumped against her hip, eliciting a muffled *thump*. Her sewing shears—shoved in while she rushed Ewan through her shop—must have settled against the wooden box.

Fie! She did not want to draw the attention of thieves. Exhaling a nervous sigh, she urged Ewan to a faster pace and rammed the satchel with her elbow. The coins inside clinked, a reminder of the urgency of her escape . . . and the choice before her, as real as the shadows crowding in upon them.

She had enough silver to hire a wagon and driver, flee Clovebury, and never look back. To realize her dream that had sustained her. She could abandon all she loathed—and *loved*—in exchange for freedom. Her past would become a secret, held tight within her, never to be spoken of again.

"Mama." Ewan pulled on her hand. "I . . . Sir Smug is scared."

Glancing down at her son's upturned face, she squeezed his fingers. "We will be fine."

*We.* How she and Dominic had spoken of each other, that summer, when they lay together in the meadow.

The night breeze stirred her hair and forced her to blink

several times. What had happened to Dominic? Had he escaped Crenardieu's men? Was he badly injured?

Foolish, mayhap, to worry. He had survived crusade. With his cleverness and fighting skills, he would vanquish the thugs at the first opportunity, force them to reveal the location of the rest of the stolen silks, and then return for Crenardieu. Dominic was, after all, a warrior.

Part of her began to weep while she urged Ewan on. Despite the miracle of her and Dominic reuniting, and the son conceived from their love, they could never be together. She had knowingly lied to Dominic and deceived him. She deserved to be punished to the full extent of de Lanceau's authority. Moreover, Dominic would never want to be bound to a common-born woman who had betrayed his friend and lord—even if she was the mother of his son.

Long ago, she had prided herself for always doing what was right. Before Ryle had cut her breast and threatened to harm Ewan, as well as everyone else she cherished.

If only she had options other than those dictated by desperation.

Ewan yanked on her hand again. "Where are we going? To find Dominic?"

*Oh, Button.* "Nay," she said, struggling to keep her voice from wobbling. "You and I are traveling far from here." She tried to smile. "'Twill be an adventure."

How it hurt to speak each word. While Dominic

had most likely escaped, the lovesick part of her desperately wanted—*needed*—to know he was all right.

What if he hadn't managed to elude his captors? What if he were still being beaten, or . . . worse? An unbearable thought.

Ewan halted in the middle of the alley, almost pulling her off balance. "I want Dominic."

His face looked heart-wrenchingly defiant in the moonlight. Tears glistened in his eyes. "I know you do, Button."

"We must find him."

"Ewan—"

"He needs us, Mama."

*He needs us.* The words drove deep, finding the part forever devoted to her and Dominic's love. *Aye*, her soul answered. *He does.*

A sudden sense of purpose washed through her. A sense of . . . rightness. A *knowing* that before her lay only one true course.

The realization was so intense, she trembled. When the breeze blew again, bringing with it off-key singing from the tavern, she smiled. Among the men at The Stubborn Mule, she would find a driver with a wagon for hire. For a few extra coins, they would be willing to travel at night.

She'd pay whatever they asked.

"Come on," she said, coaxing Ewan back to a walk. They hurried into the next street.

Footfalls and grumbles came from the blackness ahead. Someone headed their way with determined strides.

One of the thugs she and Ada had earlier rendered unconscious? Had the man awakened, overpowered Ada, and come looking for her? Had he overheard her conversation moments ago?

Gisela looked at Ewan. Pressing a finger to her lips, she motioned to the side of the nearby building. They would crouch there, concealed by the shadows. With luck, the man would walk past them.

She darted in that direction, pulling Ewan after her, but his little fingers twisted free from hers. Spinning on her heel, she reached for him again, but he had marched on ahead into a swath of moonlight.

Ewan stood in plain view, his feet planted apart and Sir Smug flung over his right shoulder. Brandishing his sword, the little boy shouted, "Who goes there?"

"Ewan!" Gisela whispered.

"Do not worry, Mama. I will protect you."

A startled grunt came from the darkness before a tall, broad-shouldered figure emerged and halted before Ewan. The man's hair and garments glowed an eerie white.

The little boy gasped. His sword wavered, and he stumbled backward. "A ghost."

Gisela rushed to Ewan's side. Pushing her son back behind her, she stared at the man who strongly resembled the baker. Yet, why was he stomping around at night, covered in white powder?

The baker planted his hands on his hips. A fine white dust puffed into the air. "I did not expect to see ye in the night street," he said, looking first at her, then at Ewan, peering out from behind her.

"We did not expect to see you," Gisela answered. "What happened? Are you all right?"

The man's mouth pursed. Dipping his head to indicate his garments, he said, "I am not all right. Far from it, Anne." He ran his fingers through his hair, loosing another cloud of dust, and sighed.

"Why do you look like a ghost?" Ewan asked.

"Wretched thieves broke into my shop. I was at the tavern, enjoyin' a drink with me friends. Did not know what 'ad 'appened 'til I returned 'ome."

"I am sorry," Gisela said. She could well imagine the destruction wrought by the thugs.

"They smashed the front of me shop, broke me tables, ruined me breads"—the baker gestured to the powder clinging to his clothes—"and cut most of me flour sacks. 'Twill cost me nigh a month's wages, I vow, to straighten out the mess." Shaking his head, he said, "I reckon they was called away afore they finished. They did not damage all me flour, or steal me 'orse and wagon. They would 'ave done, I vow."

A knowing ache gnawed at Gisela. The thugs were likely Crenardieu's men, called away to subdue Dominic.

"'Tis all 'is fault," growled the baker. "That deceitful, clever-mouthed—"

"Crenardieu," Gisela said with a firm nod.

"Eh?" The baker's scowl darkened. "Not that French swine. The peddler who was not in truth a peddler at all. Me friends believe they saw 'im at the tavern, wearin' fine clothes."

"His name is Dominic," Gisela said. "He—"

"Ye know 'is *name*?" The baker wagged a floury finger. "Anne, stay away from him. 'E is a—"

"—knight in the service of Lord Geoffrey de Lanceau."

In mid-sentence, the baker quit talking. His mouth gaped. "What?"

"Dominic was sent here to investigate the recent cloth thefts. To spy for de Lanceau." Raising her eyebrows, she added, "A very important duty."

The baker's raised hand shook. "Oh." Curling his fingers into a loose fist, he cleared his throat. "Ye mean, I pummeled an innocent man? De Lanceau's man?"

Gisela nodded.

"Uh-oh," Ewan said.

Dismay clouded the baker's face. He groaned and dragged a hand over his mouth.

The sense of purpose glowed anew inside Gisela. Smiling, she touched his arm. "Do not worry."

"Why would I *not* worry? Me shop is destroyed. I wounded de Lanceau's spy."

"You still have a horse and wagon, aye?"

The baker blinked. "Aye."

Gisela reached into her satchel and withdrew the jingling bag of coins. She offered it to him.

His eyes grew wide. "Anne—"

"My real name is Gisela," she said.

"Gisela." He frowned. "Why, then, did ye tell me yer name was Anne? Why—?"

"Later, I will explain." She pushed the bag into his hands. "There is enough here to pay for repairs to your shop and to sustain you over the next few months."

"Why are ye givin' it ta me? What of yer tailor's shop?" Glancing at Ewan, who had finally stepped out from behind her, he said, "Ye have a growin' child ta raise."

Gisela drew in a tremulous breath. "Days ago, you told me if I ever needed help, to ask you."

"True."

"I am asking now. I need you to take us to Branton Keep."

"De Lanceau's castle?" The baker's eyes widened even further. "Tonight?"

Gisela nodded. "I must speak with de Lanceau as soon as possible. Dominic's life may be in terrible danger."

The baker shifted the coin bag in his palm. "But I hit de Lanceau's spy."

"Please." She pressed her hands over his. Unable to stop her voice from breaking, she said, "'Tis my life's savings. Every last bit of silver I own. I beg you, please help me. Together, we will do what is right. We will save Dominic's life."

# CHAPTER SEVENTEEN

"Kick him again."

Crenardieu's voice cut into Dominic's slowly returning consciousness. He fought a groan, refusing to yield to the pain throbbing in every muscle in his body. He would *not* think about the impending kick. Neither would he recall how, after the last lash of the rope, his surroundings had faded to black.

Fear and physical pain would never break his spirit. *Never!*

Drawing in a breath, Dominic ignored the mutterings of the thugs around him and concentrated instead on the coolness of the dirt floor on which he'd collapsed, the mustiness of damp earth, and the breeze caressing his cheek. He forced himself to recall the meadow where he and Gisela had made love, to focus on the happiness of that memory. Blue sky. Cornflowers. Daisies. Tufted grasses that flattened to the perfect bed.

How gentle the hut's draft felt against his bruised skin. Like the meadow breeze and Gisela's lovely fingers skimming over him—

A booted foot plowed into his belly again. Dominic tried to smother another groan, but the sound escaped, raw and fraught with exhaustion.

Crenardieu laughed.

His delighted guffaw sliced deeper than sharpened steel. The idyllic memory faded away, devoured by a scarlet blur. Dominic ground his teeth, tasting dirt. Torture he could endure. The Frenchman's vile pleasure in eliciting pain, he could not. How wondrous 'twould be to finally slam his fists into Crenardieu's gut.

Filling his lungs with another breath, Dominic gathered his dwindling strength. His physical endurance might be strained, but his spirit demanded he get his arse up off the floor and fight. And so he would.

Dominic cracked his puffy eyes open. Four men stood hovering nearby. From their disgruntled scowls, they were disappointed he hadn't made their work easy.

Ha! One small triumph for him.

A grin tugged at his lips. Tensing his aching muscles, he waited for a thug to kick out again. He watched the lout's boot swing toward him. Before it connected with his stomach, he caught the boot in both hands. He held tight, keeping the man's foot immobile.

With a startled yelp, the thug hopped on one foot. He fell to the ground.

Dominic chuckled and struggled to rise.

Snarling an oath, Crenardieu crouched beside Dominic, grabbed a fistful of his hair, and yanked his head back. The sudden movement, combined with the unnatural strain on his neck, sent pain shooting through Dominic's skull.

"You are a stupid man, *mon ami.*"

Dominic smothered a gasp. "I told you before, I will never betray de Lanceau."

A thin smile twisted Crenardieu's lips, a look that implied he hadn't yet run out of methods of coercion. "We shall see."

*Aye, you French whoreson, we shall.*

Crenardieu wrenched his hand from Dominic's hair and stood, snapping his fingers. Before Dominic could push up to sitting, two lackeys stepped forward and hauled him to his feet.

Nausea slammed through him, bringing fresh perspiration to his brow. His legs felt unbearably weak. Still, he thrust up his chin to meet Crenardieu's stare.

The Frenchman was still smiling. "If you refuse to talk to me," he said, wiggling his ringed fingers as though discarding ripped-out strands of Dominic's hair, "mayhap Gisela will help me."

*Gisela.* Dominic's mouth went dry. He had tried not to contemplate what might be happening to her and

Ewan, with Ryle in her home. Worry threatened to drive him mad, to uproot his strength of will and leave him emotionally vulnerable.

Gisela had lied to him about the stolen silks and Ewan, transgressions he couldn't easily forgive. However, the thought of her enduring more cruelty, from Ryle or Crenardieu . . .

Fear for her, as fierce as a call to battle, ran in his blood. Ah, God, he mustn't allow himself to become distracted. He must escape. He must protect her and his son.

Dominic forced a careless expression. "Gisela can tell you naught."

The Frenchman's smug smile did not waver. He seemed to know every thought undermining Dominic's courage.

Shame swept through him. How stupid of him to fall prey to Crenardieu's taunt. For not being strong enough to hide his weakness.

"How do you know Gisela cannot help me?"

By sheer strength of will, Dominic managed a disparaging laugh. "She is but a tailor."

"You visited her shop more than once. She is far more than an acquaintance to you, *oui*?"

*Bastard!*

Dominic refused to cower to the Frenchman's probing stare.

Crenardieu's mouth curled into a sneer. "Did you really believe others would not notice the way you look upon her? The affection you bestow upon her in every glance and word?"

Dismay sank like a rock into the pit of Dominic's stomach. He scrambled for a way to cast doubt upon Crenardieu's words. "There, you are wrong."

"Ryle will know for certain."

"What do you mean?" Rage hammered in Dominic's temple. His arms, pinned by Crenardieu's thugs, shook with the force of his fury. If that dragon of a man dared to set one hand upon her . . .

With agonizing slowness, Crenardieu inspected the largest of his rings, then glanced back at Dominic. "What did you tell de Lanceau in your other letters to him?"

Dominic clamped his jaw.

The Frenchman nodded.

Close behind him, Dominic heard the ominous *hiss* of uncoiling rope. *Not again!*

He lunged forward, hoping to break the thugs' hold. How he craved the moment he walloped Crenardieu!

The thugs' fingers dug into his arms. Yanked him back. Forced him, kicking and thrashing, down on his knees.

The rope whistled, an instant before it lashed across his back.

Dominic bit down on his lip, fighting a scream. He crumpled forward, his arms imprisoned by the two thugs. His hair brushed the dirt. His eyes watered with the agony searing through him. Beneath the bandages still wrapped around his ribs, he felt the warm trickle of blood.

Closing his eyes, he focused on a vision of Gisela, standing as he'd last seen her in her shop. So beautiful, despite the fear in her eyes. Fear, aye, but also iron resolve.

As the rope whistled again, bringing more excruciating pain, the image in his mind sharpened. Her flaxen hair streaming behind her like a banner, Gisela stood with her hands clenched around the hilt of a glinting sword. Determination blazing in her eyes, she raised her weapon.

She lunged toward a fire-breathing dragon.

"Only a few more leagues to go," the baker called over his shoulder, his voice barely audible over the wagon's jarring sqeak and rumble.

Seated in the back, Gisela nodded at him. As she jostled from side to side, her gaze shifted to the pinpoints of light ahead—the torches on the battlements of Branton Keep.

Apprehension shuddered through her, colder than the night breeze tousling her hair and numbing her hands. She glanced down at Ewan, curled up beside her. Sound asleep, he lay with his head resting on a folded blanket in her lap. Sir Smug peeped out from under his arm. In the moonlight, Ewan's face looked utterly peaceful, his mouth slightly open, his lashes dark feathers against his cheeks.

*My sweet child. How I love you. Know that I will always love you, even if we cannot be together as before.*

Tears dampened Gisela's eyes while she tucked the coarse blanket, provided by the baker, more carefully about her son's shoulders. How she cherished these quiet moments with him, the contentment of holding him close.

The wagon bounced down into a rut, then out again with a loud *squeak*. Ewan stirred and mumbled in his sleep, but did not wake.

The baker muttered under his breath before clucking to his horse. "Easy now, lovey. I know ye are tired, but we are almost there." Then, as if noticing flour on the clean garments he had donned before their journey, he swatted at his sleeve.

They passed a stand of trees, standing like silent guards beside the road, and then a stretch of field dotted with slumbering sheep. Stones rattled under the wagon's wheels as they took the road toward the castle.

Square and imposing, Branton Keep loomed ahead. Moonlight swept over the fortress, lighting sections of the thick stone walls while hiding others. A moat surrounding the castle glistened a cold, steel gray.

Shouts echoed into the night. The guards at the gatehouse had noted their approach.

The baker moaned and shook his head. "'Twill be the coldest, darkest dungeon cell fer me. I am certain of it. Once de Lanceau 'ears 'ow I 'it 'is spy—"

Gisela smothered a sigh. "At this moment, finding

Dominic is far more important."

"Aye, true. But—"

"There is no need to mention the fight in the stable."

"Aye, but—"

*God above!* "If the matter arises, I will say you mistook Dominic for one of the thugs responsible for the break-ins in Clovebury. Moreover, I will insist how very noble you were to drive the roads at night. Being a man of honor, loyal to your lord, you understood the urgency of my plea tonight and did not hesitate to help. Especially when you learned Dominic's life could be in jeopardy."

"Oh." He pushed back his shoulders, pride now in the tilt of his head. He sat straighter on the wagon's front seat. After a few silent moments, he glanced back at her, worry again creasing his brow. "Do ye think he will believe ye?"

Gisela shrugged aside a twinge of doubt. She smiled. "From all I have heard, de Lanceau is a reasonable man. He will appreciate what you have done for Dominic."

Shouts carried from the keep's battlements. Men were relaying orders. Moving figures dotted the wall walk now. Archers, most likely, aiming their bows and arrows at them.

The enormity of what she must do pressed down upon Gisela, as tangible as Ewan's sleeping weight upon her legs. Anxiety threatened to rip her confidence into tiny, irreparable shreds. Yet, what she was about to do was *right*. She must focus on her conviction, not her unease.

"Halt!" a man's voice boomed into the night.

The baker muttered worried words and slowed the wagon. It ground to a stop a short walk from the edge of the moat.

Gisela sensed the suspicious stares of the sentries in the gatehouse, as well as the men on the battlements. Her pulse thundered against her ribs, but, with gentle hands, she moved Ewan off her lap to lie in the wagon bed.

"Mama?" He rubbed his eyes with his fists.

"I love you," she whispered, kissing his brow. Blinking away tears, she stood.

"Who goes there?" the voice boomed again.

"I . . . I am but a . . . a s-simple man from C-Clovebury," the baker said.

Gisela braced her hands on the wagon's wooden side, sat for a moment on the makeshift ledge, and slid down to the ground. Mutters rippled through the darkness above. Holding her head high, she called, "I am Gisela Anne Balewyne. I must speak with Lord de Lanceau."

More muttering.

"You are a noblewoman?" the voice asked. "An acquaintance of his lordship?"

"Nay, a tailor from Clovebury."

A curse echoed, followed by disbelieving laughter. "A commoner, then?"

*As humble as a daisy growing in the hedgerow.* "Aye," she said.

"Lord de Lanceau is abed." The speaker sounded

annoyed. "Return in the morn."

Gisela drew a nervous breath. She had expected such a response. Looking up at the battlements near the gatehouse—where the voice originated—she said, "I am here on an important matter. It concerns Dominic de Terre."

Shocked mutters this time.

"What do you know of Dominic?"

*He is the father of my son. The man I will love until the day I die.* "He is in danger."

"How do you know?"

She glanced about. Shadows loomed like monsters, waiting to lunge. From behind her came the creak of the wagon. She sensed Ewan's gaze upon her and knew he peered over the wagon's side, watching all that transpired.

Squaring her shoulders, she said, "What I have to say must be relayed to Lord de Lanceau. In private."

"She is a stubborn wench," another man groused.

"What might she know about Dominic?" the first voice said, sounding concerned. "Mayhap she speaks true."

Frustration churned inside her, making her stomach gurgle. "Every moment you delay is a moment lost. Please! Dominic may . . . *die.*" Her voice cracked with the agony of that word.

Weariness and the strain of the night's events brought a rush of scalding tears. "Nay," she said under her breath, fingering away the tears. "I will not cry. I will not!"

A small, warm hand caught hold of hers. Ewan stood beside her, holding his toy sword. "I love you, Mama."

A sob stuck in her throat. "Button."

Her little boy scowled at the castle. "Those men will let you in. I will break down the drawbridge. Just watch me—"

"Thank you, Ewan. 'Tis a very gallant offer, but—"

A metallic *squeal* erupted from the keep. A moment later, the drawbridge began to lower.

Relief almost knocked Gisela to her knees.

Ewan dashed forward, pulling her along after him. "Hurry, Mama." Looking back at her, his eyes bright, he whispered, "We are going inside a keep."

"I . . . ah . . . will await ye here," the baker called after them.

Gisela beckoned to him. "Come on."

Bowing his head, the baker mumbled what sounded like a frantic prayer. With a reluctant flick of the reins, he urged the horse onward.

Gisela tripped on a half-buried rock, caught her balance, and matched Ewan's stride. The scents of old stone and water wafted from ahead, a reminder of how very near she was to facing de Lanceau.

Suppressing a shudder, she stood with Ewan in the shadow of the keep and watched the drawbridge lower to the dirt bank. Boots rapped on the wooden planks as four men-at-arms strode out to meet them.

The leader, a young man with corn-silk blond hair, gave her an assessing glance-over. He held a primed crossbow. From his expression, she didn't doubt he knew how to use the weapon.

"You may enter," he said, gesturing to the darkness beneath the gatehouse. His voice revealed him as the man who had questioned her from the battlements.

Gisela nodded and, holding tight to Ewan's hand, stepped onto the drawbridge. Moments later, she heard the *clip-clop* of hooves and rumble of wagon wheels as the baker followed.

Ewan glanced to and fro, his mouth open in awe, while they walked under the teeth of portcullis into the gatehouse's dank shadows and on into the torch-lit bailey. "Mama," he whispered. "There are many warriors here."

Indeed, there were. All watching her and Ewan. When Gisela murmured, "Aye," the blond man glanced at her. His mouth curved into a faint smile.

After handing his crossbow to another guard, he escorted them into the keep's enclosed forebuilding, up the stone stairs, and into the great hall. At the top of the steps, Gisela hesitated, the expansive, shadowed hall more imposing than she ever imagined.

Across the room, a low fire flickered in the hearth far larger than the one in her home. Men, women, and children—the castle's servants—slept on pallets on the rush-strewn floor. Where she and Ewan would sleep, if they lived at the keep. Soft snores carried, along with the restless stirring of dogs. When Gisela and Ewan started down the space between the pallets, mongrels dozing between the warm bodies pricked up their ears and watched them.

The blond man started up a flight of wooden stairs leading to an upper level. His boots made a dull *thud* on the planks.

"Mama," Ewan whispered, "where are we going?"

Glancing back at them, the man murmured, "To see Lord de Lanceau, of course."

"Why must we go upstairs? Will we visit his bed-chamber?" Ewan's hushed voice grew louder with each word. "What does a lord wear to bed? Does he have special nightclothes? Does he sleep in his undergarments?"

Gisela's face burned. "Ewan, hush."

"But, Mama—"

"Rather than speak with you in the hall, which would mean waking the servants," the man said, clearly trying hard not to grin, "he will receive you in another chamber."

Gisela murmured her thanks, grateful Ewan had heeded her request for silence. Yet, with each step, her trepidation grew. Each stair brought her closer and closer to the moment she must admit her deceptions, and, also, her responsibility for what had happened to Dominic. If she'd been honest with him about the hidden silks the first time he'd mentioned the shipment, he wouldn't be in danger now.

Smoke from the fire hovered at the upper level, making her eyes burn. As she and Ewan crossed the narrow landing and stepped into the corridor beyond, she prayed Dominic was all right. *I love you, Dominic. More than you can ever know. I will do all I can to save you.*

The blond man led them past an imposing set of doors. Farther down the passage illuminated by torches along the wall, he motioned them into a chamber. "Wait here."

Gisela stepped inside. A red woolen blanket stretched across the floor. A small, wooden wagon, carved animals, a wooden castle, and soldiers lay scattered across the blanket as though whoever arranged them had left in mid-play. Her gaze fell upon a cloth dragon, lying atop of a large oak chest, an instant before Ewan gasped, twisted his hand free, and rushed over to it.

He picked up the toy. "Mama, look!"

She crossed to her son's side. "'Tis a magnificent beast." The dragon's embroidered scales were exquisitely rendered with gold thread. De Lanceau's lady wife, Elizabeth, was said to be a very talented embroiderer.

The *click* of a closing door, then booted footfalls, carried in the passage.

*Oh, God, give me strength for what I must say and do.*

Linking her clammy hands together, she turned to face the doorway. A tall man halted just outside, raking his fingers through his brown, sleep-tousled hair. Frowning at the blond man, who stood just inside the chamber, he said, "Aldwin."

"Milord." Aldwin tipped his head toward Gisela.

As de Lanceau's steel-gray gaze shifted to her, Gisela shivered. She dropped to her knees on the blanket, pulling Ewan down beside her. "Lord de Lanceau," she said, staring at the blanket's rolled edge.

The rap of boots on the plank floor told her he approached.

"You are?" he asked.

"Gisela Anne Balewyne," she said, unable to keep from shaking. "This"—she pointed—"is my son, Ewan."

"Gisela," de Lanceau murmured with considerable surprise. Her name seemed familiar to him, as though someone had recently spoken of her. "Dominic mentioned you in his earlier missive," he added.

"H-he did?" Oh, God. What had Dominic said? Did he know, when he sent the missive, about the silk hidden beneath her floorboards? Unable to suppress a stab of anxiety, she raised her lashes to glance up at de Lanceau.

He met her gaze. His handsome face, bronzed by days spent in the sun, eased into a smile. Extending his hand, he said, "Please, rise. I have spent enough time on that floor to know 'tis not very comfortable."

Gisela blinked. "But, milord—"

Before she could say more, he caught her hand and drew her to her feet.

"Can I stay down here?" Ewan squinted up at them. His sword pushed to one side, he glanced longingly at the wooden toys.

"*May* I, milord," Gisela quickly corrected. "I do apologize, Lord de Lanceau, for his lack of propriety. We are not used to speaking with noblemen of your importance . . . I mean, well . . . we are very common folk."

Inwardly, she cringed. Could she have sounded more like a witless fool?

To her astonishment, de Lanceau's smile did not falter. "My lady wife and I also have a son, named Edouard. He is younger than your Ewan. Young boys can be most . . . stubborn." Shaking his head, his expression becoming grave, he said, "Now, I am told you bring word of Dominic."

She nodded. "I fear his life is in danger. This eve, he was beaten and dragged away—"

"Beaten!" Anger glinted in de Lanceau's eyes. "By whom?"

"Varden Crenardieu's men." She moistened her dry lips. "He is a wealthy merchant who controls our town, Clovebury. He is responsible for . . . He stole your cloth shipment."

De Lanceau's gaze sharpened. He glanced at Aldwin, then back at her.

"Dominic confided in me about his mission to find the silks," she went on. "He discovered Crenardieu's treachery and tried to send you a missive yester eve, but they found out and captured him."

"God's blood." He sounded furious and worried. "You know this man, Crenardieu?"

"Aye." Her stomach tightened. She braced herself to reveal her involvement. "He and his lackeys often visited my tailor's shop. I must confess, milord, I—"

"Mama," Ewan piped up, "tell how you bashed that thug over the head."

She gasped. "Ewan."

Holding a wooden soldier in each hand, the little boy whacked them together. "*Crash!* The bowl smashed into lots of pieces. Just like when you hit Father."

De Lanceau's eyebrows raised. He clearly expected her to explain.

Gisela bit back a groan. Not only had she spoken like a dimwit earlier, now he thought her a bowl-smashing madwoman. Pressing a hand to her brow, she said, "Milord, I assure you, I had reason for my actions. You see, I—"

"Geoffrey?" A feminine voice and the whisper of silk carried from the doorway. A young woman, her belly rounded with child, hurried into the chamber, smoothing the sleeves of her embroidered green gown. Left unbound, her black hair cascaded in glossy curls to the small of her back. "What is the news of Dominic?"

Gisela dropped to her knees again, pulling her little boy over beside her. "Milady." She sensed the woman's gaze traveling over them.

"Elizabeth," de Lanceau said, "this is Dominic's Gisela."

"I see." From the woman's voice, she had heard of Gisela before, too. "This is your son, Gisela?"

"Aye. He is named Ewan." She dared to raise her gaze. "Please, milord, do not think me impertinent, but

I am not 'Dominic's Gisela.'"

The lady was smiling. A warm, knowing smile. Curiosity swirled up inside Gisela like a hundred tossed petals. The lady did not look upon her as though she were a deceitful thief. What, exactly, did Lady Elizabeth know about Gisela?

"She was just telling me about Dominic," de Lanceau said.

"Good." Standing at his side, Lady Elizabeth smoothed a hand over her bodice. "I will listen, too."

His lordship frowned. "This matter is not of your concern." His expression softened a fraction as he pressed a tender hand to her belly. "You look weary, damsel. Why do you not return to bed? In the morn, I will—"

"Not tell me a thing," she said, with a defiant jut of her chin. "I will stay. Dominic is a dear friend of mine, as well."

De Lanceau scowled. A flush darkened his cheekbones. "Elizabeth."

She smiled most sweetly. "Geoffrey."

The two stared at each other, locked in a silent battle of wills. Uncertain quite what to say or do, Gisela rose to her feet, then glanced down at Ewan. He sat in the midst of the toys, looking wide-eyed at his lord and ladyship.

"Mama," he whispered. "I hope she does not hit him with a bowl."

De Lanceau laughed.

Lady Elizabeth exhaled on a chuckle. "What?"

Grinning, his lordship said, "Ewan told me his

mother bashed men over the head with bowls."

"I see." Admiration glowed in the lady's eyes. Slanting her husband a wry look, she said, "Was she trying to knock some sense into them?"

Gisela blushed. "Oh, nay! You misunderstand. I—"

"You had best tell us all," de Lanceau said, and his lady wife nodded. "Start from the very beginning of your tale, Gisela. Be sure to reveal all you know of Dominic's predicament."

# CHAPTER EIGHTEEN

"Mama, you must eat some bread." Ewan stuffed more of the grainy loaf into his mouth while he spoke. "'Tis delicious."

"Mmm," Gisela said, picking at the wondrously soft, fresh bread before her. She should try to break her fast . . . but her stomach still clenched with nerves.

She and her little boy sat in the great hall, cleared of the sleeping servants. The pallets on the floor were gone, replaced by trestle tables arranged in rows. Servants hurried about the hall, some adding logs to the hearth blaze, others delivering wooden boards of bread and jugs of ale to the tables. A wolfhound sat at Ewan's elbow, watching every morsel that went into his mouth.

The frantic activity began after she finished telling Lord and Lady de Lanceau her tale. Gisela relayed the events in detail, including her involvement with the stolen silks. Holding de Lanceau's gaze and confessing her deceptions was difficult. However, at the same time, a tremendous weight lifted from her conscience.

She withheld naught. Naught, that is, except Ryle's slashing of her breast. While Ewan knew she was unwell months ago, she had never shown him the wound or told him of it, and she still preferred to spare him the grim truth. Neither did she reveal Ewan was Dominic's son. Until she and Dominic were able to tell the little boy themselves, she reserved the news to share with de Lanceau in private.

As soon as she finished, de Lanceau turned to Aldwin. "Rouse the servants. Rally the men-at-arms. Tell them to break their fast and prepare to ride."

"Aye, milord." Aldwin strode away.

His gaze returning to her, de Lanceau said, "You have given me much to consider, Gisela, including your role in what has happened."

"I do not deny my guilt," she said quietly. "I will accept whatever punishment you wish, milord. Please, I ask only that you . . . that Ewan is well cared for."

If necessary, she would fall to the floor and beg him to keep her son at Branton Keep. Her little boy would fit in among the servants. Now and again, she might be allowed to see him. To still be part of his growing up, even if their lives must be separate.

As though attuned to her desolation, the lady's face

shadowed with sorrow.

De Lanceau's mouth flattened. "We will speak again, Gisela." He nodded to his lady wife and walked out of the room.

Fighting to hold back her tears, Gisela smiled down at her son, standing at her side, holding tight to the embroidered dragon.

"Mama," he whispered. "What will happen to you? What about me?"

"Well . . ." How did she tell him they might be separated? Pressing her hands over her heart, Gisela tried to quell the ache threatening to destroy the last of her composure.

"You must both be hungry," Lady Elizabeth said, "and weary after your journey. Come with me to the great hall, and I will have one of the servants bring you some fare."

Ewan's face brightened. "I am starved."

The lady smiled. "I imagine a growing boy like you is always hungry, just like my Edouard." Turning with an elegant swish of her gown, she said, "Follow me."

Gisela carefully took the dragon from Ewan, set it back on the oak chest, and then led him out of the chamber.

At an insistent tap on her hand, Gisela blinked. "Mama, you are not listening."

The memory of heading down to the hall dissipated, and Gisela was aware again of the servants rushing around the tables, the excited chatter, and the tang of a recently stoked fire. Men-at-arms tromped into the hall, many wearing chain-mail armor. Talking among themselves, they sat on benches along the tables.

"Look at Lord de Lanceau, Mama."

Gisela glanced in the direction her son pointed. His lordship stood before the raised dais, on which rested the dining table reserved for him, his family, and their noble guests. He was speaking with Lady Elizabeth, who offered him a goblet of wine. A chain-mail hauberk draped to his knees. A broadsword hung by his side, while he carried an iron helm tucked under his arm. Sipping his wine, nodding as his wife spoke, he looked every bit the ruler of an important castle.

De Lanceau handed back the wine goblet. The lady touched his arm, but he shook his head. Gisela fought a jolt of misgiving. Something in his expression . . .

He glanced her way.

When he started toward her, dread cinched her innards.

She forced herself to calm. Now was not the time to succumb to despair. Whatever punishment he meted out for her crimes, she would accept it with courage and dignity. She must be a good example for her son, in the few free moments she might have left with him.

Gisela bowed her head. "Milord."

De Lanceau halted before their table, his wife strolling close behind. When he frowned down at her, Gisela shivered.

"What is wrong with the bread?" he asked.

"Naught, milord. 'Tis very good. I . . . am not hungry."

He nodded, as though he understood perfectly the emotions roiling inside her. She swallowed again, wishing desperately that whatever he had to say, he would say it quickly and be done with it.

Tension lined his mouth. "My men and I leave for Clovebury shortly. You will stay here, until my return."

As she expected, he ordered her to remain at the keep, likely under armed guard. Mayhap even in a dungeon cell. Even as his judgment settled in her mind, the sense of rightness burned within her again. She could *not* stay here, imprisoned within Branton Keep's walls, while Dominic's life was threatened.

For the love they once shared, for all that he meant to her, she must be brave enough to voice what was in her heart.

Drawing a fortifying breath, she looked up at de Lanceau. "I respect your decision, milord, and vow to abide by it . . . upon my return to the keep."

His eyes flared. "Return—?"

"Aye, milord. You see, I must come with you."

"God's blood!"

Fear fluttered beneath her determination, like a butterfly trapped under ice. She didn't intend to sound disloyal or insolent. She had to make him understand. "I know Clovebury's streets," she said quickly. "I know Crenardieu."

De Lanceau's lips tautened.

"Geoffrey—" The lady again placed a hand again upon his arm.

He thrust up his palm, a clear refusal of his wife's protests. "I will not be distracted by fear for Gisela's safety. The situation could be extremely dangerous."

"I am aware of the dangers," Gisela said. "Yet, I cannot sit idle while Dominic may be suffering. I am to blame for what happened to him."

"Mama." Ewan snatched up his wooden sword lying on the table. "I want to come, too."

"Nay, my son," she said gently. "You must stay here, because"—*I could not bear for aught to happen to you*—"you are needed to help protect the castle."

Doubt shadowed his eyes.

"'Tis an excellent plan," Lady Elizabeth said with a smile. "You can patrol the battlements with the other guards."

Ewan's eyes grew huge. "Really?"

De Lanceau sighed. "Damsel!"

Gisela sensed her opportunity slipping away. Never must she lose her chance to save Dominic. She rose from the bench, then dropped to her knees on the rushes by de Lanceau's boots, her drab gown pooling around her.

"Please. I beg you. Let me journey with you."

"Gisela—"

"I love him."

De Lanceau stood motionless. "What did you say?"

"I love him. Very much." Her tone roughened with anguish. "I have not yet told him."

De Lanceau was silent a moment. "By law, you are wed to another. But you love Dominic?"

Another confession she must make, but she'd not let de Lanceau believe she had any loyalty to Ryle. "Aye, milord, I married because I had no other choice. However, I call no man husband now, and for good reason."

"Indeed?"

Gisela met his keen gaze, hoping he'd realize she couldn't divulge more with Ewan nearby. "I will be glad to tell you all, when we return."

His expression sober, thoughtful, he studied her.

"Let me go with you. Please, milord."

"Gisela, you remind me of my lady wife," he said softly. "She is equally as stubborn."

Lady Elizabeth chuckled, a throaty sound rich with love. Leaning forward, she kissed her husband's cheek.

Gisela pushed to her feet, hope surging inside her. "Milord, do you mean . . ."

De Lanceau's mouth ticked up at one corner. His gaze slid to Ewan, then back to her. "My men and I will await you in the bailey. Do not be long."

"'E looks pretty calm fer a man who's goin' ta die."

Despite his black eye, Dominic glared at the two

louts who rode ahead of him carrying burning reed torches to light their route. Glancing back over their shoulders, the men spoke of him as though he were as deaf as a tree. The number of times they'd beaten him over the past night, mayhap he should be.

Swaying to and fro on the back of a lumbering mount, his hands bound behind him, he squinted ahead at the horse-drawn wagon leading the way. The gritty *clop* of hooves and juddered creaks of the cart reverberated into the surrounding blackness. Eerily silent, the world seemed to wait in breathless anticipation to see what would happen to him next.

Scowling, he blew away stringy hair fallen across his face. Whatever transpired, he did not intend to die. Not this day, and not at the hands of these bastards.

His gaze fixed on Crenardieu, seated at the front of the wagon. Moments ago, the thugs had hauled Dominic from the cold, fireless wooden hut into the even chillier outdoors and propped him up beside a horse. Before they forced him up onto the mount, he heard the Frenchman speaking to one of his lackeys.

"—bring them back here," he said. "Ryle is to come, as well." Glancing over at Dominic, the Frenchman smiled. "Balewyne will enjoy the bloodletting."

A chill had crawled down Dominic's spine. Grinning, the man swung up onto his horse, took a torch handed up to him by another thug, and galloped off.

Then, Crenardieu drew aside the canvas sheet covering the wagon bed. Inside, lying in orderly lines, were bolts of shimmering cloth. De Lanceau's stolen shipment. On the top were the blue silk and garments from Gisela's shop. After smirking at Dominic, Crenardieu repositioned the canvas again and ordered his cohorts to move out.

A loud snort reached Dominic. The louts were laughing at him again.

*Let them laugh. Not for much longer, by God.*

He pointedly blocked out their chuckles and the conversation of the thugs riding close behind him. He shut out the agony in his bones that threatened to steal his consciousness and send him careening off the horse onto the ground. At the same time, he discreetly twisted his tied hands. The rope gnawed into his flesh, pressing against tender wounds. His fingertips grazed the knot. Wiggling his fingers, he began to explore the bindings.

The damp, earthy scent of water lingered on the breeze, indicating the river flowed close by. Where, though, in relation to the road they traveled? Dawn hadn't yet encroached on the shadows, although the first hint of light brushed the sky.

His fingers slid off the knot to touch soft fabric. Silk. The scrap he'd found at Gisela's and tied around his wrist. He had taken care during his captivity to keep it pushed up his forearm, out of sight. With him sitting upright, it had slipped down to his bonds.

A plan glimmered to life in his mind, just as a loud

*thump*, then a *creak*, came from ahead. The sniggering thugs instantly sobered.

"*Merde*," Crenardieu growled. The wagon rested at an odd angle in the middle of the road. The right back wheel was lodged in a rut.

Holding his torch high, Crenardieu jumped down from the wagon, his cloak billowing behind him like disfigured wings.

"Get down and help!" he bellowed to the two louts ahead of Dominic.

Anticipation whispered inside Dominic with delicious temptation. Two fewer men to guard him. A rare opportunity. If only his wretched bindings were not so tight . . .

The men dismounted. The taller one motioned to Dominic. "What about 'im?"

"If he tries to escape," Crenardieu said to the men behind Dominic. "Shoot him with the crossbow."

Bile burned the back of Dominic's mouth. He knew exactly how much damage such a weapon could cause, especially at close range. A crossbow wound had almost killed Geoffrey several years ago. A miracle, indeed, he had survived. Many said he would have died, had his and Lady Elizabeth's love not been so strong.

The memory of Gisela's pale, lovely face filled his mind. For her, he would not risk escape now. For her— the chance to see and love her again—he'd leave behind a clue.

His fingers brushed the silk again. With careful movements, he maneuvered the scrap until he located the knot. With his fingers and nails, he began to loosen it.

Muttering coarse French oaths, Crenardieu tossed the blazing torch into the dewy grasses along the road-side, where it slowly smoldered. He stormed to the back of the wagon, the two thugs by his side. They braced their weight against the cart. Crenardieu yelled at the wagon driver. The stuck wheel spun, spewing dirt, before the cart bounced forward, mobile once again.

The silk's knot eased free. Smothering a smile, Dominic curled his palm around the silk.

His face set in a scowl, Crenardieu strode back to retrieve the torch. It had burned out. Tossing it into the middle of the road, he climbed back onto the wagon. It rumbled on.

The thugs remounted their horses. "Not even a word o' thanks," the taller thug mumbled. "'E'd best not be stingy with 'is promised coin."

"We get the silver today," the other man said. "As soon as those merchants from London pay 'im."

"Shh!" came a sharp reprimand from behind them.

The taller thug swiveled. "Why?" Wrapping the reins of Dominic's horse around his wrist again, he said, "'E's a dead man. 'E will tell no one."

Dominic shrugged away a twinge in his right shoulder. His gaze settled on the torch, lying in the road, and he fought a grin. *Foolish oaf, you are the dead man. Just you wait . . .*

The thug pulled on Dominic's horse's reins, and they began to walk again. Opening his hand, he released the silk. He dared not glance back to see where it had landed.

On they journeyed, while the road and its surroundings surrendered to the dawn light. Water glistened, visible here and there through the trees alongside the road. They traveled through a forest.

Birds shrilled overhead, while light slipped through the trees, illuminating lush patches of ferns and nettles. A doe and her fawn, grazing on roadside flowers, raised their heads and then bounded away into the brush. As Dominic watched the young deer's leggy gait, he suddenly thought of Ewan and Gisela. Were they all right? If only he knew.

Just as Dominic shifted his leg, which had gone numb, Crenardieu ordered the wagon down a pitted road winding into the forest. Jarring on the rough ground, the wagon rolled down through the trees to a wide, cleared stretch along the riverbank. A crude wooden dock stretched out into the water. Rowboats rocked on the gentle current. By the opposite bank, ducks paddled and bobbed for minnows.

Crenardieu leapt down from the wagon. "Stand guard with the cloth," he ordered his cohort, who began to climb down.

The thugs ahead of Dominic halted their horses. Crenardieu's boots crunched on the dirt while he strode toward them.

Twisting his hands, Dominic felt the rope's knot give slightly. Ah. Excellent.

"The buyers will be here soon," Crenardieu said to his men. "When the merchants arrive, I want you to stand watch by the silks. Naught is to be loaded into the boats until they have handed over the coin."

"Aye, milord," the men said.

Crenardieu's gaze sharpened. A chill prickled the hairs on Dominic's nape as the Frenchman inhaled a dramatic breath of the crisp, fragrant air, then smiled at him. "A fine place to die, *oui*?"

"I cannot say," Dominic said with a careless smile, "for I do not intend to perish here."

Crenardieu snorted. "Still, you believe you will escape? That your loyalty to de Lanceau means aught?" He spat on the ground.

"Killing me will not stop de Lanceau. He has many trusted men in the riverside towns, and he will find you. When he does . . ."

"Ha! Once the silk is gone"—the Frenchman waved his hand—"who is to say I stole it? Who will tell de Lanceau?" He grinned. "Not I. Not you. And not your Gisela."

Dominic's pulse lurched at the mention of Gisela. Rage burned the back of his eyes, but he fought the urge to acknowledge Crenardieu's taunt. "What of your men?" He raised an eyebrow. "They are loyal to you? You pay them well enough to ensure their silence?"

An inkling of doubt shadowed the Frenchman's gaze. Then, he smiled. "You are a clever one, de Terre. Yet, I grow weary of our talk." Addressing the thugs, he said, "Get him down from the horse."

"When do we slay 'im?"

"When the negotiations are done. Then we may take as long as we like. No one will stop us."

Anger boiled inside Dominic. The impulse to dig his heels into the horse, to spur the animal to a gallop, screamed in his wounded muscles. But, the man with the crossbow would slaughter him before he reached the trees' protective cover. Better to wait until a more opportune time. Better yet, until he'd seen the faces of the London merchants who would dare to buy de Lanceau's stolen cloth.

The man by the wagon waved his hand. "Milord."

Crenardieu's head swiveled. "What is it?"

"Four boats, headed in this direction."

The Frenchman's expression hardened. "Did they give the signal?"

The thug squinted, then nodded.

Crenardieu laughed. With a swirl of his cape, he turned and strode down toward the dock. "Tie de Terre to one of the trees. Shove a rag in his mouth, so he cannot interfere." Glancing back, he said, "Count your breaths, Dominic, for they are your last."

# CHAPTER NINETEEN

When de Lanceau led his contingent of men-at-arms into the dark street by her shop, Gisela fought a rush of panic. Her hands clenched on her horse's reins. The steady ring of hooves, creak of leather, and chime of bridles became a discordant melody echoing inside her head. Would Ryle still be sprawled on the floor of her home? Or had he and the thugs awakened and overpowered Ada? They might be hiding inside, waiting to attack as Gisela entered.

Astride his huge gray destrier, holding aloft a burning torch, de Lanceau turned to look at her. His long cloak rippled as he moved. "Which shop?"

"The one with the door ajar, milord."

De Lanceau frowned at her premises. Even in the predawn darkness, the building appeared run-down, the wooden walls grayed and peeling. With the door ajar, it appeared . . . deserted.

Nay, never deserted. Apart from Ryle possibly being inside, there were too many memories within, clinging like cobwebs, lingering in the shadows.

Thrusting his torch high, de Lanceau drew his horse to a halt. The men-at-arms halted their mounts, as well. Where once there had been a host of sound, the street fell silent, save for the swish of horses' tails.

One hand on his sword, de Lanceau dismounted. He motioned his men-at-arms to do likewise. Swallowing down chafing fear, Gisela slid down from her horse and hurried to him.

De Lanceau's sword hissed from its scabbard. A magnificent weapon. The metal gleamed in the torchlight. Some of his men drew their swords and hurried along the front of her premises to assume a defensive position. Others stood wary and resolute beside their lord.

He glanced at her. "Stay here, Gisela."

Oh, God, nay. She couldn't have any deaths upon her conscience. "Milord, what if Ryle is inside? What if—?"

"He is no match for my men." With a brisk tilt of his head, he motioned his warriors to move to either side of the doorway.

Weapons raised, the men pushed in the door. It flew inward, meeting the wall with a *crash*.

Boots pounded on the boards. Torchlight flickered off the walls. Shouts echoed. The door into her home banged open. More harsh voices.

A moment later, de Lanceau returned to her. "Come inside."

A command she must obey. Yet, his grim tone—a warning—brought a painful tightness to her chest. Curling her sweaty hands into her skirts, she walked in. The familiar scents and coolness of her shop enveloped her. Her worktable appeared as she'd left it, thread, candles, and implements scattered across the surface.

She stepped into her home. Men-at-arms stood by her trestle table, their presence seeming to suck the air from the interior. As her gaze moved about the room, she gasped.

Her and Ewan's pallets were slashed by knife marks. Straw was scattered in clumps, obviously ripped from the beds during a screaming rampage. The bench alongside the table lay in pieces. Gouges marred the tabletop like dragon-claw scratches.

A hand at her throat, she stepped into her kitchen area. Earthenware shards covered the floor. Judging by the marks on the walls, Ryle had thrown most of the bowls to smash them into insignificant bits.

He had destroyed her home. Left his hallmark on each symbol of her independent life.

Pain stabbed through her scarred breast. Pressing her hand to her old wound, she trembled.

"Is this Ryle's doing?" de Lanceau asked from behind her. Disgust dripped from every word.

She nodded.

"The man has a violent temper."

A sob welled, but she refused to release it, or the moisture trying to well over her lashes. What Ryle had done was beyond tears. He did not deserve such respect.

How she hated him for the senseless ruination of all she'd worked to establish.

Hated, hated, *hated!*

A harsh, rasping sound broke through the fury burning in her mind. With a start, she realized she heard her own breathing.

A hand fell upon her shoulder. She turned around to see de Lanceau studying her, concern in his gaze. "Gisela?"

"He did this because I left him," she ground out. "Because I would not tolerate his drunken cruelty."

"He is gone now," he said, squeezing her arm. The torch in his hand hissed, spewing black smoke.

"For how long?"

Footfalls sounded on her shop's planked floor. "Milord," said one of the men-at-arms. "A woman outside says she must speak with you."

"What does she want? Who is she?"

"I do not know, milord, but she says her name is Ada."

"Ada," Gisela echoed, glancing at the man-at-arms. "Please, milord, may I see her?"

Motioning to the sentry, de Lanceau said, "Show her in."

The torchlight playing across the plank floor shifted,

murmurs sounded outside, and then Ada appeared, wrapped in a woolen cloak. Her worried face softened with a smile. "Gisela."

Tears welled again. Gisela hurried to Ada, meeting her at the inner doorway. Throwing her arms around the older woman, Gisela hugged her tight.

Sniffling, pulling back, she asked, "Are you harmed? What happened?"

"I will tell ye all," Ada said, gently extricating herself from Gisela's arms. She dropped into a low curtsy. "Milord."

"Ada stayed here while Ewan and I traveled to Branton Keep," Gisela explained.

"I remember. You were her accomplice in the bowl-smashing antics," de Lanceau said, mirth in his gaze.

"Aye, milord." Ada flushed and tugged at her cloak. "I kept watch o'er Ryle and the two other men. After a while, I grew 'ungry and weary. I did not want ta fall asleep on such an important duty." She shook her head. "They appeared ta be oblivious, so I left for me 'ome for a quick meal. Well"—she looked sheepish—"right as I was about to return 'ere, I 'eard voices outside."

"Whose voices?" Gisela asked.

"I recognized Ryle's." Ada shuddered. "Unmistakeable, 'is. 'E was furious, cursin' Gisela's name, rammin' his foot—or maybe his fist—into a wall close by . . . *Slam, slam, slam,* it went." She shuddered again.

Gisela slid her arm around the woman's shoulders.

She could imagine what a frightening experience that was.

"Did you hear what they said?" de Lanceau asked, his frown deepening.

"They discussed the fastest way ta meet up with Crenardieu. The thugs wanted their share o' coin, promised to them after Crenardieu sold the cloth ta the London merchants."

"God's blood!" de Lanceau growled.

"When was the meeting to take place?" Gisela asked.

"This morn at dawn. At the old dock along the river."

De Lanceau ran a hand over his jaw. "Which one?"

"There are several docks close by," Gisela said in dismay. "There are others on Clovebury's outskirts."

Ada nodded. "Ryle did not want ta simply follow the other men. 'E wanted specific directions. They told 'im ta go through Clovebury, travel to a forest, and the dock would be there."

"A rather vague account," de Lanceau said. "Still, my men and I will find them." He nodded to the older woman and turned to walk out.

A dismissal. De Lanceau intended to leave them behind.

Sliding her arm from around Ada, Gisela darted in front of him to block the doorway out into the shop. Determination blazed in her veins with the scorching heat of a summer day.

He leveled her with a cool glare. The torch in his hand crackled.

Gisela shivered at the intensity of his stare. She had no right to stand in his way. If she had any sense, she would humbly apologize and step aside, before she added to her list of offenses for which he would punish her. However, the nagging sense of rightness inside her wouldn't be quelled. Until Dominic was safe—until she embraced him, kissed him, and told him how much she loved him—'twould never be silenced.

"Stand aside, Gisela."

His tone warned her not to disobey. Yet, if she did as he bade, she forfeited her own promise to help Dominic. A betrayal she couldn't abide.

Folding her arms across her bosom, she did not move. "Will Dominic be at the dock, milord?" How she despised the way her voice wavered, making her sound consumed with worry rather than a fearless, determined woman. However, she could no more control the tremor rippling through her than she could stop her heart from beating.

De Lanceau's mouth tightened, but she saw a glimmer of sympathy in his eyes. "I expect so."

"We must hurry. We have to find him, before . . ." *he is murdered*, her mind finished for her. *Before Ryle reaches him and takes out his anger with me upon Dominic.* She couldn't say those terrible words.

Flexing his fingers on the torch handle, de Lanceau said, "You will stay here. I will assign men-at-arms to wait with you."

"Milord, I go with you."

"Nay."

Fighting a growing sense of despair, she said, "When I asked to ride with you, I meant every league of the journey to save Dominic."

De Lanceau's steely gaze did not waver. "When I agreed to your request, I was not aware of Ryle's temperament. You saw what he did to your home. 'Tis impossible to know what he"—de Lanceau paused—"might be capable of doing."

*Committing murder. The killings he vowed months ago. That is what he is capable of.*

How chivalrous of his lordship to try to protect her sensibilities. But the ache in her disfigured breast couldn't be more poignant, or more compelling. "I know exactly what he is capable of, milord. He is not a man, but a vicious monster. That is why I do not consider him my husband—and why I must come with you."

De Lanceau's eyes narrowed. She sensed his unspoken question: *What did he do to you, Gisela? What did you not tell me before, because Ewan was close by?*

Before he could speak, she said, "You have my son, milord—my most cherished possession—within your keep's walls. 'Twas a very difficult decision, to leave him behind. I would not have done so, unless I felt 'twas the only choice for him."

De Lanceau growled. "Gisela."

"I will not try to flee. I will not deceive you. I give you my word, as a woman who accepts full responsibility for her misdeeds. And, milord, as a mother. Please. Do not make my decision to leave Ewan be one made in vain."

Looking away, he cursed under his breath. "You are willing to risk your life? What if you are wounded or even killed? Your son needs his mother."

She could not resist a wobbly smile. "Ewan also needs his father."

"His . . . *father?*" Shaking his head, de Lanceau said, "You mean Ryle?"

"Nay, milord. I could not tell you earlier because Ewan was with me. He does not yet know."

De Lanceau's eyes widened. "Dominic—?"

She nodded. "—Is Ewan's father."

"God's teeth!" Glancing over at the scratched table, de Lanceau asked quietly, "Does Ryle know?"

"He does." Her voice trembled. "He promised to kill Dominic if he ever met him. 'Tis why he insisted upon directions to the dock. He plans to murder Dominic."

"If Crenardieu does not kill him first," de Lanceau muttered. "Gisela, my patience has ended. Step aside. *Now!*"

"Forgive me, milord, but I cannot. Not until you agree I can ride with you."

"Guards!" he bellowed.

Tromped footfalls sounded behind her. From de Lanceau's ominous stare, she guessed they were coming to forcibly remove her.

"Milord, I know Ryle better than you," she said in a frantic rush. "I can help you defeat him, as well as

Crenardieu. If there is aught I can say, or do, to sway him from murdering Dominic, I will. If I can give you and your men even the slightest advantage to save Dominic, I will."

De Lanceau shook his head.

Struggling against the men grabbing her arms, she cried, "Please! 'Tis my solemn oath. A vow as binding as a knight's. A pledge I champion with my soul. A vow I make not for myself, but for a little boy—"

"Gisela!"

"—who has been denied so much." Her tone hoarsened on a sob. "Most of all, his father's love."

Raising a hand, De Lanceau halted his men. His gaze softened. "Eloquent words."

"I meant every one," she whispered, "milord."

"Very well. Release her," he commanded. As the rough hands fell away, he said, "To your horse, Gisela."

His gaze fixed upon Crenardieu and the four finely dressed merchants chatting on the dock, Dominic dug his nails into the ropes binding his wrists. The bastards had tied him to a tree out of clear view of the approaching buyers. With the crossbow aimed squarely at his chest, the men had bound his hands behind the trunk. A rope around his chest pinned him against the rough bark, which caught at his hair like fingers. More ropes secured his feet. After grinding a scrap of linen in the loamy soil, laughing with each scrape of their boots, they tied it in his mouth.

He was securely fettered. Like a sheep waiting to be slaughtered.

*Never.*

He swallowed, tasting dirt from the tight gag. The boughs above him sighed, casting a lazy pattern across the ground, while his nails dug deeper into the grooves between the bonds. They had not restrained him as efficiently this time. They obviously saw no need. Gloating over the imminent bloodletting, eager for their payment, Crenardieu's men had sniggered while they tied him. They sauntered away to stand by the trees closest to the wagon, near enough to keep watch on him, but also to overhear Crenardieu's bartering.

Wincing as bark scraped against his tender skin, Dominic wiggled his wrists back and forth. The rope gave a little. A fraction more than the last time he tried.

*If you do not hurry, idiot, you will lose your chance!*

He blocked out the voice shouting inside his head. He tried not to think what might happen if he didn't manage to get free. To never see Gisela again, to never taste the sweetness of her dewy mouth, to never sink with a groan into the wetness of her body . . .

Crenardieu's laughter echoed out across the river. The dark-haired merchant beside him, wearing a sumptuous brown cloak, extended his hand.

*Hurry!*

Dominic dragged in a breath. The scents of damp earth, water, horse—of *life*—taunted him to fight harder.

After shaking hands, Crenardieu and the merchant strode across the dock and up the bank, followed by the three other men. Other merchants waited in the boats rocking gently on the water. Sunlight slanted over the walkers, illuminating their features—the indulgent faces of men who got rich on others' hard work and misfortune. Dominic committed the faces to memory, his gaze sharpening as the group approached the wagon. The merchants clearly wanted to inspect the cloth before handing over their coin.

The louts standing nearby shifted, a restless sound matched by the whisper of the wind.

*Hurry, idiot.*

Dominic dug his nails in again, and the ropes gave a little more. The canvas fluttered away from the cloth, revealing the brilliant jewel tones of the fabric within. The merchants murmured. A smile lit the dark-haired buyer's face. Reaching out, he fingered the yellow silk, and then the cornflower blue.

"Magnificent," he said. "As you promised."

Crenardieu's chest swelled like an arrogant cockerel's. "My asking price is fair, *oui*, considering the quality?"

The man pushed aside several bolts and examined others. Silence spread across the riverbank. Even the birds seemed to have stopped warbling, as if they, too, waited for the man's final word.

"Agreed." The merchant motioned to the men in the boats. "We will pay your price."

"*Bon.*" Crenardieu beamed. The thugs close to Dominic slapped their hands together and hollered. Water sloshed against the dock. One of the men stepped out of his swaying boat and strode up the bank, carrying a leather sack under his arm.

Taking the bag from his lackey, the merchant handed it to Crenardieu. "'Tis all there."

"I wish to count it. Of course, you understand."

His smile thinning slightly, the merchant nodded.

Crenardieu took a blanket down from the front of the wagon, spread it on the ground, and dumped out the sack's contents. Gold shimmered.

*Hurry, fool! Hurry! Once he has counted the coins, the men will load the silks into the boats and sail away. You will have failed!*

Sweat beaded on Dominic's brow. Tipping his head back against the trunk, he stared up at the sky, the same exquisite blue as the day he and Gisela first made love.

The day they created a new life. Together.

*Together.*

How had their lives become so desperate, danger-ous, and . . . separate?

Squeezing his eyes shut, swallowing down grit, Dominic rubbed his wrists against each other. Along with the chafe of rope, he felt a leggy insect—a spider, mayhap—scrambling over his hand.

Tree boughs shifted overhead. As the wind began to fade, he caught a familiar sound. Faint at first, but growing in volume.

*Thud-thud-thud. Thud-thud-thud. Thud-thud-thud.*

Horses approached at a gallop.

Geoffrey had found him! He'd seen the scrap of silk on the road and traced Dominic to this isolated location. Buoyed by a burst of hope, Dominic worked again at the ropes. Once free, he would charge into the battle. Crenardieu and his men wouldn't escape the retribution they deserved.

Muttering between themselves, the merchants drew weapons and slunk into the underbrush beneath the trees. Rage tightening his features, Crenardieu glared at his men. "Go see who draws near," he snapped. "If you do not recognize them, kill them."

His thugs disappeared into the forest, while the dark-haired merchant—clearly uneasy, but unwilling to leave his gold—drew his sword and faced the road. Drawing his weapon, as well, Crenardieu placed it on the blanket. Faster now, he counted the coins. *Clink. Clink.*

Voices carried from the road winding down to the riverbank. Dominic strained to hear. Muffled by the breeze, what he heard didn't sound like the shouts of armed men attacking foes.

The hoofbeats slowed to a rhythmic *clip-clop*. Moments later, three men, riding behind Crenardieu's brisk-striding thugs, came into view.

A cry, sharp with worry, welled up inside Dominic. *Gisela. Oh, God. Gisela!*

For riding toward the river were the two thugs Crenardieu had ordered to guard her shop.

And an angry-looking Ryle.

# CHAPTER TWENTY

Following behind de Lanceau and Aldwin, her gaze upon the crumbling wall and riverbank meadow where she and Dominic had talked yester eve, Gisela did not notice the man until she heard him say, "Milord."

Something in the voice made her glance his way. His head bowed in a gesture of respect, he guided his horse onto the grassy verge to let de Lanceau's contingent go past. Winded from a fast run, the animal snorted loud breaths.

When she drew alongside the man, he raised his head slightly. Their gazes locked. Her pulse gave a stunned jolt.

One of Crenardieu's lackeys.

He had visited her shop with the Frenchman many times.

The man's eyes flared. Perspiration glistening on his

face, he tightened his hold on the horse's reins, preparing to gallop off.

"Lord de Lanceau!" she shrieked.

De Lanceau looked back at her, just as the man spurred his mount to a canter. He was headed into Clovebury. He would easily be lost in the maze of streets.

She thrust her hand in the thug's direction. "Crenardieu's man!"

"Aldwin!" de Lanceau snapped, wheeling his steed around while motioning to other men-at-arms. "You are with me. Gisela, wait here with the rest."

De Lanceau, Aldwin, and five others raced toward the town. Dust blew up from the road, motes glittering in the early dawn light.

She yearned to kick her horse into motion, to rush with them into the pursuit. The thug likely knew where his cohorts took Dominic. The sooner he divulged that critical information, the sooner they rescued Dominic. However, she knew naught about chasing criminals eager to avoid capture, and might well hinder rather than help the pursuit. Far wiser to obey de Lanceau and stay put.

The pounding of hooves faded. Moving their horses closer to each other, the other men-at-arms began to talk amongst themselves. The breeze whispered through the meadow, stirring the grasses and sleepy wildflowers raising their heads toward the sun. How empty the meadow seemed, save for a few birds flitting between the branches of the huge tree.

Anxiety gnawed at her, making her belly gurgle. After checking her satchel was still securely fastened to her saddle, Gisela looked at the nearest man-at-arms, who had leaned forward to pat his horse's neck. He gave her a kindly smile.

"Will they catch that man?"

"Aye. De Lanceau is a very clever lord. He will not let him get away."

Moments passed. The sun crept higher in the sky, spreading light across the meadow and taking the chill from the early morning. Just when she thought she could bear the waiting no longer, riders appeared on the road. She recognized de Lanceau in the lead, with Aldwin and the others close behind. When they drew nearer, she saw the lackey riding between them, his mount pinned in the center of the group. His hands were bound to his saddle. Sullen, he refused to meet her gaze.

"Milord," Gisela said, words rushing from her lips. "Does he know where—?"

De Lanceau raised a hand. "I gave him the journey here to decide whether to speak of his own will." Glancing at the man, he said, "Well?"

The lackey's lips flattened.

Flicking his hand, de Lanceau said, "Tie his horse to that tree, Aldwin."

The man glanced at the tall oak de Lanceau had indicated, which shaded part of the verge. Worry shadowed his gaze.

"Aldwin is extremely skilled with a crossbow," de Lanceau went on in a mild tone, while Aldwin led the lackey's horse to the oak and secured the reins to one of the lower boughs. "A few years ago, he almost killed me with a bolt through the chest, the day I fought my lady wife's father for the great keep at Wode." He smiled. "Aldwin fired a clean shot from a good distance away. Do you recall that battle? 'Tis mentioned in many *chansons* here in Moydenshire."

Sweat began to run down the man's temple. Aldwin guided his horse away, leaving the man alone on the verge. Glancing down at his bound hands, he struggled to get free.

"Aldwin is so skilled, he can shoot the ears right off your head. One by one. Then shoot holes clean through each of your arms. Not intending to kill you, of course. Nay, he would render you helpless, toy with you for long, painful moments before that happened. He enjoys making his victims suffer. And the blood—"

Covering her mouth, Gisela fought a horrified gasp.

As though noting her distress, de Lanceau glanced at her . . . and winked.

His expression grim, Aldwin rode a short distance down the road toward the river. Then, he turned and halted his horse.

The lackey whimpered.

With an ease that bespoke his mastery of the weapon, Aldwin picked up the crossbow, fitted with a deadly, steel-tipped bolt. The man's eyes bulged.

His gaze narrowing, Aldwin aimed the weapon.

The lackey moaned.

"Tell us where to find Crenardieu and Dominic," de Lanceau said, "and spare yourself torment."

"Aaahhh—"

The trigger clicked. The bolt hissed from the crossbow. Whizzing past the man's head, it lodged in the tree beside him with a *thwack*. Bark flew off the trunk, hitting the man on the arm.

He shrieked. His face crumpled, and he looked on the close to tears.

"Hmm. Somehow, I missed." Aldwin reached for another bolt. "This time, milord, I will not fail to take his ear."

"The left one first," de Lanceau said.

"As you command, milord." The blond warrior cocked the crossbow again.

"Nay! Please. I w-will t-tell you," the man blubbered.

"Where is Dominic?" de Lanceau demanded.

"H-he . . . Ah . . ."

De Lanceau nodded.

Raising the weapon, Aldwin aimed at the left side of the man's head.

"T-the d-dock by the river. Not far."

"Crenardieu?"

"T-there, too."

"Why were you traveling into Clovebury?"

"T-to fetch R-Ryle Balewyne a-and the others." His gaze slid to Gisela, then away.

De Lanceau frowned. "The other men are to help with the cloth sale?"

Nodding, the man swallowed with great effort. "And a-also . . ."

"Aye?"

"T-to kill Dominic once the d-deal is complete."

"Oh, God," Gisela whispered. The faint drone of the insects in the nearby meadow seemed to rise in volume, to become a shrill scream echoing within her.

His lip curling back from his teeth, de Lanceau spurred his horse closer to the lackey. "You will take us there. Without delay. I warn you now, if you try to betray us, or give so much as a whisper of warning to your cohorts"—he tipped his head at Aldwin—"he will shoot your ears off. To begin. Understood?"

The man's head bobbed.

Looking at Gisela, then his men, de Lanceau said, "Keep alert."

While Aldwin kept the crossbow trained on the lackey, another of the men-at-arms untied the horse's reins and led it back onto the road. The crunched *clop* of hooves resumed. De Lanceau rode in the lead, the lackey close behind surrounded by the men-at-arms, with Aldwin at his back.

Gisela shuddered a sigh. *We are on our way, Dominic, my love. Do not lose hope. We will find you.*

They followed the road running parallel to the river. The forest thickened. The shadows grew deeper, the rich scents of leaves and decaying wood wafting from the forest floor.

Impatience in the slant of his mouth, de Lanceau glared back at the lackey. "How much farther?"

"N-not far," said the man.

Aldwin snarled. "For your sake, I hope you do not speak falsely."

They rode on, following the road's twists and turns. An object, caught in the light dappling the shaded road, seized Gisela's attention. Leaning forward, she peered at the ground. "Look!"

De Lanceau frowned in the direction she indicated. "Fresh dirt thrown up by a wagon wheel. A cart must have become stuck in the rut."

"There is a torch," one of the men-at-arms noted. "Mayhap they traveled before dawn? Crenardieu would likely have done so."

"Any traveler could have discarded that torch," de Lanceau said, urging his men on.

"Wait!" Gisela drew her horse to a halt and dismounted.

"Gisela!" de Lanceau growled.

She dashed forward, stooped, and snatched up the object that glimmered with such vibrancy against the dirt.

A scrap of blue silk. The bit Dominic had taken from Ewan's sword. Of that, she was certain.

With careful fingers, she brushed dirt from the

scrap. "Milord, Dominic dropped this."

"How do you know?"

"He found this in my home. Proof that I deceived you."

De Lanceau held her gaze. Instead of commenting on her admitted deception, he said, "Dominic dropped it on purpose."

"I expect so." Standing in the road, looking up at him, she could not help but smile.

His mouth twisted in an answering grin. "We will find him, Gisela." He raised a brow. "Once you get back on your horse."

Silently resolving to tuck the scrap into her satchel, she hurried back to her mount. "Aye, milord," she said. "We *will* find him."

# CHAPTER TWENTY-ONE

Dominic watched, anger and worry threatening to choke him, while Ryle dismounted and tethered his horse to a tree. Rage underscored each of Ryle's movements. His face, which some women might consider handsome, looked flushed and taut with barely leashed fury.

Fear trailed down Dominic's spine. What had made Ryle so angry? What had happened at Gisela's house?

Finished counting the coins, the Frenchman shoved them back into the bag and pushed to his feet. He nodded to the London merchant. "The cloth is yours."

The man gestured to his lackeys emerging out of the undergrowth. "Start loading the boats," he said, heading down to the wagon.

Ryle stormed toward Crenardieu. Dominic stood utterly still, listening, anxious not to miss a word.

"Good morn," the Frenchman said.

Gisela's former husband scowled. Reaching into his cloak, he yanked out a flask and gulped the liquor inside.

"What is the matter?" As he glanced over at his two lackeys securing their mounts, one of whom had injured his shoulder, Crenardieu frowned. "Where is the man I sent to fetch you?"

Ryle wiped his mouth with the back of his hand. "No man came to find us."

"I sent him a while ago." Suspicion in the slant of his eyes, Crenardieu said, "Where are Gisela and the boy?"

Ryle drank again. "They got away."

"*What?*" Crenardieu snapped.

Tremendous relief whooshed through Dominic. *Thank God.*

"She hit me with a bowl." Ryle touched the back of his head and winced. "Gave me a lump the size of an egg. Bloody *bitch!*" he bellowed, his curse echoing out into the forest.

"Keep your voice down!" Crenardieu spat a crude French oath. "You *promised* me. You said you would watch them."

His face an ugly red, Ryle said, "I did not expect her to knock me senseless."

Laughter, smothered by the gag, tickled Dominic's throat. *Well done, Gisela. You are a warrior just like our son.*

Ryle glanced about the riverbank. "Where is he?"

"Dominic?" Crenardieu waved an indolent hand in

his direction.

When Ryle's furious gaze fixed on him, Dominic refused to avert his gaze. Never would he admit the fear crawling down into his gut.

Ryle's hands clenched, as though squeezing around someone's neck. "I cannot wait to—"

"And you shall. First, let us be done with the cloth."

"You deal with the merchants," Ryle growled. "I will finish him."

"Nay, leave him." Stopping Ryle with a firm hand upon his arm, Crenardieu said, "I will not have you scaring off my buyers. Your grudge will wait." His lips curled in a depraved smile. "He cannot escape. He will still be there when the merchants row their boats away." Glancing down at the dock, he said, "Let us offer our help, shall we? The sooner the cloth is loaded into the boats, the sooner we can kill him."

Ryle did not move. Drinking again, he stared at Dominic, loathing blazing in his eyes.

"Do not be a fool," Crenardieu sneered and strode on ahead. With reluctant strides, Ryle followed.

Twisting his hands, Dominic struggled again with his bonds. Gisela and Ewan had escaped Ryle, but where had they gone? He had to find them. He *had* to.

He exhaled a sharp breath through his nostrils and focused on the knot. Over the rough scraping of rope, he heard a rustling sound behind him.

He froze. Listened.

The noise originated from the ground.

An animal? Nay. More likely one of Crenardieu's thugs, sneaking up behind him to indulge in the first stab.

He jerked his head sideways, trying to see.

Cold metal pressed against his wrists.

Thrusting up his hand, de Lanceau drew his horse to a halt. His men immediately reined in their mounts.

Gisela's pulse lurched into a more urgent rhythm. She, too, had heard the shout. "Milord," she said. "'Twas Ryle. He yells like that when drunk."

Crenardieu's lackey shifted on his horse.

De Lanceau tipped his head, a slight but deliberate gesture. The closest man-at-arms whacked the thug on the back of the head. With a groan, he slumped forward.

"Bind him to a tree," de Lanceau said quietly without looking back. "We will collect him upon our return. Leave the horses here, as well. We will proceed on foot."

The men-at-arms slid down from their mounts, silent but for the creak of leather and jangle of tack. Several of the guards drew the unconscious lackey down to the ground and began to tie him.

Drawing Aldwin and another man aside, de Lanceau spoke to them in hushed tones. The two nodded, then slunk into the undergrowth, no doubt sent to assess the situation.

Gisela dismounted from her horse and untied her satchel. She slung the strap over her shoulder. The bag's weight settled by her hip.

While de Lanceau relayed instructions to the rest of his men, the distant voices carried again. *Oh, Dominic.* Fear squeezed her innards, along with a desperate need to know he was all right. If Ryle decided to take out his rage upon Dominic . . .

"Gisela, you will stay here."

Disappointment flooded through her. "Milord—"

"'Tis safest for you." De Lanceau turned to a broad-shouldered guard armed with a bow and arrows. "Watch over the horses and prisoner."

Underbrush rustled close by.

The men immediately fell silent. Swords hissed from their scabbards before Aldwin loped out of the forest, his expression grim. "The silks are there, milord. So is Crenardieu. Men are loading the cloth into boats. They are almost done."

"Dominic?"

"I did not see him."

A worried frown creasing his brow, de Lanceau beckoned to his warriors. "Come."

The men stole into the woods. The muted crunch of leaves and brush faded to forest silence.

Gnawing her lip, Gisela glanced at the slumbering lackey, securely bound. The tethered horses nibbled at grass alongside the road. Standing on a rise of ground nearby, the bowman returned her gaze before staring past her into the forest.

How could she just stand here and wait for the men to return?

*I love you, Dominic. I love you!*

Twigs snapped in the woods behind the guard. He turned and scanned the undergrowth.

Gisela darted into the forest. The carpet of forest leaves whispered under her shoes. Fern fronds slipped against her skirts as she headed toward the riverbank, paying no heed to the bowman's muffled oath.

Movement ahead captured her attention. Through a gap in the trees, she saw Crenardieu, bold as a peacock, standing by the river. Ryle stood beside him. Panic lanced through her, almost causing her to fall.

Another movement, closer to her, snared her focus. She blinked, trying to discern exactly what she saw. Hands. Twisting.

Scarcely visible to her, a man stood bound to a tree. She crept closer. Measured step by measured step.

*Dominic!*

Her heart pounded so fiercely she thought the sound would echo up to the sky. Barely resisting the need to rush forward and throw her arms around him, she edged nearer.

His struggles ceased. Had he sensed her approach?

Tears dampened her eyes. A filthy gag bound his mouth. His clothes were torn and bloodstained. His swollen face proved the cruelty he had endured. *Cut him free!* her mind screamed. *Quickly. Get him to safety. Later, you can talk, kiss him, and weep over his wounds.*

Biting her bottom lip, she moved directly behind him, slipped her sewing shears from her satchel, and nudged the blades against his bindings.

A muffled hiss broke from him. He fought to look at her.

"Hold still," she whispered, squeezing his fingers in reassurance.

His body went utterly still. "Mffmmm?"

"Aye. De Lanceau is here, too, with his men-at-arms." She dared a glance at the riverbank. The men continued talking and loading the boats. None of Crenardieu's thugs had noticed her. "Do not move. I will cut you free."

She tried not to look at the bruises coloring his wrists, the flesh worn raw by ropes and . . . God knew what else.

He made a low sound of distress. A sound that, somehow, conveyed every physical pain and frustration he experienced.

With careful snips, she cut the ropes. Each metallic *clip* of the shears raised the hairs on her nape, for any moment, Crenardieu's men might hear.

Moments seemed to stretch into the space of tormented breaths before the ropes finally fell away from his wrists. Dropping to her knees, she cut the rest of his bindings. When she rose, he stood before her, yanking away the gag.

For a breathless moment, she could only stare at him. Words bubbled inside her, jamming together. What did she say to him? How did she begin to convey the emotions knotting up inside her with excruciating intensity?

In two strides, he crossed to her. His arms closed around her. A sound like a sob broke from him before his hungry lips closed over hers.

She kissed him back, frenzied, ravenous, tasting his pain and uncertainties. Each sweep of her tongue, each gasped breath, told him of her anguish at being apart. "Dominic," she whispered between kisses. "Oh, Dominic."

He shuddered against her. "Thank God you are all right."

"What they did to you—"

"Do not speak of it now." Catching her hand, he linked his fingers through hers. "We must get you away from here. Any moment, Ryle is coming to kill me."

"But—"

Moisture glistened in his eyes. "Gisela, please. I lo—"

A roar erupted behind them.

Dominic spun around, blocking her with his body. Yet, in the moment before he whirled to protect her, she saw Ryle standing by the tree. Less than three steps away.

Ryle tossed aside the flask in his hand. Men crashed through the brush, surrounding them. Her fingers still entwined with Dominic's, Gisela pressed against him, terror's bitter taste scalding her mouth.

"Bring them out here," Crenardieu said, his drawn sword glinting. Thugs seized Gisela's arms, while Ryle and two others grabbed hold of Dominic. They dragged both of them onto the expanse of ground leading down to the dock.

Gisela straightened, shivering when Crenardieu's hard gaze fixed upon her.

"How did you come here?" he demanded.

"I rode my horse."

"Alone?" He adjusted his grip on his weapon. "How did you find this place?"

Dominic wavered on his feet. Ryle jerked hard on his arm, causing him to lurch forward. Dominic gasped. His face contorted with pain.

"Stop!" Gisela shrieked. "He is wounded enough."

Ryle's lips drew back in a cruel smile. "I have not even begun to hurt him."

Fear seared through her, along with the urge to lower her gaze, to acknowledge Ryle's power over her. If she looked away, he might be merciful.

Fie! She couldn't let Ryle win. For those she loved, she would not yield.

Forcing her trembling chin higher, she stared at him. Her eyes burned. Her body shook, betraying her inner turmoil. But she did not look away. "Do not hurt Dominic."

Slowly lowering his hand from Dominic's arm, Ryle laughed. His teeth, yellowed like a dragon's, glinted in the sunlight. "You will stop me?"

"Aye."

"*You?*" He laughed. The men around them chortled.

She sensed his fluctuating mood, smelled the drink he'd consumed. She also saw his fingers curling. Before she could turn her face away, his fist slammed into her jaw.

"Gisela!" Dominic cried.

The impact snapped her head back, smacking it into the face of the man behind her.

"My nose!" Releasing her, he clutched at his face.

Pain seared through the side of Gisela's face. She reached up to touch it, hot, angry tears welling in her eyes. Through blurred vision, she saw Dominic struggling against the two men who pinned him. Twisting free, he punched Ryle in the stomach. Ryle grunted and clutched at his belly. He straightened, massaging his gut. His hand reached to his belt.

He drew out a knife.

*Oh, God! Oh, God!*

Icy fear whooshed through Gisela. She stared at the dagger. She tried to move, to wipe away the sickly sweat beading on her brow, but her limbs seemed paralyzed.

*Oh, God! Oh, God!*

Sounds broke through the shrill humming in her ears. Battle cries, emanating from the forest. De Lanceau's men streamed out of the woods.

"Crenardieu!" a lackey yelled. More shouts, followed by the *clang* of swords. De Lanceau's men split into two groups. Following their lord, some of the guards rushed toward those surrounding her and Dominic. Aldwin and the others charged down to the dock.

Halting a few paces away, de Lanceau glared at Ryle. "Put down the dagger."

"Who in hellfire are you?" Ryle sneered.

"Geoffrey de Lanceau, Lord of Branton Keep."

Ryle spat on the ground. "I know your name well—"

"Ryle!" Crenardieu said, warning in his glare.

"—for you ruined my cloth business. You ruined *me!*"

When Ryle's fingers flexed on the knife, Gisela's hand flew to her aching scar. Down by the docks, swords clashed. A man screamed, followed by a splash. Ryle, too, would not yield without a fight. Men would die before this battle ended.

De Lanceau's face hardened with anger. "Balewyne, set down your knife. The rest of you, throw down your weapons. You are all under arrest. No one steals my cloth and sells it to other merchants."

"Arrest *him!*" Ryle shouted, thrusting a finger at Dominic. "I caught him with my wife, embracing and kissing her. A moment more, and they would be fornicating there in the woods. Ask the others. They saw, too."

"Gisela is not your wife," Dominic said. "You do not deserve her."

"I married her. By law she is mine. She will obey me as her wedded husband."

"Never," Gisela said, resolve giving her voice. "Never again."

Wrath lit Ryle's eyes. "Shut up!"

"You shut up," Dominic shot back. "By law, you never were her husband."

"Lying bastard!"

Gisela shuddered at the violence of Ryle's tone, even as a brittle laugh broke from Dominic. Waving a hand at the surrounding men, he said, "Admit it, if you have the ballocks. Your marriage was never consummated."

Gisela's breath locked in her lungs. *Oh, Dominic! Beware!*

"That means your and Gisela's marriage is not—and never was—legally binding."

Ryle's face turned scarlet. "I care not what you say. She is my wife."

Arching an eyebrow, Dominic said, "Nay. You were not *man* enough to make her so. Not on your wedding night, or any instance after that."

A wary scowl creased Crenardieu's brow. "How would you know?"

"Gisela told me."

Sucking in a furious gasp, Ryle glared at her. He looked angry enough to exhale flames.

Crenardieu swallowed as though to rid his mouth of a foul taste. "*C'est impossible.* Ryle has a son—"

"Nay," Dominic ground out.

"—whom he sold to me for fifty silver coins. To help pay off some of his debts."

"*Sold?* Like an *animal?*" Gisela glared at Ryle.

Disgust rose so hot within her, she almost choked on it. "How could you?"

"Easily," Ryle bellowed. "The sniveling little whelp—"

"How *dare* you speak of him so?" Fury crackled in Dominic's voice. "His name is Ewan. He is a clever, ambitious boy who deserves his sire's love. A son who will know the truth about his father."

"I *am* his father," Ryle said, spittle whitening his lips. "He is my son. I do with him as I please."

Dominic's hands balled into fists. He clearly fought to restrain his temper.

Ryle pointed at Gisela. "She birthed my son."

Dominic shook his head. "Gisela bore *my* son."

"*What?*" Crenardieu said.

"Ewan is my child." Dominic's steady, determined gaze slid to Gisela, and tingling warmth swirled in her belly. "Tell these men how you conceived him that day in the meadow when we made love, days before I left for crusade. Tell them how your family forced you to marry Ryle to spare them the shame of an unwed, pregnant daughter."

His impassioned tone brought fresh tears to her eyes. "'Tis true," she said.

"Including what he said about your marriage not being consummated?" asked de Lanceau.

Heat burned her face. Refusing to acknowledge Ryle's lethal glower, she said, "Aye."

"Bitch!" Ryle roared. He raised his knife.

In a blur of a moment, Dominic lunged, catapulting

into Ryle. Crenardieu spun, his cloak whirling about him. The *clank* of swords echoed, followed by pounded footfalls. Glancing over her shoulder, Gisela spied the Frenchman running to the dock, de Lanceau's men in pursuit.

"Dominic!" de Lanceau yelled. As the two fighting men broke apart, he tossed Dominic a knife, then raced down to the riverbank.

Dominic drew the dagger and tossed the leather sheath aside.

Ryle chuckled. A terrifying sound.

Gisela dried her sweat-coated palms on her gown. Ryle must not win this fight. He must *not* triumph to ride away from this place, boasting how he vanquished de Lanceau's most loyal, trusted knight. Weakened, wounded, Dominic would soon tire, and then . . .

A sickening realization filled her. A decision.

She swallowed down a surge of bile. Reaching into her satchel, she drew out her sewing shears. Her only weapon. Yet, 'twould do.

With a gruesome snarl, Ryle swung the knife toward Dominic.

Dominic dodged, his movements obviously slowed by his injuries. "You missed."

Snarling again, Ryle lashed out. His dagger flashed. Dominic jumped back, avoiding the strike. However, Ryle lunged forward again, grazing Dominic's shoulder. His slashed tunic gaped, revealing a light cut across his shoulder blade. Dominic winced.

His face twisting into a grin, Ryle again poised the dagger.

"Ryle!" Gisela shrieked.

His breathing harsh, he turned to face her. Blood glistened on the knife's tip. Memories of his slashing her breast, months ago, tore through her mind.

Her blood that night. Dominic's today.

*Never again.*

His dagger still raised to strike, Ryle glanced at Dominic. Blood staining his shoulder, sweat streaming down his face, Dominic stared back. How ashen he looked. She sensed the tremendous effort it cost him to fight.

Ryle's lip curled, and Gisela fought a despairing cry. She knew with absolute certainty this time, he meant for Dominic to die.

She tightened her grip on her sewing shears. "'Tis me you want, Ryle."

"Gisela!" Dominic rasped. "Do not goad him."

Aye, she would—*must*—goad him, as a knight provoked a dragon. "I ran away," she went on, as Ryle's eyes cinched into slits. "Remember how I left you? Remember how I betrayed you?"

Ryle glowered at her. "I remember."

She edged closer, holding the shears against her skirt. "Never again will I run from you."

"*Gisela!*" Dominic gasped.

Surprise widened Ryle's eyes. His knife wavered. For a moment, his face twisted into an expression akin to anguish. "At last, will you love me?"

*Love him?!* "Nay. Always, I will love Dominic."

Throwing his head back, Ryle roared like an angry dragon. The very moment his body began to swivel toward Dominic, she rushed forward. Raised the shears. Slammed them down into Ryle's chest. Stumbled back.

He dragged in a shrill, disbelieving gasp. Gaped at the wrought-iron handles protruding from his torso. Blood oozed in a crimson stain.

Moaning, he clutched at the shears. "Look what you have done!"

"She has killed a dragon," Dominic murmured.

Ryle fell to his knees. Swayed. "Bitch!" he spluttered, his voice trailing off on another moan.

His gaze lost focus. Dimmed. His lips parted, as if to spit his last words. With a gurgled hiss, he collapsed sideways on the ground and lay still.

Sobs welled inside Gisela. She pressed her hands over her breast, unable to tear her gaze away from Ryle's corpse and the blood seeping into the dirt.

"Gisela." Dominic slid an arm around her waist.

The sob burst free, becoming a wail.

"Gisela," he said again, gently turning her so she faced him. Holding her close, he kissed her hair, her brow, the side of her cheek.

Sobs racked her body. Leaning against him, she wept like a woman lost.

Nay, she was not lost. Finally, she was free. She

was alive, in the arms of the man she loved. Never again would she live in fear of Ryle.

Trembling, she looked up at Dominic. Tears ran down his face. He didn't speak, but his gaze seemed to convey every tangled thought and emotion coursing through her. Dipping his head, he kissed her, very gently.

"I killed him," she whispered. "I took . . . his life."

With a small grunt of pain, Dominic hugged her tighter. "You saved mine—and no doubt, the lives of others. You were incredibly brave, Gisela."

"I agree." De Lanceau strode toward them, sheathing his broadsword.

"You saw what happened?" Dominic asked.

De Lanceau nodded, and Gisela shuddered as his gaze settled upon her. "You may be common born," he said with a smile, "but you are as noble as any highborn lady."

"Gisela, the Fair Lady Warrior," Dominic added with a wink.

She smiled, and de Lanceau chuckled.

Shouts drew her gaze to the riverbank. Standing by the dock, their hands bound, a scowling Crenardieu and the London merchants stood under the watchful guard of de Lanceau's men-at-arms. Three thugs lay dead, their bodies sprawled in the shallows. Aldwin stood on the dock, relaying orders while helping the other men transfer the silks from the boats back into the wagon.

"We will soon return to Branton Keep," Gisela said, unable to stop her voice from catching. How she longed to take her little boy in her arms and hug him tight, to rejoice in knowing at last, he was safe from Ryle. But, upon her return, she must accept her punishment from de Lanceau.

Dominic eased her away. "A word, milord." Touching her sleeve, he said, "I will be but a moment."

She watched him stride away, speaking in low tones to de Lanceau. She hugged herself, unable to stifle a chill. How handsome Dominic looked, despite his tattered garments and wounds. Naught could disguise his noble strength. Standing beside de Lanceau, he clearly belonged among the highborn. Far beyond her common reach.

Loneliness pressed down upon her, crushing her earlier bloom of relief. Whatever her fate, she would accept it.

De Lanceau nodded and grinned. Then, he clapped Dominic on the back before they walked back to her.

"I have considered all that occurred today," de Lanceau said, warmth in his compelling gray gaze. "Above all, the fact that you selflessly risked your own life to save Dominic's. I have also taken into regard your earlier revelations at Branton Keep and at your home."

Gisela bit down on her lip. "Aye, milord."

*I have sentenced you to my dungeon for the rest of your living days.*

"While I cannot condone all of your decisions, I believe you did what was necessary to protect not only your own life, but that of your young son." He paused. "Dominic's child."

Blinking hard, she nodded.

"Therefore—"

*Please, God, let him be merciful. Please, do not take Ewan from me. Please, please . . .*

"—since your decisions were made for the well-being of his son—"

*Please, please!*

"I leave any punishment entirely up to Dominic."

Exhaling a stunned breath, Gisela said, "Dominic?"

Slipping his arm around her waist, he kissed her cheek. "Since I am heartily glad Ryle is dead, you kept my son safe from his murderous rage, and all of Geoffrey's silks were recovered"—he shrugged—"I see only one resolution, really."

She gasped. "Oh!" Then she frowned. "What resolution?"

De Lanceau clapped his hands together. "'Tis settled, then."

Confusion bubbled up inside Gisela. "Dominic?"

Mischief glinted in his eyes. "We will discuss it, Sweet Daisy, on our return to Branton Keep."

# CHAPTER TWENTY-TWO

Seated behind Gisela on her horse, Dominic took her to the meadow close to Branton Keep. Standing on the nearby hill, the castle looked down over the expansive field brightened by poppies, daisies, and cornflowers.

Four times she'd asked that he reveal her fate. Four times, smothering a smile, he refused.

Drawing the horse to a halt in the middle of the meadow, he slid down, and then helped her dismount. Leaving the animal to graze, he caught Gisela's hand. He led her farther into the wildflowers and grasses, rousing butterflies and bumblebees as he walked.

"Dominic, please! Will you tell me now?"

She sounded so frantic, he paused and faced her. How beautiful she looked standing amid the flowers, her hair tangled from their ride. She looked more lovely than years ago. He fought the desire to pull her into his arms, kiss her until her mouth was as red as poppies, and then draw her down among the grasses.

Instead, he slipped his hand from hers and picked a daisy.

"I cannot bear not knowing," she said.

"Very well." He handed her the bloom. "I never want us to be apart again."

She took the daisy. Elation filled her eyes, but also painful doubt.

"Never again," he whispered, reaching for her.

She hesitated, her eyes brimming with tears. Then, with a sobbed sigh, she melted into his embrace. His lips found hers, and he kissed her, deeply, urgently, starved for her essence.

Placing her hands on either side of his face, she kissed him back. Without restraint. With a hunger that roused his to a fever pitch. Groaning, he urged her down to the ground. She lay on her back, while, careful of his wounds, he reclined beside her, one hand clasping hers. "I love you, Gisela."

She gazed up at him, tears shimmering on her lashes. "As I love you."

"Marry me."

She froze. Her throat moved with an awkward swallow before she said, "'Tis impossible. I am a commoner."

"I care not. Neither does de Lanceau. He is in favor of our marriage. As a wedding gift, he will award me one of his small estates." He kissed her hand. "My mother would be proud."

"Aye, she would." Gisela's lips formed a shaky smile. "So, I vow, would your father."

Indeed, he might. But at this moment, Dominic had more important matters to consider.

A dull ache spread through his chest. Gisela hadn't accepted his proposal. Did she not wish to wed him?

"Please, Gisela, marry me. You are the mother of my son. The woman who saved my life." He pressed her fingers. "I want no one else."

"Oh, Dominic." She sniffled. Gently touching his bruised face, she whispered, "How many nights I dreamed of lying with you again. Of being together."

His brow creased in a mock frown. "Hmm. Are you saying 'aye' to my proposal?"

"Hmm . . ." she repeated, mischief in her eyes. "I believe . . . Aye."

"At last," he murmured, sweeping his lips over hers.

Gisela smiled up at him, joy in her eyes. "Ewan will be so excited."

"I cannot wait to tell him he is my son." Dominic imagined the little boy's face brightening when they told him the news. How he looked forward to embracing his son. To teaching him the nuances of swordplay, archery, and . . .

"Imagine," Dominic said. "A family of warriors."

She giggled, and he kissed her again, with all the love

pouring from his soul. His hands trembling, he removed her garments until she lay naked before him. With a coy smile, she helped him remove his tunic and hose. Then, the linen bandages still wrapped around his ribs.

As the extent of his beatings was revealed, concern filled her gaze, but Dominic firmly shook his head. "Our lovemaking may not be quite as . . . lusty on this occasion"—he winked—"but my wounds will heal quickly."

"They will," she agreed, "for I will ensure they do." While she spoke, her fingers brushed the swollen heat of him, as though discovering him anew. Closing his eyes, Dominic shuddered with pleasure. How he had missed coupling with her.

Leaning forward, he kissed her throat, shoulder blade, and the valley between her breasts.

Her hands flitted up to cover her scar.

"Gisela." He nibbled her fingers before drawing them away. Anguish clouded her gaze, but he kissed her scar's ragged line. "You are more beautiful to me now, Sweet Daisy."

"Really?" she whispered.

He nodded. "This scar is a mark of honor. Proof of the dragon you battled—and defeated."

Kissing her again, he moved over her. When their bodies touched, she sighed and arched up, answering the bold insistence of his manhood. "Aye, Dominic," she whispered. "Aye."

He slid into her. Groaned.

*Ah, God!*

A ragged cry broke from her. "Dominic," she whimpered.

And he was lost.

As he surrendered to the rhythm of long ago, he savored the joy of pleasuring Gisela. The relief they would never again be apart. The knowledge that, at long last, she belonged to him.

The greatest reward of all.

Don't miss the next exciting historical romance by
# CATHERINE KEAN

# A Knight's Temptation

Aldwin Treynarde, a squire who shot Lord Geoffrey de Lanceau with a crossbow bolt after being deceived by Baron Sedgewick, is ordered to retrieve a stolen ruby pendant before it falls into the Baron and Veronique's hands. Haunted by his guilt over being manipulated by the baron years ago, Aldwin wants to prove his worth to his lord. If he excels in his duty, he might even be awarded knighthood. Such an honor would also help redeem himself to his respected parents who, ashamed by his reckless near-murder of de Lanceau, told him never to return home.

Lady Leona Ransley, in an effort to help her depressed father, only wants to hand over the pendant, collect the reward, and vanish. When she arranges a meeting in a seedy tavern, she never expected to face Aldwin, who almost caused her death twelve years ago when they disturbed a bee's nest during a childhood game. Although Aldwin does not recognize her, he is reminded of Leona and is haunted by his belief that she died from the bee stings from that day twelve years prior. Believing that the woman before him is a courtesan and has information on the conspirators' whereabouts, he takes Leona hostage and spirits her away, meaning to deliver her and the pendant to de Lanceau.

She, however, fights him at every chance. He desires his warrior captive more than any noble woman he has ever met, and when he discovers who she really is, he knows he has one last chance to protect his lady's life. Only by resolving what happened between them and by fighting side by side can Aldwin and Leona defeat the conspirators and surrender to their greatest temptation—love.

ISBN# 9781933836522
Jewel Imprint: Sapphire
Historical Romance
US $7.95 / CDN $8.95
APRIL 2009

# CATHERINE KEAN
# A Knight's Vengeance

### A quest for revenge . . .

Geoffrey de Lanceau is a knight, the son of the man who once ruled Wode. His noble sire died, however, branded as a traitor. But never will Geoffrey believe his father betrayed their king, and swears vengeance against the man who brought his sire down in a siege to take over Wode.

### A quest for love . . .

Lady Elizabeth Brackendale dreamed of marrying for love, but is promised by her father to a lecherous old baron. Then she is abducted and held for ransom by a scarred, tormented rogue who turns out to be the very knight who has sworn vengeance against her father.

### A quest for truth . . .

The threads of deception sewn eighteen years ago bind the past and present. Only by Geoffrey and Elizabeth championing their forbidden love can the truth — and the lies — be revealed about . . .

A Knight's Vengeance.

ISBN# 9781932815481
US $6.99 / CDN $9.99
Historical Romance
Available Now
www.catherinekean.com

# CATHERINE KEAN

# My Lady's Treasure

## *The Treasure of Love . . .*

Facing the tall, brooding rider by the stormy lakeshore, Lady Faye Rivellaux clings to her goal — to rescue the kidnapped child she vowed to protect. At all costs, she must win back the little girl she loves as her own. When the stranger demands a ransom she can never pay, Faye offers him instead her one last hope — a gold cup.

Brant Meslarches is stunned to see the chalice. Worth a fortune, it's proof a lost cache of wealth from the legendary Celtic King Arthur does exist, as Brant's murdered brother believed. Brant can't return the little girl to the lady whose desperate beauty captivates him. Yet, now that he's seen Lady Faye, he can't let her escape his grasp; she is the key to his only means of redemption.

The last thing Faye wants is an alliance with a scarred knight tormented by secrets. But, she has no other way to rescue the child. Risking all, she joins Brant's quest. And finds some things are more valuable than gold.

ISBN# 9781932815788
US $6.99 / CDN $8.99
Historical Romance
Available Now
www.catherinekean.com

# CATHERINE KEAN

# DANCE of DESIRE

Desperate to save her brother Rudd from being condemned
as a traitor, Lady Rexana Villeaux must dance in disguise at
a feast for the High Sheriff of Warringham. Her goal is to
distract him so her servant can steal a damning missive from
the sheriff's solar. Dressed in the gauzy costume of a desert
courtesan, dancing with all the passion and sensuality in
her soul, she succeeds in her mission. And, at the same
time, condemns herself.

Fane Linford, the banished son of an English earl, joined
Richard's crusade only to find himself a captive in a hellish
eastern prison. He survived the years of torment, it's
rumored, because of the love of a Saracen courtesan. The
rumors are true. And when he sees Rexana dance . . .

Richard has promised Fane an English bride, yet he desires
only one woman — the exotic dancer who tempted him.
Then he discovers the dancer's identity. And learns her
brother is in his dungeon, accused of plotting against the
throne. It is more temptation than Fane can resist.

The last thing Rexana wants is marriage to the dark and
brooding Sheriff of Warringham. But her brother is his
prisoner, and there may be only one way to save him.
Taking the greatest chance of her life, Rexana becomes the
sheriff's bride. And learns that the Dance of Desire was
only a beginning . . .

ISBN#9781932815351
US $6.99 / CDN $8.99
Historical Romance
Available Now
www.catherinekean.com

# Lisa Manuel

# Fortune's Kiss

Moira Hughes's stepfather has died, and although the bulk
of the family holdings must pass to a relative, a codicil to his
will secures her and her mother's future — or so she believes.
When their London solicitor denies all knowledge of this
codicil, practical, country bred Moira must put aside both
pride and propriety, travel to London and press her rights.
Once there she resolves to confront her stepfather's heir, the
dashing black sheep of the family whom she believes has
unlawfully withheld her rightful share of the family fortune.

Graham Foster, treasure hunter and Egyptian antiquities
expert, must leave his adventurous life to return to England
and claim the barony left him by a distant cousin. Upon his
arrival he discovers his estranged and spoiled family making
free with his inherited home and fortune, while a dazzling,
dark-haired step-cousin several times removed adamantly
accuses him of foul play. There are times he feels his only
true friend is his pet African Sun Spider . . .

Coming to a wary truce and teetering on a middle ground
of irresistible if imprudent desire, Graham and Moira team
up to hunt for her lost treasure. A trail of fraud, deceit and
murder leads them through the streets of London and into
each other's arms, and to the most unlikely of conclusions.

ISBN# 9781933836355
US $7.95 / CDN $8.95
Historical Romance
MARCH 2008
www.lisamanuel.com

# Judith James
# BROKEN WING

Abandoned as a child and raised in a brothel, Gabriel
St. Croix has never known tenderness, friendship, or affection. Although fluent in sex, he knows nothing of love. Lost
and alone inside a nightmare world, all he's ever wanted was
companionship and a place to belong. Hiding physical and
emotional scars behind an icy façade, his only relationship is
with a young boy he has spent the last five years protecting
from the brutal reality of their environment. But all that is
about to change. The boy's family has found him, and they
are coming to take him home.

Sarah Munroe blames herself for her brother's disap-
pearance. When he's located, safe and unharmed despite
where he has been living, Sarah vows to help the man who
rescued and protected him in any way she can. With loving
patience she helps Gabriel face his demons and teaches him
to trust in friendship and love. But when the past catches up
with him, Gabriel must face it on his own.

Becoming a mercenary, pirate and a professional gam-
bler, Gabriel travels to London, France, and the Barbary
Coast in a desperate attempt to find Sarah again and all he
knows of love. On the way, however, he will discover the
most dangerous journey, and the greatest gamble of all, is
within the darkest reaches of his own heart.

ISBN# 9781933836447
US $7.95 / CDN $8.95
Historical Romance
NOVEMBER 2008
www.judithjamesauthor.com

# BLAZE OF
# LIGHTNING ROAR OF
# THUNDER

## HELEN A. ROSBURG

Louisa Rodriguez was out on the desert gathering fuel when the scalp hunters came, massacred her family and all the people of her village, shot her in the head and left her for dead. Regaining consciousness, she buried the people she had loved, and when she was done she stripped off her bloody clothes and walked naked into the mountains. Where she was reborn.

When horse wrangler Ring Crossman came across the half-wild woman in the western wilderness, she would not tell him her name. So he gave her one. Blaze, for the lightning-like streak of white in her long, black hair where a bullet had creased her skull. He gave her his heart, too, although he knew there was no room in her life for anything but revenge.

Vengeance consumed Bane as well. His life was devoted to finding the man who raped his Apache mother and fathered him. Then The Bringer of Thunder, as he was called by his people, crossed trails with the only human being whose thirst for a man's blood was as great as his own. And when they discovered they stalked the same prey, the destructive power of the storm they unleashed consumed all around them. Including themselves.

ISBN# 9781932815641
US $7.95 / CDN $8.95
Historical Romance
AUGUST 2008
www.helenrosburg.com

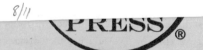